The Catholic Beethoven

The Catholic Beethoven

NICHOLAS CHONG

Oxford University Press is a department of the University of Oxford.
It furthers the University's objective of excellence in research, scholarship,
and education by publishing worldwide. Oxford is a registered trade mark of
Oxford University Press in the UK and in certain other countries.

Published in the United States of America by Oxford University Press
198 Madison Avenue, New York, NY 10016, United States of America.

© Oxford University Press 2024

All rights reserved. No part of this publication may be reproduced, stored in a retrieval system, transmitted, used for text and data mining, or used for training artificial intelligence, in any form or by any means, without the prior permission in writing of Oxford University Press, or as expressly permitted by law, by license or under terms agreed with the appropriate reprographics rights organization. Inquiries concerning reproduction outside the scope of the above should be sent to the Rights Department, Oxford University Press, at the address above.

You must not circulate this work in any other form and
you must impose this same condition on any acquirer

CIP data is on file at the Library of Congress

ISBN 9780197752920

DOI: 10.1093/9780197752951.001.0001

The manufacturer's authorised representative in the EU for product safety is
Oxford University Press España S.A. of El Parque Empresarial San Fernando de Henares,
Avenida de Castilla, 2 – 28830 Madrid (www.oup.es/en or
product.safety@oup.com). OUP España S.A. also acts as importer into Spain
of products made by the manufacturer.

For my family

Contents

List of Figures	ix
List of Music Examples	xi
Acknowledgments	xiii
List of Abbreviations	xv
Note to the Reader	xvii

Introduction	1
1. German Catholicism in Beethoven's Time: Enlightenment and Restoration	25
2. Beethoven and the Catholic Enlightenment in Bonn	47
3. Beethoven's Religious Works before the *Missa solemnis*: The Gellert Lieder, *Christus am Ölberge*, and the Mass in C	71
4. Religion in Beethoven's Library: Christoph Christian Sturm and Ignaz Aurelius Feßler	128
5. Beethoven and Johann Michael Sailer	160
6. The *Missa solemnis*	201
Conclusion	271
Works Cited	289
Index	305

Figures

I.1	Ernst Julius Hähnel's statue of Beethoven (1845), Münsterplatz, Bonn	2
I.2	Ernst Julius Hähnel's statue of Beethoven (1845), Münsterplatz, Bonn, pedestal (detail)	3
2.1	Cover of a French Bible in the Port-Royal (Sacy) translation	62
4.1	Cover of an edition for Catholic readers of Christoph Christian Sturm's *Betrachtungen über die Werke Gottes*	140
4.2	Statement of ecclesiastical approval in a Catholic edition of Christoph Christian Sturm's *Betrachtungen über die Werke Gottes*	141
5.1	Latin quotation used by Beethoven as it appears in Sailer's *Goldkörner der Weisheit und Tugend*	166
5.2	Cover page showing the compilation of Johann Michael Sailer's *Kleine Bibel* and *Neue Beyträge zur Bildung des Geistlichen* in a single volume	197
6.1	Portrait of Beethoven by Joseph Karl Stieler (1820)	203

Music Examples

All examples come from works by Beethoven.

3.1	Gellert Lieder, "Die Ehre Gottes aus dem Natur," op. 48 no. 4, mm. 19–27	82
3.2	*Abendlied unterm gestirnten Himmel*, WoO 150, mm. 10–14	83
3.3	*Der Wachtelschlag*, WoO 129, mm. 1–8	84
3.4	Gellert Lieder, "Die Liebe des Nächsten," op. 48 no. 2, mm. 2–7	89
3.5	*Christus am Ölberge*, op. 85: No. 6, mm. 95–105	90
3.6	Mass in C major, op. 86: (a) Kyrie, mm. 2–5, choral soprano part; (b) Gloria, mm. 190–93, choral alto part	99
3.7	Mass in C major, op. 86, Credo, mm. 160–64	103
3.8	Mass in C major, op. 86, Credo, mm. 172–77	103
3.9	Mass in C major, op. 86, Credo, mm. 221–26	104
3.10	Mass in C major, op. 86, Agnus Dei, mm. 58–78	106
3.11	Mass in C major, op. 86, Gloria, mm. 339–53	110
3.12	Mass in C major, op. 86, Credo, mm. 302–14	112
3.13	Mass in C major, op. 86, Kyrie, mm. 37–56	123
6.1	*Missa solemnis*, op. 123, Gloria, mm. 35–48	213
6.2	*Missa solemnis*, op. 123, Kyrie: (a) mm. 182–83; (b) mm. 190–93	216
6.3	*Missa solemnis*, op. 123, Credo, mm. 29–33	218
6.4	*Missa solemnis*, op. 123, Credo, mm. 257–64	219
6.5	*Missa solemnis*, op. 123, Gloria, mm. 514–17	221
6.6	*Missa solemnis*, op. 123, Gloria, mm. 426–42	224
6.7	*Missa solemnis*, op. 123, Kyrie, mm. 88–93	229
6.8	*Missa solemnis*, op. 123, Credo, mm. 67–71	231
6.9	*Missa solemnis*, op. 123, Credo, mm. 117–36	233
6.10	*Missa solemnis*, op. 123, Credo, mm. 184–202	237
6.11	*Missa solemnis*, op. 123, Sanctus, mm. 104–20	244

6.12 *Missa solemnis*, op. 123, Sanctus, mm. 140–50   251

6.13 *Missa solemnis*, op. 123, Credo, mm. 141–42   258

6.14 *Der Wachtelschlag*, WoO 129, mm. 51–58   265

6.15 Mass in C major, op. 86, Agnus Dei, horn part:
(a) mm. 114–18; (b) mm. 178–82   266

Acknowledgments

This book is the product of a long and challenging intellectual journey, and I would not have finished this project without the support and encouragement of many people. Numerous scholars offered advice, suggestions, and very helpful critiques at various stages of my research and writing. Among music scholars, I wish especially to thank Joanna Biermann, Mark Evan Bonds, Susan Boynton, Erica Buurman, Jen-yen Chen, Daniel Chua, Walter Frisch, James Hepokoski, the late Warren Kirkendale, Birgit Lodes, Nicholas Mathew, Jeremiah McGrann, Elisabeth Reisinger, Julia Ronge, Elaine Sisman, Stephen Rumph, James Webster, John Wilson, and the anonymous reviewers solicited by Oxford University Press. I am also grateful for assistance given by the following historians and theologians, who have been patient and welcoming to someone seeking to engage with their disciplines from the outside: Michael Bangert, Shaun Blanchard, Euan Cameron, Ulrich Lehner, and Andrei Pesic. Some of those just named may not realize how much help they have given me: often it takes only a brief conversation or a casual remark to stimulate one's thinking or to inspire new ideas. I also wish to acknowledge the support and intellectual friendship offered by Christy Thomas Adams, Eric Bianchi, Mia Chung, Julia Doe, and Lucy Turner, as well as by Nathaniel Peters and his staff at the Morningside Institute in New York City.

My current and former faculty colleagues at the Mason Gross School of the Arts, Rutgers University, have been extremely supportive of my work and my development as a scholar. I would like to express particular thanks to Rebecca Cypess, Christopher Doll, Amanda Eubanks Winkler, Patrick Gardner, Eduardo Herrera, Douglas Johnson, Steven Kemper, Scott Ordway, Nancy Rao, George Stauffer, and Kristen Wallentinsen. I am especially grateful for the many helpful words of encouragement I have received from my colleagues during moments of self-doubt.

At Oxford University Press, Suzanne Ryan expressed initial interest in this project, and Norman Hirschy and Laura Santo, along with other members of their editorial staff, were indispensable in seeing the publication process through to its conclusion. I also wish to thank Bonnie Blackburn for copyediting and indexing assistance, and Lynette Bowring for helping tidy up and proofread my music examples.

For help with retrieving items, and for granting permission to reproduce images of them, I would like to acknowledge the following staff members at various libraries: Timothy Noakes at Stanford University; Renée Ann Bosman at the University of North Carolina at Chapel Hill; Sara Weber at the University of Notre Dame; and Gertrud Oswald and Hans-Peter Zimmer at the Austrian National Library in Vienna. My research has also benefited tremendously from access to the Burke Library at Union Theological Seminary in New York City, one of the premier collections of material on theology and religious history in the United States. I have lost count of the number of times I stumbled upon an obscure but valuable source while surveying bookshelves in the stacks.

Portions of chapters 1, 5, and 6 first appeared in "Beethoven's Theologian: Johann Michael Sailer and the *Missa solemnis*," *Journal of the American Musicological Society* 74, no. 2 (2021): 365–426. I thank the University of California Press for permission to reproduce this material.

Finally, I would like to express my deepest gratitude to my family for their unwavering support: especially my wife, Erin, who has been a loving and devoted partner; my sons Alexander and Oliver; my parents Choon Nean and Sue; and my brother Adam. Alexander tells me all the time that he wants to write a book when he grows up: I hope that with this work I have done something small to inspire him. Thank you for always being there for me: I love you all.

Abbreviations

Albrecht	Albrecht, Theodore, ed. and trans. *Letters to Beethoven and Other Correspondence*. 3 vols. Lincoln: University of Nebraska Press, 1996.
Anderson	Anderson, Emily, ed. and trans. *The Letters of Beethoven*. 3 vols. New York: St. Martin's Press, 1961.
BCB	Albrecht, Theodore, ed. and trans. *Beethoven's Conversation Books*. Rochester, NY: Boydell and Brewer, 2018– (4 of 12 projected volumes published so far).
BGA	Brandenburg, Sieghard, ed. *Ludwig van Beethoven: Briefwechsel Gesamtausgabe*. 7 vols. Munich: Henle, 1996.
Biamonti	Biamonti, Giovanni. *Schema di un catalogo generale cronologico delle musiche di Beethoven, 1781–1827*. Rome: Mezzetti, 1954.
BKh	Köhler, Karl-Heinz, Grita Herre, and Dagmar Beck, eds. *Ludwig van Beethovens Konversationshefte*. 11 vols. Leipzig: VEB Deutscher Verlag für Musik, 1968–2001.
Schätzungsprotokoll	Albrecht, Theodore, ed. and trans. "Appraisal of the Value of Beethoven's Library." In *Letters to Beethoven and Other Correspondence*, 3:231–38. Lincoln: University of Nebraska Press, 1996.
Tagebuch	(English) Solomon, Maynard, ed. and trans. "Beethoven's Tagebuch." In *Beethoven Essays*, 233–95. Cambridge, MA: Harvard University Press, 1988. (German) Solomon, Maynard, ed., *Beethovens Tagebuch*. Bonn: Beethoven-Haus, 1990.

Note to the Reader

Throughout this study, I use the adjective "German" in the broad sense, to refer to the entire German-speaking cultural area of Central and Eastern Europe: what in modern German might be referred to as the German *Sprachgebiet*. Terms such as "German-speaking lands," "German lands," "German Catholicism," and "German Catholic Church" should thus be understood in this manner. As will be evident in the titles of many of the sources I have cited, historical scholarship often employs the noun "Germany" in this same sense, especially when dealing with the time period prior to the formation of the modern nation-state of Germany in 1871—a state that most notably excluded Austria. (There are writers who do, however, adopt a definition of Germany that is separate from Austria even when discussing periods earlier in the nineteenth century.) I have chosen to avoid the unqualified use of the noun "Germany" in order to prevent confusion with the other, narrower definitions of the word to mean the more limited geographical region encompassed by the present-day Federal Republic of Germany, or by the German state constituted in 1871.

Additional complications are introduced by the terms "Holy Roman Empire" and "Habsburg lands" in reference to the period before 1806. Most, though not all, of the Habsburg lands (other equivalent terms include "Habsburg Monarchy," "Austrian Monarchy," and "Danubian Monarchy") were part of the Holy Roman Empire—Hungary was a notable exception—and the head of the House of Habsburg since the fifteenth century had almost always been elected Holy Roman Emperor. Conversely, most of the Holy Roman Empire was not ruled directly by the Habsburgs, though all of its constituent states, at least theoretically, owed limited allegiance to the (Habsburg) Holy Roman Emperor. The Holy Roman Empire itself did not encompass all of what might be called the German cultural region; German-speaking Switzerland, for instance, lay outside it. These distinctions are crucial for the purposes of this study because in relation to historical movements such as the German Catholic Enlightenment I shall deal with both trends that apply generally to the German cultural region as a whole, and specific versions that differed from region to region. In addition, cultural ties were a separate issue from political boundaries. For instance, Josephinism, as a manifestation of the German Catholic Enlightenment, was official policy only in the Habsburg lands, but, as will be discussed, it also exerted a significant influence on non-Habsburg lands such as Bonn, where Beethoven grew up. Conversely, Bavaria was not a Habsburg territory, but Johann Michael Sailer, who was based there, was a well-known figure throughout the German lands, including in Habsburg Vienna.

༄ ༄ ༄

For primary biographical sources related to Beethoven—such as correspondence, conversation books, the *Tagebuch*—I employ, where available, the standard editions commonly cited in the Beethoven literature. The list of abbreviations used for these standard editions has been provided in the previous section. Unless there is a compelling reason to do otherwise, I refer to published English translations of this material where they exist, with citations—and where appropriate, quotations—of the original German provided in footnotes or the main text. Places where I have found it necessary to amend these standard translations are clearly indicated. In all other cases, translations of non-English sources are my own, unless otherwise stated or a published translation is explicitly cited. In translating from the German, I have attempted, to the extent possible, to retain the German word order, unless doing so would obscure the meaning of the English. I have thus allowed some translations to come across as a little unidiomatic or stilted in English in order to give the reader a more literal sense of the original German.

In quotations from standard editions of Beethoven biographical sources, whether in German or English, I retain the formatting and orthography employed in those editions. An exception to this practice is the omission of slashes used to indicate line breaks in both the English and German versions of Beethoven's conversation books: Albrecht, ed., *Beethoven's Conversation Books* (*BCB*); and Köhler, Herre, and Beck, eds., *Ludwig van Beethovens Konversationshefte* (*BKh*). In the standard German edition of Beethoven's correspondence—Brandenburg, ed., *Ludwig van Beethoven: Briefwechsel Gesamtausgabe* (*BGA*)—underlined text indicates emphasis in the original, while the use of italics indicates text Beethoven wrote in the Latin rather than the German variety of cursive script (*Kurrentschrift*).

Citations of Beethoven's correspondence, the posthumous inventory of Beethoven's library (Albrecht, ed., "Appraisal of the Value of Beethoven's Library"), and the catalog of Beethoven's works by Giovanni Biamonti are by item number, rather than by page number. Citations of the *Tagebuch* are similarly by entry number: the same numbering is utilized in the standard German and English editions of the *Tagebuch*, both of which have been edited by Maynard Solomon.

Dates for Beethoven's correspondence follow *BGA*. Dates for the conversation books follow the English translation in *BCB*, where such a translation has already been published; in other cases, dates will be those given in *BKh*.

Biblical quotations use the Revised Standard Version (RSV).

Music examples, all from works by Beethoven, were prepared on the basis of the following score editions:

- Lieder (including the Gellert Lieder): Ludwig van Beethoven, *Sämtliche Lieder für eine Singstimme und Klavier*, ed. Helga Lühning, 2 vols. (Munich: Henle, 1990)
- *Christus am Ölberge*: Ludwig van Beethoven, *Christus am Ölberge, Opus 85*, ed. Anja Mühlenweg (Munich: Henle, 2008)
- Mass in C: Ludwig van Beethoven, *Messe C-Dur, Opus 86*, ed. Jeremiah W. McGrann (Munich: Henle, 2004)
- *Missa solemnis*: Ludwig van Beethoven, *Missa solemnis, Opus 123*, ed. Norbert Gertsch (Munich: Henle, 2000)

In addition, I used the following vocal scores for keyboard reductions of instrumental parts in the Mass in C and *Missa solemnis*: Ludwig van Beethoven, *Mass in C major, Opus 86* (Kalmus vocal score 6077); and Ludwig van Beethoven, *Missa solemnis, Opus 123*, ed. Kurt Soldan (Frankfurt: Peters, 1952). Minor corrections have been made to these reductions for the sake of greater clarity, or to ensure conformity with the full scores cited above.

Space constraints have limited the number of music examples that could be supplied. In situations where an example is not provided, the reader is invited to consult their own copy of the score. Scores for all of the works under discussion are widely available, including on the internet.

Introduction

On the Münsterplatz in Bonn stands a large statue of Beethoven by Ernst Julius Hähnel (see figure I.1). Perhaps the most famous of the numerous monuments erected in the composer's honor during the nineteenth century, it was unveiled in August 1845 in conjunction with a grandiose, three-day festival celebrating the seventy-fifth anniversary of his birth, a public event of sufficient importance to warrant the attendance of the Prussian royal family and even Britain's Queen Victoria.[1] In Hähnel's monument, the towering figure of Beethoven stands atop a pedestal featuring four reliefs, each representing a musical genre associated with the composer: fantasy, referring to piano music; the symphony; dramatic music; and sacred music, unmistakably depicted by the figure of St. Cecilia playing an organ (see figure I.2).[2]

From our vantage point today, it is hardly surprising that Hähnel's monument highlights piano music and the symphony: Beethoven's works in both of these genres have long been unquestioned staples of the core repertoire of Western art music. The references to dramatic and sacred music, on the other hand, pose more of a challenge to what is now the usual image of Beethoven and his music. Beethoven completed just one opera, *Fidelio*, even if he did also write works connected to spoken theater, most famously the *Coriolan* Overture, and the overture and incidental music for *Egmont*. As for sacred music, Beethoven completed only two liturgical works: the Mass in C major, and the *Missa solemnis*. Even were we to expand the definition of sacred music to include non-liturgical works with Christian content—Beethoven's lone oratorio *Christus am Ölberge* (Christ on the Mount of Olives); the Gellert Lieder, op. 48; and a few individual religious songs such as *Abendlied unterm gestirnten Himmel*, WoO150—it seems a stretch to say that sacred music was a prominent part of Beethoven's compositional identity. Sacred music forms a very small proportion of his overall output, and, more importantly, with the possible exception of the *Missa solemnis*, none of his religious works are considered quintessential Beethovenian "masterpieces," an

---

[1] Comini, *Changing Image of Beethoven*, 333–34.
[2] Comini, 332. Hähnel's drawings of the reliefs are reproduced ibid., 261.

Figure I.1 Ernst Julius Hähnel's statue of Beethoven (1845), Münsterplatz, Bonn. Photograph by the author.

Figure I.2 Ernst Julius Hähnel's statue of Beethoven (1845), Münsterplatz, Bonn, pedestal (detail). Photograph by the author.

honor usually reserved for some or all of the composer's symphonies, piano sonatas, and string quartets.[3] In addition to being depicted on Hähnel's pedestal, Beethoven's sacred music played a prominent role in the festivities surrounding the monument's inauguration. Aside from the *Missa solemnis*, the musicians present performed the Mass in C and *Christus am Ölberge*.[4] In the middle of the nineteenth century, then, Beethoven's religious music seems to have been a significant enough component of the composer's public image to be specifically highlighted in objects and activities venerating his memory. The same situation appears to have existed immediately following Beethoven's death: Franz Grillparzer's oration at the composer's funeral referred to "the humble sacrificial song of the Mass" (*Meßopfers gläubiges Lied*) as central to his musical legacy.[5]

To return to Hähnel's monument, if dramatic works such as *Fidelio*, *Coriolan*, and *Egmont* may be considered relatively atypical of Beethoven's output in terms of genre, their political content at least appears to accord with the stereotypical Enlightenment values of freedom, equality, and progress usually assumed to have been central to the composer's own worldview. The idea of Beethoven as a composer of sacred music, however, seems much more in tension with the conventional understanding of Beethoven the man. Since the middle of the nineteenth century, most accounts of the composer's religious views have tended to separate the composer from Catholicism or any other form of traditional Christianity. Writers do not agree on precisely what label is most appropriate for describing Beethoven's outlook. "Deist," "pantheist," "universalist," and "humanist" are some of the common terms employed, despite the fact that these words have quite different meanings. Nevertheless, what unites most accounts of Beethoven's religious outlook is the assumption that as a child of the Enlightenment, Beethoven was indifferent, possibly even hostile, toward organized religion, particularly the Catholic Christianity of his birth.

This book argues instead that Beethoven and his religious works were influenced by the German Catholicism of his era to a greater extent than has long been thought. My starting point is to call into question the

---

[3] The string quartet was also not a genre that Hähnel chose to feature on the monument, but it should be noted that it did not yet have the level of prominence in conceptions of Beethoven's musical identity that it would acquire in later decades: see November, *Beethoven's Theatrical Quartets*, 235–54. Over the course of the nineteenth century, the critical fortunes of Beethoven's string quartets thus seem to have undergone a process that was the reverse of what occurred with his religious music.

[4] Poppe, *Festhochamt, sinfonische Messe*, 112–15.

[5] The oration is reproduced in English translation in Thayer, *Thayer's Life of Beethoven*, 2:1057–58, at 1058. For the original German, see Kopitz and Caidenbach, *Beethoven aus der Sicht*, 1:389–91.

fundamental cultural-historical assumption implicit in much Beethoven scholarship: that the Enlightenment with which Beethoven is normally associated was the antithesis of traditional religion, especially Catholicism. Though this conception of the Enlightenment remains common in much humanistic scholarship and in the popular imagination, it has, for a number of decades now, been considered excessively simplistic, even misleading, by many historians of the Enlightenment. Beethoven's religious environment was defined by a movement known as the German Catholic Enlightenment, which sought to reconcile traditional Catholic beliefs with some aspects of the secular Enlightenment, as well as by the reaction against this movement that became more influential in the German lands over the course of the composer's lifetime. The complexity of this historical context, as I shall show, should prompt a re-evaluation of biographical evidence usually cited in relation to Beethoven's religious outlook, as well as his major musical works with a Christian, if not specifically Catholic, text: the Gellert Lieder, op. 48; *Christus am Ölberge*, op. 85; the Mass in C major, op. 86; and the *Missa solemnis*, op. 123. Broadly speaking, Beethoven's worldview was, for the most part, progressive and "enlightened," but in his time such characteristics were not necessarily at odds with a continued allegiance to the Catholic religion. Beethoven's engagement with religious ideas, along with his religious music, was shaped by an environment in which Catholicism was still prominent, though often in a form that was open to other Christian confessions as well as secular thought.

Beethoven the Lapsed Catholic?

There is no doubt that Beethoven was at least nominally a Catholic, even if not all biographical accounts draw attention to this fact.[6] The composer was born into a Catholic family. He was baptized a Catholic—the baptismal font survives today in Bonn's St. Remigius Church—and attended a Catholic grade school, the Tirocinium. All his life he lived in a Catholic world. Bonn and Vienna, his two main places of residence, were both Catholic territories within a Holy Roman Empire that had for several centuries been divided politically and culturally along confessional lines. Bonn, his hometown, was even the seat of one of the most important clerics in the German-speaking

---

[6] The biographical facts that follow are neatly summarized in Solomon, "Quest for Faith," 216.

Catholic lands—the Archbishop of Cologne, who was also a prince-elector of the Holy Roman Empire. Much of Beethoven's early musical training there took place in local Catholic churches, where he would have become familiar with church music and its place in the Catholic liturgy. At the end of his life, Beethoven was given a Catholic funeral.[7] Anton Schindler also reports that on his deathbed, the composer willingly received Last Rites from a priest.[8] Beethoven's letters, from different periods of his life, contain puns and witty remarks referring to Catholic religious practice, an indication at least of the prominent place of Catholicism in his cultural milieu. There are several examples of Beethoven playfully using Latin phrases from the Mass or from other well-known Catholic texts in more mundane contexts. In an 1801 letter to Breitkopf & Härtel, Beethoven used the phrase "pax vobiscum" (Peace be with you) as part of an attempt to downplay the irritation he felt at receiving a bad review.[9] On two separate occasions, Beethoven thanked his friend Nikolaus Zmeskall by writing, "Gratias agimus tibi" (We give thanks to you).[10] Writing to Antonie Brentano, he celebrated securing custody of his nephew Karl with the words "Te deum laudamus" (You, O God, we praise).[11]

That Beethoven grew up and lived in a culture shaped by the Catholic Church says nothing, of course, about what he actually believed. And for most writers on Beethoven, the composer's relationship with Catholicism was largely limited to the superficial connections just described. The surviving documentary evidence—especially the composer's letters, *Tagebuch*, and conversation books—shows clearly that Beethoven had a lifelong interest in religious and spiritual issues, making it impossible to claim that the composer was *anti*-religious in a more general, nonsectarian sense.

---

[7] Beethoven's funeral took place in the Dreifaltigkeitskirche (Church of the Holy Trinity), a parish church in the care of the Conventual Franciscans (*Minoriten* in German), on Alser Straße in Vienna. See Solomon, *Beethoven*, 383.

[8] Albrecht no. 479 (*BGA* no. 2291), Anton Schindler to B. Schotts Söhne, April 12, 1827. For several decades now, Beethoven scholars have called into question Schindler's reliability as a source. It has been demonstrated, for instance, that Schindler forged a number of entries in the composer's conversation books, and that his biography of Beethoven is full of embellishments and possibly even lies. The first discoveries along these lines were made by Dagmar Beck and Grita Herre: see "Anton Schindlers fingierte Eintragungen." Theodore Albrecht has, however, made the more nuanced argument that not all of Schindler's claims should be dismissed as untrustworthy, arguing that some of the conversation-book entries he falsified make claims that are actually corroborated by other sources: see "Anton Schindler as Destroyer." There exists no compelling evidence to doubt Schindler's account in the letter I have cited here.

[9] Anderson no. 48 (*BGA* no. 59), April 22, 1801.

[10] Anderson no. 494 (*BGA* no. 666), 1st half of September 1813; and Anderson no. 753 (*BGA* no. 1078), February 4, 1817.

[11] Anderson no. 607 (*BGA* no. 897), February 6, 1816.

But this evidence is almost always used to demonstrate Beethoven's supposed distrust of traditional sources of religious authority. The conventional wisdom is thus that Beethoven's religion was idiosyncratic, unorthodox, individual; not specifically Christian, and certainly not Catholic. The composer was much more concerned with ethics and morality than with dogma, hence his documented interest in non-Christian religions, especially Eastern traditions and Freemasonry.[12] Beethoven had little time for organized religion, and he certainly did not go to church.

This tendency to separate Beethoven from the Catholic religion has a very long history. Its origins can be traced back to the first edition of Anton Schindler's biography (1840), which seems to have been the first to comment specifically on Beethoven's religious attitudes, an issue not dealt with in the earlier biographies by Johann Aloys Schlosser, and by Franz Wegeler and Ferdinand Ries.[13] Schindler reported that Beethoven, though "educated in the Catholic religion" (*in der katholischen Religion erzogen*), was "inclined to deism" (*neige er sich dem Deismus zu*).[14] He maintained this description in the second edition of his biography (1845),[15] then seems to have qualified his claim somewhat in the third edition (1860): "We can ... say almost certainly that [Beethoven's] religious views were based much less on beliefs from the church than they were sourced from deism."[16] Apparently to buttress his claim of Beethoven's separation from the Catholicism of his birth, in all three editions Schindler added that Beethoven kept on his desk several inscriptions purportedly of ancient Egyptian origin: "I am that which is." "I am everything that is, that was, and that will be. No mortal man has raised my veil." "He is one, self-created, and to this oneness all things owe their being."[17]

---

[12] Beethoven scholars make this argument based mainly on evidence from the *Tagebuch*. See, e.g., the following essays by Maynard Solomon: "Beethoven's Tagebuch," 233–46; "Masonic Thread"; and "Masonic Imagination."
[13] See Schlosser, *Beethoven*; and Wegeler and Ries, *Beethoven Remembered*.
[14] See Schindler, *Life of Beethoven*, 2:162–63; and *Biographie*, 1st ed., 250.
[15] Schindler, *Biographie*, 2nd ed., 250.
[16] See Schindler, *Beethoven as I Knew Him*, 365; and *Biographie*, 3rd ed., 2:161: "Mit ziemlicher Gewissenheit kann . . . gesagt werden, daß seine religiösen Anschauungen weniger auf dem Kirchenglauben beruhten, als vielmehr im Deismus ihre Quelle gefunden haben." The English translation provided in the former source has been amended.
[17] See Schindler, *Beethoven as I Knew Him*, 365; and *Biographie*, 3rd ed., 2:161: "Ich bin was da ist." "Ich bin Alles, was ist, was war, was seyn wird, kein sterblicher Mensch hat meinen Schleier aufgehoben." "Er ist einzig von ihm selbst und diesem Einzigen sind alle Dinge ihr Daseyn schuldig." The English translation provided in the former source has been amended. Unbeknownst to Schindler, Beethoven derived these quotations from Friedrich Schiller's *Die Sendung Moses*: see Grigat, *Beethovens Glaubensbekenntnis*, esp. 8–10.

In the almost two centuries since the first edition of Schindler's biography, the overwhelming majority of writers on Beethoven and his music have continued to distance Beethoven from the Catholic religion in which he was raised, although Schindler's choice of the term "deism" has not been consistently accepted. Maynard Solomon, whose writings on Beethoven's religion have exerted the greatest influence on other English-language accounts of the last few decades, has argued that "Beethoven had little use for organized religion" and "was completely lacking in piety toward the icons and assumptions of Christianity."[18] Solomon's view—which recalls Adorno's proclamation in his famous essay on the *Missa solemnis* that Beethoven "must have stood very aloof from organized religion"—has been echoed by many others in both scholarly and popular writings on Beethoven.[19] According to Wilfred Mellers, for instance, Beethoven was "spiritually subversive" and "suspicious of the feudal hierarchy of the Church."[20] For Lewis Lockwood, "Beethoven was not a regular churchgoer, but he had a lifelong leaning to religious experience that took many forms."[21] Jan Caeyers writes of Beethoven's "aversion to the church as an institution."[22] Jan Swafford declares that Beethoven was "no lover of priests, ritual or magic," adding that the composer "had no use for dogma" because "dogma was a variety of tyranny."[23]

The persistence of such views is striking given the relative paucity and, more importantly, the ambiguity of documentary evidence regarding Beethoven's religious outlook. Often quoted in the Beethoven literature are certain statements by the composer that appear to express antipathy toward the Catholic Church, such as an April 1802 letter to the publisher Franz Anton Hoffmeister in which he appears to mock the "newly developing Christian times" (*neuangehenden christlichen Zeiten*) in the aftermath of Napoleon's Concordat with Pope Pius VII.[24] But Beethoven also made other statements hinting at a more positive attitude toward the Church, and these are rarely, if ever, cited. To Nanette Streicher, he wrote:

---

[18] Solomon, "Quest for Faith," 220.
[19] See Adorno, *Beethoven*, 138.
[20] Mellers, *Beethoven*, 3.
[21] Lockwood, *Beethoven*, 402.
[22] Caeyers, *Beethoven*, 285.
[23] Swafford, *Beethoven*, 2, 129.
[24] Anderson no. 57 (*BGA* no. 84). I shall return to this letter in chapter 2, where it will be quoted at greater length.

INTRODUCTION 9

> Train your daughter carefully so that she may become a wife—Today happens to be Sunday, and if I am to read you out something more from the Gospel, then "Love one another" etc., etc., etc.—I am closing this letter and I send you and your most excellent daughter my best greetings, and I trust that all of your wounds will be healed.[25]

In another letter, Beethoven addressed his brother Johann thus:

> Now all good wishes, most excellent little brother! Read the Gospel every day. Take to heart the Epistles of Peter and Paul. Travel to Rome and kiss the Pope's slipper. My warmest greetings to your family. Write soon. With all my heart I embrace you.[26]

And to Carlo Boldrini, a partner at the publisher Artaria, he advised, "Do not be too dissolute; but read the Gospel and be converted."[27] There is nothing in the letters from which these statements are drawn to suggest that Beethoven's remarks were anything but sincere, rather than ironic or sarcastic. Beethoven's surviving correspondence also includes seven letters to Joseph Varena in Graz, dated between 1812 and 1815, in which he refers to a group of Ursuline nuns for whose charitable concerts he provided music.[28] Beethoven appears to have held the nuns in high regard, in one instance calling them "noble-minded."[29] He also explicitly requests that Varena ask the nuns to pray for him.[30] The warm feelings the composer felt for the Ursulines seems to have been reciprocated: in one of the letters, Beethoven reports to Varena that the nuns had sent him some sweetmeats.[31]

Beethoven's connection to the Bavarian Catholic theologian Johann Michael Sailer (1751–1832) provides a more compelling reason to reconsider

---

[25] Anderson no. 789 (*BGA* no. 1142), July 20, 1817: "Halten Sie ihre Töchter fleißig an, daß sie eine Frau werde.—Heute ist eben Sonntag, soll ich ihnen noch etwas aus dem Evangelium vorlesen, 'Liebet euch untereinander' *etc. etc. etc.*—ich schließe [und] empfehle mich ihnen [und] ihrer besten Tochter bestens, wünsche ihnen Heilung aller ihrer Wunden."
[26] Anderson no. 1087 (*BGA* no. 1486), July 31, 1822: "Jetzt Lebe wohl, bestes Brüderl! lies alle Tage das Evangelium; führe Dir die *Epistln Petri* u[nd] *Paulli* zu Gemüth, Reise nach Rom, u[nd] küsse dem Papst den Pantoffl. Grüße mir die Deinigen herzlich. Schreibe bald. Ich umarme Dich von Herzen."
[27] Anderson no. 1017 (*BGA* no. 1379), April 8, 1820: "Seyd Nicht zu liderlich, leßt das *Evangelium* u[nd] bekehrt euch."
[28] Anderson nos. 378, 411, 414, 419, 424, 428, and 528 (*BGA* nos. 587, 630, 633, 653, 652, 661, and 781). See also Anderson no. 408 (*BGA* no. 631).
[29] Anderson no. 414 (*BGA* no. 633), April 8, 1813: "edlen Klosterfrauen."
[30] Anderson no. 378 (*BGA* no. 587), July 19, 1812.
[31] Anderson no. 424 (*BGA* no. 652), May 27, 1813.

10 THE CATHOLIC BEETHOVEN

the received wisdom on the composer's religious outlook. Though far from a household name today, Sailer was the preeminent Catholic theologian of his era, whose fame extended far beyond the boundaries of his own religious group.[32] Beethoven expressed a desire for his beloved nephew Karl to study under Sailer's tutelage, and evidence from both the composer's letters and the conversation books suggests that he and his close associates held favorable opinions of the theologian.[33] Beethoven also purchased some of Sailer's books.[34] Sailer's name has not been entirely absent from Beethoven scholarship, but it has tended to appear only as a passing reference within biographies, usually accompanied by a brief suggestion that the composer's connection to Sailer may have had some impact on the *Missa solemnis*, which Beethoven started working on around the same time.[35] In addition to works by Sailer, Beethoven's personal library contained other religious books that were explicitly Christian: *Betrachtungen über die Werke Gottes im Reiche der Natur und der Vorsehung* (Reflections on the works of God in the realm of nature and of Providence) by Christoph Christian Sturm (1740–1786), *Ansichten von Religion und Kirchenthum* (Views on religion and the church) by Ignaz Aurelius Fessler (1756–1839), and Thomas à Kempis's famous medieval devotional text *The Imitation of Christ*. Of these works, only Sturm's book has received significant attention in the Beethoven literature, mainly in relation to the composer's interest in the natural world.[36]

As hinted at above, the conventional view of Beethoven's religious outlook has been closely tied to the critical marginalization of his works of religious music. The *Missa solemnis* has been an obvious exception to this rule. It is, after all, hard to dismiss a piece of such complexity and scale, especially one that the composer himself described on more than one occasion as his greatest work.[37] But the *Missa* has tended to be understood as

---

[32] See Baumgartner, *Johann Michael Sailer*, esp. 21, 27, 144–45.

[33] See Albrecht no. 256; Anderson nos. 946 and 1005 (*BGA* nos. 1300 and 1365); *BCB* 1:16, 24, 29, 53, 57 (*BKh* 1:39, 44, 48–49, 68–69, 72); *BCB* 2:42, 277 (*BKh* 1:364; *BKh* 2:187–89); and E. Anderson, *Letters of Beethoven*, 3:1394. This evidence will be discussed in detail in chapter 5.

[34] See *Schätzungsprotokoll* nos. 1 and 11.

[35] See, e.g., Lockwood, *Beethoven*, 403–5; Solomon, "Quest for Faith," 222–23; and Lodes, "Probing the Sacred Genres," 234–35. Two notable exceptions to this relative neglect of Sailer in the existing literature are provided by Ito, "Johann Michael Sailer"; and Wolfsohl, "Beethoven liest Autoren," 115–17. Both these accounts argue that Sailer's ideas did not exert a significant influence on Beethoven. I will outline my disagreements with this argument in chapter 5. A recent essay by Jakob Johannes Koch ("'Von Herzen'"), which also mentions Sailer, will be discussed below.

[36] See, e.g., Witcombe, "Beethoven's Markings"; and Wyn Jones, *Beethoven: Pastoral Symphony*, 22–24.

[37] See Anderson nos. 1079 and 1270 (*BGA* nos. 1468 and 1787).

proof of Beethoven's unorthodox, idiosyncratic religious attitudes, rather than as a sincere example of Catholic church music. William Kinderman, for instance, writes of how the "Mass text is not simply affirmed in its literal content but is interpreted by means of *universal* images, thereby imposing a *broader humanistic* perspective on the received doctrines."[38] Solomon is less diplomatic: "Although we may be certain Beethoven poured his deepest religious feelings into the *Missa solemnis*, we may be equally sure it was not deference to the Catholic Church that prompted the work."[39] More recently, Jan Assmann declared that the *Missa* was the culmination of a historical process through which the Mass was "emancipated" (*emanzipierte*) from Catholic worship to become a work of art.[40]

In contrast, Beethoven's sacred works other than the *Missa solemnis* have been routinely treated as anomalies, as pieces written merely for commercial gain or to take advantage of career opportunities, rather than authentically Beethovenian works. In addition, their aesthetic value has frequently been dismissed.[41] But there is a good deal of evidence that complicates such characterizations. Using religious texts for lieder was highly unusual during Beethoven's time, so it seems difficult to claim that in composing the Gellert Lieder, Beethoven was motivated primarily by commercial reasons.[42] *Christus am Ölberge* was probably not written specifically for the 1803 Akademie where it was premiered, as has often been claimed.[43] Moreover, the texts in both these works bear strong resemblances to the Heiligenstadt Testament, in terms of general themes as well as specific words and phrases,

---

[38] Kinderman, *Beethoven*, 307 (my emphasis).
[39] Solomon, *Beethoven*, 400.
[40] Assmann, *Kult und Kunst*, 17.
[41] Critical judgments of *Christus am Ölberge* have been especially harsh. Lockwood, e.g., has described it as nothing more than a "hastily crafted effort to compete with Haydn as an oratorio composer" (*Beethoven*, 271). Solomon called it a "flawed conception," attributable to the fact that "Beethoven was temperamentally and ideologically disinclined to view Christ's crucifixion as a sorrowful but necessary submission to the Father's will" (*Beethoven*, 249). More recently, Jan Swafford proclaimed it "one of the most misconceived, inauthentic, undigested large works Beethoven ever wrote" (*Beethoven*, 317–18). For William Drabkin, both *Christus* and the Mass in C were "failed works," written in haste for specific occasions (*Beethoven: Missa solemnis*, 1). Other writers have treated Beethoven's first mass more charitably, though it is still most often viewed as a preparatory work for the *Missa solemnis*, which is considered the real masterpiece: see, e.g., Kinderman, *Beethoven*, 146; and Lockwood, *Beethoven*, 272–73.
[42] Lodes, "Probing the Sacred Genres," 219.
[43] The 1803 Akademie was probably not planned when Beethoven began composing the oratorio; moreover, he would not have needed this kind of work in order to have an Akademie put on, since we know that he was complaining during this period about having too many commissions for other works. See B. Cooper, "Beethoven's Oratorio," 23–24.

suggesting that they can be rightly understood as deeply personal, autobiographical works.[44]

In any case, neither the commercial nor the occasion-specific nature of a work automatically excludes the possibility that it also reflected Beethoven's own views. Though undoubtedly commissioned by a patron for a specific occasion, Beethoven's Mass in C was apparently of such personal significance for the composer that when confronted with Breitkopf & Härtel's reluctance to publish it, he insisted they do so without having to pay him for it, declaring the work "especially close to [his] heart."[45] And even if Beethoven was motivated to write a piece by external circumstances rather than simply because he felt inspired to do so, he would still have had considerable control over the exact way in which that piece of music was composed.[46] After all, few critics would claim that works such as the Razumovsky Quartets or the Galitzin Quartets are any less sincere or "authentically" Beethoven simply because they were commissioned by (and not just dedicated to) someone else. And the *Missa solemnis* has never been dismissed as merely an occasional work prompted by the enthronement of the Archduke Rudolph as Archbishop of Olmütz.[47]

It is impossible to deny that, numerically speaking, religious music—defined relatively narrowly as works with a Christian text—forms a small

---

[44] See B. Cooper, "Beethoven's Oratorio"; and Massenkeil, "Religiöse Aspekte," 193–94. Alan Tyson has stressed the parallels between *Christus* and *Fidelio*, written just a couple of years later. For Tyson, these works, along with the *Eroica* Symphony that Beethoven completed in between his only oratorio and his only opera, define what he calls Beethoven's "heroic phase," a period of intense interest in the theme of heroism, which arose as a means of coming to terms with the onset of his deafness—the subject, of course, of the Heiligenstadt Testament: see Tyson, "Beethoven's Heroic Phase." Tyson's argument makes sense, but it also appears to downplay the specifically Christian nature of Beethoven's oratorio, akin to the reluctance among commentators to treat the *Missa solemnis* as a Catholic work. For instance, Tyson describes Beethoven's Christ as an "*Ur*-Florestan," who, like the character in *Fidelio*, is "resigned to the will of God" despite being "under the threat of a painful death" (ibid., 140).

[45] Anderson no. 169 (*BGA* no. 331), end of July 1808: "[Die Messe] mir . . . vorzüglich am Herzen liegt." The Mass in C was commissioned by Prince Nikolaus Esterházy II, erstwhile employer of Haydn, for his wife's name day: see McGrann, "Beethoven's Mass in C," 1:49–55, 78.

[46] Joanna Biermann has made such an argument specifically in relation to *Christus*. Even if Beethoven intended *Christus* to show he could write in the oratorio genre, or he was eager to take advantage of the opportunities presented to him by his recent employment at the Theater an der Wien, this would not, in Biermann's view, explain why Beethoven chose to set the text in the way he did, or why the libretto itself depicts Christ in the way it does. See Biermann, "*Christus am Ölberge*," 296–98. See also B. Cooper, "Beethoven's Oratorio," 23–24.

[47] To be sure, the fact that Beethoven ended up writing a good amount of the *Missa* only *after* Rudolph's enthronement has probably helped critics de-emphasize the idea that it was composed for this specific occasion. On Archduke Rudolph, and Beethoven's close relationship with him, see Kagan, *Archduke Rudolph*; Novotny, "Kardinal Erzherzog Rudolph"; and Nettl, "Erinnerungen an Erzherzog Rudolph."

part of Beethoven's output. But the personal significance of such religious works, including those aside from the *Missa solemnis*, suggests that their small number says nothing about their importance to the composer. Moreover, we know that Beethoven sketched ideas for a handful of sacred works that were never completed, and he expressed an interest in composing several others that were never started, including a Requiem and a *Te Deum*.[48] If one takes into account Beethoven's intentions to compose such pieces, the religious works that he did compose, though few in number, begin to seem less anomalous.

Enlightenment Historiography and Beethoven's Religious Outlook

What underlies conventional accounts of Beethoven's religious views, and the critical marginalization of most of his sacred music that has accompanied such accounts, is an implicit reliance on a stereotyped conception of the Enlightenment as intrinsically opposed to institutional religion, especially the Catholic Church. According to this conception, Enlightenment ideas served as the basis of the political upheavals of the late eighteenth and nineteenth century, and either undermined or overthrew the old order, an important pillar of which was the institutional church, whether Catholic or Protestant. In light of this familiar narrative, many of the household names of the Enlightenment—such as Voltaire or Rousseau in France, or Hume in Britain—are famous because of their critique and even rejection of religious belief, at least in the way it had been traditionally defined by Western Christianity. The Catholic Church, in particular, perhaps because of its persistent transnational power, was a favorite whipping boy of many intellectuals, who viewed it as the prime symbol of superstition and backwardness. Prominent Enlightenment intellectuals may not all have been atheists or even agnostics, but they were at least deists, and certainly not Christians in the traditional sense. The French Revolution, that monumental political event often seen as the preeminent realization of the Enlightenment's ideas, involved, among other things, the turning of Notre Dame Cathedral into a Temple of Reason, the abolition of the Gregorian

---

[48] See Ronge, "Beethoven's Ambitions in Church Music."

calendar, and the persecution of noncompliant Catholic clergy. Put simply, the stereotypical view of the Enlightenment is that it launched the West on its path toward secular modernity. Particularly influential in the dissemination of this perspective was Peter Gay's classic two-volume history of the Enlightenment, written in the 1960s, whose preface bears the provocative title "The Rise of Modern Paganism."[49]

If this story is correct, then Beethoven, who is often believed to have sympathized with Enlightenment values such as political liberalism, rationalism, and skepticism toward traditional symbols of authority, could not possibly have been a pious and obedient devotee of the Catholic Church. The habitual attempts to distance the composer from Christianity in general, and Catholicism in particular, have thus served a broader desire to present the composer and his music as quintessentially modern. The titles of three book-length studies published in conjunction with the recent 250th anniversary of the composer's birth suggest that the image of Beethoven as "lifelong Enlightenment radical," to borrow Nicholas Mathew's phrase, remains very appealing: *Beethoven: A Political Artist in Revolutionary Times* by William Kinderman, *Beethoven: The Relentless Revolutionary* by John Clubbe, and *Beethoven: Musik für eine neue Zeit* (Beethoven: Music for a new time) by Hans-Joachim Hinrichsen.[50] Hinrichsen's book in particular exemplifies the common tendency in Beethoven scholarship to link Beethoven and his music to ostensibly progressive figures associated with the secular Enlightenment. For its author, Beethoven's musical achievements are analogous to the way Immanuel Kant's critical philosophy ushered in modern thought: "Just as the main works of Kant's critical philosophy represent nothing less than the 'foundation of modern philosophy,' in a similar sense Beethoven's mature works accomplish the foundation of modern music."[51] In the same vein, Kinderman has stressed the special importance of both Kant's and Schiller's philosophies for understanding Beethoven's music.[52]

To be clear, it is not my purpose here to deny the relevance of secular thinkers such as Kant and Schiller for Beethoven, though at least in the case

---

[49] Gay, *Enlightenment*. For succinct and informative overviews of the evolution of Enlightenment historiography since Gay's book, see De Dijn, "Politics of Enlightenment"; and Barnett, *Enlightenment and Religion*, 1–10.

[50] Mathew, *Political Beethoven*, 6; Kinderman, *Beethoven: A Political Artist*; Clubbe, *Beethoven*; Hinrichsen, *Beethoven*.

[51] Hinrichsen, *Beethoven*, 9: "In einem ähnlichem Sinne, in dem Kants kritische Hauptschriften nichts Geringeres darstellen als die »Grundlegung der modernen Philosophie«, leisten Beethovens reife Werke die Grundlegung der modernen Musik."

[52] See Kinderman, *Beethoven*, 3–15.

of Kant the extent to which Beethoven was familiar with his critical philosophy remains disputed.[53] My aim, rather, is to show that there were other "enlightened" influences on the composer that are worth taking seriously, if we adopt a broader conception of the Enlightenment than the one to which many of us are accustomed, especially with regard to religion. Over the past few decades, wide-ranging research by political and intellectual historians has called into question the idea that the Enlightenment and traditional religious beliefs were mutually exclusive. This binary view has been motivated by various ideological agendas, some dating back to the time of the Enlightenment itself, but does not account for the diversity of positions embraced by thinkers who all considered themselves "enlightened."[54] It also misleadingly assumes that what was true of the Enlightenment in France was true of the Enlightenment everywhere else in Europe.[55] As early as the 1980s, Derek Beales proposed that the Enlightenment in the German lands and Italy should be distinguished from the French, and to some extent also the British, Enlightenment.[56] Generally speaking, the Enlightenment in the German lands (and in Italy) was far less hostile to religion. Even if it was often anti-clerical, its primary concern was religious *reform*. Unlike the Enlightenment in France, which did not contain much state involvement, the German Enlightenment was often driven by the state (hence the presence of Enlightened despots such as Frederick the Great in Prussia and Joseph II of Austria, about whom more below).

More recent historians have advocated an even more pluralistic conception of the Enlightenment. David Sorkin, for instance, speaks of an "Enlightenment spectrum" and identifies what he calls a "religious Enlightenment" that overlapped with moderate versions of the secular

---

[53] I discuss this issue in "Beethoven and Kant's *Allgemeine Naturgeschichte*." See also Maier, "Beethoven liest Littrow."

[54] See Bradley and Van Kley, introduction to *Religion and Politics in Enlightenment Europe*, esp. 2–3. An important distinction should be made between how the Enlightenment was understood by various figures who saw themselves as "enlightened" at the time, and what strands of Enlightenment thinking—and which representative figures—have ended up being most influential in hindsight. There are debates to be had about both these issues, of course, but keeping them separate is essential for an accurate understanding of the Enlightenment in its time, as opposed to the later legacy of the Enlightenment over the longer term. (The work of Jonathan Israel, discussed below, is a helpful illustration of this distinction.) The religious thinkers with whose writings Beethoven engaged were much more prominent in their time than their present-day obscurity suggests.

[55] See Bradley and Van Kley, 2–5. On the historic dominance of French perspectives in Enlightenment historiography, see Edelstein, *Enlightenment*, esp. 2–6.

[56] See Beales, *Joseph II*, 1:7–8, 2:70. See also Beales, *Enlightenment and Reform*, 60–89. A more recent source that makes a similar distinction is Rady, *Habsburgs*, 201.

Enlightenment.⁵⁷ This religious Enlightenment occurred in various national strands, and across all three of Western Europe's major religious groups: Protestants, Catholics, and Jews.⁵⁸ To accept the existence of the religious Enlightenment does not require denying the obvious threat that many secular Enlightenment ideas posed to traditional religion. But it is inaccurate to reduce the Enlightenment to being simply the antithesis of religion, especially in its organized and institutional forms. Many religious leaders and intellectuals were, in fact, open to the influence of Enlightenment ideas; in some cases, it may even be said that they contributed to the Enlightenment as a broader movement. As Sorkin writes:

> Contrary to the secular master narrative, the Enlightenment was not only compatible with religious belief but conducive to it. The Enlightenment made possible new iterations of faith. With the Enlightenment's advent religion lost neither its place nor its authority in European society and culture. If we trace modern culture to the Enlightenment, its foundations were decidedly religious.⁵⁹

Many, if not most, Enlightenment thinkers were less hostile to religion than is usually assumed: a famous figure such as Voltaire is really an extreme example of an Enlightenment thinker rather than a typical one.⁶⁰ And even the familiar idea that deism was the default view among Enlightenment figures is untrue.⁶¹

The more nuanced account just described of the relationship between religion and the Enlightenment is now widely accepted among specialist historians of the Enlightenment. Tacit acceptance of it is evident even among historians who otherwise display an ideological sympathy for secularism and rationalism, most notably Jonathan Israel, whose writings—especially the books *Radical Enlightenment, Enlightenment Contested, Democratic Enlightenment,* and *A Revolution of the Mind*—have been among the most influential, albeit controversial, accounts of the Enlightenment written in the last two decades.⁶² Israel's main argument, which has been much criticized, is that only the strands of the Enlightenment that he considers "radical" (as

---

[57] Sorkin, *Religious Enlightenment*, 19.
[58] Sorkin, 1–21, esp. 3–11.
[59] Sorkin, 3.
[60] See Beales, *Enlightenment and Reform*, 60–89.
[61] Barnett, *Enlightenment and Religion*, 11–44, esp. 12–14.
[62] For an overview of critiques of Israel's work, see Eigenauer, "Meta-Analysis of Critiques."

opposed to "moderate"), by virtue of their descent from the rationalist and religiously skeptical thought of Spinoza, were ultimately influential for the later political history of the West. What is noteworthy, however, is that despite this view, Israel still takes for granted a pluralistic account of the Enlightenment— that is, the existence of multiple versions of the Enlightenment that differed considerably in their level of radicalism. Nevertheless, the older and more reductive view of the Enlightenment continues to exert a strong hold on other fields of humanistic inquiry, a situation that can be attributed at least partly to continued anti-religious bias in the historiography of the modern era.[63]

Within the broader "religious Enlightenment," itself one of many strands of the Enlightenment as a whole, there existed a specifically Catholic Enlightenment that consisted of a number of eighteenth-century intellectual, theological, and political movements that aimed to reform the Catholic Church, as well as to reconcile various ideas from the mainstream, secular Enlightenment with Catholic belief.[64] The concept of the Catholic Enlightenment (*katholische Aufklärung*) was first introduced as long ago as 1908 by the German theologian Sebastian Merkle, but it has attracted sustained scholarly interest only more recently.[65] Though Merkle meant it as a framework for understanding the *German* Enlightenment specifically, newer scholarship has sought to extend it to other national contexts.[66] (The first major English-language monograph on the Catholic Enlightenment—which

---

[63] For discussions of this state of affairs, see Printy, "History and Church History," 259; Blanchard, *Synod of Pistoia*, 44n2; Lehner, *Catholic Enlightenment*, 1–13, esp. 2–3; Lehner, *On the Road*, 1–21, esp. 5–6; Sorkin, *Religious Enlightenment*, 1; and Beales, *Prosperity and Plunder*, 9. An excellent survey of the broader historical and historiographical issues at stake in reconsidering the role of religion in the Enlightenment is provided by Sheehan, "Enlightenment, Religion." For a discussion of the impact of traditional Enlightenment historiography on art history, see Grewe, *Painting the Sacred*, 7–8.

[64] For a general introduction to the Catholic Enlightenment, see Printy, "History and Church History"; Burson, "Introduction"; and Lehner, *Catholic Enlightenment*. Some scholars have sought to distinguish between the "Catholic Enlightenment," as a description of Enlightenment-influenced ideas for church reform, and other terms referring more generally to varieties of the Enlightenment specific to Catholic societies: "Enlightenment Catholicism," "Enlightened Catholicism," "Enlightenment in Catholic Germany." See Hinske, "Katholische Aufklärung" and Klueting, "'Der Genius der Zeit.'" In the latter case, the point is to show that even the secular Enlightenment was in many cases influenced by religious issues emerging from within the Catholic Church. Other scholars seem to use these terms interchangeably: see, e.g., Forster, *Catholic Germany*, esp. p. 189 ("Catholic Enlightenment") and p. 199 ("Enlightened Catholicism"). It suffices to note for our purposes that, whatever terminology is employed, the relationship between Catholicism and the (secular) Enlightenment was dynamic and bidirectional: each influenced the other. For convenience, I shall use only the term "Catholic Enlightenment" throughout this study.

[65] See Burson, "Introduction," 1–9; and Lehner, "Introduction," 1–12. See also Printy, "History and Church History."

[66] See Printy, "History and Church History," 248–49.

goes so far as to present it as a global rather than merely Western European phenomenon—appeared as recently as 2016.)[67]

Beginning with his composition of the Gellert Lieder in 1802 through to the end of his life, Beethoven appears to have shown a consistent interest in a number of key ideas associated with the German Catholic Enlightenment. This can be discerned from the compositional circumstances and the characteristics of his major religious works, as well as from the content of the religious texts in his library cited above. Additional clues can also be found in the traditional documentary sources associated with Beethoven: his correspondence, conversation books, and *Tagebuch*. Though some of this evidence has been overlooked in prior scholarship, in other cases a more accurate understanding of Beethoven's religious-historical context leads to what I shall argue are more historically grounded interpretations of material that has previously been acknowledged. Of particular importance is the convergence of Catholic Church reform and some liberal sociopolitical ideas within the German Catholic Enlightenment, which should serve to caution against overstating the radicalism of Beethoven's views. Consider, for example, the anticlerical streak that many scholars have justifiably attributed to Beethoven, or Beethoven's apparent Masonic sympathies, which have been linked to a belief in religious tolerance and the importance of virtuous conduct over religious dogma.[68] As I shall show, none of these ideas would have been automatically considered opposed to Catholicism in Beethoven's time. In a similar vein, musical aspects of Beethoven's religious works that have often been interpreted as departing from a Christian outlook may not actually have been considered so within his historical context.

Beethoven's sympathy for the Catholic Enlightenment was probably inspired by his exposure to the movement during his youth in Bonn, which was an especially important center of efforts to reform the German Catholic Church. Complicating matters, however, is that some aspects of his outlook can be understood as deviating to some degree from the Catholic Enlightenment, though in a "conservative" direction. For reasons that will be explained in chapter 1, popular support for the Catholic Enlightenment was limited, and many reforms that were implemented in the 1770s and 1780s were rolled back in the changing sociopolitical climate generated first by the French Revolutionary and Napoleonic Wars, then by the subsequent

---

[67] Lehner, *Catholic Enlightenment*.
[68] On Beethoven and Freemasonry, see Solomon, "Masonic Thread" and "Masonic Imagination."

Restoration period, as more conservative visions of the Church regained support among many, though by no means all, German Catholics.[69] The historical literature reveals no standardized term akin to "Catholic Enlightenment" for describing this process of reaction, but, for convenience, I shall call this phenomenon the "Catholic Restoration," a term I borrow from Josef Schuh.[70] Signs of Beethoven's openness to more conservative approaches to Catholicism can be detected as early as 1803, in his oratorio *Christus am Ölberge*. In the last decade of his life, the composer's admiration for Johann Michael Sailer and some compositional features of the *Missa solemnis* also suggest at least a partial sympathy for the Catholic Restoration. The Catholic Enlightenment is thus relevant for understanding Beethoven's religious context not just by itself, but also because of the way it led to the Catholic Restoration.

This book begins by outlining in the first chapter a detailed history of the Catholic Church in the German-speaking lands during Beethoven's epoch, expanding the briefer discussion provided above. I explain the origins of the German Catholic Enlightenment as a reaction against something known as Baroque Catholicism before examining the Catholic Enlightenment itself, with a particular focus on the reformist policies of the Habsburg emperor Joseph II. The chapter then describes the decline of the Catholic Enlightenment and the accompanying rise of the Catholic Restoration.

The historical overview provided by chapter 1 lays the groundwork for the remaining chapters of the book, which, taken together, constitute a roughly chronological study of Beethoven's engagement with religious ideas throughout his life. Chapter 2 explores Beethoven's exposure to the German Catholic Enlightenment during his youth in Bonn. My account contributes to recent efforts to reevaluate the composer's Bonn years, which have often been either neglected or misunderstood.[71] I stress in particular the centrality of Catholic church reform to the Enlightenment in Bonn, which was reflected in the relative moderation of most self-identified progressive thinkers in the city, as well as the prominence of church music in Beethoven's early training.

---

[69] For general sources on German Catholicism during the Napoleonic Wars and the Restoration, see Holzem, *Christianity in Germany*, 2:978–1156; Nipperdey, *Germany from Napoleon to Bismarck*, 356–73; Hänsel, *Geistliche Restauration*; Beales, *Prosperity and Plunder*, 270–90; Blanning, "Role of Religion"; and Blanning, *French Revolution in Germany*, esp. v, 15–17, 207–54, 255–85, 312, 317–36.
[70] Schuh, *Johann Michael Sailer*, 11.
[71] See, among other sources: Wilson, "From the Chapel"; Reisinger, *Musik machen, fördern, sammeln*; Reisinger, Riepe, and Wilson, *Operatic Library*; Lodes, Reisinger, and Wilson, *Beethoven und andere Hofmusiker*; and Konrad, "Der 'Bonner' Beethoven."

Chapter 3 connects the three major religious works Beethoven wrote before the *Missa solemnis*—the Gellert Lieder, *Christus am Ölberge*, and the Mass in C—to the Catholic Enlightenment. Compositional circumstances surrounding the Gellert Lieder and the Mass in C exemplify the movement's ecumenical outlook—its openness to engagement with non-Catholics, especially Protestant Christians—and the thematization of nature and ethical conduct in the Gellert Lieder and *Christus* reflects two of its key concerns. Beethoven's musical treatment of the liturgical text in the Mass in C illustrates, though not in a straightforward way, the Catholic Enlightenment's encouragement of active participation in the liturgy among the laity. The chapter concludes by introducing a complication to my argument concerning Beethoven's Catholic Enlightenment leanings: Beethoven's highly sentimental depiction of Christ in *Christus* can be more appropriately linked to the conservative Catholic Restoration—something that was recognized even in early critical reactions to the oratorio.

Chapters 4 and 5 connect Beethoven to the religious figures mentioned above, mainly through a close examination of books by them that he had in his library. The available evidence suggests that Beethoven engaged with all of these books during the 1810s or the early 1820s, in the decade or so before the composition of the *Missa solemnis*. Chapter 4 focuses on Sturm's *Betrachtungen über die Werke Gottes* and Ignaz Aurelius Feßler's *Ansichten von Religion und Kirchenthum*. I demonstrate the way Sturm's text reflects the Catholic Enlightenment's interest in the natural world, while Feßler's book can be tied to its ecumenical concerns. (Because neither of these two authors was Catholic himself, I shall also discuss a number of reasons why it is nevertheless appropriate to interpret their books through a Catholic Enlightenment lens.) Additionally, a brief section of this chapter will address Beethoven's *Tagebuch*, which also comes from the 1810s, arguing that the prevalence of quotations from non-Christian sources need not, in the context of the time, be interpreted as antithetical to Catholic belief.

A separate chapter (chapter 5) is then devoted to Beethoven's engagement with the writings of Johann Michael Sailer, as well as with Thomas à Kempis's *Imitation of Christ*, which can be tied to Sailer for a number of reasons, including the fact that Beethoven probably read the work in Sailer's translation.[72] I accord Sailer special attention because Beethoven owned multiple books by him and because of the indirect personal contact that he had with

---

[72] See Ito, "Johann Michael Sailer and Beethoven," 90–91.

the theologian (discussed above), a situation that does not exist with regard to any other major religious figure of the time. In addition, Beethoven's interest in Sailer's writings began while he was working on the *Missa solemnis*, his most important religious work. Because some aspects of Sailer's thought show affinities with religious ideas that Beethoven had already been concerned with earlier in his life, it would be misleading to claim that Sailer's ideas caused some kind of radical change in the composer's views. More likely, they resonated with and reinforced certain views that the composer already had. That said, the relative conservatism of Sailer's theology, and his ambivalent relationship to the Catholic Enlightenment, can be read as an indication, however slight, of an increased affinity on Beethoven's part for approaches to Catholicism that deviated in crucial ways from the Catholic Enlightenment.

Finally, chapter 6 discusses the *Missa solemnis* through the lens of Sailer's theology. I interpret the work as channeling, in the religious-historical context of the time, a combination of progressive and conservative theological ideas, a blend of Catholic Enlightenment and Restoration analogous to Sailer's outlook. Though several of its key features extend compositional practices Beethoven utilized previously in the Mass in C, on the whole the greater prominence of musical characteristics seemingly reflective of the Catholic Restoration provides a further hint of the composer's growing sympathy for more conservative varieties of Catholicism toward the end of his life.

Beethoven's Catholicism and the "Beethoven Myth"

In reconsidering the conventional view of Beethoven's religious outlook, this book joins previous efforts to challenge the so-called Beethoven myth—the image, largely inherited from nineteenth-century German criticism, of Beethoven as a secular liberal Enlightenment hero. Many aspects of the myth have been shown to be false, the result of what later generations of critics and listeners have wanted to hear in Beethoven's works rather than an accurate portrayal of Beethoven the real historical figure.[73] At the very least, the Beethoven myth presents an incomplete picture of the composer and his

---

[73] See, among other sources, Solie, "Beethoven as a Secular Humanist"; Dennis, *Beethoven in German Politics*; Knittel, "Wagner, Deafness" and "Construction of Beethoven"; and Burnham, *Beethoven Hero* and "Four Ages of Beethoven."

music. Revisionist scholars have focused primarily on Beethoven's political views, and there has been relatively little reconsideration of Beethoven's *religious* attitudes in particular.[74] Nicholas Mathew and Stephen Rumph, for instance, have attempted to link Beethoven's music, especially political works such as *Wellington's Victory* and *Der glorreiche Augenblick* that were written for the Congress of Vienna, to conservative political ideologies associated with the Restoration, ideologies that were opposed to the Enlightenment in the secular-liberal sense in which it is normally understood.[75] Both Mathew and Rumph acknowledge that there was a significant religious, indeed Catholic, component to Restorationist politics, but there is little specific discussion of religion separate from politics in either study. My suggestion that there existed a notable, though not dominant, conservative component to Beethoven's Catholic outlook might seem to follow directly in the footsteps of these studies. But given the complexity of both the political and religious situations at the time, any conservative religious leanings Beethoven may have had do not automatically prove an affinity for conservative *politics*, especially in the form embodied by the political Restoration—which was not always neatly aligned with the Catholic Restoration, as I shall explain in chapter 1.

In any event, the fact that the Beethoven myth has been shown to be problematic in the political realm should encourage us also to rethink longstanding assumptions about the composer's views when it came to religious matters.[76] My attempt to question the received wisdom in this regard is not entirely without precedent, for there have been isolated examples of skepticism toward it in previous Beethoven scholarship. Martin Cooper's 1970 book *Beethoven: The Last Decade* claimed that "although Beethoven was plainly not a practicing Catholic during his lifetime, his acceptance of the

---

[74] This fact is specifically lamented by Gerhard Poppe in his study of the reception history of the *Missa solemnis*: see *Festhochamt, sinfonische Messe*, 453.

[75] Mathew, *Political Beethoven*; Rumph, *Beethoven after Napoleon*. See also Cook, "Other Beethoven." Unlike Rumph, who explicitly argues that Beethoven himself had a "change of heart" about the liberal Enlightenment ideals he once espoused (*Beethoven after Napoleon*, 93), Mathew seems to shy away from making claims about the composer's own political views in favor of focusing on the Restoration as cultural context for the *reception* of Beethoven's political music.

[76] Our understanding of the historical issue of Beethoven's religious outlook may even have ethical ramifications. As Daniel Chua argues in his recent book *Beethoven and Freedom*, the "heroic" view of freedom long associated with Beethoven, which is closely tied to the Beethoven myth, paradoxically leads to authoritarianism, or more generally to a politics of exclusion, given its monolithic focus on individual autonomy. Chua argues that it is possible to discern a different kind of freedom in Beethoven's music, one that is relational rather than individualistic. Especially in the last of his three main chapters, he implies that this "other" freedom requires that we let go of hearing Beethoven's music in exclusively secular terms, and embrace instead a Christian ethical framework.

last sacraments on his death-bed confirms the impression that he had not consciously separated himself from Church membership."[77] Cooper seems to stress that Beethoven's attitude to the Catholic Church was neither negative nor indifferent, but still errs on the side of denying that Beethoven had any kind of *active* affinity for Catholic beliefs. In a similar vein, a recent essay by Jakob Johannes Koch acknowledges the Catholic Enlightenment in Bonn and Beethoven's connection to Johann Michael Sailer, but ultimately still characterizes Beethoven's outlook as "unorthodox" (*unorthodoxe*).[78] Koch is willing to call Beethoven a Christian, but qualifies this description by stating that he was an "individual" and "spiritual" Christian who was "formed by very diverse traditions."[79] As we shall see, elements of Beethoven's religiosity that seem "unorthodox" were more often than not compatible with strands of Catholic belief that were current in his time.

For a more forceful challenge to the prevailing consensus on Beethoven's religious outlook we must go further back to a book from the 1920s: Arnold Schmitz's *Das romantische Beethovenbild*. In a chapter entitled simply "Religiosität" (Religiosity), Schmitz describes the existence of multiple theological camps even within Vienna alone, and argues that the two biggest influences on Beethoven's religious beliefs were Christoph Christian Sturm and Johann Michael Sailer.[80] Schmitz goes so far as to contend that not only was Schindler incorrect in describing Beethoven as a deist, and not only can Beethoven's religiosity not be reduced to a "crass" (*krasser*) rationalism or pantheism, but Beethoven was in fact some kind of Christian, even a Catholic.[81] Beethoven, in Schmitz's view, believed at least in Jesus Christ as Redeemer, and it would be wrong to claim that he separated himself from the Church.[82] More recent Beethoven scholars such as Solomon and Lockwood have not been unaware of Schmitz's text but have drawn from it only individual pieces of information regarding Beethoven's religious context, without mentioning Schmitz's overall conclusion about Beethoven's own beliefs—a conclusion with which they obviously disagreed.[83] As Helmut Loos has

---

[77] M. Cooper, *Beethoven*, 105–19, at 119.
[78] See Koch, "'Von Herzen,'" 32–39, 52–53, 59.
[79] Koch, 59: "Er war ein individueller, von sehr unterschiedlichen Traditionen geprägter, spiritueller Christ."
[80] Schmitz, *Das romantische Beethovenbild*, 82–101.
[81] Schmitz, 82, 91–93.
[82] Schmitz, 89.
[83] See Solomon, "Quest for Faith," 222; and Lockwood, *Beethoven*, 403. Drawing on Schmitz, Solomon acknowledges the existence of a Catholic revival in Vienna in the 1810s and the possibility that Beethoven might have been influenced by it. In the end, however, he insists that the composer's

argued, Schmitz's work has been unjustly neglected because it goes against the then- and still-prevailing secular-liberal view of Beethoven: "A musicologist describing Beethoven as a faithful Catholic and enlightened Christian disturbs this worldview immensely. Such a Beethoven does not fit into a perception of history that is dominated by a secularization theorem claiming that the progress of humankind is in fact to be measured by the rejection of religion."[84] My study shows how more recent, demonstrably even-handed research into the nature of Catholicism in Beethoven's historical milieu lends considerable credence to Schmitz's views.[85] Beethoven's religious outlook was indeed much more oriented toward the Catholic Church than most accounts have proposed since the middle of the nineteenth century. It will be the task of this book to recover the lost voice of a Catholic Beethoven.

"reconciliation with Catholicism in his last years was at best partial and ambivalent.... [H]e was too much of a child of the Enlightenment fully to yield to the comforting promises of religion" ("Quest for Faith," 221–23, 227–28). For a discussion of a similarly selective use of Schmitz's work in German Beethoven scholarship, see Loos, "Arnold Schmitz as Beethoven Scholar," 151. Elaine Sisman has pointed me to one other source from outside musicology that articulates a view very close to Schmitz's. In *The Birth of the Modern*, the historian Paul Johnson writes, "It is important to grasp that Beethoven was not consciously trying to turn music into a secular religion. He was neither agnostic nor atheist, deist nor Unitarian, but a Roman Catholic. It is significant, however, that he was a warm admirer of Father Johan [sic] Michael Sailer, a leader in the religious revival which accompanied the nationalist upsurge in Germany after the Battle of Jena in 1806" (120). Frustratingly, Johnson does not cite a source for this view.

[84] Loos, "Arnold Schmitz as Beethoven Scholar," 158.

[85] In a recent article ("Das romantische und gegenrevolutionäre Beethovenbild"), Tobias Janz situates Schmitz's work within the context of a movement of right-wing German Catholic intellectuals during the 1920s and 1930s whose antipathy toward modernity led them to varying levels of sympathy for National Socialism. Janz's argument is at odds with Helmut Loos's previous claim that Schmitz "was quite untouched by any National Socialist disposition" and held an "exceptional position within German musicology as one of very few persons who, during the time of the Third Reich, were not affected by National Socialist ideology": see Loos, "Arnold Schmitz as Beethoven Scholar," 153, 161. Janz refers to Loos's work in his article but stops short of directly refuting Loos's position. Instead, Janz implies that even if Schmitz was not actively involved in National Socialist organizations, there existed "ideological points of contact" (*ideologischen Berührungspunkten*) between his worldview and National Socialism: see "Das romantische," 119n94. However we assess Schmitz's writings in this regard, it should be made clear that my attempt in this book to revive, from a historical and biographical perspective, Schmitz's view of Beethoven's religious outlook absolutely does not entail an endorsement of his political views.

1
German Catholicism in Beethoven's Time

Enlightenment and Restoration

The religious context for Beethoven's life and music was defined both by the German Catholic Enlightenment and a more conservative "Catholic Restoration" that reacted against it. In this chapter I survey this context as a prelude to the remainder of this book, providing the necessary historical framework for interpreting evidence concerning Beethoven's religious outlook, as well as the motivations behind his religious music. As we shall see in later chapters, Beethoven's upbringing in Bonn probably gave him direct exposure to the German Catholic Enlightenment, given that the city, along with other parts of the Rhineland region, was an important center for reformist ideas associated with the movement. Catholic Enlightenment ideas then seem to have remained a prominent component of his religious outlook throughout his adult life, though there are also subtle suggestions of an openness to some aspects of the Catholic Restoration.

Baroque Catholicism in the German Lands

To understand the German Catholic Enlightenment, we must reach a little further back in time to comprehend what it was responding to: Baroque Catholicism. Historians employ this term to describe German Catholicism from the Counter-Reformation through the first few decades of the eighteenth century. Fundamentally, Baroque Catholicism can be understood as the practical manifestation of the Counter-Reformation's attempts to reassert traditional Catholic doctrine against the challenge of Protestantism. Not surprisingly, one of its most important features was a heavy emphasis on liturgy and the sacramental life of the Church, especially on the Eucharist, the dogma surrounding which was central to Catholicism's efforts at distinguishing itself from Protestantism. In particular, the liturgy and the sacraments were to be made *visible* to the faithful.[1] Gone were the medieval rood screens that hid the Eucharistic mystery from the congregation. The altar, it was stressed, was the throne of Christ, and the church was where the believer came to behold him.[2] Liturgical symbols permeated everyday life, creating what one scholar has described as a "symbolic system [that] extended prayer from the altar into every situation and place."[3] There remained very little participation by laypeople in the Mass, but this was counterbalanced by a vibrant culture of popular religious activities that were outside of the liturgy: processions, pilgrimages, and devotions to the saints and to the Virgin Mary.[4] Baroque Catholicism stressed the public and the external, and was focused on outward expression rather than private piety, resulting in a Catholicism that is often described as highly sensual and exuberant—a description that should be familiar to anyone acquainted with the ornate nature of Baroque art, architecture, and music.

Notwithstanding the pervasive influence of the Catholic Church over all aspects of society, Baroque Catholicism was also marked by considerable variation in liturgical practice and church governance from country to country, region to region, even diocese to diocese.[5] Individual bishops regularly ignored dictates from Rome, helped by the fact that the papacy was relatively weak because of the competing claims of Catholic monarchs to spiritual authority of their own.[6] This state of religious localism was particularly pronounced in the German-speaking lands, to a large extent because of their uniquely biconfessional nature.[7] Nowhere else in Europe did Protestants and Catholics interact so closely, not only because Protestant states of the Holy Roman Empire existed next to Catholic ones, but also because individual states, whether officially Catholic or Protestant, tolerated believers "from the other side." Amid competition with Protestants, church officials were often willing to turn a blind eye to departures from formally approved practices because keeping Catholic Germans within the Catholic fold was considered more important than enforcing uniformity.[8] One notable example of this

---

[1] Donakowski, "Age of Revolutions," 353.
[2] White, *Roman Catholic Worship*, 26–28.
[3] Donakowski, "Age of Revolutions," 356.
[4] See Donakowski, 353; and White, *Roman Catholic Worship*, 34–36.
[5] See White, *Roman Catholic Worship*, 31, 51–52; and Forster, *Catholic Germany*, 149.
[6] Such conflict between the pope and individual monarchs over church governance had been ongoing since the foundation of the papacy, and showed no signs of letting up in the eighteenth century. For a discussion of this issue, see Gregory, *Unintended Reformation*, 133–45.
[7] Forster, *Catholic Germany*, 4, 103, 144, 177–82. See also Zalar, *Reading and Rebellion*, 73.
[8] Forster, *Catholic Germany*, 6–8.

situation, which would go on to provide the seedbed for the diversity of viewpoints that emerged in the German Catholic Enlightenment, was the existence of a strong but highly localized tradition in the German lands of congregational singing in the vernacular, dating as far back as 1605.[9]

Compared to other regions in the German lands, Baroque Catholicism was especially pronounced in the Habsburg territories: in Austria and other eastern regions such as Bohemia, Moravia, and Hungary. As Owen Chadwick has observed, architectural evidence clearly demonstrates that the Church was more Baroque in Austria than in the Rhineland, in the countryside than in the city.[10] The particular strength of Baroque Catholicism in Austria and the eastern Habsburg possessions was due partly to the necessity for the Church there to combat Protestantism, which remained stubbornly prominent in some areas. Well into the eighteenth century, Eastern Europe was treated as a missionary land, with the Jesuit order playing an especially prominent role in re-Catholicizing the population.[11] A certain kind of externalized piety was central to the self-conception of the ruling Habsburgs, and hence also to the culture of the lands over which they ruled.[12] The veneration of the Eucharist was an important practice, which continued to flourish even during the church reforms of Joseph II, to be discussed below.[13] Attention to the Eucharist had a political dimension too, as it was prominent in legends about Rudolph of Habsburg, founder of the dynasty.[14] Those same legends also emphasized Marian piety, and the cultural and political importance of Mary was further buttressed by the role she was believed to have played in saving Vienna from Turkish invasion.[15] Marian devotions, especially Marian pilgrimages, were thus a prominent part of Austrian Catholic devotional practice.[16] In addition, starting around 1700, the popular cult of the Sacred Heart of Jesus, a characteristic feature of Baroque Catholicism more generally, gained a strong following in Austrian and especially Viennese piety.[17]

---

[9] See White, *Roman Catholic Worship*, 43; and Chadwick, *Popes and European Revolution*, 72–75.
[10] Chadwick, *Popes and European Revolution*, 80.
[11] Beales, *Joseph II*, 1:31, 362.
[12] Coreth, *Pietas Austriaca*, 1–7.
[13] Coreth, 23–27.
[14] Coreth, 14–16.
[15] Coreth, 47, 58.
[16] Coreth, 66.
[17] Coreth, 81.

The German Catholic Enlightenment

The German Catholic Enlightenment, whose beginnings can be detected around the middle of the eighteenth century, was to a considerable degree a self-conscious repudiation of Baroque Catholicism, especially what educated Catholics perceived as its ostentatious sensuality. In other ways, however, elements of Baroque Catholicism provided the conditions necessary for the development of Catholic Enlightenment ideas. Like the Enlightenment as a whole, the German Catholic Enlightenment was far from a monolithic phenomenon. Individual figures had in common a desire to reform the Catholic Church in the German lands, but had varying views on what specific reforms ought to be implemented, and how much reform was needed.[18] Movements for church reform involved the development of new ideas by theologians and clergy, as well as actual policies implemented by both secular rulers and church leaders.[19] In both cases, three main issues were at stake: dogma; religious practice, including liturgy and church discipline; and the nature of church authority, especially in relation to the state. These issues were often, though not always, connected. Catholic Enlightenment thinkers who focused on the first of these issues—dogma—were among the most radical reformers, though such thinkers would be far less influential in the long run than those devoted to the other two issues.[20] The variety of views held by Catholic Enlightenment figures owed much to the religious localism, described above, that had already existed in the German lands under Baroque Catholicism. It should be stressed that, even if they held views in tension with official church positions, whether in their own time or in later historical periods, none of these reformist figures saw themselves as being *against* the Church; indeed, most, if not all, of them regarded the reforms they desired as more faithful to the spirit of the Catholic religion than the status quo.

Notwithstanding this diversity of opinion within the German Catholic Enlightenment, it is possible to outline a list of interrelated ideas in which

---

[18] Lehner, "Introduction," 38. Though Lehner does not refer to the *German* Catholic Enlightenment explicitly, the content of his essay indicates an almost exclusive focus on the German context. This situation reflects the specifically German origin of the Catholic Enlightenment as a concept, as discussed in this book's introduction. See also Burson, "Introduction," 17.

[19] Beales, *Joseph II*, 1:477.

[20] Nichols, *Catholic Thought since the Enlightenment*, 16–19. Nichols also draws attention to the fact that though Kant's attempt to separate religion from reason did exert some influence on the Catholic Enlightenment, few Catholic thinkers actively embraced Kant.

most, if not all, of its prominent figures were interested.[21] The German Catholic Enlightenment favored a more "rational" approach to religion, compared to the perceived sensuality of Baroque Catholicism. Given the challenge posed by the rationalism of the secular Enlightenment to religious belief generally, theologians were keen to demonstrate the ways in which faith could be compatible with reason.[22] In addition, the secular Enlightenment's interest in the rational workings of the natural world was translated by the Catholic Enlightenment into "physico-theology," which emphasized nature as a reflection of God's glory.[23] Physico-theology was especially prominent among Austrian Catholic thinkers, who liked to emphasize the link between ethics, aesthetics, and nature. As Jakob Johannes Koch has noted, it is this aspect of the Catholic Enlightenment in Austria that is reflected in Gottfried van Swieten's librettos for Haydn's two great oratorios, *The Creation* and *The Seasons*.[24]

The Catholic Enlightenment also adopted a more positive view of human nature, a tendency often referred to as "anthropocentric" theology. This resulted in a shift in emphasis away from Catholicism's dogmatic claims toward the benefits that its ethical precepts could contribute to civil society.[25] The individualism so often associated with the Enlightenment as a whole manifested itself in increased attention to personalized, individual piety (as an adjunct to public liturgical worship) among ordinary Catholics. Efforts were made to improve religious education for clergy and laity alike.[26] Movements for broader clerical reform were inspired by a desire for priests to be moral educators for their parishioners, not just ministers of the sacraments. The sermon (or homily), for instance, assumed a larger

---

[21] In what follows I shall synthesize material from a number of different historical sources, but a succinct account of the key ideas of the German Catholic Enlightenment is provided by Lehner, "Introduction," esp. 12–38.

[22] Lehner, "Introduction," 2.

[23] Lehner, 12. See also Beutel, *Aufklärung in Deutschland*, 203–6, 226–28; and Lehner, *Catholic Enlightenment*, 41–46, 127–30.

[24] Koch, *Heiliger Haydn?*, 180–81.

[25] Lehner, "Introduction," 12. The significance of this shift can be hard for us to comprehend, given that in our own time, where religious pluralism is taken for granted in Western societies, the Catholic Church's engagement in public debates tends to focus on ethical issues such as sexual morality or capital punishment, rather than on dogmas such as the virginity of Mary or the Real Presence of Christ in the Eucharist. In the eighteenth and nineteenth centuries, traditionalists worried that excessive emphasis on ethics risked undermining the Church's exclusive claim to doctrinal authority by promoting religious indifferentism: the idea that dogmatic disagreements among different religious groups, especially between Catholics and non-Catholic Christians, could be downplayed if those groups shared the same ethical beliefs.

[26] See Lehner, "Introduction," 19–24, 40–42.

role both in seminary instruction and in the average Catholic's experience of the Mass.[27] This emphasis on the educative function of the church's liturgy was related to a general preference for simplified, less elaborate liturgy, as well as the discouragement of supposedly "superstitious" Catholic practices that had been popular under Baroque Catholicism, such as pilgrimages and devotions to Mary and the saints.[28]

Somewhat paradoxically, however, the new emphasis on individual piety also led to an increased stress among some German Catholic Enlightenment thinkers on the role of feelings and emotions, including a revived interest in ascetic and mystical theology.[29] There was thus a tension within the movement between a rationalist side and what could be called a sentimentalist side—the latter itself an outgrowth of religious individualism. The coexistence of rationalistic and sentimentalist strands within the German Catholic Enlightenment might be understood in analogous terms to the role that Lutheran Pietism played in the secular German Enlightenment, but with the process reversed. As a religious movement within Lutheranism emphasizing personal faith over more intellectual approaches to religious belief, Pietism, as many intellectual and religious historians have argued, laid the groundwork for a more secularized and rationalistic individualism that emerged a little later.[30] In the case of the German Catholic Enlightenment, a later phenomenon than Pietism, it may have been the individualism of the secular Enlightenment that led in some cases to a more emotionalist understanding of religion via an emphasis on individual piety.[31] As Conrad Donakowski has pointed out, Enlightenment religion, broadly speaking, produced two extremes: impersonal deism on the one hand and a kind of hyper-personal "Inner Light" theology that "pursued the experience of Jesus Christ as personal Savior."[32] Both groups had a distrust of religious ritual and clerical

---

[27] See White, *Roman Catholic Worship*, 67–69; and Chadwick, *Popes and European Revolution*, 165–72.

[28] Nichols, *Catholic Thought*, 16–17.

[29] Lehner, "Introduction," 24–26.

[30] Shantz, *Introduction to German Pietism*, 273–81. Sorkin has drawn attention to the close links between Pietism, which emerged in the late seventeenth century, and the early German Enlightenment of the first half of the eighteenth century: *Religious Enlightenment*, 115–63.

[31] Given the slight chronological discrepancy, there was not a direct connection between Pietism and the German Catholic Enlightenment, but an indirect connection can be found through a shared link to a French theological movement known as Jansenism. Pietism was closely linked to Jansenism. As will be described in the next section, Jansenism heavily influenced the reform program of Emperor Joseph II, which sought to put Catholic Enlightenment ideas into practice. See Lehner, "Introduction," 15–16; Melton, "Pietism"; and Van Kley, "Piety and Politics," 132–34.

[32] Donakowski, "Age of Revolutions," 366.

authority, but for different reasons. In this sense, the tension between rationalist and sentimentalist strands within the German Catholic Enlightenment was typical of its historical era.

With regard to issues of church governance, the German Catholic Enlightenment, while not going as far as to question the primacy of the pope, pushed for individual national churches to have greater autonomy. This was one area in which the Catholic Enlightenment extended rather than reversed a trend that was already a feature of Baroque Catholicism in the German lands. In line with such a decentralized conception of the church, for instance, many reformers supported the use of the vernacular in the liturgy.[33] The reformers relied heavily on the idea that greater autonomy of local and national churches from Rome represented a return to the way the German Catholic Church had operated in the Middle Ages and earlier, before the increased centralization of papal power.[34] From this perspective, changes to the Church that supporters of the status quo regarded as radical were paradoxically portrayed by the reformers as a recovery of neglected traditions. The idea of greater local autonomy in church governance was also very attractive to secular rulers, from individual Catholic princes to the Holy Roman Emperor himself, who saw an opportunity to increase their power versus that of the pope. Changes such as the clerical reforms discussed above could be exploited for political purposes. In a society where the Church had long been a social as well as a religious institution, individual clergy within a Church under stronger state control could be reconceived as civic leaders, even as bureaucrats, in addition to their role as religious leaders.[35]

If some of the ideas advocated by the Catholic Enlightenment that I have just described sound Protestant, that is because the movement was indeed influenced not just by the secular Enlightenment, but also by Protestant theology. The biconfessional situation in the German lands allowed Catholic clergy and laity to have greater exposure to, and, in many cases, sympathy for Protestant religious ideas than elsewhere in Europe.[36] Catholic Enlightenment thinkers encouraged an "irenic" attitude toward Protestants—the prioritization of shared beliefs over doctrinal disagreements—and emphasized the cross-confessional unity of Christians: a position commonly denoted by

---

[33] See Lehner, "Introduction," 21–22; White, *Roman Catholic Worship*, 67; and Ward, "Late Jansenism and the Habsburgs," 169.
[34] Printy, *Enlightenment*, 27.
[35] Printy, 166–84.
[36] Printy, 144–45.

the term "ecumenism." German Catholic theologians engaged in an active dialogue with their Protestant counterparts, some even going as far as to advocate ecclesial reunion with German Protestants.[37] Irenicism and ecumenism formed part of a broader project of religious tolerance that included non-Christian religions.[38] Many supporters of the Catholic Enlightenment, for instance, were active Freemasons who saw no contradiction between Catholicism and Masonry, despite official church prohibitions on Masonic membership.[39] Indeed, dialogue between Catholics and Protestants was often facilitated by their common involvement in Freemasonry.[40]

The German Catholic Enlightenment "in Real Life": Josephinism

A series of church reforms in the Habsburg lands in the 1770s and 1780s constituted the most significant means by which the ideas of the German Catholic Enlightenment were put into actual practice. This reformist project is usually given the label "Josephinism," since it was enacted by Joseph II, Holy Roman Emperor from 1765 to 1790. Joseph's reforms began during the period (1765–1780) when he was co-ruler of the Habsburg lands with his mother, Maria Theresa, but reached their apogee in the decade from 1780 to 1790, when he became sole ruler after his mother's death.[41] Though the Josephine reforms officially applied only to the Habsburg territories directly under Joseph's rule, they inspired similar policies in other German Catholic lands, including in Bonn, where Beethoven was born and raised. As we shall see in the next chapter, Josephinism is relevant to Beethoven not just because

---

[37] See Lehner, "Introduction," 36–38; and Printy, *Enlightenment*, 36, 51, 144–45.
[38] Blanchard, *Synod of Pistoia*, 49.
[39] See Lehner, "Introduction," 40–41; and Ward, "Late Jansenism," 177. See also Beales, *Enlightenment and Reform*, 99–100. Beales cites Mozart as an example of a figure for whom Catholicism and Masonry were not opposed (ibid., 107).
[40] See Printy, *Enlightenment*, 145.
[41] For an overview of Josephinism, see Beales, *Joseph II*, 1:439–79 and vol. 2. Beales uses the term "Josephism," but "Josephinism" has become standard in more recent scholarship. The co-ruling arrangement between Maria Theresa and her son resulted from the so-called Pragmatic Sanction of 1713, promulgated by her father, the Holy Roman Emperor Charles VI. As a woman, Maria Theresa had only been allowed to inherit the Habsburg dominions because of Charles's decree. After Charles died, a number of major European powers refused to accept her succession, leading to the War of the Austrian Succession (1740–1748), during which the Habsburgs lost territory to the Prussians and the Spanish. To strengthen her political position, Maria Theresa appointed first her husband Francis Stephen, then after his death her son Joseph, as co-rulers. A woman could not succeed to the imperial throne—which, in any case, was technically an elective office—so during Maria Theresa's reign, Francis Stephen (as Francis I) and then Joseph II served as Holy Roman Emperor. See ibid., 1:17–28.

of its influence on the cultural environment in the composer's home city, but also because of his own apparent admiration for the emperor.

Joseph's ideas about reforming the Catholic Church in the lands over which he ruled stemmed from his exposure during his youth to two important, and interrelated, movements. Both movements had French roots and heavily influenced the German Catholic Enlightenment as a whole. They were, in addition to German Protestant theology, the major sources for many of the ideas described in the previous section. The first was Jansenism, a theological movement that arose in seventeenth-century France, named after one of its founding theologians, the Dutchman Cornelius Jansen (1585–1638). Jansenism emphasized moral rigor and placed a strong Augustinian stress on faith and grace over works, which led to frequent accusations that its supporters were secret Calvinists.[42] The Jansenists also advocated liturgical simplification as well as the encouragement of lay Bible reading in the vernacular. They opposed monasticism and papal infallibility. Though decisively condemned by the papal bull *Unigenitus* of 1713, many churchmen, including some high-ranking clergy, continued to be sympathetic to Jansenism, and the movement was especially influential in German Catholicism. Bishops with Jansenist sympathies were common in the Habsburg lands, the most prominent being Cardinal Christoph Anton Graf von Migazzi, who was archbishop of Vienna for almost all of the second half of the eighteenth century (1757–1803).[43] A significant number of high-ranking court officials in Vienna also held Jansenist views, including Gerard (Gerhard) van Swieten (1700–1772), Maria Theresa's physician and trusted advisor, and father of Gottfried van Swieten (1733–1803), the famous patron of Haydn, Mozart, and Beethoven.[44] Joseph II's contact with Jansenist ideas most likely came through reading works by the Italian priest and historian Ludovico Antonio

---

[42] Beales, *Joseph II*, 2:83–84. For a detailed overview of Jansenism in its original French context, see McManners, *Church and Society*, 2:346–480.

[43] Hochstrasser, "Cardinal Migazzi and Reform Catholicism," esp. 17–19, 22.

[44] See Chadwick, *Popes and European Revolution*, 392–94; and Klueting, "Catholic Enlightenment in Austria," 139. For more information on Gerard van Swieten and his son Gottfried, see Scholz, "Die geistigen Wurzeln," 169–94. Gerard van Swieten had moved with his family to Vienna from Leiden in the Netherlands, one of the many advisors Maria Theresa sought out from more far-flung regions of her empire. Though he and his family considered themselves Catholic, he had been exposed to Jansenist ideas both in Leiden and during university studies in Louvain. Leiden had also been a religiously diverse place, which probably inspired Gerard van Swieten's commitment to religious tolerance. Despite his undeniable sympathy for some Jansenist views, he cannot be considered a committed Jansenist. While working as imperial censor, he even banned the dissemination of some explicitly Jansenist writings, and was considered sufficiently orthodox in his religious views to be appointed ambassador to the Vatican in 1769. Gottfried van Swieten, on the other hand, was more radical than his father. See Biba, "Gottfried van Swieten."

Muratori (1672–1750), whose views, much admired by Cardinal Migazzi, were characterized by contemporaries as being Jansenist.[45]

The second influence on Joseph's reformist leanings was a movement called Febronianism, which was initiated by the publication in 1763 of a controversial book entitled *De statu ecclesiae et legitima potestate Romani pontificis* (On the state of the Church and the legitimate power of the Roman pontiff), whose author used the pseudonym Justinus Febronius.[46] The author's real name was Johann Nikolaus von Hontheim (1701–1790) and he was a coadjutor bishop of Trier. Hontheim argued for defined limits on papal power. He favored increased authority for local bishops as well as the idea that supreme authority in the Church was vested not in the pope alone, but in ecumenical councils of bishops, a position variously termed "episcopalism" or "conciliarism." Hontheim's position was essentially the German equivalent of what is called Gallicanism in France, a movement that had a longer history in that country, and one with which the Jansenists were unsurprisingly sympathetic.[47] Some of Hontheim's ideas, though, were more radical than the Gallicanism from which they were derived. He argued, for instance, that power in the Church resides originally in all the faithful collectively, with the clergy and the pope holding leadership roles only by convention.[48] Hontheim's book was condemned by Rome soon after its publication, but its ideas nevertheless continued to gain a sympathetic hearing from many reformists within the German Catholic Enlightenment.[49]

As advocates of greater limits on papal power, both the Jansenists and the Febronians, along with other eighteenth-century Catholic reform movements in the German lands and elsewhere, took particular aim at the Society of Jesus, more commonly known as the Jesuits. The Jesuit Order had long been perceived as an instrument for the exercise of papal power away from Rome, especially since they made a special vow of obedience to the Roman Pontiff.[50] Jesuit power was particularly pronounced in the German Catholic lands, because competition from Protestants there meant that a continued need was perceived for missionary activity well into the eighteenth century.[51] The order was especially dominant in its control of educational

---

[45] Beales, *Joseph II*, 1:60, 2:78. See also Blanchard, *Synod of Pistoia*, 73–78.
[46] Beales, 1:443, 2:78.
[47] See White, *Roman Catholic Worship*, 31–33, 53; and Lehner, "Introduction," 35.
[48] Useful overviews of Febronianism can be found in Blanchard, *Synod of Pistoia*, 53–55; and Printy, *Enlightenment*, 15–16, 51–53.
[49] Printy, *Enlightenment*, 42–54.
[50] See Chadwick, *Popes and European Revolution*, 346–47.
[51] Beales, *Joseph II*, 1:31, 362.

institutions.[52] For these reasons, the Jesuits were also hated by Protestants and secular Enlightenment thinkers with strong anti-Catholic feelings.[53]

The Jesuit order, as a transnational vehicle for papal power, thus threatened anyone who believed that local clerical and secular authorities ought to have a greater say in the running of the Church within their own territories.[54] Hostility toward the Jesuits on such political grounds was widespread not just in the German Catholic lands but in all the Catholic countries of Europe, and culminated in what came to be known as the Suppression of the Jesuits. Starting in the 1760s, the Catholic monarchs in Europe, taking advantage of papal political weakness, began banning the order in their own kingdoms, and eventually, in 1773, Pope Clement XIV gave official sanction to these actions.[55] Anti-Jesuit feeling was actually less severe in the lands governed by Maria Theresa and Joseph II than elsewhere in Europe.[56] One historian has even argued that Maria Theresa defended the order before changing her mind for political reasons.[57] Nevertheless, the Suppression was very much welcomed by those German Catholic clergy and political leaders who were eager to see further curbs placed on papal power.

While not technically a part of the Josephine church reforms, the Suppression of the Jesuits paralleled a key feature of Josephinism: its suppression of various other religious orders, this time those of a monastic nature. Under the influence of Jansenism, hostility to monasticism in general was common among many thinkers of the German Catholic Enlightenment, who perceived monks as far less socially useful than parish priests.[58] Joseph II put this hostility into practice by dissolving monasteries across the lands over which he ruled.[59] Unlike a similar event in England in the reign of Henry VIII, however, the money derived from this policy was not stolen and given to political cronies but was put into the foundation and maintenance of parish churches.[60] The new state-driven funding structure created

---

[52] Klueting, "Catholic Enlightenment in Austria," 135–39.
[53] Chadwick, *Popes and European Revolution*, 346–47.
[54] Beales, *Joseph II*, 1:443.
[55] Beales, 1:256.
[56] Beales, 1:461.
[57] Loidl, *Geschichte des Erzbistums Wien*, 150.
[58] See Beales, *Prosperity and Plunder*, 36–37, 81; Beales, *Enlightenment and Reform*, 232; and Chadwick, *Popes and European Revolution*, 235–40. Johann Pezzl's "Sketch of Vienna," which has been cited by H. C. Robbins Landon as an important contemporary source concerning the social and cultural life of Vienna during the time of Mozart and Haydn, includes a sharp critique of monasticism. Pezzl was a strong supporter of the Josephine reforms. See Robertson, "Johann Pezzl"; and Landon, *Mozart and Vienna*, 51–191, at 58–59.
[59] Beales, *Enlightenment and Reform*, 227–55.
[60] See Beales, *Joseph II*, 2:77–78.

by Joseph's dissolution of the monasteries made it easier for the state to control individual parishes, but Joseph claimed that in increasing the number of parishes, he was making the clergy more directly accessible to ordinary Catholics.[61] Using an argumentative strategy that was common in the German Catholic Enlightenment as a whole, Joseph also maintained that greater state control over the local Church represented a return to the practice of "primitive" Christianity.[62] A couple of minor anecdotes from Beethoven's life suggest that the composer was probably familiar with Joseph's monastic policies. As described in the introduction, Beethoven expressed admiration for a group of Ursulines in Graz in a series of letters from the 1810s. The Ursulines were among the few religious orders allowed to remain open: they were considered useful given their educational mission.[63] In addition, the last building in which Beethoven lived, the so-called Schwarzspanierhaus, was a cloister that had been dissolved as a result of the Josephine reforms.[64]

A similar desire for a more "rational" church led to official discouragement of pilgrimages and Marian devotions, which were perceived as too "superstitious."[65] Efforts were also made to simplify the Catholic liturgy.[66] Joseph attempted, through the so-called *Gottesdienstordnung* (Order on worship) of 1783, to limit both the use of musical instruments in church and the broader influence of secular music, especially opera, on sacred works.[67] Musical settings of the Mass were also to be shortened.[68] In addition, efforts were made to introduce vernacular elements into the liturgy, especially German congregational singing, both of hymns (*Kirchenlieder*) and of parts of the Mass text itself (*Singmessen*).[69] Aside from decrees governing liturgical music, Joseph tried to limit the frequency of Masses, and even ordered newly built churches to be less architecturally ornamented.[70] The emperor insisted that such liturgical changes did not in any way indicate a turning away from

---

[61] Beales, *Enlightenment and Reform*, 237–42, 249.
[62] Beales, *Joseph II*, 2:76–77.
[63] Loidl, *Geschichte des Erzbistums Wien*, 177.
[64] Loidl, 180.
[65] Beales, *Joseph II*, 1:155, 197.
[66] See Loidl, *Geschichte des Erzbistums Wien*, 165–66; and Coreth, *Pietas Austriaca*, 66, 85.
[67] Joseph's restrictions on church music constitute an aspect of the German Catholic Enlightenment that has received some attention in musicological studies; see Pauly, "Reforms of Church Music"; Chen, "Catholic Sacred Music in Austria," 88, 98, 106–7; and Black, "Mozart," 4, 21–39.
[68] Chen, "Catholic Sacred Music in Austria," 98.
[69] Pauly, "Reforms of Church Music," 374–76. See also Loidl, *Geschichte des Erzbistums Wien*, 166; Chen, "Catholic Sacred Music in Austria," 99; and Heer, "Zur Kirchenmusik und ihrer Praxis," 132–33.
[70] Loidl, *Geschichte des Erzbistums Wien*, 166.

piety but represented acts of humility paralleling attempts to reduce the overall extravagance of court life.[71]

In line with the Catholic Enlightenment's advocacy of religious toleration, Joseph removed many of the civic restrictions under which non-Catholics had previously been forced to live.[72] On this issue Joseph disagreed with his mother Maria Theresa, who throughout her life never wavered from her belief that as a Catholic monarch it was her duty to promote Catholicism against Protestantism.[73] Joseph, by contrast, went so far as to reform Catholic seminaries so that they taught Protestant as well as Catholic theology.[74] More than any of Joseph's other policies, religious toleration rankled the Vatican. Pope Pius VI regarded it as so offensive that he personally traveled to Vienna in 1782 in a vain attempt to convince Joseph to change his mind—the first papal trip outside of the Papal States in two and a half centuries.[75] While most historians agree that Joseph's decision on toleration was motivated at least in part by a desire to buy the loyalty of his non-Catholic subjects, the Emperor himself believed that toleration as a gesture of goodwill could be a way of winning back religious dissenters for the Catholic Church.[76] Joseph's policy of religious toleration was also tied to attempts to relax censorship laws, which encouraged the publication of heterodox theological works, including some with strong Masonic sympathies.[77]

The "Catholic Restoration"

As we shall see in subsequent chapters, the concept of the German Catholic Enlightenment provides a much-needed corrective to the false binary between enlightened ideas and traditional religious belief, especially Catholicism, that has long been prevalent in accounts of Beethoven's life and music. But the Catholic Enlightenment is not the only historical

---

[71] Beales, *Joseph II*, 1:155, 197.
[72] See Beales, *Joseph II*, 2:168–211. (For a more concise account, see Klueting, "Catholic Enlightenment in Austria," 149–50.) The extent of the toleration granted varied depending on geographical region and on the religious group in question. Notably, Jews were still subject to more restrictions than Protestants or the Greek Orthodox.
[73] Beales, 1:465–73.
[74] Wallnig, "Franz Stephan Rautenstrauch," 213.
[75] Beales, *Joseph II*, 2:169.
[76] See Beales, 2:179.
[77] Beales, 1:168. Conversely—and hypocritically—government censors banned Catholic books considered overly "superstitious": see ibid., 2:93–94.

phenomenon relevant for understanding Beethoven's religious outlook. As early as the time he left his native city for Vienna in late 1792, a movement was taking root in German Catholicism that, over the next few decades, would result in a decisive turn away from the Catholic Enlightenment. What has been termed the "Catholic Restoration" was a revival of a more conservative vision of Catholicism, including a return to many aspects of Baroque Catholicism that the Catholic Enlightenment had sought to marginalize.[78]

The roots of the Catholic Restoration can be traced to the unpopularity of many aspects of the Catholic Enlightenment among ordinary Catholics. Most notably, the Josephine reforms were perceived as attempts by the state and educated elites to eradicate Baroque devotional traditions to which they remained loyal.[79] Joseph's suppression of monasteries also deprived the lower classes of an important source of formal education.[80] The limitations on elaborate church music imposed by the *Gottesdienstordnung* were routinely ignored in Vienna.[81] Though some of the Josephine reforms would remain in place through the first decades of the nineteenth century, others were rolled back as early as the reign of his brother and successor Leopold II (1790–1792).[82] For instance, Leopold revived some monasteries and eased the restrictions of the *Gottesdienstordnung*.[83] Such was Josephinism's unpopularity that Leopold felt compelled to pursue such actions even though he largely shared his late brother's progressive outlook.[84]

More significant than the unpopularity of specific Catholic Enlightenment reforms were the political and cultural upheavals caused first by the French Revolution, then by the subsequent French Revolutionary Wars (1792–1802) and Napoleonic Wars (1803–1815). The Catholic Restoration reflected a general trend all across Europe: resistance to French occupation

---

[78] As described in the introduction, I have borrowed the term "Catholic Restoration" (*katholische Restauration*) from the theologian Josef Schuh: see Schuh, *Johann Michael Sailer*, 11. Unlike "Catholic Enlightenment," I have detected no standardized term for this historical phenomenon in the current scholarly literature.

[79] See Lehner, "Introduction," 43–44; and Bowman, "Popular Catholicism in *Vormärz* Austria," 51–53.

[80] See Beales, *Joseph II*, 1:458–60; and Loidl, *Geschichte des Erzbistums Wien*, 176–83.

[81] Pauly, "Reforms of Church Music," 377–78; Fellerer, "Beethoven und die liturgische Musik," 69.

[82] Ingrao, *Habsburg Monarchy*, 236–38.

[83] See Beales, *Enlightenment and Reform*, 249–50, and Chen, "Catholic Sacred Music in Austria," 88. Sales records for musical instruments and sheet music indicate that following the relaxation and eventual lifting of restrictions on elaborate church music, there was enormous popular demand for such music, even in rural, less well-endowed churches. See Riedel, "Kirchenmusik," 57. This fact may be a sign of the unpopularity of the *Gottesdienstordnung*.

[84] See Okey, *Habsburg Monarchy*, 52; and Ward, "Late Jansenism," 177–79.

during these wars, as well as negative views of the revolution that had led to these conflicts, resulted in either the persistence or the revival of traditional religious attitudes.[85] This situation was part of a broader reaction against ideas perceived as progressive, whether in society as a whole or within a religious group like the Catholic Church. Such ideas were, in the minds of many, tied to the Revolution specifically and to the Enlightenment more broadly. Though this conservative turn occurred to varying extents depending on both location and the individual, it took place as much among intellectual and artistic elites as among ordinary people.

In the German lands, many who held progressive political views initially welcomed the French Revolution and in some cases even the subsequent invasion of French armies. But the violent and repressive conduct of the occupation forces quickly turned many ordinary people against the French and what the French stood for.[86] Historians have also pointed out that even those who were willing to collaborate with French authorities were more likely to do so for pragmatic reasons, such as a desire for political stability in their homelands, than because they were ideologically aligned with their occupiers.[87] Many enlightened German intellectuals who had been sympathetic to the Revolution became disillusioned as it became more anarchic and unstable, and even more so once that revolution led to decades of armed conflict across Europe.[88] Examples included figures as prominent as Goethe and Schiller.[89] Such disillusionment became particularly pronounced in the aftermath of Napoleon's rise to power in 1799.[90]

A similar evolution of views took place among the Habsburg rulers in Vienna. Even though some of their officials were ideologically opposed to it from the beginning, both Joseph II and his successor Leopold II reacted quite positively at first to the Revolution, especially because it led to the introduction of a constitutional monarchy in France—a development that aligned with their progressive outlooks.[91] What changed their minds was the

---

[85] For general sources on this topic, see Broers, *Europe under Napoleon*, esp. 99–143; Blanning, "Role of Religion"; and the essays in Broers, Hicks, and Guimerá, *Napoleonic Empire*.
[86] See Blanning, *French Revolution in Germany*, v, 15–17, 317–36.
[87] See, e.g., Aaslestad, "Napoleonic Rule," 162.
[88] See Blanning, *French Revolution in Germany*, 260–70; and Blanning, *Reform and Revolution in Mainz*, 303–34. See also Broers, *Europe under Napoleon*, 115–22.
[89] See Broers, *Europe under Napoleon*, 107–8; and Blanning, *French Revolution in Germany*, 312. Schiller's well-known *Letters on the Aesthetic Education of Man* was written in response to his disillusionment with the course the Revolution had taken.
[90] Blanning, *French Revolution in Germany*, 285. See also Broers, *Europe under Napoleon*, 105–6.
[91] See Beller, *Habsburg Monarchy*, 12; Rady, *Habsburgs*, 225; and Wangermann, "Austrian Enlightenment," 5–6.

increasingly radical direction taken by the Revolution, especially for Leopold the overthrow and execution of Louis XVI in 1792–1793.[92] (That Louis XVI's queen Marie Antoinette, who was later executed herself, was Leopold's sister must not have helped matters.) Leopold's successor Francis II—who ruled as Holy Roman Emperor from 1792 to the empire's dissolution in 1806, then as Francis I of Austria from 1804 to 1835—was a more reactionary ruler. But it is uncertain whether Francis was always this way, or whether events in France prompted a change of heart.[93]

Francis's accession was characterized by an increase in censorship and the repression of perceived political radicals.[94] With the help of his chancellor Clemens von Metternich (1773–1859), he then become more absolutist in the years after Napoleon's defeat in 1815.[95] Historians continue to debate the extent to which Francis's rule should be considered authoritarian, even during the Metternich era. As Pieter Judson has recently remarked, "while many histories portray Metternich's regime as a dictatorship that successfully repressed all demands for enhanced participation in civic life, Metternich's police state was never the totalizing dictatorship that both he and his opponents liked to claim that it was."[96] In any event, what is noteworthy is that the emperor's policies were much more in harmony with public opinion than might be imagined. Hostility to the French, and the political ideals they were held to represent, was widespread, and Francis himself was a popular ruler known for his ability to connect with ordinary people.[97] This situation is not surprising when one considers the horrendous impact of the conflict that the French had started. Taken together, the French Revolutionary Wars and the subsequent Napoleonic Wars, as historian David A. Bell has argued,

---

[92] Rady, *Habsburgs*, 225.
[93] Beller, *Habsburg Monarchy*, 12.
[94] Wangermann, *Austrian Achievement*, 162–66.
[95] Robertson, *Crossroads of Civilization*, 137–38, 150.
[96] Judson, *Habsburg Empire*, 106. For other accounts that have argued against overstating the extent of Francis's authoritarianism, see Ingrao, *Habsburg Monarchy*, 260–68; Rady, *The Habsburgs*, 239; and Beller, *Habsburg Monarchy*, 35–36. There has been a recent trend among historians to paint a more positive picture of Habsburg rule than that which has been traditional, especially in the English-speaking world. As Steven Beller has argued, anti-Catholic bias has played a major role in fostering negative views of the Habsburgs: e.g., the narrative that they were an imperial power bent on suppressing the nationalist aspirations of various ethnic groups. Revisionist accounts have focused instead on the diversity and the adaptability of the Habsburgs, including their willingness to embrace reform. See Beller, *Habsburg Monarchy*, 15–21.
[97] See Ingrao, *Habsburg Monarchy*, 253–54; and Robertson, *Crossroads of Civilization*, 117. Alex Balisch has argued that the increasing negativity of public opinion in Vienna toward the French is reflected in the evolving tone of press coverage in the *Wiener Zeitung*, the city's main daily newspaper: see "*Wiener Zeitung* Reports."

constituted the "first total war."[98] In the "scope and intensity of warfare," especially in the amount of suffering induced for civilians, this conflict was unprecedented for its time—a fact that is easily obscured by the even greater horrors humanity would witness in the following century's two world wars.[99] Bell attributes this situation to a new "culture of war" that emerged in Europe starting in the middle of the eighteenth century, which made warfare more extreme and unrestrained.[100] The first five years of war with France—the so-called War of the First Coalition (1792–1797)—resulted in 100,000 Austrian soldiers dead, another 100,000 wounded, and 220,000 taken prisoner.[101] In 1809, at the Battle of Wagram on the outskirts of Vienna, Napoleon crossed the Danube with an army about the size of that which landed in Normandy on D-Day; the Battle of Leipzig, in 1813, involved half a million men.[102] (I have chosen the two examples here because of their geographical proximity to Beethoven in Vienna.) Most people, including those who held progressive political views, thus welcomed Napoleon's eventual downfall and the peace and stability brought about by the Congress of Vienna in 1814.[103] Indeed, an influential narrative of Napoleon as the leader who spread the idea of political liberty from revolutionary France to the rest of Europe arose only later— the product of radicals who were too young to have personally experienced the period from the French Revolution to Napoleon's defeat.[104]

The Catholic Restoration in the German lands emerged out of these decades of political turmoil and military conflict initiated by the French Revolution, which encouraged not just a general growth of religious fervor, but an increasing preference for approaches to Catholicism that were in tension with the German Catholic Enlightenment.[105] A more detailed discussion of how this Catholic Restoration played out specifically in Bonn and Vienna—the two cities most relevant to Beethoven's life—will be deferred to later chapters. Here it suffices to point out that just as the German Catholic

---

[98] See Bell, *First Total War*.
[99] See Bell, 7.
[100] See Bell, 1–20, esp. 5–13. In Bell's telling, there were two important components of this new conception of war: the social separation of the military from the rest of the society (which had been far less pronounced in previous historical eras); and the rise of modern "militarism," defined as an attitude that considers military life to be superior to ordinary civilian existence. Bell argues that these two phenomena persist in our society today.
[101] Robertson, *Crossroads of Civilization*, 90.
[102] Roberts, *Napoleon*, 518, 675.
[103] Broers, *Europe under Napoleon*, 267–68.
[104] Broers, 273–74.
[105] For overviews of this process, see Holzem, *Christianity in Germany*, 2:978–1156; Nipperdey, *Germany from Napoleon to Bismarck*, 356–73; and Hänsel, *Geistliche Restauration*.

Enlightenment encompassed reformist positions of different natures and extents, those figures who can be considered part of the Catholic Restoration held different views on which reforms to roll back, or how much of the Catholic Enlightenment should be rejected. In other words, such "conservatism" as there was existed to varying degrees. Even so, it is possible to outline four main ideas that could be said to have defined the Catholic Restoration. These ideas are interrelated but distinguishable; importantly, not all Catholic Restoration thinkers embraced all of them, or to the same extent.[106]

First, there existed a close connection between Catholic Restoration and political absolutism, a situation that should be unsurprising given how closely intertwined political and religious factors were in the reaction to the French Revolution and its aftermath. Especially after the political settlement provided by the Congress of Vienna, absolutist monarchy benefited from the endorsement of a more conservative Catholic Church, while the Church gained the protection of the state.[107] Put another way, the Catholic Restoration can be understood to some degree as the religious dimension of the more familiar *political* Restoration that usually describes the historical era following Napoleon's defeat, an authoritarian brand of conservatism famously represented by Metternich. That said, figures associated with the Catholic Restoration insisted that political absolutism must be tempered by Christian mercy and, more importantly, be counterbalanced by the spiritual authority of the pope. This crucial nuance brings us to the second major component of the Catholic Restoration: ultramontanism, a belief about church governance that places a strong emphasis on the pope's authority over that of local ecclesiastical figures like bishops. This position put the Catholic Restoration at odds with the Catholic Enlightenment's preference for giving greater authority for church governance to individual bishops and even to Catholic monarchs.[108] A stronger papacy was intended as a way of protecting the Church from excessive state interference.[109] The Catholic Restoration feared not only strands of political liberalism that were hostile

---

[106] My explanatory model here is inspired by Aidan Nichols, *Catholic Thought since the Enlightenment*, 23–42. Though he cites a number of examples specific to the German lands, Nichols's account concerns reactions against strands of the Catholic Enlightenment throughout Western Europe. For this reason, I shall synthesize his account with material drawn from other sources, as indicated in the next several footnotes.

[107] See Holzem, *Christianity in Germany*, 2:1023–40, 1048–49, 1082–85; Nipperdey, *Germany from Napoleon to Bismarck*, 372; and Hänsel, *Geistliche Restauration*, 125–36.

[108] See Nichols, *Catholic Thought since the Enlightenment*, 41.

[109] See Holzem, *Christianity in Germany*, 2:1090–98, 1132–45; and Nipperdey, *Germany from Napoleon to Bismarck*, 362–63, 367.

to traditional religion, but also absolutist monarchs seeking to exploit the Church for political gain. At the Congress of Vienna, though the so-called Holy Alliance of Russia, Austria, and Prussia agreed to restore Christian principles to their states, they showed little interest in restoring the *temporal* power of the Roman Catholic Church. The ultramontanism of the Catholic Restoration thus reflected a lack of trust even in conservative political forces otherwise sympathetic to the Church.[110]

The third major feature of the Catholic Restoration was its emphasis on the epistemological value of tradition, in particular the idea that religious and moral truths are more reliable when derived from corporate, rather than individual, reason.[111] This conception of tradition was famously associated with Edmund Burke in his *Reflections on the Revolution in France* (1790), and, separate from its implications for religion, its appeal grew among German intellectuals at the turn of the nineteenth century precisely because of the influence of Burke's thought, which was pronounced even among figures whose political outlooks were relatively progressive.[112] One important translation of Burke's *Reflections* was published in 1793 by Friedrich von Gentz (1762–1832), later to become a close associate of Metternich in Vienna, as well as a friend of Beethoven's patron Count Razumovsky.[113] In the specific context of the Catholic Restoration, the increasing regard for tradition encouraged a renewed focus on the communal nature of the Church and on continuity with the Church's past, in contrast to the Catholic Enlightenment's emphasis on individual piety.

Finally, the Catholic Restoration devoted renewed attention to emotion, sentiment, and mysticism, in reaction against those strands of the Catholic Enlightenment, especially Josephinism, that were perceived as overemphasizing reason.[114] This aspect of the Catholic Restoration was heavily influenced by the contemporaneous Romantic movement in the

---

[110] See Schaefer, "Program," 437; Chadwick, *Popes and European Revolution*, 535–37; and Nichols, *Catholic Thought since the Enlightenment*, 41.

[111] See Nichols, *Catholic Thought since the Enlightenment*, 31–35; and Nipperdey, *Germany from Napoleon to Bismarck*, 274–80.

[112] Blanning, *Reform and Revolution in Mainz*, 314.

[113] See Nipperdey, *Germany from Napoleon to Bismarck*, 12, 17–18; Eakin, "Between the Old"; and Ferraguto, "Beethoven à la moujik," 109n75.

[114] See Nichols, *Catholic Thought since the Enlightenment*, 26–30; Holzem, *Christianity in Germany*, 2:1074–90; Nipperdey, *Germany from Napoleon to Bismarck*, 363–65. Owing to the internal tensions within the Catholic Enlightenment discussed above, this facet of the Catholic Restoration might alternatively be understood as emerging from the Catholic Enlightenment's sentimentalist side. In this respect, at least, it would be going too far to characterize the Catholic Restoration as a complete repudiation of the Catholic Enlightenment.

arts and philosophy, whose foundation is often traced to the formation of the so-called Romantic circle in Jena in 1796.[115] The relationship between the Catholic Restoration and Romanticism was complex and bidirectional. On the one hand, several important early German Romantic artistic figures came under the spell of conservative varieties of Catholicism. (Some prominent examples from the Viennese context will be discussed in chapter 4.) Such a connection between Romanticism and Catholicism was already recognized at the time: in his essay "The Romantic School," Heinrich Heine criticized numerous early German Romantic artistic figures for their Catholic sympathies, at one point designating them with the pithy label "restorers of Catholicism."[116] Conversely, there were a good number of German Catholic theologians of the early nineteenth century who were influenced by Romantic artists, as well as by secular philosophers associated with them.[117]

Though the beginnings of the Catholic Restoration can be detected as early as the 1790s, it was ultimately a gradual process that took place over several decades. But the eventual result was that by the liberal revolutions of 1848, the German Catholic Church came to be dominated by a self-conception that was antimodern and antiliberal, one that retrospectively conceived of the Enlightenment as its enemy, and held a more or less negative view of the reformist vision previously advocated by Catholic Enlightenment. This state of affairs would continue for many decades to come, prompted above all by the growing power of political liberalism.[118] Some German Catholics, especially educated urban elites, did continue to seek a reconciliation between their faith and liberal ideals, and can be thought of as the heirs of Josephinism and the German Catholic Enlightenment.[119] In the 1840s, the most extreme

---

[115] Though one can identify many distinctive forms of Romanticism—as applied to philosophy, theology, or different artistic media, or to different national traditions—early German Romanticism can, broadly speaking, serve as the originating movement for Romanticism writ large. As Julia Lamm has written in an essay on the influence of Romanticism and pantheism on Christian theology, "There were many kinds of Romanticisms and pantheisms in nineteenth-century religious thought, art, and literature—each distinctive in its own way, and yet most of which can be traced back to Germany in the 1790s" ("Romanticism and Pantheism," 167).

[116] Heine, "Romantic School," at 24.

[117] The two most influential groups of theologians influenced by Romanticism during this period were known as the Munich School and the Tübingen School. Both groups were attracted by the idealist philosophy of Friedrich Schelling. See Dietrich, *The Goethezeit*; and O'Meara, *Romantic Idealism and German Catholicism*.

[118] For general sources on this topic, see Clark, "New Catholicism"; Sperber, *Popular Catholicism in Nineteenth-Century Germany*; Gross, *War against Catholicism*; Blaschke, "Das 19. Jahrhundert"; and Graf, *Die Politisierung des religiösen Bewußtseins*.

[119] See Printy, *Enlightenment*, 7.

among them created a movement known as *Deutschkatholizismus* (German Catholicism), which advocated a German national church with significant autonomy from Rome.[120] Such liberal Catholics were, however, very much a minority. The majority felt threatened by the increasingly anticlerical attitudes of political liberals and became more ultramontane in their outlook. A more powerful papacy, they felt, was the best defense against political forces who were threatening their Church.[121] The resulting growth of papal authority coincided with a hardening of the Vatican's attitudes toward modernity in general and decreasing tolerance of theological views that did not accord with the scholastic tradition of Thomas Aquinas, which by the middle of the nineteenth century was becoming the dominant school of thought in Rome.[122] Two events are often cited by historians as symbolic of these trends. In 1864, Pope Pius IX issued the *Syllabus of Errors*, a document condemning many key tenets of Enlightenment and post-Enlightenment thought.[123] And in 1870, the First Vatican Council defined papal infallibility as dogma.[124] The thorny theological issues and disputes surrounding this doctrine need not concern us here, but what is crucial is this event's importance as an example of the Catholic Church's increasingly antagonistic relationship with the modern world through the nineteenth century, a situation that would arguably persist until the Second Vatican Council of the 1960s.[125]

From the vantage point of Beethoven's lifetime, these developments in the history of German Catholicism were several decades into the future, but as we shall see in the conclusion, they bear upon the reception of Beethoven's sacred works after his death. In the first three decades of the nineteenth

---

[120] See Holzem, *Christianity in Germany*, 2:1145–56; and Nipperdey, *Germany from Napoleon to Bismarck*, 364–65.
[121] See Gross, *War against Catholicism*, 21–24, 32, 116; Sperber, *Popular Catholicism in Nineteenth-Century Germany*, 155–87; and McCool, *Catholic Theology*, 25–26, 133.
[122] See Nichols, *Catholic Thought since the Enlightenment*, 72–74; and McCool, *Catholic Theology*, 27–36.
[123] Nichols, *Catholic Thought since the Enlightenment*, 61–63.
[124] Nichols, 64–71.
[125] Indeed, sustained interest in the German Catholic Enlightenment and in German theology of the early nineteenth century was reawakened, albeit in a limited way, during the years surrounding the Second Vatican Council of the 1960s, as reformist theologians, this time of the mid-twentieth century, found inspiration in the work of thinkers who had been excluded for decades from officially permissible Catholic thought. A number of the Council's most important initiatives echo proposals made by the German theologians of those earlier eras: e.g., the introduction of vernacular liturgy and the encouragement of dialogue with non-Catholics. See Blanchard, *Synod of Pistoia*; Lehner, *On the Road*, 1–21; Burson, "Introduction," 7–9; and Lehner, "Introduction," 6.

century, however, the Catholic Restoration was in the ascendancy, but not yet dominant. German Catholicism at this time was thus characterized by the coexistence of—and conflict between—many different views on what being Catholic meant and on what a Catholic could permissibly believe, even if the endpoint would ultimately be the triumph of the Catholic Restoration. In Marc Forster's words, during this period "individuals had considerable freedom to choose the kind of Catholicism they preferred."[126]

Starting around the time he moved to Vienna in the early 1790s, this complex situation defined German Catholicism for the entirety of Beethoven's adult life. In the remainder of this book, we shall consider how this context might have shaped both the composer's religious outlook and his sacred music.

---

[126] Forster, *Catholic Germany*, 197.

2
Beethoven and the Catholic Enlightenment in Bonn

The German Catholic Enlightenment played an especially important role in the political and cultural life of Bonn, the city in which the composer was born and raised. As John Wilson has pointed out, both popular and scholarly accounts of Beethoven's life and music have long tended to neglect the composer's Bonn years, or else they have constructed myths about this period of his life that are only weakly substantiated by the available historical evidence.[1] This situation has begun to be rectified in recent years, most prominently in multi-year research projects led by Birgit Lodes concerning the contents of the music library of the city's electoral court.[2] Beethoven biographies have also started to devote proportionally more attention to the Bonn years.[3]

Bonn as Progressive City

Most discussions of Beethoven's life have depicted Bonn as a kind of hotbed of progressive Enlightenment thought, notwithstanding the city's political status as the capital of Cologne, an ecclesiastical state ruled by an elector-archbishop.[4] Bonn's forward-looking cultural environment thus exerted a lifelong influence on the composer's worldview, especially given specific evidence of the young composer's interactions with a number of prominent

---

[1] Wilson, "From the Chapel," 1–3. See also Konrad, "Der 'Bonner' Beethoven."
[2] See Lodes, Reisinger, and Wilson, *Beethoven und andere Hofmusiker* (2018); Reisinger, Riepe, and Wilson, *Operatic Library* (2018); Reisinger, *Musik machen, fördern, sammeln* (2020). Additional volumes associated with these projects are forthcoming. See also the website associated with these projects: https://musikwissenschaft.univie.ac.at/forschung/projekte/abgeschlossene-projekte/the-music-library-of-elector-maximilian-franz/, accessed August 1, 2024.
[3] See, e.g.: Caeyers, *Beethoven*, 15–67; B. Cooper, *Beethoven*, 1–40; Wyn Jones, *Life of Beethoven*, 1–27.
[4] For two recent examples, see Kinderman, *Beethoven: A Political Artist*, 3–32; and Hinrichsen, *Beethoven*, 25–32.

The Catholic Beethoven. Nicholas Chong, Oxford University Press. © Oxford University Press 2024.
DOI: 10.1093/9780197752951.003.0003

intellectuals in the city. Indeed, not just Bonn but the larger Rhineland region was noted for its openness to new social and political ideas.[5] The local population was highly educated by the standards of the time, and religious tolerance was encouraged by the presence of sizable minorities of Protestants and Jews, despite the numerical dominance of Catholics.[6] This image of the Rhineland is buttressed by its subsequent history after the French Revolution and the invasion of French armies. At least initially, there was a considerable amount of local support for the French, who helped establish the first modern republic on German soil in Mainz in 1792–1793.[7]

Writers have frequently pointed to the centrality of Freemasonry to the dissemination of progressive ideas in the city.[8] A Masonic lodge was established in Bonn no later than 1776. In 1780, a branch of a secret society known as the Illuminati was also founded there, a few years after the group as a whole was conceived by Adam Weishaupt (1748–1830) in Bavaria.[9] Though not officially Masonic, Weishaupt's organization was heavily infused with Masonic ideas.[10] Unlike the local Masonic lodge, whose members were all aristocrats, the membership of the "Minervalkirche Stagira," as the Bonn chapter of the Illuminati was known (after the birthplace of Aristotle), was more diverse in terms of social class: merchants and artists participated alongside prominent court officials.[11] Beginning in 1785, both the Illuminati and Freemasonry in general were suppressed throughout the Holy Roman Empire by order of Emperor Joseph II, who, though sympathetic to many Masonic ideas, began to fear their potential for fomenting political discontent.[12] In the aftermath of this policy, many of the members of the Bonn Minervalkirche formed a new organization called the "Lesegesellchaft" (Reading society), which was less secretive than its predecessor and operated with the explicit approval of the ruling elector-archbishop Maximilian Franz.[13]

There is no evidence of the young Beethoven actually being a member of either the Minervalkirche or the Lesegesellschaft. (In the case of the

---

[5] Rowe, *From Reich to State*, 1–3.
[6] See Rowe, 21–22, 25–27; and Brophy, *Popular Culture*, 23.
[7] See Rowe, *From Reich to State*, 3, 40; and Rowe, "A Tale of Two Cities," esp. 127–28. I shall complicate this description below.
[8] This topic is discussed in many writings on Beethoven, but a succinct and informative account has recently been provided by Wolfshohl, "Nichts weniger als Atheisten."
[9] For an overview of the Illuminati in Bonn, see Braubach, "Neue Funde und Beiträge"; and Dotzauer, "Die Illuminaten im Rheingebiet," esp. 139–45.
[10] Wolfshohl, "Nichts weniger als Atheisten," 217.
[11] Wolfshohl, 217.
[12] Beales, *Joseph II*, 2:526–27, 537–43.
[13] Wolfshohl, "Nichts weniger als Atheisten," 224–29.

former, he would have been too young.)[14] But Beethoven knew a number of people who were active in these organizations. Most notably, the composer Christian Gottlob Neefe (1748–1798), whom many sources have characterized as Beethoven's most important teacher in Bonn, was a founding member of the Minervalkirche and served as its leader for a period of time.[15] Nikolaus Simrock (1751–1832), the horn player and later music publisher who was a lifelong friend of Beethoven's, was a member of both organizations. Simrock published political writings attacking fanaticism and despotism that were more radical than the views held by most other members of these groups. Later, after the French invasion of the Rhineland, he was publicly regarded as a French sympathizer.[16] Other known associates of Beethoven who were affiliated with either the Minervalkirche or the Lesegesellschaft included Franz Anton Ries, Beethoven's violin teacher, concertmaster of the Bonn Hofkapelle, and father of Beethoven's student and friend Ferdinand Ries; and Count Waldstein, a prominent liberal nobleman who arrived in Bonn from Vienna in 1787 and would soon become one of Beethoven's important patrons.[17] Several members of the Lesegesellschaft were also part of what scholars have termed the Zehrgarten Circle, a group of people whom Beethoven got to know from frequenting the tavern Zum Zehrgarten.[18] The composer was on close enough terms with these people to have received the so-called *Zehrgarten Stammbuch*, an autograph book presented as a gift upon his departure for Vienna in 1792.[19] The *Stammbuch* contains fourteen messages from members of the Zehrgarten circle as well as the tavern's owner Matthias Koch and members of Koch's family.[20] The messages include a number of literary quotations and allusions, mostly

---

[14] Wolfshohl, 229–30.
[15] See Braubach, "Neue Funde und Beiträge," 159–62; and Kinderman, *Beethoven: A Political Artist*, 10–11. As will be discussed below, some recent scholarship has expressed significant doubts concerning the level of influence Neefe had over Beethoven both musically and personally.
[16] See Braubach, "Neue Funde und Beiträge," 164–65; and Kinderman, *Beethoven: A Political Artist*, 33–35. See also Biermann, "Bonn *Aufklärer* Nikolaus Simrock."
[17] See Kinderman, *Beethoven*, 19; and Solomon, *Beethoven*, 50.
[18] See Wolfshohl, "Nichts weniger als Atheisten," 229–30; and Braubach, "Beethovens Abschied von Bonn," 25–31, 37–40.
[19] The *Zehrgarten Stammbuch* is translated in Albrecht no. 13(a–n). For a facsimile of the original book, see Braubach, *Die Stammbücher Beethovens*, 1–32. In this source, a transcription is provided by Michael Ladenburger on pp. 5–22 of an accompanying booklet ("Textübertragung"). The German text is also available in Thayer, *Ludwig van Beethovens Leben*, 1:467–74.
[20] Albrecht, *Letters to Beethoven*, 1:15n1. The *Stammbuch* is perhaps best known for containing Count Waldstein's famous remark that Beethoven "shall receive *Mozart's spirit from Haydn's hands*" (emphasis original): "Durch ununterbrochenen Fleiß erhalten Sie: *Mozart's Geist aus Haydens* [sic] *Händen.*" See Albrecht no. 13g, and Thayer, *Ludwig van Beethovens Leben*, 1:471.

sourced from notable secular Enlightenment thinkers such as Schiller and Klopstock.[21] Ethical and moralistic statements, whether original or quoted, are particularly prominent.

In addition to the role of Freemasonry in Bonn, scholars have also suggested that the young Beethoven was exposed to progressive ideas at the local university, whose faculty was dominated by supporters of the critical philosophy of Immanuel Kant.[22] The university was also home to Eulogius Schneider (1756–1794), perhaps the most politically radical thinker in Bonn.[23] A former Franciscan friar, Schneider was appointed a professor of aesthetics in 1789, just before the outbreak of the French Revolution. His views would prove to be too extreme even for Bonn, and he was dismissed just two years later. Among the justifications given for his dismissal were his critique of priestly celibacy, his publication of erotic poems, his explicit celebration of the French Revolution, and his mocking attitude toward the Catholic Church. After a brief period in Mainz, he ended up in Strasbourg, where he became involved in the French Revolution as a Jacobin, serving as a public prosecutor responsible for sentencing people to death. Eventually, he went to the guillotine himself in 1794. Beethoven's name appears on a list of subscribers to a 1790 collection of Schneider's poems, one of which celebrates the author's newfound freedom from Catholic theology.[24] As a member of the Lesegesellschaft, Schneider was also the organizer of a memorial service mourning the death of Joseph II, for which the young Beethoven composed his *Cantata on the Death of Emperor Joseph II* (*Kantate auf den Tod Kaiser Josephs II.*, WoO 87), setting a text written by Severin Averdonk, a local poet.[25] (This work was not eventually performed, most likely because it was decided to hold the service in dim lighting, which made a musical component logistically difficult.)[26]

---

[21] The Schiller allusions and quotations occur in the messages by Baron Carl August von Malchus, Anna Maria Koch, Matthias Koch, and Jakob Klemmer (Albrecht nos. 13a, 13b, 13e, and 13n). The quotations from Klopstock occur in the messages by Matthias Koch and Peter Joseph Eilender (Albrecht nos. 13e and 13l).

[22] See, e.g., Kinderman, *Beethoven: A Political Artist*, 10–11; Hinrichsen, *Beethoven*, 28–30; Lockwood, *Beethoven*, 35; and B. Cooper, *Beethoven*, 14.

[23] See Höyng, "'Denn Gehorsam ist die erste Pflicht,'" esp. 313–21.

[24] Kinderman, *Beethoven: A Political Artist*, 12–15. A more detailed discussion of Schneider's poems is provided by Höyng, "Codependent Polarity."

[25] Kinderman, *Beethoven: A Political Artist*, 12–15; Reisinger, "Prince and the Prodigies," 60. Two notable passages from the cantata were reused in *Fidelio*: see Kinderman, *Beethoven*, 24.

[26] Reisinger, "Prince and the Prodigies," 60. Two passages from the cantata were later reused in Beethoven's opera *Fidelio*: see Kinderman, *Beethoven: A Political Artist*, 24–27.

As William Kinderman has suggested, a sign of Schneider's influence on Beethoven might be detected in the parallel between Schneider's use of the phrase "Ein freier Mann" (A free man) in a poem extolling the French Revolution and the title of Beethoven's song *Der freie Mann* (WoO 117; The free man), which he began composing in Bonn in 1792 but subsequently revised in 1794 after he moved to Vienna.[27] *Der freie Mann* features a strophic setting of a text by Gottlieb Conrad Pfeffel, a Protestant school administrator who was a regular contributor to the Hamburg *Musenalmanach*, and whose writings also reveal a sympathy for the French Revolution.[28] The ten stanzas of the poem evoke several stereotypical Enlightenment themes, notably the Kantian idea of freedom as freedom to self-legislate (stanzas 1 and 2) and social egalitarianism (stanza 5). The references to religion in stanzas 3 and 4 were considered radical enough to have been suppressed by the publisher in the first edition.[29] Stanza 3 describes a free man as "he whose radiant faith / no rude mockery can take away / no priest can overcome" (*Wem seinen hellen Glauben / Kein frecher Spötter rauben, / Kein Priester meistern kann*). In stanza 4, the free man is one who is able to recognize "virtue" (*Tugend*) even in the "heathen" (*Heiden*). Paul Reid has explicitly linked this song to Beethoven's exposure to Masonic ideals in Bonn, an argument that is reinforced by the fact that Beethoven's friend Franz Wegeler published a version of the song in 1806 with the title "Maurerfragen" (Masons' questions).[30]

Bonn and the Catholic Enlightenment

Some Beethoven scholars have urged caution in assessing the influence that apparently progressive figures in Bonn might have had on the young composer.[31] Ulrich Konrad, for instance, points out that though we may know Beethoven attended lectures at the local university, it remains uncertain what specific lectures he went to. Konrad argues further that Beethoven might have been shaped just as much from the religious preaching to which he was exposed in many years working as a church musician in Bonn—a topic to which I shall return below—as he was by those university lectures. Other

---

[27] Kinderman, *Beethoven: A Political Artist*, 22.
[28] Reid, *Beethoven Song Companion*, 100, 284.
[29] Reid, 100.
[30] Reid, 101.
[31] Konrad, "Der 'Bonner' Beethoven," 72.

scholars have also questioned whether Neefe was as important a teacher and mentor for Beethoven as has long been assumed.[32]

In any event, what is more problematic about most accounts of Beethoven's Bonn years is that they seem to assume the overly reductive definition of the Enlightenment discussed in the introduction: the simple equation of Enlightenment with political egalitarianism and freedom from the oppression of traditional religious institutions. Concerning the religious situation in Bonn, Maynard Solomon's description is typical: "Enlightened and especially Kantian conceptions of morality served Beethoven and many of his compatriots in Bonn as a substitute theology."[33] In terms of politics, the presence of nominal aristocrats like Count Waldstein in the young Beethoven's social milieu cannot be denied, but what is invariably stressed is the way such figures embraced progressive ideas in a manner at odds with their class position. A pluralistic and more complex conception of the Enlightenment should, however, complicate our understanding of the city that nurtured Beethoven in his youth. In this regard, historians have cautioned against overstating the radicalism of the Bonn Enlightenment, especially as represented by organizations like the Minervalkirche and Lesegesellschaft.[34] Most such organizations, Michael Rowe writes, "dedicated themselves to the propagation of useful knowledge rather than radical politics."[35] The prominent role played by aristocrats and even monarchical rulers like Maximilian Franz and Joseph II in the promotion of Enlightenment ideas was also not some kind of exception to the rule but entirely typical of the Enlightenment in the German context, in comparison to the situation in France and even Britain. Indeed, recent research into Beethoven's Bonn years has called into question long-standing narratives about the composer's having been emancipated from an older model of aristocratic patronage.[36] As Elisabeth Reisinger has argued, ideological prejudices against aristocracy as a form of sociopolitical organization have led most scholars to ignore the role of aristocratic institutions for musical activity even after the French Revolution and the continued relevance of the "court-musician" model for Beethoven's artistic identity.[37] The fact that Beethoven would go on to make numerous

---

[32] See Loos, "Christian Gottlob Neefe."
[33] Solomon, *Beethoven*, 54.
[34] See Rowe, *From Reich to State*, 24–25; and Blanning, *French Revolution in Germany*, 37–47.
[35] Rowe, *From Reich to State*, 25.
[36] See Lodes, Reisinger, and Wilson, introduction to *Beethoven und andere Hofmusiker*, 1; and Reisinger, "Sozialisation, Interaktion, Netzwerk."
[37] Reisinger, "Sozialisation, Interaktion, Netzwerk," 179–80.

attempts to secure a court position over the course of his career should thus be unsurprising.[38]

More importantly given the subject of this book, any suggestion that the Bonn Enlightenment simply involved the replacement of religious ideas with enlightened ones is misleading. As Rowe has stressed, "Within the Rhenish context, the Enlightenment should be seen primarily as a religious reform movement."[39] The Enlightenment in Bonn was a Catholic Enlightenment, a manifestation of the broader German Catholic Enlightenment described in the previous chapter. With very few exceptions, self-identified progressives in Bonn sought to reform the Catholic Church rather than to overthrow it.

The two elector-archbishops who governed Bonn during Beethoven's youth both pursued a program of reform very much in line with the German Catholic Enlightenment. Maximilian Friedrich, who ruled from 1761 to 1784, reduced the number of feast days and placed limitations on religious processions and pilgrimages.[40] It was Maximilian Friedrich who was primarily responsible for establishing what would become the University of Bonn out of what had been the former Jesuit Gymnasium, after the continent-wide suppression of the Jesuit Order. And he did this precisely to create a reformist counterweight to the theological faculty in Cologne, whom he thought to be too conservative. As Rowe writes, the new university became a "center of radical thought and attracted Kantians fleeing from the unpropitious surroundings in Cologne."[41] Maximilian Friedrich was succeeded by Maximilian Franz, younger brother of the emperor Joseph II. Maximilian Franz, who ruled from 1784 until the invasion of French forces ten years later, had an outlook similarly shaped by the Catholic Enlightenment. Like his brother, he was known to be very sympathetic to Jansenist ideas.[42] He was also partial to Febronianism: along with the other three prince-archbishops of the Holy Roman Empire, he convened in 1786 an event known as the Congress of Ems, which led to a demand for greater independence from papal governance over individual ecclesiastical territories.[43] Both Maximilian Friedrich

---

[38] Bonds, "Court of Public Opinion," 17–24.
[39] Rowe, *From Reich to State*, 45.
[40] Wolfshohl, "Nichts weniger als Atheisten," 213–15.
[41] Rowe, *From Reich to State*, 26.
[42] Ward, "Late Jansenism and the Habsburgs," 175.
[43] Blanning, *Reform and Revolution in Mainz*, 220–27. The other three participants were the elector-archbishops of Mainz and Trier and Prince-Archbishop Colloredo of Salzburg, who is well known in music history as the patron of Mozart. The archbishops' demand was unsuccessful, mainly because Joseph II ultimately refused to give them his full support: he was worried about giving them too much political power in relation to himself.

and Maximilian Franz cultivated religious tolerance. Two examples related to Beethoven can be cited in this regard. Beethoven's teacher Neefe was appointed court organist by Maximilian Friedrich despite being a Calvinist.[44] And Maximilian Franz allowed the sister of Heinrich Struve, a diplomat whom Beethoven got to know in Bonn as part of the Zehrgarten Circle, to be buried in the city cemetery when she died in 1789, even though she was a Protestant. The incident was reported in a local newspaper as an example of the elector's enlightened nature.[45]

Private reading circles like the Lesegesellschaft were entirely typical of the German Catholic Enlightenment, and reflected a devotion to books among lay Catholics that was especially strong in the Rhineland.[46] In addition, the Minervalkirche exemplifies the way in which, in the context of the Catholic Enlightenment, it was common for reform-minded Catholics to perceive no incompatibility between their religion and Freemasonry. Out of its twenty-eight known members, no fewer than eleven were Catholic priests.[47] That Neefe, who was for a time a leader of the Minervalkirche, was a Calvinist also illustrates the way that Masonic organizations throughout the Rhineland were important settings for Catholics and Protestants to interact, a situation that was typical of the German Catholic Enlightenment as a whole (see chapter 1).[48] There is no doubt that Neefe saw himself as a kind of enlightened Christian. Neefe's writings, heavily influenced by the thought of Johann Georg Sulzer (1720–1779), put forward the then widely held view that aesthetic taste was closely tied to moral conduct. But this view did not entail a rejection of Christianity; for Neefe as for Sulzer, morality was still defined in Christian terms.[49] Neefe also expressed sympathy with Christian writers who sought to push back against the perceived excesses of the Enlightenment, especially atheism.[50] Therefore, even if we were to set aside the more fundamental question (discussed above) of whether Neefe should be considered a significant influence on the young Beethoven, Neefe's extensive Masonic connections, including leadership of the Minervalkirche,

---

[44] Wolfshohl, "Nichts weniger als Atheisten," 215.
[45] Ronge, "'When Will the Time,'" 7.
[46] See Lehner, "Introduction," 40–41; and Zalar, *Reading and Rebellion*, 65.
[47] Wolfshohl, "Nichts weniger als Atheisten," 217–18.
[48] See Rowe, *From Reich to State*, 24.
[49] Loos, "Christian Gottlob Neefe," 402–3.
[50] Loos, 392–99. Neefe also had no problem having his children baptized as Catholics in Bonn (ibid., 407). Neefe's Christian leanings were deliberately excised from nineteenth-century accounts of the composer's life. Friedrich Rochlitz went so far as to edit Neefe's autobiography to remove all references to Christianity. See ibid., 395–99.

did not mean that he left Christianity behind. As Helmut Loos has argued, he simply should not be characterized as an "enlightened enemy of the church" (*kirchenfeindlicher Aufklärer*).[51]

It is still true, of course, that the young Beethoven interacted with figures like Simrock and Schneider, whose beliefs were more radical than Neefe's. But even in such cases, the available evidence must be interpreted with caution. What we know of Simrock's outlook concerns mainly his political views: however progressive these may have been, it should not automatically be assumed that they would have led to a rejection of traditional religious belief. It is worth mentioning in this regard that the *Zehrgarten Stammbuch*, in addition to containing quotations from familiar Enlightenment heroes like Schiller and Klopstock, also includes a biblical quotation from Paul's first letter to the Thessalonians (5:21): an exhortation to Beethoven to "investigate all and retain the good."[52] And this quotation was inscribed by Johann Joseph Eichhoff, who later became an enthusiastic supporter of the French Revolution and served as mayor of Bonn during the French occupation.[53] Even Schneider's radicalism should not be overstated, at least in terms of his religious outlook. As Peter Höyng has argued, though he rejected many official Catholic beliefs from an early point in his career, Schneider's attempt "to reconcile his Christian upbringing with basic principles of the Enlightenment represents a stylistic leitmotif that would surface throughout his brief life."[54] In any case, even in the context of Bonn's generally progressive atmosphere, Schneider was an outlier in terms of his radicalism, a fact that explains his dismissal from the university. None of Schneider's theological colleagues eventually left the priesthood as he did; some even experienced notable conservative turns during the 1790s, in line with the Catholic Restoration described in chapter 1.[55] Most of the university's faculty were progressive only to the extent that they supported the Josephine church reforms. Broadly speaking, the overall intellectual and political climate in

---

[51] Loos, 407.

[52] Albrecht no. 13f; Thayer, *Ludwig van Beethovens Leben*, 1:469: "Prüfe Alles und das Gute behalte." The *Stammbuch* contains an additional link to the religious Enlightenment, though to its Jewish rather than Catholic strand. Heinrich Struve (who will be discussed in more detail below) wrote down a quotation from Moses Mendelssohn: "To discern *Wisdom*, / to love *Beauty*, / To desire *Good*, to do the *Best*" (Albrecht no. 13i, Struve's emphasis). For the German original, see Thayer, *Ludwig van Beethovens Leben*, 1:472: "*Wahrheit* erkennen, *Schönheit* lieben. / *Gutes* wollen, das *beste* thun." For a discussion of Moses Mendelssohn in the context of the religious Enlightenment, see Sorkin, *Religious Enlightenment*, 165–213.

[53] See Braubach, "Neue Funde und Beiträge," 167–68; and "Beethovens Abschied von Bonn," 39.

[54] Höyng, "'Denn Gehorsam,'" 315, 325–26.

[55] See Braubach, "Neue Funde und Beiträge," 187–96.

Bonn was, even within the framework of the Catholic Enlightenment, less radical than in places to the south, especially Mainz.[56]

The young Beethoven's engagement with apparently progressive ideas in the *Joseph* Cantata and *Der freie Mann* can also be understood in light of the Catholic Enlightenment. The advocacy of religious tolerance and suspicion of clerical power in *Der freie Mann* is more correctly understood as an expression of a reformist mentality within a Catholic context than as a rejection of the church itself. In the text of the *Joseph* Cantata, which otherwise consists mostly of hyperbolic praises for the emperor, the one aspect of Joseph's governance that is mentioned specifically is his vanquishing of "fanaticism" (*Fanatismus*)—a term that probably refers to the rationalistic aspects of his church reforms, especially the discouragement of "superstitious" religious practices, but may also have included his support for religious toleration:

Ein Ungeheurer,	A monster,
sein Name Fanatismus,	its name fanaticism,
stieg aus den Tiefen der Hölle,	arose from the depths of Hell,
dehnte sich zwischen Erd' und Sonne,	stretched itself between Earth and the Sun,
und es ward Nacht!	and it became night!
Da kam Joseph,	Then came Joseph,
mit Gottes Stärke,	with the strength of God,
riß das tobende Ungeheurer weg,	he tore the fuming monster away,
weg zwischen Erd' und Himmel	away between Earth and Heaven
und trat ihm auf's Haupt.	and trod on its head.

Shortly after completing the *Joseph* Cantata, Beethoven composed a second cantata, this time for the accession of the new emperor, Leopold II (*Kantate auf die Erhebung Leopolds II. zur Kaiserwürde*, WoO 88). As with the first cantata, it was probably commissioned by the Lesegesellschaft, and its text was once again provided by Averdonk.[57] Leopold's own sympathies for the Catholic Enlightenment, described in the previous chapter, help explain the confidence expressed in the *Leopold* Cantata that the new ruler would

---

[56] Rowe, *From Reich to State*, 22–26.
[57] Reisinger, "Prince and the Prodigies," 60–61.

continue Joseph's policies: "You who called Joseph your father, / weep no more! / Great as he whom we called father / is he [Leopold] also" (*Ihr, die Joseph ihren Vater nannten, / weint nicht mehr! / Gross wie der, den wir als Vater kannten, / ist auch er*).

Beethoven and Church Music in Bonn

Understanding Beethoven's youth in Bonn through the lens of the Catholic Enlightenment is important not only as a corrective against the false opposition between Enlightenment and Catholicism that has so often been assumed in previous scholarship. It also helps draw attention to the role of church music in the composer's upbringing—a topic that has been unjustly neglected, as John Wilson has recently pointed out.[58] Despite their progressive outlooks, the attitudes of both Maximilian Friedrich and Maximilian Franz regarding church music were not straightforward. In line with Catholic Enlightenment principles, Maximilian Friedrich attempted to simplify liturgical music and move away from the elaborate Italian-influenced church music with instrumental accompaniment that had been popular in Bonn since at least mid-century.[59] However, he did so by advocating a renewal of Gregorian chant. This policy diverged from the growing popularity in the German Catholic lands of using liturgical music with vernacular texts, a practice advocated by many Catholic Enlightenment thinkers, and which had already taken partial root in Bonn.[60] Beethoven, who came from a family of church musicians, received his earliest musical training under Willibald Koch, a Franciscan friar and organist, who had his young student play the organ at Mass.[61] It seems almost certain that the composer's first experiences with church music were shaped by Maximilian Friedrich's policies favoring chant. Among Beethoven's duties under Koch's tutelage was the improvisation of preludes based on chant melodies, and we have sketch evidence of him writing out

---

[58] Wilson, "From the Chapel," 7–11. See also Sanda, "Enlightened Practice of Sacred Music."
[59] McGrann, "Beethoven's Mass in C," 1:20–29.
[60] McGrann, 1:20–29. See also Chen, "Catholic Sacred Music in Austria," 99.
[61] See Wilson, "From the Chapel," 7–11; McGrann, "Beethoven's Mass in C," 1:34; and Fellerer, "Beethoven und die liturgische Musik," 61. The young Beethoven also played the organ at Siegburg Abbey, just outside Bonn: see Heer, "Zur Kirchenmusik und ihrer Praxis," 132.

harmonizations for the Lamentations of Jeremiah, presumably for the Tenebrae liturgy of Holy Week.[62]

Going against the tastes of his predecessor as well as his brother Joseph II, Maximilian Franz encouraged elaborate church music, even if liturgical reforms inspired by Josephinism did reduce the number of occasions for performing such music.[63] Surviving examples of church music in Maximilian Franz's library include works by the court trumpeter and violinist Johann Ries, which John Wilson has described as "exuberant sacred compositions . . . replete with horn calls and trumpet fanfares."[64] At the same time, however, Maximilian Franz also actively promoted vernacular church music. This diverged from his predecessor's preference for chant and led to a decline of chant in Bonn.[65] In 1784, for instance, he approved the publication in Bonn of Johann Kohlbrenner's *Deutsche Singmesse*, a Mass-setting in the vernacular, which had been popular in Austria since it had been first published there in 1777.[66] The widespread use of Kohlbrenner's mass in Bonn and the surrounding areas is attested to by its frequent appearance in local choirbooks.[67] Maximilian Franz's music library included a copy of a widely circulated collection of vernacular *Kirchenlieder* for congregational singing, first published in Vienna at the direction of Maria Theresa.[68] The Bonn Hofkapelle was also noted for publishing its own series of similar vernacular hymnbooks.[69] In line with the tenets of the Catholic Enlightenment, Maximilian Franz's ultimate goal

---

[62] McGrann, "Beethoven's Mass in C," 1:34, 36–37. The practice of using chordal organ accompaniment with chant melodies in Bonn predated Maximilian Friedrich's reign (ibid., 1:20).

[63] Reisinger, *Musik machen, fördern, sammeln*, 174. Contrary to previous scholarship, Reisinger argues that a reduction in the quantity of such music should not be taken as evidence that there was a decline in its importance to musical life at the Bonn court. She also comments that generally speaking, Maximilian Franz was more enthusiastic about the political aspects of Josephinism than its prescriptions regarding church music (ibid., 102).

[64] Wilson, "From the Chapel," 9.

[65] McGrann, "Beethoven's Mass in C," 1:29–31. See also Heer, "Zur Kirchenmusik und ihrer Praxis," 130–31, 136; and Fellerer, "Beethoven und die liturgische Musik," 65.

[66] Kohlbrenner's mass appeared in his hymnal *Der heilige Gesang zum Gottesdienste in der römisch-katholischen Kirche*, the most important German hymnal of its time in the Austrian territories. See Pauly, "Reforms of Church Music," 375; and Heer, "Zur Kirchenmusik und ihrer Praxis," 135.

[67] Heer, "Zur Kirchenmusik und ihrer Praxis," 135.

[68] Modena, Gallerie Estensi, Biblioteca Estense Universitaria, Mus.F.1578. See the entry in the recently prepared catalog of Maximilian Franz's music library: https://www.univie.ac.at/muwidb/sacredmusiclibrary/entry/119, accessed August 1, 2024. The full title of the score is *Katholisches Gesangbuch auf allerhöchsten Befehl Ihrer k. k. apost. Majestät Marien Theresiens zum Druck befördert, Wien, im Verlag der katechetischen Bibliothek*. See also Reisinger, *Musik machen, fördern, sammeln*, 102n445.

[69] McGrann, "Der Hintergrund zu Beethovens Messen," 123–24.

in promoting vernacular church music was to enable greater congregational participation.[70] Reformist thinkers in Bonn believed, too, that vernacular music would help to explain the meaning of the liturgy to the laity.[71] In an article in a local journal, Ferdinand d'Antoine, a member of both the Minervalkirche and the Lesegesellschaft, argued that a close connection between words and music should be prioritized in church music, which ought not just to express adequately the meaning of individual words but also their broader moral implications.[72] D'Antoine thus objected to the infiltration of church music by theatrical musical styles: church music ought not to inspire dance but *Andacht* (devotion)—a word that later appeared as a direction in Beethoven's sacred works, famously in the *Missa solemnis* but also in the Gellert Lieder. Unlike Joseph II in his *Gottesdienstordnung*, however, d'Antoine was not bothered specifically by excessive musical complexity or emotional intensity: his main concern was propriety of expression.[73] In this regard, d'Antoine's outlook might be seen as straddling the divide between the rationalist and sentimentalist strands of the Catholic Enlightenment discussed in the previous chapter. On the one hand, his desire that liturgical music communicate the meaning of the text accords with the Catholic Enlightenment's emphasis on religious education and an active engagement of the laity with the liturgy. On the other hand, his tolerance of music that was emotionally exuberant was somewhat at odds with the liturgical simplicity demanded by the Josephine reforms in particular. Wilson has pointed to examples in Maximilian Franz's library of sacred works that appear to have been inspired by d'Antoine's views, in particular four pieces composed by the tenor Ferdinand Heller between 1787 and 1792: two masses, a requiem, and a *Te Deum*.[74] The young Beethoven was probably exposed to such works, and more generally to the combination of both highly elaborate and simple reformist church music that proliferated in Bonn.[75] As we shall see in later chapters, aspects of the mature composer's sacred compositions bear obvious traces of ideas about church music that he would have come into contact with during his youth.

---

[70] McGrann, "Beethoven's Mass in C," 1:29–31.
[71] McGrann, "Der Hintergrund zu Beethovens Messen," 123–24.
[72] McGrann, 122–23. See also Fellerer, "Beethoven und die liturgische Musik," 64–65.
[73] McGrann, "Der Hintergrund zu Beethovens Messen," 123.
[74] Wilson, "From the Chapel," 11.
[75] See McGrann, "Beethoven's Mass in C," 1:38.

Beethoven's Bible

The historical context provided by the German Catholic Enlightenment might also help us understand what comes across as an oddity in the posthumous inventory of Beethoven's books: a Bible in French translation, published in Liège in 1742.[76] Even if Beethoven was relatively competent in French, it seems strange that the one copy of the Bible he apparently owned would be in a language other than his native German.[77] As Beate Kraus has pointed out, however, in Beethoven's time it was not uncommon for educated Germans to read the New Testament in French, especially in the Rhineland.[78] In addition, both Alexander Wolfshohl and Theodore Albrecht have suggested that, given its place of publication, the Bible in question was inherited from the composer's grandfather, also named Ludwig.[79] The elder Ludwig, a choral singer, was born in 1712 in Mechelen in Flanders and was employed in both Leuven and Liège before moving to Bonn in March 1733.[80] Though neither Wolfshohl nor Albrecht has commented on the fact that the Bible was published *after* the elder Ludwig left Flanders, it is certainly possible it was acquired on a subsequent visit back to the region of his birth.

There may, however, be more to this story. Though we cannot be absolutely certain given that the original book is lost, it is extremely likely that, based on the date and place of publication, Beethoven's French Bible was a copy of the *Bible de Port-Royal*, a version also known as the "Sacy Bible" after its principal translator, Louis-Isaac Lemaistre de Sacy (1613–1684).[81] At the time of this writing, the WorldCat website (worldcat.org) lists eleven copies of Bibles published in French in Liège in 1742 that are held by libraries that share cataloging information with the site. All of these Bibles are in

---

[76] *Schätzungsprotokoll* no. 44.
[77] On Beethoven's knowledge of French, see Kraus, "Beethoven liest international," 78–79, 83–91.
[78] Kraus, 76.
[79] See Wolfshohl, "Beethoven liest Autoren," 109n11; and Albrecht, *Letters to Beethoven*, 3:238n44.
[80] Caeyers, *Beethoven*, 3–4. Ludwig van Beethoven the elder was probably recruited by Maximilian Friedrich's predecessor as elector-archbishop, Clemens August of Bavaria, on a visit to Liège. The city of Mechelen is also referred to by its French name, Malines, and the anglicization "Mechlin."
[81] For an introduction to the *Bible de Port-Royal*, see Chédozeau, "Bibles in French," 291–304. See also Chédozeau, *La Bible et la liturgie* and *Port-Royal et la Bible*; and Delforge, *La Bible en France*, 139–41. The translation was the result of a long process. The New Testament was published first, in 1667, as the *Nouveau Testament de Mons*. The books of the Old Testament came out in installments between 1672 and 1693, before the New Testament translation was revised between 1696 and 1708. Sacy died in 1684, well before the whole project was completed, but most of the work that led to the final product has been attributed to him. I thank Euan Cameron for first alerting me to the likelihood that Beethoven's copy of the Bible was a Sacy Bible.

the Sacy translation. Figure 2.1 shows the cover page of a copy at Stanford University.[82] Though neither "Port-Royal" nor Sacy's name appears on the cover, the book's preface (not shown in the figure) clearly identifies the translation. Port-Royal, an abbey outside Paris, was the most important center for Jansenism: the French theological movement of the seventeenth and eighteenth centuries that has been discussed in the previous chapter as a key influence on the German Catholic Enlightenment, especially Josephinism. In later eras, the *Bible de Port-Royal* would become one of the most popular French versions of the Bible and exerted a significant impact on newer translations.[83] But in the early eighteenth century, it was widely denounced by church officials for its Jansenist leanings, not only in the translation itself but also in Sacy's prefaces and annotations.[84] The translation project that produced the *Bible de Port-Royal* was inspired by the Jansenists' promotion of vernacular Bible reading, which went as far as advocating that for the ordinary lay Catholic, the practice should not only be permitted but was in fact a religious obligation—a view later explicitly condemned by the papacy.[85] Though papal limitations on the dissemination of vernacular Bibles had often been ignored since the Reformation—especially in France, the Low Countries, and the German-speaking lands—the prohibition was not officially lifted until as late as 1757.[86]

Though Jansenism was ostensibly a French movement, it became popular among lay Catholics and rank-and-file priests in the nearby Low Countries, especially in Liège and Mechelen—two of the Flemish cities associated with the elder Ludwig van Beethoven. Liège was second only in importance to Port-Royal as a geographical center for the spread of Jansenism, especially as a location for the printing of Jansenist books.[87] (J. F. Broncart, who published the copy of the Sacy Bible in figure 2.1, was known specifically as a Jansenist publisher.)[88] In Mechelen, conflicts between pro- and anti-Jansenist clerics were particularly fierce in the late seventeenth and early eighteenth centuries,

---

[82] Call number BS230 1742 F. I wish to thank Timothy Noakes for his assistance in locating this item at Stanford. In this Bible, the biblical text itself (not shown in the figure) is presented in a bilingual format, with the Latin Vulgate in the right column of each page and Sacy's French translation in the left column.

[83] Sayce, "Continental Versions," 349.

[84] Agten, *Catholic Church*, 146–71.

[85] See Agten, 4, 146–71; and Blanchard, *Synod of Pistoia*, 58, 66–67.

[86] See Chadwick, *Popes and European Revolution*, 75–76.

[87] Addison, "Bibliographie liégeoise," 122. See also Crahay, "Les tensions réligieuses"; and Agten, *Catholic Church*, 315.

[88] Addison, "Bibliographie liégeoise," 136.

LA SAINTE BIBLE

TRADUITE EN FRANÇOIS,
LE LATIN DE LA VULGATE A CÔTÉ,
AVEC DE COURTES NOTES TIRÉES DES SAINTS PERES
& des meilleurs Interprêtes, pour l'intelligence des endroits les plus dificiles;

ET

LA CONCORDE DES QUATRE EVANGELISTES,
en Latin & en François.

NOUVELLE ÉDITION,
ENRICHIE DE CARTES GEOGRAPHIQUES ET DE FIGURES,

Avec les Traitez de Chronologie & de Geographie, les Sommaires des Livres tant du Vieux que du Nouveau Testament, & toutes les Tables tirées de la grande Bible Latine d'ANTOINE VITRE':

De plus une Idée generale de l'Ecriture Sainte, avec diferentes Manieres & diverses Regles pour l'expliquer.

Le tout augmenté d'une Table très-ample des Matieres en François & en Latin.

TOME PREMIER,

Qui contient la Genese, l'Exode, le Levitique, les Nombres, le Deuteronome, Josué, Juges, Ruth, les quatre Livres des Rois, les deux des Paralipomenes, les deux d'Esdras, Tobie, Judith, Esther & Job.

A LIEGE, chez J. DELORME DE LA TOUR, Marchand Libraire, au Palais de S. A.
ET SE VEND
A AMSTERDAM, chez { P. MORTIER. / J. F. BERNARD. } A UTRECHT, chez SAVOYE.
A LAHAYE, chez { J. NEAULME. / VAN DUREN. / P. DE HONDT. / ADRIEN MOETJENS. } A COLOGNE, chez METTERNICH.
A FRANCFORT ET A LEIPSIK, { En tems de Foires, chez } P. MORTIER. ET VAN DUREN.

De l'Imprimerie de J. F. BRONCART, avec Privilege, Approbation & Permission des Superieurs.

M. DCC. XLII.

Figure 2.1 Cover of a French Bible in the Port-Royal (Sacy) translation (Liège: J. F. Broncart, 1742). Image courtesy of the Department of Special Collections, Stanford University Libraries.

a situation probably encouraged by the status of the city as the primatial see of the Low Countries.[89]

If the younger Ludwig van Beethoven's copy of the Sacy Bible was indeed first purchased by the composer's Flemish grandfather, the likelihood that the older Ludwig's ownership of the Bible reflected sympathy for Jansenism seems high. Support for vernacular Bible reading among the laity was widely associated with Jansenism throughout the Low Countries, even if not all Catholic figures who supported the practice would have self-identified as Jansenists.[90] At the very least, the older Ludwig would have been aware of Jansenism, for he was able to obtain a job at a church in Leuven as the result of a purge of suspected Jansenists from the church choir.[91] Whether the younger Ludwig, several decades later, remained aware of the wider significance of his grandfather's Bible cannot be determined with certainty. But the historical connections described earlier in this chapter between Jansenism and the German Catholic Enlightenment suggest that the possibility ought not to be ruled out. Any exposure that Beethoven had to the Catholic Enlightenment might have come not just from the cultural environment in Bonn, but may have been rooted in a family history of sympathy for reformist visions of Catholicism going back to his grandfather's origins in Flanders.

Beethoven's Outlook during His First Decade in Vienna

The historical framework provided by the German Catholic Enlightenment thus permits a more nuanced understanding of Beethoven's upbringing in Bonn than that which has been usual in the Beethoven literature. Beethoven was indeed raised in an enlightened milieu, but one where, at least to reform-minded Catholics, the Enlightenment tended to be connected to the Catholic religion, rather than opposed to it. As discussed in the previous chapter, however, around the time that Beethoven left Bonn for Vienna in late 1792, the Catholic Restoration's process of reaction against the Catholic Enlightenment was beginning, even if that process was very gradual and would only reach its endpoint with the liberal revolutions of 1848, some

---

[89] See Agten, *Catholic Church*, 14, 35, 53–59, 111–20, 182–84, 273–74, 336–37. It is worth mentioning too that Cornelius Jansen, whose ideas inspired the Jansenist movement after his death in 1638, was Flemish, and had been ordained a priest in Mechelen.
[90] Agten, 386, 4.
[91] Caeyers, *Beethoven*, 3–4.

two decades after the composer's death. For almost all of Beethoven's adult life—he left Bonn a month shy of his twenty-second birthday—the Catholic Enlightenment was, if not in decline, then at least threatened by competing and more conservative visions of the Church. Was Beethoven's religious outlook affected by these developments? To what extent did the ideas of the German Catholic Enlightenment that were so prominent in the Bonn of his youth remain attractive into his adulthood?

In a sense, these are the overarching questions for the remainder of this book, especially as we investigate Beethoven's mature religious works in subsequent chapters, along with certain religious texts that he probably read. But for the moment, I shall conclude this chapter by examining the small amount of evidence concerning Beethoven's worldview that dates from his first decade in Vienna. The majority of this evidence seems to refer to politics rather than religion. However, given that reaction to the French Revolution and the warfare that resulted was a key factor in the Catholic Restoration, Beethoven's political views during this period might provide at least indirect hints as to his religious outlook.

The one piece of documentary evidence from this time that contains an explicitly religious reference comes from April 1802, right at the end of the period under discussion here. In a letter to the publisher Franz Anton Hoffmeister, Beethoven expressed annoyance at an apparent request for a piano sonata celebrating the French Revolution:

> Has the devil got hold of you all, gentlemen?—that you suggest that *I should compose such a sonata*—Well, perhaps at the time of the revolutionary fever—such a thing might have been possible, but now, when everything is trying to slip back into the old rut, now that Buonaparte has concluded his Concordat with the Pope—to write a sonata of that kind?—If it were even a Missa pro Sancta Maria a tre voci, or a Vesper or something of that kind— In that case I would instantly take up my paint-brush—and with fat pound notes dash off a Credo in unum. But, good heavens, such a sonata—in these newly developing Christian times—Ho ho—there you must leave me out— you won't get anything from me.[92]

---

[92] Anderson no. 57 (*BGA* no. 84), April 8, 1802 (Beethoven's emphasis): "Reit euch den der Teufel insgesammt meine Herrn?—mir Vorzuschlagen eine Solche <u>Sonate zu machen</u>—zur Zeit des *Revoluzions*fieber's nun da—wäre das so was gewesen aber jezt, da alles wieder in's alte Gleiß zu schieben sucht, *buonaparte* mit dem Pabste das *Concordat* geschlossen—so eine Sonate?—wär's noch eine *Missa pro sancta maria a tre vocis* oder eine *Vesper etc*—nun da wollt ich gleich den Pinsel in die hand nehmen—und mit großen Pfundnoten ein *Credo in unum* hinschreiben—aber du lieber

It is tempting to treat these remarks as evidence of Beethoven's radical political outlook, including an antipathy toward traditional Christianity.[93] According to this interpretation, the composer wistfully recalls a more progressive time—"the time of the revolutionary fever"—and regards Napoleon's recent concordat with Pope Pius VII as a betrayal of French revolutionary ideals, an attitude that foreshadows his famous removal of the *Eroica* Symphony's dedication to Napoleon two years later. Beethoven then goes on to mock ("Ho ho") "these newly developing Christian times," a sign of his unhappiness at the revival of conservative religious attitudes occurring in response to the upheavals caused by war and revolution—in other words, the Catholic Restoration.

Read in this manner, the letter accords with conventional accounts of Beethoven's reaction to the political landscape of Vienna during the 1790s. Such accounts have tended to depict the city as a conservative, even authoritarian place, in contrast to the progressive Bonn that the young composer had left behind.[94] As a result of the repressive atmosphere introduced under the reign of Francis II/I, Beethoven was unable to express himself freely. Many writers have thus interpreted the paucity of surviving statements concerning the political situation to be a sign that Beethoven felt forced to keep silent in order to avoid getting into trouble with the authorities,[95] even if this state of affairs might be due simply to the lower rate of survival of Beethoven's correspondence in the earlier part of his life.[96] The composer's true beliefs, according to this narrative, had to be channeled into various works in his musical oeuvre, most of which were written later, after the 1790s. Indeed, specific resemblances between Beethoven's music and French revolutionary musical styles have been noted since the composer's own lifetime.[97] Beethoven also publicly expressed admiration for Cherubini—a figure who was not politically innocent in terms of his active association with the Revolution.[98] Emperor Francis himself is reported to have worried about the

---

Gott eine so[l]che Sonate—zu diesen neuangehenden christlichen Zeiten—hoho—da laßt mich aus—da wird nichts draus."

[93] See Kinderman, *Beethoven: A Political Artist*, 66; Lockwood, *Beethoven*, 184; and Solomon, *Beethoven*, 176–77.
[94] See, e.g., Kinderman, *Beethoven: A Political Artist*, 3–32.
[95] See, e.g., Solomon, *Beethoven*, 115.
[96] See Albrecht, "Anton Schindler as Destroyer," 174.
[97] See Jones, "Beethoven and the Sound," 950–56.
[98] Jones, 956.

66 THE CATHOLIC BEETHOVEN

"revolutionary" nature of Beethoven's music, and it is even possible that the composer himself was placed under surveillance.[99]

Beethoven's reported interactions with the French ambassador in Vienna, Jean-Baptiste Bernadotte, lend support to claims of the composer's affinity for forbidden radical politics in the 1790s. Bernadotte, who would later become one of Napoleon's generals, introduced Beethoven to the violinist Rodolphe Kreutzer, later the dedicatee of the op. 47 violin sonata.[100] Other suggestive clues can be found in a recently discovered letter that Beethoven wrote in 1795 to the diplomat Heinrich Struve, whom he had known in Bonn through the Zehrgarten Circle. As Julia Ronge has commented, "No other autograph document has been preserved that states his political attitudes so plainly."[101] Struve was stationed in Russia at the time, a country Beethoven describes disapprovingly as a "cold land, where humanity is treated so very far beneath its dignity."[102] The composer then asks, "When will the time finally come when there will only be *humans*[?]"[103] The letter's explicit advocacy for egalitarian political ideals resonates strikingly with similar sentiments expressed in Schiller's ode "An die Freude," which Beethoven first came across two years earlier, in 1793.[104] Just as provocative, if not more so, is another letter Beethoven wrote to Nikolaus Simrock in August 1794, describing the political situation in Vienna:

> Here various *important* people have been locked up; it is said that a revolution is about to break out—But I believe that so long as an Austrian can get his *brown ale* and his *little sausages*, he is not likely to revolt. People say that the gates leading to the suburbs are to be closed at 10 p.m. The soldiers have loaded their muskets with ball. You dare not raise your voice here or the police will take you into custody.[105]

---

[99] Kopitz and Cadenbach, *Beethoven aus der Sicht*, 1:258; Haag, "Beethoven," 112–13.
[100] Kinderman, *Beethoven: A Political Artist*, 60.
[101] Ronge, "'When Will the Time,'" 13. This letter remained undiscovered until 2012 (ibid., 1).
[102] Quoted in Ronge, 9: "Kalten Lande, wo die Menschheit noch so sehr unter ihrer Würde behandelt wird." The translation is by Stephen M. Whiting.
[103] Quoted in Ronge, 9 (Beethoven's emphasis): "Wann wird auch der Zeitpunkt kommen wo es nur Menschen geben wird[?]" The translation is by Stephen M. Whiting.
[104] Ronge, 8–13. See also Dennis, *Beethoven in German Politics*, 26.
[105] Anderson no. 12 (*BGA* no. 17), August 2, 1794 (Beethoven's emphasis): "Hier hat man verschiedene Leute von Bedeutung eingezogen, man sagt, es hätte eine Revolution ausbrechen sollen—aber ich glaube, so lange der österreicher noch Braun's Bier und würstel hat, *revoltirt* er nicht, es heißt, die Thöre zu dem vorstädten sollen nachts um 10 uhr gesperrt werden. die Soldaten haben scharf geladen. man darf nicht zu laut sprechen hier, sonst giebt die Polizei einem *quartier*."

Especially in light of Simrock's own support for the French (discussed above), most commentators have interpreted this letter as a kind of anguished complaint: Beethoven, nurtured in the more progressive city of Bonn, chafes at the repressive environment he found in Vienna, and at the political passivity of that city's inhabitants.[106]

But complicating this image of Beethoven as oppressed radical is the fact that later in the very same letter, the composer expresses a desire to return to his previous life as a court musician for Maximilian Franz, a desire eventually thwarted only because the elector's rule was ended by the fall of Bonn to French forces.[107] Even if Beethoven sympathized to some degree with the ideals of the French Revolution, such sympathy may not have led him to a wholesale rejection of Habsburg authority. Such an attitude is no contradiction but accords with the nature of the Enlightenment in his native Bonn, where progressive ideas circulated within the framework of traditional political and religious institutions rather than seeking their overthrow.

In any case, Beethoven's account of the political situation in Vienna occurs in a letter that is otherwise full of mundane details about his life in the city. In context, therefore, Beethoven's comments need not be interpreted as anything more than a simple description of the facts on the ground. As David Wyn Jones has argued:

> Beethoven's comments on the placid Austrians are all too easily interpreted as sympathy towards France and criticism of Austria. They are more appropriately read as casual ones, accepting rather than judgment. Beethoven was a Habsburg loyalist, brought up in a court in Bonn ruled by Maximilian Franz, the brother of Joseph II and Leopold II, and someone who had written cantatas to commemorate the death of the first and the succession of the second.[108]

In addition, historians of the period routinely caution against overstating the severity of Francis's supposed authoritarianism. Charles Ingrao, for instance, has argued that "the Franciscan reaction did not constitute an outright rejection of the Enlightenment."[109] A relatively liberal conception of the rule of law continued to prevail, even when it came to censorship: no one was

---

[106] See, e.g., Kinderman, *Beethoven: A Political Artist*, 33–34.
[107] See Wyn Jones, *Music in Vienna*, 123.
[108] Wyn Jones, 123.
[109] Ingrao, *Habsburg Monarchy*, 260.

68 THE CATHOLIC BEETHOVEN

punished merely for expressing pro-French views.[110] Even political agitators who were executed were, in Ingrao's view, guilty of treason under any reasonable definition.[111] Wyn Jones's more prosaic reading of the "brown ale and sausages" letter might also encourage greater caution in interpreting Beethoven's 1802 letter to Hoffmeister quoted above. Could Beethoven's tone in that letter have been merely light-hearted rather than scornful or sarcastic? Could his irreverent "Ho ho" have been a reference less to a perceived revival of Christianity than to the unfashionable nature of Hoffmeister's request for a revolution-themed sonata? Is criticism of a corrupt alliance between the Church and an authoritarian political leader necessarily equivalent to a more fundamental rejection of Christian religious ideas?

Wyn Jones's use of the label "Habsburg loyalist" to describe Beethoven, which is provocative given its contrast with the received wisdom about Beethoven's worldview, is credible not just in light of the composer's continued affinity for aristocratic patronage discussed above. Two years after writing this letter, Beethoven went so far as to compose two songs gushing in their praise not only for Austria and her people but, more importantly, for Austria's rulers: *Abschiedsgesang an Wiens Bürger* (Farewell song to the citizens of Vienna, WoO 121) and *Kriegslied der Österreicher* (War song of the Austrian, WoO 122). These songs prefigure the even more chauvinistic political works like *Wellington's Victory* and *Der glorreiche Augenblick* that Beethoven wrote around the time of the Congress of Vienna, apparently in support of the Habsburg monarchy.[112] The third line of *Kriegslied* is far from subtle: "For our Prince is good, our courage is raised!" (*Denn unser Fürst ist gut, erhaben unser Mut!*). These songs were both written in response to declining Austrian morale in the face of French military successes during the latter stages of the War of the First Coalition.[113] This context hints at a slightly different possibility concerning Beethoven's outlook in the 1790s: the composer's attitudes toward the French Revolution might have become more negative over time, given the increasingly illiberal course taken by the Revolution and the belligerence of French armies across Europe. In light of the historical context discussed in the previous chapter,

---

[110] Ingrao, 261, 254.
[111] Ingrao, 254.
[112] On the works associated with the Congress of Vienna, see Cook, "Other Beethoven"; Mathew, "History under Erasure"; and Mathew, "Beethoven's Political Music."
[113] See Mathew, *Political Beethoven*, 143–50.

such a shift—however slight, or however hesitant—would have been far from unusual among people of his time.

Notwithstanding the lack of clearcut surviving evidence, it is hard to imagine that Beethoven was unaware of the particular impact of French military actions back in the Rhineland of his birth. French armies first invaded the Rhineland as early as the autumn of 1792, and had taken Mainz (in the southern part of the region) by the time of Beethoven's departure from Bonn. Barry Cooper has speculated that the composer's departure from his hometown might well have been hastened by the political situation in the region, though Bonn itself would not end up falling until 1794.[114] Antipathy toward the French was widespread in the Rhineland.[115] As alluded to earlier in this chapter, there was undoubtedly a notable amount of sympathy for the French Revolution in the region, and even for the French armies after their occupation began. But *resistance* to the French was the much more common position.[116] In this regard, figures like Nikolaus Simrock and Eulogius Schneider, who were connected to Beethoven in Bonn, may not have been unique in their support for, or even outright collaboration with, the French—but they were also not typical. As was true in many occupied areas, collaboration was not necessarily prompted by a genuine allegiance to the French or the political ideas they were perceived to represent, but was often motivated by practical reasons such as a desire for peace and order.[117] In any case, the conduct of the French armies in the Rhineland quickly eliminated whatever goodwill toward them might have existed among the local population. Such was the frequency of violence and corruption that characterized the occupation that the French even managed to alienate political radicals who would otherwise have been ideological allies.[118]

Opposition to the French was prompted not only by material hardship or patriotic sentiment, but by religious concerns. In Bonn, popular hatred of the occupation was stimulated by what were perceived as insults against Catholicism, for instance the parading of a "goddess of reason" in the city, or the use of the baptismal font in the Bonn Minster to store rancid meat.[119] Given the hostility of the local population, the French authorities

---

[114] B. Cooper, *Beethoven*, 39.
[115] Rowe, *From Reich to State*, 40–49.
[116] Rowe, 40–49.
[117] See Rowe, 81–83.
[118] Blanning, *French Revolution in Germany*, 255–85.
[119] Chadwick, *Popes and European Revolution*, 498; Zalar, *Reading and Rebellion*, 46–48.

found it difficult to enforce bans on particular religious activities, especially pilgrimages.[120] A similar nexus between religion and patriotism was present in Vienna in the 1790s, albeit in a different manner given that the city was not yet subject to French occupation, as would occur twice in the decade after. (I shall return to this topic in chapter 4.) As Wyn Jones has documented, war with France stimulated a profusion of musical and literary responses, many of which were replete with religious references.[121] This is the cultural context for the patriotic songs by Beethoven discussed above, as well as for Haydn's composition of his famous *Kaiserhymne* (Emperor's hymn) in honor of Emperor Francis II/I.[122] The practice of congregational singing played an especially important role in the cultivation of popular patriotism. As Nicholas Mathew has written, "Religious worship provided one of the most influential models according to which entire peoples were encouraged to join in—a paradigm for active participation in the corporate projects of state and civil society."[123] Congregational singing thus seems to have been an aspect of the Josephine church reforms that retained broad support.

The remainder of this book will demonstrate how, starting with the Gellert Lieder of 1802, Beethoven, in both his sacred works and in his engagement with various religious thinkers, showed a consistent interest in a number of ideas that can be tied to the German Catholic Enlightenment. This aspect of his religious outlook was most likely rooted in his upbringing in Bonn, an important center of Catholic reform in the second half of the eighteenth century. But as we shall see, there are also hints of an openness to ideas more in line with the conservative Catholic Restoration. Such hints appear especially in the composer's early oratorio *Christus am Ölberge* and are more pronounced in the *Missa solemnis*. If this is correct, it is possible that disillusionment or at least ambivalence toward the French Revolution—a common reaction at the time to the upheavals of war and occupation wrought by French armies—played some role in encouraging a partial turn in his worldview toward the Catholic Restoration.

---

[120] Blanning, *French Revolution in Germany*, 231.
[121] Wyn Jones, *Music in Vienna*, 122–26. See also Hugo Schmidt, "Origin."
[122] Hugo Schmidt, "Origin."
[123] Mathew, *Political Beethoven*, 142.

3

Beethoven's Religious Works before the *Missa solemnis*

The Gellert Lieder, *Christus am Ölberge*, and the Mass in C

Beethoven's letter to Hoffmeister quoted in the previous chapter, apparently rejecting a request for a sonata celebrating the French Revolution, was written in April 1802. To interpret this letter as expressing a negative view of Christianity, as one might be tempted to do, creates a tension with the fact that around the same time, Beethoven completed his first mature work of religious music: the *Sechs Lieder von Gellert* (Six songs by Gellert), op. 48, usually referred to more simply as the Gellert Lieder. In these songs for voice and piano, Beethoven set six poems by Christian Fürchtegott Gellert (1715–1769), a Protestant pastor who had been based in Leipzig. Though the songs were first published in August 1803, a full manuscript copy exists from as early as March 1802.[1] Also in 1803, Beethoven wrote his only completed oratorio, *Christus am Ölberge* (Christ on the Mount of Olives), op. 85, on the subject of Christ's Passion. The piece was premiered in April of that year, but Beethoven may have begun work on it as early as November 1802.[2] Maynard Solomon has suggested that "there may have been a stirring of religious impulses in Beethoven at this time," given the close composition dates of these two works, along with *Der Wachtelschlag*, WoO 129, another religious song that was eventually published in 1804.[3] This situation was almost certainly connected to a personal crisis: the composer's realization that he was

---

[1] See Biermann, "Cyclical Ordering," 170–74. The cycle was published a second time by Hoffmeister & Kühnel a few months after it was first published by Artaria in August 1803, with the order of the six songs slightly altered. Biermann argues that the Hoffmeister edition was also authorized by Beethoven.

[2] See Mühlenweg, "Ludwig van Beethoven," 1:5–11, 17. The oratorio was not published until 1811. The extensive process of revision that occurred before that time, especially to the text, is relevant to understanding the work as reflective of Beethoven's religious outlook, and will thus be discussed in detail below.

[3] See Solomon, *Beethoven*, 247; and Reid, *Beethoven Song Companion*, 117–20.

The Catholic Beethoven. Nicholas Chong, Oxford University Press. © Oxford University Press 2024.
DOI: 10.1093/9780197752951.003.0004

72 THE CATHOLIC BEETHOVEN

losing his hearing, as famously documented in the Heiligenstadt Testament, which dates from October 1802, as well as in several letters shortly before this time.[4]

Though caution is always required in treating musical works as reflections of composers' own views, in the case of these religious works of 1802–1803, we have good reason to interpret these pieces as important documents of Beethoven's religious outlook. As Paul Reid has argued, Beethoven's songs in general provide useful clues concerning his personal beliefs, because in most cases their texts set were "carefully and deliberately chosen by the composer to reflect and parallel his own world view."[5] With regard to the Gellert Lieder, Beethoven's drew his texts from the poet's fifty-four *Geistliche Oden und Lieder* (Sacred odes and songs), published in Leipzig in 1757. The poems in Gellert's original collection were not divided into groups, nor were they ordered in a particular way based on subject matter.[6] Beethoven thus had to take great care in choosing just six poems that presumably were of special significance for him, and, as we shall see below, he seems to have cared a great deal about how those poems were to be ordered. A contrast can be drawn with C. P. E. Bach, who simply set the entirety of Gellert's collection to music a year after the poems were published.[7] Gellert's poetry had been extremely popular in the middle of the eighteenth century: during his lifetime, only the Bible was more widely read in German-speaking lands.[8] But it was no longer so by the time Beethoven wrote his songs.[9] And in any event, lieder with religious texts were generally out of fashion at the beginning of the nineteenth century.[10] To compose songs on Gellert's poetry thus appears to have been a very deliberate and personal choice on Beethoven's part.

---

[4] See "The Heiligenstadt Testament," in Anderson, *Letters to Beethoven*, 1351–54 (*BGA* no. 106); and Anderson nos. 51, 53, and 54 (*BGA* nos. 65, 67, and 70). The earliest letter referring to Beethoven's deafness (Anderson no. 51/*BGA* no. 65) dates to June 1801. As Maynard Solomon has noted, the Testament survives as a fair copy, meaning that it cannot be interpreted as a spontaneous emotional outburst, nor as a passing comment. Rather, Beethoven seems to have intended it as a polished, deliberate statement of his personal views. See Solomon, *Beethoven*, 154.

[5] Reid, *Beethoven Song Companion*, 5. For Reid, this autobiographical aspect to many of Beethoven's songs is a key reason for devoting greater attention to the composer's lieder output than has traditionally been the case in Beethoven scholarship.

[6] Biermann, "Cyclical Ordering," 168–69.

[7] See Biermann, 169; and Reid, *Beethoven Song Companion*, 154.

[8] Schneiderwirth, *Das katholische deutsche Kirchenlied*, 9: "Kaum hat je ein deutscher Dichter bei seinen Lebzeiten eine ähnliche Berühmtheit erlangt, wie Gellert" (Hardly has a German poet gained a similar fame during his lifetime as Gellert did).

[9] See Massenkeil, "Religiöse Aspekte in den Gellert-Liedern," 193; and Herttrich, "Beethoven und die Religion," 27.

[10] Lodes, "Probing the Sacred Genres," 219. Haydn's own setting of four of Gellert's *Geistliche Oden* as part songs (Hob. XXVc:1–9 and XXVb:1–4) would constitute an exception to the general trend. Haydn considered Gellert a favorite writer and owned the poet's complete works. While the

Moreover, resonances between the texts of the Gellert Lieder and the actual content of the Heiligenstadt Testament suggest that the songs were written as a direct response to the emotional crisis prompted by Beethoven's encroaching deafness.[11] For instance, the third song in the Gellert Lieder, "Vom Tode" (On death), speaks of the importance of being prepared for death, a theme that is also prominent in the Testament, which repeatedly emphasizes the necessity of stoicism in the face of suffering and mortality.[12] As Stephen Rumph has demonstrated, a more precise textual parallel even exists between the line "Stündlich eil' ich zu dem Grabe" (With each hour I hasten toward the grave) in Gellert's poem and Beethoven's "Mit Freuden eil ich dem Tode entgegen" (Joyfully I go to meet Death) in the Testament.[13] "Vom Tode" was a poem that seems to have meant a lot to Beethoven. In addition to the setting in the Gellert Lieder, drafts for three other settings have survived in Beethoven's sketches. The earliest of these dates to late 1798, the second to late 1803, shortly after the publication of the Gellert Lieder, and the latest to 1822.[14]

A personal investment in the text is something that is also evident with *Christus am Ölberge*, which Theodore Albrecht has pithily labeled "an autobiographical oratorio."[15] The main themes of *Christus* clearly overlap with those of the Heiligenstadt Testament: undeserved suffering, loneliness, fear of death, stoicism, and the overcoming of adversity.[16] Close textual similarities exist between lines from the Testament and lines from the *Christus* libretto, and Barry Cooper goes so far as to argue that "the oratorio text is often closer to the Heiligenstadt Testament than to the original Biblical narratives on which it is

---

possibility that Beethoven was influenced by Haydn's admiration for Gellert cannot be ruled out entirely, Haydn's songs were not published until shortly after Beethoven completed his Gellert Lieder. There are also no poems that are common to both Haydn's and Beethoven's settings, though they both seem to have emphasized the themes of death and thanksgiving in choosing which poems to set from Gellert's collection. See Schroeder, "Haydn and Gellert," 8; and Komlós, "Miscellaneous Vocal Genres," 172–75.

[11] My argument here echoes that made by Joanna Biermann: see "Cyclical Ordering," 176.
[12] See "The Heiligenstadt Testament," in Anderson, *Letters to Beethoven*, 1351–54 (BGA no. 106). See also Lodes, "Probing the Sacred Genres," 218.
[13] See Rumph, *Beethoven after Napoleon*, 39; and "The Heiligenstadt Testament," in Anderson, *Letters to Beethoven*, 1351–54, at 1353 (BGA no. 106, p. 123).
[14] Biermann, "Cyclical Ordering," 163–64.
[15] Albrecht, "Fortnight Fallacy," 276.
[16] B. Cooper, "Beethoven's Oratorio," 19–20. As Alan Tyson has pointed out, these themes are also central to Beethoven's opera *Fidelio*, which he wrote just two years after *Christus*: see "Beethoven's Heroic Phase."

based."[17] To cite just one example, the unusual description of Christ as "Verbannte" (the banished one) in the oratorio's fifth number, the *Chor der Krieger* (Chorus of soldiers), matches Beethoven's use of the same word in the Testament.[18] Beethoven worked unusually closely with the librettist Franz Xaver Huber on the content of the text: he appears to have chosen the theme of *Christus* as a way of dealing with his personal crisis, then assisted Huber with the libretto.[19] Moreover, at the time that Beethoven wrote his oratorio, the dominance of Haydn's *Creation* and *Seasons* meant there was little commercial demand for new oratorios in Vienna.[20] It is thus unlikely that Beethoven chose the subject matter of *Christus* to follow some kind of trend, especially since there had also been no recent oratorio setting of the Passion subject in particular.[21] As with the Gellert Lieder, *Christus* was not a commission, nor was composing it simply a good career move on Beethoven's part. These pieces were motivated primarily by events in the composer's life, in particular his despair at losing his hearing.

Following the religious works of 1802–1803, Beethoven's next foray into religious music would have to wait a few more years until the Mass in C major, op. 86. This work premiered in September 1807 but was probably commissioned in late 1806 by Prince Nikolaus Esterházy II, better known as Haydn's last patron, for his wife's name day.[22] The Mass in C may not have been as disconnected from the earlier religious works as this chronological gap suggests. As early as 1804, Beethoven made brief sketches for a mass in A major. These do not appear to have been directly related to the Mass in C, but they do suggest that Beethoven was interested in writing a mass well before the commission he eventually received.[23] This fact also speaks against casting doubt, as some commentators have done, on its sincerity as

---

[17] B. Cooper, "Beethoven's Oratorio," 20. Cooper's detailed study also shows parallels between the *Christus* libretto and the letters Beethoven wrote before the Heiligenstadt Testament referring to his deafness (see above).

[18] B. Cooper, 20.

[19] See B. Cooper, 20–23; Biermann, "*Christus am Ölberge*," 281; and Albrecht, "The Fortnight Fallacy," 273–74. Cooper's account is the most thorough and presents persuasive sketch evidence to support this argument.

[20] Biermann, "*Christus am Ölberge*," 280–81. See also Smither, *History of the Oratorio*, 4:62.

[21] Lodes, "Probing the Sacred Genres," 220. The oratorio version of Haydn's *Seven Last Words* might be considered an exception. Though it was performed for the first time in Vienna back in 1796, it was not published until 1801 (by Breitkopf & Härtel), a date that would put it closer in time to Beethoven's oratorio. See Landon, *Haydn*, 97–98, 180–83. The possibility that Haydn's *Seven Last Words* influenced Beethoven's interest in the topic of Christ's Passion thus cannot be ruled out.

[22] See McGrann, "Beethoven's Mass in C," 1:48–81; and Knapp, "Beethoven's Mass in C major," 200–1.

[23] See McGrann, "Der Hintergrund zu Beethovens Messen," 124.

an expression of the composer's own religious beliefs.[24] Though Beethoven's first completed mass was written, indeed commissioned, by a patron for a specific occasion, the commission, rather than being the sole impetus for the work, seems to have provided Beethoven the chance to fulfill a desire that he already had to write a mass. (As we shall see in chapter 6, a similar situation would apply in the case of the *Missa solemnis*.)

More importantly, Beethoven himself indicated on several occasions that the work was of profound personal importance to him.[25] As discussed in the introduction, Beethoven refused to accept his publisher Breitkopf & Härtel's argument that there was a lack of demand for church music. In letters from 1808 he pressed the firm to publish the work anyway, even if it meant that he himself would not be compensated. The composer declared, "Notwithstanding the utterly frigid attitude of our age to works of this kind, the Mass is especially close to my heart."[26] Four years later, after multiple delays in the publication of the piece, the seemingly impatient Beethoven asked Breitkopf: "When is [the Mass] to be presented to our devout Catholics?"[27] In another letter, Beethoven also described the kind of religious message he wished to convey in the Mass:

> The general character of the Kyrie ... is heartfelt resignation, deep sincerity of religious feeling ... yet without on that account being sad. Gentleness is the fundamental characteristic of the whole work. . . . Cheerfulness pervades this Mass. The Catholic goes to church on Sunday in his best clothes and in a joyful and festive mood.[28]

The level of detail in this description of the Kyrie is striking; it brings to mind the composer's infamously fussy tempo marking for the same movement—Andante con moto assai vivace quasi Allegretto ma non troppo—which was

---

[24] See, e.g., Drabkin, *Beethoven: Missa solemnis*, 1.
[25] See McGrann, "Beethoven's Mass in C," 1:112.
[26] Anderson no. 169 (*BGA* no. 331), end of July 1808: "[Die Messe] mir ... vorzüglich am Herzen liegt troz aller Kälte unseres Zeitalters gegen d[ie] g[leichen]." See also Anderson no. 168 (*BGA* no. 329), Beethoven to Breitkopf & Härtel, c. July 10, 1808.
[27] Anderson no. 351 (*BGA* no. 555), February 28, 1812: "Die *Missa*, wann wird sie den andächtigen Katholiken vorgelegt werden?" See also Anderson nos. 272, 294, 297, 325, 379, 380, and 383 (*BGA* nos. 465, 484, 486, 523, 588, 591, and 594).
[28] Anderson no. 294 (*BGA* no. 484), January 16, 1811: "der allgemeine character ... in dem *Kyrie* ist innige Ergebung, woher innigkeit *religiöser* Gefühle ... ohne deswegen Traurig zu seyn, sanfthaft liegt dem Ganzen zu Grunde. . . . So ist doch heiterkeit im Ganzen, Der Katholike tritt sonntags geschmückt festlich Heiter in seine Kirche."

added only after the premiere.[29] As Jeremiah McGrann has pointed out, it was highly unusual for the composer to comment to such an extent about the expressive intentions behind one of his musical works.[30] There can be no doubt that Beethoven cared deeply about how this piece sounded in performance, and about the emotions it aroused in his listeners.

Whatever personal motivations may have been behind Beethoven's composition of these religious works during the first decade of the nineteenth century, specific details concerning these pieces suggest that his broader outlook continued to be shaped by the Catholic Enlightenment to which he had been exposed in Bonn. Considered as a group, these works reflect several themes associated with the German Catholic Enlightenment that were previously discussed in chapter 1: ecumenism and religious tolerance; the presence of God in the natural world; ethical conduct; and the importance of an active engagement with the liturgy among ordinary Catholics. Complicating this argument, however, are certain features that conflicted with Catholic Enlightenment principles. The emotional exuberance and structural complexity of the Mass in C would have violated the preference for liturgical simplicity that characterized the Josephine reforms, even if these characteristics of the work seem paradoxically to have been inspired by Beethoven's desire to abide by the Catholic Enlightenment's outlook on the liturgy in other ways. In *Christus am Ölberge*, the highly sentimental manner in which Beethoven's oratorio depicts Christ is more readily tied to the Catholic Restoration than to the Catholic Enlightenment. As will become clearer in chapters 5 and 6, these suggestions of an openness to departing from the Catholic Enlightenment, and even to embracing certain aspects of the Catholic Restoration, foreshadow Beethoven's apparent admiration for the theologian Johann Michael Sailer, as well as several features of the *Missa solemnis*.

The Gellert Lieder and the Ecumenical Concerns of the Catholic Enlightenment

The circumstances surrounding the composition of the Gellert Lieder and later the Mass in C can be tied to the ecumenism typical of the German

---

[29] McGrann, "Beethoven's Mass in C," 1:135.
[30] McGrann, 1:123. McGrann's observation echoes similar comments by Adorno on Beethoven's statements regarding the *Missa solemnis*: see *Beethoven*, 138, 143–44.

Catholic Enlightenment, which encouraged dialogue and interaction between Catholics and Protestants.

With the Gellert Lieder, this spirit of ecumenism is evident not only in the superficial fact that Beethoven was interested in a Protestant poet, though he himself lived only in Catholic environments, but in the status of Gellert himself. Though he was a Protestant, Gellert's writings were as popular among German Catholics as they were within his own religious community; indeed, historians have cited this specific fact as a notable example of the openness to Protestant religious writing that was a key feature of the German Catholic Enlightenment.[31] It is likely that Beethoven became familiar with Gellert's poetry during his youth in Bonn. Neefe was known to have admired Gellert's works,[32] and the music library of Bonn's electoral court included a musical setting of the *Geistliche Oden* by an unspecified composer.[33]

But Gellert was important for the Catholic Enlightenment for a still more specific reason. As Matthaeus Schneiderwirth showed in an exhaustive but now-forgotten study published in 1908, Gellert—along with Klopstock, another Protestant writer beloved by Beethoven—was an enormous influence on the development of the Catholic *Kirchenlied* during the second half of the eighteenth century.[34] Gellert himself was very interested in religious music, and intended the poems in his *Geistliche Oden* to be sung. For each poem in the collection, he suggested existing Lutheran chorale melodies that could be employed.[35] Gellert emphasized the role of religious poems and songs in encouraging moral behavior, hence the heavy stress on ethics and the didactic tone of many of his poems.[36] His habit of making frequent scriptural references in his poetry seems to have been another way in which he sought to teach religious lessons to ordinary believers and to cultivate individual piety rooted in knowledge of the Bible.[37] These were all ideas shared by

---

[31] See, e.g., Printy, *Enlightenment*, 145; and Swidler, *Aufklärung Catholicism*, 21–22.
[32] Loos, "Christian Gottlob Neefe," 396–99.
[33] Modena, Gallerie Estensi, Biblioteca Estense Universitaria, Mus.F.1327. See the entry in the recently prepared catalog of Maximilian Franz's music library: https://www.univie.ac.at/muwidb/sacredmusiclibrary/entry/33, accessed August 1, 2024. The printed title is *C. F. Gellerts geistliche Oden und Lieder mit neuen Melodien zum Singen beym Claviere, für eine und mehrere Stimen* [sic]. The score was published in 1777 by Heinrich Steiner in the Swiss city of Winterthur.
[34] Schneiderwirth, *Das katholische deutsche Kirchenlied*.
[35] Reid, *Beethoven Song Companion*, 154.
[36] Schneiderwirth, *Das katholische deutsche Kirchenlied*, 10–11.
[37] See Schneiderwirth, 13. See also Reid, *Beethoven Song Companion*, 154.

Catholic Enlightenment thinkers and by church musicians influenced by the movement, especially the composers of vernacular Catholic *Kirchenlieder*.[38] German Catholic hymnbooks of the time, including one published in Vienna under the explicit instructions of Maria Theresa, even contain hymns using Gellert's own words, or texts clearly adapted from Gellert's poetry.[39] At least four of the texts in Beethoven's selection were used for hymns in actual German Catholic hymn books published in the late eighteenth century: "Bitten" (Petitions), "Die Liebe des Nächsten" (Love of neighbor), "Vom Tode," and "Gottes Macht und Vorsehung" (God's power and providence).[40] (In the Gellert Lieder, these poems correspond respectively to song numbers 1, 2, 3, and 5.)

Gellert's historical importance for the development of the vernacular *Kirchenlied* makes it possible to connect Beethoven's writing of the Gellert Lieder to his own exposure to vernacular Catholic liturgy during his youth in Bonn. More obvious evidence of this connection is observable in Beethoven's musical treatment of Gellert's poems, at least in the first five songs. In these Beethoven sets the texts strophically, with only the first stanza given with the musical notation and the text for the remaining stanzas listed separately, as is common practice in hymn books. The fourth song, "Die Ehre Gottes aus der Natur" (The glory of God from nature), constitutes a slight exception in that *two* stanzas of text correspond to one musical strophe, producing a double-strophic structure, but musical notation is still only provided for the first two stanzas. Beethoven's music often appears to have been written with only the first stanza of the text in mind, a fact confirmed by evidence from the composer's sketches.[41] The later stanzas often do not fit the music as well, either metrically or in terms of which words are emphasized by particular musical devices.[42] However, it seems fair to say, as Günther Massenkeil has argued, that all the stanzas

---

[38] Schneiderwirth, *Das katholische deutsche Kirchenlied*, 15–20.
[39] Schneiderwirth, 16–26. One of the most important composers of German Catholic vernacular hymns in this period was Ignaz Franz (1719–1790), a follower of Gellert's. Franz's biggest claim to fame is the hymn "Grosser Gott, wir loben dich," which is frequently found to this day in Anglophone Catholic hymnals as "Holy God, We Praise Thy Name."
[40] Schneiderwirth, 42–43.
[41] Massenkeil, "Religiöse Aspekte in den Gellert-Liedern," 199–200.
[42] Reid, *Beethoven Song Companion*, 157, 159, 164.

for each of the strophic songs played a part in Beethoven's conception of these pieces.[43] There would otherwise have been no reason for the "extra" stanzas to be printed, and Beethoven took care that not one of Gellert's original stanzas was omitted. This is true even in the case of the second song, "Die Liebe des Nächsten," which has fourteen stanzas, and the fifth song, "Gottes Macht und Vorsehung," which has fifteen. One can imagine a performer choosing certain preferred stanzas much as a church musician might choose particular verses of a hymn for a particular liturgical occasion. (It is hard to believe that Beethoven would have intended all the stanzas in these songs to be sung in any single performance.) Beethoven's evocation of hymnody in the first five songs is also apparent in the relatively simple and emotionally restrained musical style employed to set Gellert's words. The vocal melody is predominantly conjunct, and is often doubled by the piano. Consonant harmonies prevail, despite the occasional judicious use of dissonance. The text-setting is almost always syllabic. Chordal hymn textures make an appearance in three songs: "Bitten" (mm. 36–44), "Die Ehre Gottes" (mm. 1–18, 29–42), and "Gottes Macht" (mm. 1–14). In addition, the plain tonic chords in the piano that begin "Die Liebe des Nächsten" and "Vom Tode" seem to evoke the liturgical practice of playing such chords on the organ as a way of giving the congregation the correct starting pitch.

Nature and Ethical Conduct in the Gellert Lieder and *Christus am Ölberge*

Beethoven's religious works of the first decade of the nineteenth century can also be connected to the German Catholic Enlightenment in terms of the themes prominent in their texts. The poems that Beethoven chose to set in the Gellert Lieder, for instance, highlight two key ideas associated with the Catholic Enlightenment: the presence of God in the natural world and an emphasis on ethical conduct. The fourth and fifth songs, "Die Ehre Gottes" and "Gottes Macht," both depict physical nature as a source of knowledge about God. "Die Ehre Gottes" draws particular attention to the awe induced by the natural world, an awe that invites the listener to recognize the creative power of God:

---

[43] Massenkeil, "Religiöse Aspekte in den Gellert-Liedern," 199–200.

Vernimm's, und siehe die Wunder der Werke,	Hear it, see the wonders of the works
Die die Natur dir aufgestellt!	That nature has assembled for you!
Verkündigt Weisheit und Ordnung und Stärke	Do not wisdom and order and strength
Dir nicht den Herrn, den Herrn der Welt?	Proclaim to you the Lord, the Lord of the world?
Wer trägt der Himmel unzählbare Sterne?	Who sustains the innumerable stars?
Wer führt die Sonn' aus ihrem Zelt?	Who leads the sun out of its resting place?
Sie kommt und leuchtet und lacht uns von ferne	It comes and shines and laughs to us from afar
Und läuft den Weg gleich als ein Held.	And runs its course just like a hero.
Mein ist die Kraft, mein ist Himmel und Erde;	Mine is the power, mine is heaven and earth;
An meinen Werken kennst du mich.	Through my works you know me.
Ich bin's, und werde sein, der ich sein werde:	I am and shall be what I shall be:
Dein Gott und Vater ewiglich.	Your God and Father eternally.
Kannst du der Wesen unzählbare Heere,	Can you contemplate the innumerable armies of beings,
Den kleinsten Staub fühllos beschaun?	The tiniest dust without feeling?
Durch wen ist alles? O gib ihm die Ehre!	Through whom does everything exist? O give him the glory!
Mir, ruft der Herr, sollst du vertraun.	In me, the Lord exclaims, should you trust.
Mein ist die Kraft, mein ist Himmel und Erde;	Mine is the power, mine is heaven and earth;
An meinen Werken kennst du mich.	Through my works you know me.
Ich bin's, und werde sein, der ich sein werde:	I am and shall be what I shall be:
Dein Gott und Vater ewiglich.	Your God and Father eternally.

Ich bin dein Schöpfer, bin Weisheit und Güte,	I am your Creator, I am wisdom and benevolence,
Ein Gott der Ordnung und dein Heil;	A God of order and your salvation;
Ich bin's! Mich liebe von ganzem Gemüte	I am he! Love me with your whole mind
Und nimm an meiner Gnade Teil.	And partake of my grace.

As noted above, this song is the only one of the five strophic songs in the collection that sets *two* poetic stanzas to a single musical strophe. The likeliest explanation for Beethoven's deviation from a more straightforward strophic structure is to enable him to place special stress on the first two lines of the second stanza, which refer to the stars and the sun (see example 3.1). Beethoven's setting of these lines dramatizes in a particularly vivid manner a feeling of awe before the divine. In context, this eight-measure passage is strikingly different from what comes before and after: the piano part is more thickly voiced, and the vocal part is not doubled by the piano. The piano plays a series of quarter-note chords throughout these measures, with each sonority repeated multiple times: the passage begins, for instance, with seventeen iterations of the same E-flat major chord.

The chords here are clearly meant to depict pictorially the "innumerable stars" referred to in the text.[44] (Though the strophic structure means that the same music would also be sung for stanzas 4 and 6, only the text of this second stanza is actually printed with the musical notation.) Beethoven's keen attention to the portion of Gellert's poem that evokes the stars accords with his lifelong fascination with astronomy.[45] As we shall see in chapter 4, one of the religious books in the composer's library, Christoph Christian Sturm's *Betrachtungen über die Werke Gottes*, similarly connects the stars to the divine. Later in his career, Beethoven would set other texts linking the stars and the divine in a similar way as in "Die Ehre Gottes." A famous example occurs in the finale of the Ninth Symphony, where Beethoven has repeated pianissimo triplet chords accompany the text "über Sternen muß er wohnen" (mm. 650–54; above the stars [the Creator] must dwell).[46] Another instance is found in *Abendlied unterm gestirntem Himmel* (Evening song under the starry sky, WoO 150), a religious song Beethoven wrote in 1820 whose text

---

[44] See Lodes, "Probing the Sacred Genres," 219.
[45] On Beethoven and astronomy, see Solomon, "Some Romantic Images," 53.
[46] I discuss in greater detail elsewhere Beethoven's use of repeated chords to draw a link between the stars and the divine: see Chong, "Beethoven and Kant's *Allgemeine Naturgeschichte*."

Example 3.1 Gellert Lieder, "Die Ehre Gottes aus dem Natur," op. 48 no. 4, mm. 19–27

uses the stars as a metaphor for heaven. In this song, repeated triplet chords accompany the lines in which the stars are explicitly mentioned: "wenn die Sterne prächtig schimmern, / tausend Sonnenstraßen flimmern" (when the stars resplendently shimmer, / a thousand ways of the sun flicker; see example 3.2).

The idea of learning about God from nature also appears in Beethoven's song *Der Wachtelschlag*. The text, by the poet Samuel Sauter, has the poetic speaker hearing in the call of a quail exhortations to fear, love, praise, thank,

Example 3.2 *Abendlied unterm gestirnten Himmel*, WoO 150, mm. 10–14

seek, and trust God. As Paul Reid has pointed out, in German folk poetry of the eighteenth century, the call of a quail was commonly interpreted in religious terms, as "a command to love, trust and obey the Lord."[47] Unlike most of Beethoven's early lieder, *Der Wachtelschlag* is through-composed, a fact that he boasted about to Breitkopf & Härtel in a letter of September 1803.[48] There is not even a hint of strophic repetition, and the music in voice and piano changes flexibly, following the text. This gives the song a kind of episodic structure, a sense reinforced by the relatively large number of key areas (at least seven) the song passes through in its various sections.[49] What unifies the disparate sections is the repetition of the dotted-rhythm motive that begins the whole piece, which is clearly meant to imitate the call of the quail to which the poem refers (see example 3.3). Beethoven sets each of the

---

[47] Reid, *Beethoven Song Companion*, 118. See also Jander, "Prophetic Conversation," 525.
[48] Anderson no. 81 (*BGA* no. 158).
[49] Reid, *Beethoven Song Companion*, 119. Reid goes so far as to describe the piece as a "small cantata."

Example 3.3 *Der Wachtelschlag*, WoO 129, mm. 1–8

imperative sentences in the poem—"Fear God!," "Love God!," "Praise God!," "Thank God!," "Ask God!," "Trust God!"—to this recurring "quail" motive. Put simply, the quail serves as the religious preacher, and Beethoven emphasizes this point in his musical setting. The notion of nature as teacher about the divine is quite literal here!

In the Gellert Lieder, the link between God and nature is also established in a slightly different way, through the concept of divine providence: the notion that God intervenes actively in the world and guides the course of historical time. The word "providence" (*Vorsehung*) appears explicitly in the title of the fifth song, "Gottes Macht und Vorsehung"

(God's power and providence). Gellert's poem emphasizes the care that God has for human beings, as expressed through the gifts of the natural world:

Du tränkst das Land,	You water the land,
Führst uns auf grüne Weiden;	lead us into green pastures;
Und Nacht und Tag und Korn und Wein und Freuden	And night and day and grain and wine and joys
Empfangen wir aus deiner Hand.	We receive from your hand.

Similar ideas are evoked in *Der Wachtelschlag*:

Siehst du die herrlichen Früchte im Feld,	If you see the glorious fruits of the field,
Nimm es zu Herzen, Bewohner der Welt!	Take this to heart, dweller of the world!
Danke Gott!	Thank God!
Danke Gott!	Thank God!
Der dich ernährt und erhält!	Who feeds and preserves you!

The text of "Gottes Macht" further points out that God is near to his creation:

Er ist um mich,	He is around me,
Schafft, daß ich sicher ruhe;	Makes me rest safely;
Er schafft, was ich vor- oder nachmals tue,	He brings about what I have done, or shall do,
Und er erforschet mich und dich.	And he searches me and you.

Er ist dir nah,	He is near to you,
Du sitzest oder gehest;	Whether you sit or work;
Ob du ans Meer, ob du gen Himmel flöhest:	Whether you flee to the sea, or up to the sky:
So ist er allenthalben da.	He is everywhere.

In this regard, "Gottes Macht" balances the awe-inducing image of the divine emphasized by "Die Ehre Gottes," the previous song in the collection. God may indeed be powerful, even to the point of appearing incomprehensible, as suggested by the appearance of the word "erhaben" (sublime) in the performance directions for "Die Ehre Gottes"—the only time it occurs in all of

Beethoven's compositional output. But he is also a God who is close to his creatures. This idea may explain Beethoven's specific use of the word "providence" to address God in the Heiligenstadt Testament: "Oh Providence—do but grant me one day *of pure joy.*"[50] The God who provides, through the gifts of the natural world, is also a God who is intimate rather than remote.

The close connection between nature and the divine in the Gellert Lieder and *Der Wachtelschlag* unavoidably brings to mind a better-known Beethoven work written a few years later: the *Pastoral* Symphony (Symphony No. 6), especially the fifth and final movement. As Richard Will has pointed out, Beethoven's treatment of this movement's principal theme recalls hymnody: the theme is subject to frequent verbatim repetition and near the end of the movement it appears in chordal homophony, reminiscent of a chorale (mm. 237–44). The prominent arpeggiated horn parts also constitute a stylistic borrowing of a feature commonly employed in religious music that includes references to the pastoral.[51] In the first edition of the score, the programmatic title for the movement appears as "Hirtengesang. Frohe und dankbare Gefühle nach dem Sturm" (Shepherd's song. Glad and thankful feelings after the storm). But an earlier version of this title, as well as statements in Beethoven's sketches for the movement, suggests that for Beethoven the attitude of thanksgiving being evoked here was an explicitly religious act. In both the autograph score and the instrumental parts used at the work's premiere, the title read instead, "Hirtengesang. Wohlthätige mit Danck [*sic*] an die Gottheit verbundene Gefühle nach dem Sturm" (Shepherd's song. Beneficent feelings combined with thanks to God after the storm).[52] In addition, alongside sketches for the chorale-like appearance of the main theme mentioned above, the composer wrote "Ausdrucks des Danks O Herr wir danken dir" (Expression of thanks. O Lord, we thank

---

[50] "The Heiligenstadt Testament," in Anderson, *Letters to Beethoven*, 1351–54, at 1354 (Beethoven's emphasis); *BGA* no. 106, p. 123: "O Vorsehung—laß einmal einen reinen Tag *der Freude* mir erscheinen."

[51] See Will, *Characteristic Symphony*, 182. Generally speaking, the pastoral as musical trope was much more common in church music than in secular instrumental music in Beethoven's Vienna. Pastoral references were also frequent in instrumental interludes played during Catholic Masses. See Wyn Jones, *Beethoven: Pastoral Symphony*, 15–16.

[52] See Will, *Characteristic Symphony*, 181–82. The reasons for the change in title for the first edition remain unclear. The word "Gottheit," which Beethoven also employed in the Heiligenstadt Testament, the *Tagebuch*, and the title of the "Heiliger Dankgesang" movement in the op. 132 string quartet, has often in the Beethoven literature been translated as "Godhead," rather than "God," seemingly to distance the composer from traditional Christian conceptions of the divine. As will be discussed in chapters 4 and 5, this translation is misleading.

you).⁵³ More subtle religious references can also be discerned in the earlier movements of the symphony. For instance, the second movement includes music depicting the call of the quail, explicitly labeled as such by Beethoven, along with bird calls from the nightingale and the cuckoo (mm. 129–36). As discussed above with regard to *Der Wachtelschlag*, the quail call had religious connotations during Beethoven's time: it was commonly interpreted as an exhortation to follow God's will.⁵⁴ (Indeed, the rhythmic figure that Beethoven uses to depict the quail call is the same in both the symphony and *Der Wachtelschlag*.) In the fourth movement, the depiction of the storm might be situated within a long tradition in Western culture of storms as settings for God to appear, a trope that persisted in examples from German literature of Beethoven's era.⁵⁵

To return to the Gellert Lieder, Beethoven's songs reflect the concerns of the Catholic Enlightenment not only in their focus on nature, but also in their emphasis on the importance of ethical conduct. (This theme is prominent, too, in the Heiligenstadt Testament, which, as Solomon has observed, alternates between "touching expressions of Beethoven's feelings of despair at his encroaching deafness and stilted, even literary formulations emphasizing his adherence to virtue.")⁵⁶ The second of the six Gellert songs, "Die Liebe des Nächsten," contains a highly moralistic text stressing the importance of charitable acts toward others. Befitting the Catholic Enlightenment context, this kind of text was actually very common in Catholic *Kirchenlieder* of the second half of the eighteenth century.⁵⁷ The first two verses are typical of the didactic nature of the poem as a whole:

---

⁵³ Weise, "Einleitung," in *Beethoven: Ein Skizzenbuch zur Pastoralsymphonie*, 1:17. The original sketch is found in the sketchbook Landsberg 10, p. 164. Owen Jander has claimed that Beethoven also wrote the words "Heilig im Kirchenstil" (Holy in church style) to accompany a different set of sketches for the same musical material: see Jander, "Prophetic Conversation," 549–50. An examination of the sketchbook that Jander cites reveals that this is a mistake: see Weise, *Beethoven: Ein Skizzenbuch zur Chorfantasie*, 92, which transcribes fol. 16ᵛ of the sketchbook Grasnick 3. As Dagmar Weise explains, Beethoven's words here refer not to the *Pastoral* Symphony, but to the Mass in C, and most likely pertain to the composer's effort to find a suitable German text as an alternative to the liturgical Latin, a topic that is discussed in a later section of this chapter: see Weise, "Einleitung," in *Beethoven: Ein Skizzenbuch zur Chorfantasie*, 12–13. That said, other comments related to the symphony do appear on the same page of the sketchbook (at the top). Notwithstanding Jander's error, therefore, it is possible that the proximity of sketches for the Mass in C to sketches for the *Pastoral* Symphony points to a close link in Beethoven's mind between the two works.
⁵⁴ See also Jander, "Prophetic Conversation," 525.
⁵⁵ Will, *Characteristic Symphony*, 179–81.
⁵⁶ Solomon, *Beethoven*, 154.
⁵⁷ Pauly, "Reforms of Church Music," 375.

So jemand spricht: Ich liebe Gott!	If anyone says: I love God!
Und haßt doch seine Brüder,	And yet hates his brothers,
Der treibt mit Gottes Wahrheit Spott	He makes a mockery of God's truth
Und reißt sie ganz darnieder.	And rips it completely apart.
Gott ist die Lieb' und will, daß ich	God is love and he wishes, that I
Den Nächsten liebe, gleich als mich.	Love my neighbor as myself.
Wer dieser Erden Güter hat	Whoever has the goods of this earth
Und sieht die Brüder leiden,	And watches his brothers suffer
Und macht den Hungrigen nicht satt,	And does not satisfy the hungry,
Läßt Nackende nicht kleiden;	And does not clothe the naked;
Der ist ein Feind der ersten Pflicht	He is an enemy of the first duty
Und hat die Liebe Gottes nicht.	And has not the love of God.

Beethoven vividly dramatizes the textual reference to hypocrisy by setting the first two lines to sharply contrasting music (see example 3.4). The first line, "So jemand spricht: Ich liebe Gott!" (If anyone says: I love God!), is sung mostly to half notes. With the exception of the ornament in the piano on "spricht," the first four notes are monophonic: the piano plays just one musical line and it is identical to the vocal part. At least compared to what follows, the next four notes of the melody ("Ich liebe Gott") are then supported by relatively consonant harmony: an overall tonic-to-dominant motion is decorated by a passing tone (C), a neighbor tone (A-natural), and a 4–3 suspension (created by the E-flat). In contrast, the next line, "Und haßt doch seine Brüder" (And yet hates his brothers), is sung to shorter quarter notes, with staccato marks in the piano added for good measure. The harmonic major seconds in the piano also make this passage sound more dissonant than what came before.

The importance of neighborly love is also a prominent concern in *Christus am Ölberge*. The final number of the oratorio dramatizes Jesus's arrest in the Garden of Gethsemane, and begins with Jesus, aided by a Seraph, seeking to convince a sword-wielding Peter not to attack those who had come to arrest

Example 3.4 Gellert Lieder, "Die Liebe des Nächsten," op. 48 no. 2, mm. 2–7

him. Peter eventually agrees to back down.[58] The reference to this incident seems by itself unremarkable in a work about Christ's Passion. What is remarkable is the disproportionate attention that the incident is given within the overall narrative. Beethoven devotes considerable musical attention to depicting the evolution of Peter's emotional state. Peter's initial outburst of anger ("In meinen Adern wühlen / unbändig Zorn und Wut"; m. 34ff.) receives first a response from Christ ("Du sollst nicht Rache üben"; m. 53ff.), then a separate response from the Seraph ("Merk auf, o Mensch und höre"; m. 69) reinforcing Christ's lesson about neighborly love. Almost as if they realize that Peter is not getting the point, Christ and the Seraph eventually join forces at measure 95 to sing together words reiterating the lesson they have both been teaching:

---

[58] The libretto takes liberties with the scriptural narrative here. In John's Gospel (18:10–11), to which the libretto apparently refers, Peter does strike a slave of the high priest with a sword, cutting off his ear. Jesus then tells Peter to put his sword away but, unlike in the libretto, he does not explain his command in terms of rejecting violence; rather, he asks that Peter not prevent him from fulfilling his salvific mission. The synoptic Gospels have slightly different accounts of this incident. First of all, in Matthew, Mark, and Luke, the attacker is named only as a follower of Jesus. In Matthew's Gospel, Jesus explains that all who live by the sword will perish by it (26:52), so it is possible that the libretto of *Christus* might have sought to amalgamate the Matthean and Johannine versions. In Luke, Jesus heals the high priest's slave (22:50–51).

90 THE CATHOLIC BEETHOVEN

O Menschenkinder fasset	O human children, grasp well
dies heilige Gebot:	this holy commandment:
liebt jenen, der euch hasset,	love those who hate you,
nur so gefallt ihr Gott.	only thus will you be pleasing to God.

Over the next ten or so measures, Christ and the Seraph sing conjunct melodic lines, mostly homorhythmically in parallel motion. This creates a stark contrast with Peter, who—stubbornly refusing to accept Christ's teaching—continues simultaneously to babble on in rage, his melody angular and more rhythmically active (see example 3.5). Peter goes on to persist with his rant while Christ interjects three times, "Du sollst nicht Rache üben" (mm. 105–17; You should not seek revenge). Finally, Christ, as if tired of Peter's obstinacy, sings one last time in a sparsely accompanied, recitative-like passage with a heroically high vocal tessitura: "Ich lehrt euch bloß allein / die Menschen alle lieben, / dem Feinde gern verzeihen" (mm. 118–24;

Example 3.5 *Christus am Ölberge*, op. 85: No. 6, mm. 95–105 (vocal parts only)

Example 3.5 Continued

I taught you only / to love all people, / to forgive your enemy gladly). This emphatic plea at last does the trick. In the next section (m. 125ff.), Peter joins Christ and the Seraph in singing the words they had previously been singing: "O Menschenkinder fasset . . .". Peter's anger has been calmed by Christ's teaching, and he finally accepts that he must love his enemies.

The sheer length of the exchange between Christ, Peter, and the Seraph—it occupies about one-third of the entire final number—requires some suspension of disbelief on the part of the audience, for it seems temporally out of proportion with what comes before and after. The soldiers were just about to arrest Christ when this scene began; that they would willingly wait around while Christ lectures Peter with a long lesson on loving his enemies seems scarcely believable. (In John's Gospel, to which this part of the libretto apparently refers, this portion of the Passion story is told in just a few lines.) The narrative time seems to stop at this moment, or is perhaps stretched out, in order to emphasize the moral lesson here: "Love your enemy, love your neighbor." The soldiers and disciples, who were present in the previous two numbers, seem to disappear temporarily from the scene. Therefore, when

Christ uses the second-person *plural*, he could just as easily be understood as breaking the fourth wall, addressing the audience itself: "Ich lehrt euch bloß allein / die Menschen alle lieben, / dem Feinde gern verzeihn" (I taught you only / to love all people, / to forgive your enemy gladly).

The whole scene is thus given a very strong moralistic flavor. Its ethical focus and didactic nature not only reflect the concerns of the Catholic Enlightenment, but constitute typical features of a specific variety of oratorio that in Beethoven's time would have been associated with north German Protestantism: what Howard Smither has labeled the "lyric" oratorio.[59] Traditionally, the oratorio had been a "dramatic" genre: though an oratorio differed from an opera in being unstaged (and in always having a sacred subject), it had a plot and included named characters. (In some oratorios—which Smither labels "narrative-dramatic," rather than simply "dramatic"—the storytelling could be partially carried out by a narrator, instead of through the characters alone.[60]) By contrast, the lyric oratorio sought to distinguish the oratorio from opera to a greater extent, by eschewing theatricality and de-emphasizing its narrative aspect.[61] The listener's knowledge of the plot is assumed, and the emphasis is shifted to edification, the intention being that the listener should play a more active role, identifying with characters who express their feelings about the story: the moral of the story, so to speak, is regarded as more important than the details of the plot itself. The overall musical language in this kind of oratorio could also be quite emotionally restrained.[62]

The lyric oratorio had emerged in the mid-eighteenth century, specifically in a Protestant context, in north German regions.[63] Beethoven was most likely exposed to this particular conception of the oratorio through his reading of Johann Georg Sulzer's aesthetic writings. Sulzer assumes this kind of oratorio as standard—not even mentioning the dramatic oratorio—and discusses in detail *Der Tod Jesu* (1755) by Carl Heinrich Graun (1704–1759),

---

[59] See Biermann, "*Christus am Ölberge*," 276–80; and Smither, *History of the Oratorio*, 3:331–39. Biermann's essay ultimately argues that the influence of the lyric oratorio genre on *Christus* was only partial: more significant are the ways in which Beethoven and his librettist Huber *departed* from that generic model. As will become apparent in a later section of this chapter, I concur with Biermann's judgment in this regard.
[60] Smither, *History of the Oratorio*, 1:3–4.
[61] Smither, 3:356–69.
[62] Smither, 3:406.
[63] Smither, 3:331–39.

a work heavily inspired by Lutheran Pietism, and by far the best-known example of the lyric oratorio in the second half of the eighteenth century.[64] (As described in the previous chapter, Beethoven's teacher Neefe was an admirer of Sulzer's thought.) In contrast to the dominance of the lyric oratorio in Protestant regions, Catholic areas, though not entirely untouched by the influence of the lyric conception of the genre, continued to emphasize the more traditional dramatic oratorio.[65] Within this religious context, the aspects of *Christus am Ölberge* that recall the lyric oratorio thus had a specific denominational connotation. As a composer working in Catholic Vienna, Beethoven, in pursuing a distinctively Protestant approach to the oratorio, might be viewed as exemplifying the type of Catholic–Protestant interaction described in the previous two chapters as being typical of the Catholic Enlightenment. In a later section of this chapter, however, I shall present a more complicated view concerning the confessional identity of Beethoven's work.

Christian Schreiber's German Text for the Mass in C

The first edition of the Mass in C—which was finally published in 1812, several years after Beethoven composed the work—appeared with a German text in the score in addition to the liturgical Latin. (Though the first part of the Mass Ordinary, the Kyrie, is technically Greek, it is rendered in the liturgical text in a Latin transliteration.) While not entirely unprecedented, the publication of a bilingual edition of Catholic liturgical music was still relatively unusual, especially where the published score (as for the Mass in C) had the German text laid under the Latin one, and not just included as an appendix.[66] What is noteworthy is that the initiative for including the German text came from Beethoven himself. As early as July 1808, less than a year after the work's premiere, Beethoven wrote to Breitkopf & Härtel suggesting that a suitable translator be found. The composer then returned to this subject in no fewer

---

[64] See Biermann, "*Christus am Ölberge*," 277–80; and Kramer, "Beethoven and Carl Heinrich Graun."

[65] See Biermann, "*Christus am Ölberge*," 278, 280; and Smither, *History of the Oratorio*, 3:358.

[66] McGrann, "Zum vorliegenden Band," xii. A digitization of the original edition is available at the website of the Beethoven-Haus in Bonn: https://www.beethoven.de/en/media/view/67400 31603474432/, accessed August 1, 2024. Bilingual editions existed of the Requiems by Mozart and Salieri: see Hettrick, "Antonio Salieri's Requiem Mass," 37–38.

than five subsequent letters, the last of which written as late as 1811.[67] It is particularly striking that he brought this specific issue up repeatedly when, as previously discussed, Breitkopf were reluctant even to publish the mass at all.

Beethoven's keen interest in having a German text is also apparent from a page in the sketchbook Grasnick 3, dating from Autumn 1808, which contains German translations of three fragments of the Mass text written in Beethoven's hand.[68] For the opening line of the Gloria, "Gloria in excelsis Deo" (Glory to God in the highest), Beethoven writes, "Ruhm sei Gott in der höh." The word "Sanctus" (holy) is then rendered as "Heilig." And an additional line from the Sanctus, "Pleni sunt coeli [et terra gloria tua]" (Full are heaven [and earth with your glory]), is translated as "Es jauchzen die Himmel [und] die Erde" (literally: "Heaven [and] earth rejoice"). At the very bottom of the page, the composer also encouraged himself to consult "Gellert's songs"—meaning either Gellert's poems themselves or his own musical settings of Gellert from a few years earlier—in deciding how to render the Mass text into German: "Gellerts [L]ieder können gute Dienste thun" (Gellert's songs can be of good service).

Except for "Heilig," Beethoven's translations in this sketchbook differ from the German text eventually published in the 1812 first edition. The latter was prepared by Christian Schreiber, who was also the author of a revised libretto that Breitkopf desired for *Christus am Ölberge*, a topic to which we shall return below.[69] For "Gloria in excelsis Deo" Schreiber has instead "Preis sey dir, Lieb' und Dank / ström aus der Herzen Glut zu dir auf!" (Praise be to you, may love and thanks / flow up to you from the fervor of the heart!). He renders "Pleni sunt coeli et terra gloria tua" thus: "Voll deines Ruhmes ist aller Lebendigen Odem / Himmel und Erde sind deiner Güte voll" (Full of your glory is the breath of all living things / Heaven and earth are full of your goodness). (Schreiber's text is able to use many more words in German than in the original Latin because Beethoven's musical setting repeats some of the Latin words.) The discrepancy between the German translations in Grasnick 3 and Schreiber's published text for the Mass in C indicates that Schreiber's involvement came only later: indeed, as we shall see, Beethoven was still quibbling over the acceptability of Schreiber's text as late as January 1811. Beethoven was clearly already set on having a German text even before Schreiber came into the picture.

---

[67] See Anderson nos. 168, 169, 187, 245, 281, and 294 (*BGA* nos. 329, 331, 348, 423, 474, and 484).
[68] See Weise, *Beethoven: Ein Skizzenbuch zur Chorfantasie*, 92, which transcribes fol. 16ᵛ of the sketchbook Grasnick 3. See also Weise, "Einleitung," in ibid., 7–14, esp. 12.
[69] Schreiber's text is reproduced in McGrann, "Kritischer Bericht," 289–91.

These circumstances surrounding Beethoven's composition of the Mass in C can be connected to the ecumenical concerns of the German Catholic Enlightenment. As several scholars have suggested, the composer's desire for a German text may have been motivated by a wish to make the work usable by Protestants.[70] Beethoven's several letters to Breitkopf on the issue do not mention this intention explicitly, though they do express a desire for the work to be performed in the publisher's own city of Leipzig, a Protestant city.[71] We know, too, that Schreiber regularly collaborated with Breitkopf on the specific task of rendering Catholic works suitable for Protestant use.[72] As we shall see in chapter 6, when Beethoven wrote his *Missa solemnis*, he again asked that that piece be published with a German text, though his request went unfulfilled. In the case of his later mass, his letters do make clear that the German text was meant specifically for Protestants. It thus seems likely that he had similar motivations in mind for the Mass in C.

It is hard to imagine that there were not commercial reasons behind Beethoven's desire for the Mass in C to appeal to Protestants. But the evidence suggests that the inclusion of a German text was more than just a market expansion strategy. In one of his earlier letters to Breitkopf concerning a German text, Beethoven allowed that the "result need not be a masterpiece, provided the words really fit the music."[73] Later, however, upon receiving Schreiber's text, he became much fussier:

> The translation of the Gloria I consider very suitable, but that of the Kyrie not so good. Although the beginning "tief im Staub anbeten wir" is very appropriate, yet several expressions, such as "ew'gen Weltenherrscher" and "Allgewaltigen" seem to fit the Gloria better. The general character of the Kyrie (I consider that in a translation of this kind only the general character of each movement can be indicated) is heartfelt resignation, deep sincerity of religious feeling, "Gott erbarme dich unser," yet without on that account being sad. Gentleness is the fundamental characteristic of the whole

---

[70] See, e.g., Herttrich, "Beethoven und die Religion," 33; McGrann, "Zum vorliegenden Band," xi; and Knapp, "Beethoven's Mass in C Major," 202–3. This explanation was already offered in E. T. A. Hoffmann's 1813 review of the work: see Review of Beethoven's Mass in C, 340.

[71] See Anderson no. 168 (*BGA* no. 329), c. July 10, 1808; and Anderson no. 169 (*BGA* no. 331), end of July 1808.

[72] Mühlenweg, "Ludwig van Beethoven," 1:49.

[73] Anderson no. 187 (*BGA* no. 348), Beethoven to Joseph August Röckel, before December 22, 1808: "Es braucht eben kein Meisterstük zu seyn, wenn es nur gut auf die Musik paßt." A similar sentiment is expressed in Anderson no. 281 (*BGA* no. 474), Beethoven to Breitkopf & Härtel, October 15, 1810.

work. And here the expressions "Allgewaltiger" and so forth do not seem to convey the meaning of the whole work. Apart from "Eleison erbarme dich unser"—cheerfulness pervades this Mass.[74]

Beethoven's fairly detailed critique of Schreiber's text suggests that he did not, after all, just want a text that would do the job. Rather, he was acutely concerned that the German text should convey to his Protestant listeners the specific religious lessons he was seeking to impart through the work.

Beethoven's interest in reaching out across the denominational divide resonates with the ecumenism fostered by the German Catholic Enlightenment. The composer wished not just that Protestants purchase his work, but that their version of it properly communicated the meaning of the original Catholic text as he saw it. Beethoven would be concerned about finding the right German text for the Mass in C well into the last years of his life. Sometime in the 1820s, possibly after he had already completed the *Missa solemnis*, he received a new German text for the Mass in C, written by Benedict Scholz (c. 1760–1824), a Silesian music director. The new translation was unsolicited, and Scholz seems to have acted on his own initiative.[75] Beethoven was profoundly moved by Scholz's translation, which brought him to tears, and later wrote to the publisher Schott suggesting that a new edition of the Mass in C be published with Scholz's text instead of Schreiber's.[76]

Schreiber's text for the Mass in C can be connected to other aspects of the German Catholic Enlightenment aside from ecumenism. From a strictly practical perspective, as Jeremiah McGrann has suggested, the provision of a German text would have been useful for performances in Catholic regions to get around prohibitions on non-liturgical performances of musical masses.[77]

---

[74] Anderson no. 294 (*BGA* no. 484), Beethoven to Breitkopf & Härtel, January 16, 1811: "Die Ubersezung zum *gloria* scheint mir sehr gut zu paßen zum *Kyrie* nicht so gut obwohlen der Anfang „tief im Staub anbeten wir" sehr gut paßt, so scheint mir doch bey manchen Ausdrücken wie „ew'gen Weltherrscher" [„] Allgewaltigen" Mehr zum *gloria* tauglich. der allgemeine charakter (Bey solch einer übersezung sollte nur wie mir scheint der allegmeine Karakter jedes Stücks angegeben seyn) in dem *Kyrie* ist innige Ergebung, woher innigkeit *religiöser* Gefühle [der Karakter] „Gott erbarme dich unser" ohne deswegen Traurig zu seyn, sanftheit liegt dem Ganzen zu Grunde, hier scheint mir die Ausdrücke Allgewaltiger nicht im sinne des Ganzen obwohlen „*eleison* erbarme dich unser"—so ist [je]doch heiterkeit im Ganzen."

[75] See Anderson no. 1188 (*BGA* no. 1662), Beethoven to Anton Felix Schindler, June 1, 1823. It is unclear how much time had passed between the arrival of Scholz's text and this letter to Schindler. Scholz's text is reproduced in McGrann, "Kritischer Bericht," 291–94. Given Beethoven's interest in the stars as symbols for the divine, discussed above, he would have been especially enamored of two references to stars in Scholz's text for the Credo: "Es ist ein Gott! / der über Sternen wohnet" (There is one God! / who lives above the stars) and "die stumme Nacht flammend Ihn / im hellen Sternen lichte" (The silent night names Him [God] / in the bright flaming light of the stars). The first of these quotations is very similar to the famous line from Schiller's text for Beethoven's Ninth Symphony: "über Sternen muß er wohnen."

[76] See Anderson no. 1368 (*BGA* no. 1966), May 7, 1825; McGrann, "Zum vorliegenden Band," xi; and Gülke, "'mein Größtes Werk,'" 272.

[77] McGrann, "Zum vorliegenden Band," xii.

Indeed, German texts may have been employed when two movements of the Mass in C (the Gloria and Sanctus) were performed at the famous Akademie concert of December 1808, alongside the Fifth and Sixth Symphonies, the Fourth Piano Concerto, and the *Choral Fantasy*.[78] But a mass with a German text also accords with the encouragement of church music in the vernacular that was an important component of programs for liturgical reform within the context of the Catholic Enlightenment. It is true that, as reflected in the examples cited above, Schreiber's German text for the Mass in C is less a translation than a free poetic rendering of the Latin. But, broadly speaking, the thematic content of the original is preserved and, more importantly, the structure of the text seems to preserve a close connection to the Catholic liturgy. Schreiber separates his text into three "hymns": the German versions of the Kyrie and Gloria are combined to form the first hymn, the Credo becomes the second hymn, and the Sanctus and Agnus Dei together make up the third hymn. This arrangement continues to reflect the liturgical function of each individual part of the Mass Ordinary. The first hymn corresponds to the two parts sung in succession during the introductory rites. The third hymn combines the two parts sung during the liturgy of the Eucharist. The second hymn, like the Latin Credo, stands alone in between.

Nevertheless, Schreiber's translation—if it can even be called one—remains noteworthy for its looseness, especially when compared to the more literal translations Beethoven wrote down in Grasnick 3. But this looseness results in a kind of exegesis of the original liturgical text, suggesting other spiritual ideas that might be evoked through, or associated with, what is literally meant by the Latin words. In this sense, Schreiber's German text can also be understood as aligning with the Catholic Enlightenment desire to make the meaning of the liturgy accessible to ordinary believers. For example, these are the original Latin words in the Credo describing Christ's life on earth:

Et incarnatus est	And he was incarnate
de spiritu sancto	by the Holy Spirit
ex Maria virgine,	of the Virgin Mary,
et homo factus est.	and was made man,
Crucifixus etiam pro nobis,	he was also crucified for us
sub Pontio Pilato	under Pontius Pilate
passus et sepultus est.	he suffered and was buried.

---

[78] Though the announcement of the concert in the *Wiener Zeitung* seems to imply the contrary, a letter written by Beethoven that same month suggests that German texts were indeed used at the December 1808 Akademie concert. Compare E. Anderson, *Letters of Beethoven*, 3:1436; and

And here is Schreiber's German rendering:

Und schon entfesselt sich	And already is freed
mein Geist von den Banden	my spirit from the bonds
seine Erdenstaubes,	of its earthly dust,
der täuschend, der ihn umfangen hält,	which deceitfully surrounds it,
und Verlangen glüht in meinem Innern,	and longing glows inside me,
heisser Durst, mich kühn empor zu schwingen,	fervid thirst, to send me bravely upwards,
auf zu ihm, den kein Gedank erschöpfet,	up to him, whom no thought exhausts,
zu ihm, den Unerschaffnen,	to him, the Uncreated,
sehnend empfind' ich, dass seines Geschlechts wir sind,	longingly I sense that we are of his lineage,
zwar zum Staub verbannt.	though in fact banished to the dust.

Though deviating considerably from the literal meaning of the Latin original, Schreiber's version explains a deeper theological meaning behind the coming of Christ. Through Christ, human beings are set free from the bonds of death and sin ("schon entfesselt sich / mein Geist von den Banden / seine Erdenstaubes") and reunited with God ("sehnend fühl' ich, dass seines Geschlechts wir sind"). The original text states the major events of Christ's earthly life; Schreiber's rendering elaborates on those events by explaining their implications for human salvation. To cite another example, the first line of Schreiber's text has the phrase "Tief im Staub anbeten wir" (Deep in the dust we adore) in place of "Kyrie eleison" (Lord, have mercy). The German may be very far from a strict translation of the original, but it poignantly describes the emotional state of the penitent believer, brought low ("deep in the dust") by sin. (As described above, Schreiber's text here drew Beethoven's praise for its propriety.) This initial association of dust with the lowliness of

---

Anderson no. 187 (*BGA* no. 348), Beethoven to Joseph August Röckel, before December 22, 1808. The fragmentary German translations in Grasnick 3 described above date from shortly before this time. It is thus likely that these were portions of a complete German text that was used at the concert, assuming a German text was employed at all, and this text was distinct from that by Schreiber later published in the 1812 first edition. See Weise, "Einleitung," in *Beethoven: Ein Skizzenbuch zur Chorfantasie*, 7–14, at 12.

the sinful human being reappears at another moment in the mass where the original text is a plea for mercy: the "miserere nobis" (have mercy on us) in the Gloria. Here, Schreiber describes how God is close to humanity in spite of its lowliness: "auch dem Staube bist du nah" (even to the dust you are near). Schreiber's text thus identifies a theme common to two separate parts of the Mass.

The Mass in C as Musical Exegesis of the Liturgical Text

What Schreiber does in effectively providing an exegesis of the Mass text finds an analogue in what Beethoven does in the Mass in C—but through music rather than in words. Indeed, the manner in which Schreiber's text draws a link between "Kyrie eleison" and the words "miserere nobis" in the Gloria, as has just been described, corresponds roughly with what Beethoven does with the music in setting these two different sections of the Mass. In the Gloria, the words "miserere nobis" are sung to a melody that sounds very similar to the motive heard in the first measures of the whole piece, for "Kyrie eleison" (see examples 3.6a and 3.6b). This motivic recall is made more noticeable by its occurrence only when "miserere nobis" is repeated, after these words were previously sung to a different melody (mm. 181–88). It is true that the correspondence between what Beethoven does with his music and what Schreiber does with his text is not exact. In the first edition of the score, Schreiber has "und er denkt und fühlt dich, und ist göttlich" (and [the dust] thinks of you and feels you, it is divine) as

Example 3.6a Mass in C major, op. 86, Kyrie, mm. 2–5, choral soprano part

Example 3.6b Mass in C major, op. 86, Gloria, mm. 190–93, choral alto part

the German text for this precise iteration of "miserere nobis" in the Gloria, rather than "auch dem Staube bist du nah"—the phrase in his text that would have created a more direct parallel with "Tief im Staub anbeten wir" at the beginning of the Kyrie, which also refers to dust. Nevertheless, the general principle of illuminating a common theme between two disparate parts of the Mass text applies in Beethoven's music as it does in Schreiber's text. Beethoven uses musical means to highlight the fact that "miserere nobis" in the Gloria, like the first line of the Kyrie, is a plea for God's mercy.

A more obvious connection between two parts of the Mass also involves the opening measures of the Kyrie. The music heard in these measures returns in the final measures of the Agnus Dei, such that the concluding iterations of the words "Dona nobis pacem" are sung to the same music as that to which "Kyrie eleison" had been sung at the beginning of the whole work. Haydn had employed this technique in two of his masses: the *Nicolaimesse* (1772) and the Missa brevis in F major, Hob. XXII:1 (c. 1750).[79] But the fact that what Beethoven has done here was not unprecedented makes no difference to the impact it creates. With regard to any particular part of the Mass text, Beethoven would have had to choose from the multiplicity of compositional models that previous mass settings provided him, and what model he chose to follow was presumably connected to the spiritual meaning he wished to convey, even if how he chose to set certain words was not entirely novel. More than just a musical device unifying the mass by bookending the work as a whole, to create a link between "Kyrie eleison" and "Dona nobis pacem" helps to explain the overall narrative implicit in the Mass text: the sinner's plea for mercy at the beginning is answered by Christ in the Eucharist, the ritual with which the Dona nobis text is associated. Just as he illustrates a relationship between "Kyrie eleison" and "miserere nobis" in the Gloria, Beethoven is engaging here in a kind of musical exegesis.

This exegetical exercise occurs throughout the Mass in C in a manner even more explicit than the establishment of musical connections between different parts of the liturgical text. Perhaps the most striking thing about the work is the length to which Beethoven goes to portray through various musical devices the meaning of individual phrases, even individual words, in the text. Very often, what could fairly be described as musical pictorialism leads to a sense of disjunction at the musical surface, as the music shifts abruptly

---

[79] Knapp, "Beethoven's Mass in C Major," 207.

between relatively brief sections of sharply contrasting material to go along with the changing text. The opening measures of the Gloria provide a particularly striking example of this phenomenon. After a loud and energetic tutti beginning on the words "Gloria in excelsis Deo" (Glory to God in the highest; mm. 1–17), the music suddenly softens and the texture reduces to just first violins and cellos, which descend melodically to a lower register for the next chorus entrance on "Et in terra pax hominibus" (And on earth peace to people; mm. 21–24). Then, at "bonae voluntatis" (of good will; m. 28), a forte dynamic abruptly returns, along with a sense of rhythmic energy, this time generated by the chorus parts singing in imitation. Several measures later (mm. 46–53), Beethoven introduces an extremely sudden drop in dynamics and register for just two words—"adoramus te" (we adore you)—before a fortissimo explosion for "glorificamus te" (we glorify you). As Michelle Fillion has observed, such attention to the meaning of the text follows, in a general sense, a model provided by Haydn's masses in drawing on the "long-standing tradition of rhetorical and symbolic figures derived from *stile antico* and eighteenth-century liturgical practices as well as older traditions of Biblical exegesis."[80] But compared to Haydn, Beethoven took things to an extreme, employing such "rhetorical and symbolic figures" at every possible opportunity.[81] Moreover, he does not smooth over the resulting surface contrasts through formal procedures, such as sonata form, borrowed from instrumental music: with the exception of the Benedictus, which is in sonata form, the musical structure is driven mainly, and in some cases even exclusively, by the text. In his earliest surviving letter to Breitkopf concerning the work, Beethoven boasted to his publisher, "I think that I have treated the text in a manner in which it has rarely been treated."[82] Tempting though it may be to dismiss this remark as mere bombast, a sign of a particularly aggressive sales pitch, even the most cursory examination of the Mass in C suggests that he was not exaggerating.

From the perspective of the Catholic Enlightenment, Beethoven's musical treatment of the Mass text both accords with and deviates from prevailing ideas concerning liturgical reform, especially those advocated by

---

[80] Fillion, "Beethoven's Mass in C," 3. See also Webster, "Haydn's Sacred Vocal Music"; and Beghin, "*Credo ut intelligam*."
[81] Fillion, "Beethoven's Mass in C," 3. For a similar argument, see Larsen, "Beethovens C-Dur-Messe," 16–18.
[82] Anderson no. 167 (*BGA* no. 327), June 8, 1808: "Jedoch glaube ich, daß ich den *text* behandelt habe, wie er noch wenig behandelt worden." Early reviews of the work also consistently stressed the novelty of Beethoven's approach to the text: see McGrann, "Beethoven's Mass in C," 1:5–8.

Josephinism. In this regard, he seems to have been influenced by the views of Ferdinand d'Antoine described in the previous chapter. Conceptually, Beethoven's obvious desire to "explain" the meaning of the text to his listeners through musical means seems to align with the Catholic Enlightenment's encouragement of church music that helped the listener engage with the meaning of the liturgy, which in turn reflected a broader concern for the pastoral education of the laity. *Musically*, however, this "minute focus on the individual word and phrase,"[83] to borrow Fillion's characterization, leads to an emotional exuberance, as well as an increased structural complexity, that departs from the simplicity advocated by Josephinist musical tastes.[84]

"Personalizing" the Mass Text

The sense of disjunction that is so often felt in the Mass in C is not always motivated by Beethoven's obsession with reflecting the meaning of the text musically. On certain occasions, we get the sense instead that the composer is attempting to dramatize an individual believer's spontaneous, personal response to the liturgy. This is reflected, for instance, in the deliberate alterations that Beethoven made to the Mass text, apparently for rhetorical effect. Minor changes to the liturgical text, especially the repetition of certain words or phrases, are not uncommon in musical settings of the Mass, but what Beethoven does at several points in the Mass in C is more drastic.

In the Credo, Beethoven highlights the seemingly minor words "et" and "non" in the textual phrases "et sepultus est" (and was buried; mm. 160–77) and "cuius regni non erit finis" (of whose kingdom there will not be an end; mm. 216–26). First, in measures 160 and 161, the word "et" is sung twice in succession (see example 3.7). A little over ten measures later, however, "et" is again sung multiple times, but this time Beethoven goes beyond mere repetition by rhythmically isolating the word, interpolating rests in between successive iterations of it (see example 3.8). Haydn did something similar several times in his *Nelson* Mass (or *Missa in angustiis*, Hob. XVII:11) and *Creation* Mass (Hob. XVII:13): see measures 128, 138, 142, 145, 150–51, 165, 184, and 200 in the *Nelson* Mass, and measure 11 in the *Creation* Mass.[85] It is reasonable to

---

[83] Fillion, "Beethoven's Mass in C," 3.
[84] Jeremiah McGrann has made a similar argument: see "Der Hintergrund zu Beethovens Messen," 133.
[85] See Beghin, "*Credo ut intelligam*," 265–66.

Example 3.7 Mass in C major, op. 86, Credo, mm. 160–64 (vocal parts only)

Example 3.8 Mass in C major, op. 86, Credo, mm. 172–77 (vocal parts only)

suppose that Beethoven was inspired by Haydn's example here, but it is worth noting that in only one of those instances—measures 150–51 in the Credo of the *Nelson* Mass, on "et mortuos"—did Haydn go so far as to have "et" sung *three* consecutive times, as Beethoven does. In the Beethoven example, moreover, the emphasis on "et" is more pronounced, and sounds stranger, given the longer temporal gaps separating the statements of "et"—note both the slow tempo and the number of beats between each "et"—along with the syncopated entry of the final "et." The text thus comes across as a kind of grief-filled stutter in response to Christ's death—"And . . . and . . . and he was buried"—as if the speaker had trouble continuing. For "non erit finis," Beethoven again follows an example from Haydn in stating the word "non" no fewer than five times: compare measures 161–62 in the *Nelson* Mass. But unlike Haydn, two iterations of "non" come *after* "erit finis," so that the sentence actually ends with "non" rather than "finis" (see example 3.9). What we have here is not simply textual repetition but a substantial change in the order of the words used. The last two statements of "non" thus seem especially gratuitous, an expression of either overflowing joy or stubborn assurance in response to an important tenet of faith: "No, no, no, his kingdom will have no end! No! No!" The repetition of

Example 3.9 Mass in C major, op. 86, Credo, mm. 221–26 (vocal parts only)

these seemingly unimportant words turns the text into something that sounds more conversational than formal or ritualistic.[86]

Another alteration to the liturgical text occurs in the Agnus Dei, where the composer has the text "miserere nobis" (have mercy on us) return unexpectedly—and in violation of standard liturgical practice—shortly after the words "dona nobis pacem" (grant us peace) are first introduced (see example 3.10). The initial entry of "dona nobis pacem" (m. 40) had been marked by a change of meter to common time and a shift to the major mode. In the section preceding this moment, from the beginning of the movement to measure 40, the music had been in the minor mode and a ponderous 12/8 meter, and had made frequent use of dissonant chords. The reason for the change of mood is obvious: Jesus Christ has indeed removed the sin invoked by the words "Agnus Dei, qui tollis peccata mundi, miserere nobis" (Lamb of God, who takes away the sins of the world, have mercy on us). The plea "Dona nobis pacem" can thus be said with a greater confidence that God's peace will erase the emotional turmoil of the penitent. The sudden intrusion of "Agnus Dei, qui tollis . . . miserere nobis" into this more tranquil Dona nobis section—along with a return of the minor mode, harsh dissonances (note the clash of D against E-flat in measure 73), and tortured syncopations—seems to imply that the believer suddenly feels unsure of God's mercy. The believer has to call out desperately for that mercy one last time before an assurance of forgiveness returns. The Dona nobis section then almost literally has to begin again (compare measures 82–95 with measures 36–45).

What is going on in these examples of textual manipulation is a personalization of the liturgical text on Beethoven's part. The words are no longer merely formulaic but have almost become words that could have come from Beethoven's own mouth. Both the repetition of "et" and "non" and the intrusion of "miserere nobis" after "Dona nobis pacem" occur suddenly, and come across as spontaneous interjections—words spoken, as it were, in the heat of the moment. This feeling of a spontaneous response to the text is evoked in other ways. Several times in the Mass in C, we encounter rhythmically anticipated entries of single choral parts. These are instances when

---

[86] James Webster has explored Haydn's tendency to emphasize "little" words such as "et" (and), "non" (not), and "te" (you) in his sacred vocal music: see "Haydn's Sacred Vocal Music," 57–61. If by "little," Webster means how short or common the word is that is emphasized, I would argue instead that what matters more is the relative importance of the word for the overall meaning of the text. In this regard, "et," being a conjunction, is a much odder word to stress in a musical setting than "non."

Example 3.10 Mass in C major, op. 86, Agnus Dei, mm. 58–78

Example 3.10 Continued

Example 3.10 Continued

one section enters just slightly ahead of the other three, such that that section sounds like it has come in too early. (I am not referring here to the far less remarkable situation where more than one choral section, or even the whole chorus, enters together in a weak metrical position.) Examples can be found in the Kyrie (sopranos on the word "Kyrie" in measure 25), Gloria (basses on "Gloria" in measure 10), and Agnus Dei (sopranos on "pacem" in measure 61; tenors also on "pacem" in measure 63; see example 3.10). A similar sense of interruption occurs at two moments in the work featuring what I would describe as "stranded" solo passages: one involving the soprano soloist at the end of the Gloria, on "Amen" (see example 3.11), and the other involving the alto soloist at the end of the Credo, on "et vitam venturi saeculi amen" (and the life of the world to come, amen; see example 3.12). Elsewhere in Beethoven's Mass, the soloists always sing in pairs, in threes, or all together, and they do so either at the same time or in conversation with each other. Exceptions occur when one soloist sings for an *extended* section (e.g., in the Gloria: mm. 75–121 for the tenor, mm. 139–53 for the alto). In the case of these two "stranded" solos, however, one—and only one—of the vocal soloists sings a *short* passage that intrudes in between two musical sections for chorus alone. The "stranded" solo thus comes across as an unexpected, and fairly brief, interruption by an individual voice within a section of music that is otherwise given over to the chorus. In both the instances I have cited, the context makes it sound as if the soloist has come in at the wrong time, at the spur of the moment. The normal practice elsewhere in the work leads us to expect that the soloist will soon be joined by other soloists, or that she will sing a longer passage in dialogue with the chorus. Instead, the soloist sounds isolated, cutting in for a short time before the chorus takes over again.

In different ways, then, the alterations Beethoven made to the liturgical text, the rhythmically anticipated choral entries, and the "stranded" solo passages I have described create the impression of being spontaneous outcries in response to the liturgical text, resembling a person who speaks out of turn, compelled to express an emotion that cannot be held back. The words of the Mass come across as sincere utterances that come directly from the heart of the believer rather than merely statements that are to be repeated strictly according to a liturgical "script." In this way, Beethoven's setting of the Mass portrays an attitude of vigorous personal engagement with the meaning of the liturgy. Such engagement was something that the German Catholic Enlightenment aimed to foster among ordinary Catholics, and was a central component of the movement's interest in the improvement of

Example 3.11 Mass in C major, op. 86, Gloria, mm. 339–53

Example 3.11 Continued

Example 3.12 Mass in C major, op. 86, Credo, mm. 302–14

Example 3.12 Continued

Example 3.12 Continued

religious education among the laity. The average German Catholic, it was hoped, would no longer be merely a passive spectator, but an active participant in the Church's liturgical life. But as with his efforts at musical exegesis described above, Beethoven's dramatization of an engaged believer's response to the Mass results, paradoxically, in an overall emotional exuberance at odds with Josephinist demands for liturgical simplification.

The Highly Sentimental Depiction of Christ in *Christus am Ölberge*

The complex relationship of Beethoven's treatment of the text in the Mass in C to the Catholic Enlightenment's ideas about liturgy suggests that while the Catholic Enlightenment may have played a significant role in shaping the composer's outlook, he was also open to religious approaches that were not exactly aligned with it. A more explicit sign of this situation can be found in *Christus am Ölberge*. Earlier in this chapter, we observed that *Christus* adheres in some respects to the model of the lyric oratorio, a new approach to the oratorio that emerged in the middle of the eighteenth century, specifically in a north German Protestant context. But this was to tell only half the story, so to speak. On balance, the work actually accords to a greater degree with the generic expectations of the more traditional dramatic oratorio, which, as has been explained, had come to be associated primarily with Catholic regions of the German-speaking lands.[87] As Joanna Biermann has pointed out, unlike a typical lyric oratorio (such as Graun's *Tod Jesu*), *Christus* has no narrator and no "idealized, unnamed personages."[88] There is, instead, an unusual concentration on the person of Jesus, far exceeding what had been conventional in previous musical accounts of the Passion.[89] Christ is a character who functions as any normal theatrical protagonist would. Further evidence that the work was inspired by a fundamentally dramatic conception of the oratorio is provided by the existence of actual stage directions—as for a conventional spoken play—in the libretto for the original 1803 version of the work.[90] (As has been discussed, Beethoven probably collaborated closely with the writer Franz Xaver Huber in the production of this libretto.) It is not clear why these directions were removed in later versions of the work, but they do not come across as extraneous: as Anja Mühlenweg points out, they actually fill in various gaps in the narrative provided by the text alone.[91] If the Protestant lyric oratorio attempted to increase the distinction between oratorio and the dramatic aspects intrinsic to opera, to write an oratorio with stage directions does the opposite, emphasizing the narrative and the theatrical beyond what is normal for the oratorio genre.

The failure of *Christus* to abide by the expectations for the lyric oratorio was central to the negative criticism it received during Beethoven's time, including in an influential anonymous review in the *Allgemeine musikalische Zeitung* (AmZ) from 1812 that may have been written by E. T. A. Hoffmann.[92] This review's author took aim not only at the dramatic conception of the work discussed above but also at the directness of emotional expression in the libretto, which departs from the more restrained, delicate, and idealized manner in which the lyric oratorio preferred to depict emotions. The raw,

---

[87] See Biermann, "*Christus am Ölberge*," 278–81; and Smither, *History of the Oratorio*, 3:340, 356, 521.
[88] Biermann, "*Christus am Ölberge*," 281.
[89] Mühlenweg, "Ludwig van Beethoven," 1:30.
[90] Mühlenweg, 1:32–33, 55–56. See also Jung, "'Wahr' Mensch und wahrer Gott,'" 51–52; Biermann, "*Christus am Ölberge*," 293–94; and Brandenburg, "Beethovens Oratorium *Christus am Ölberg*," 215–16.
[91] Mühlenweg, "Ludwig van Beethoven," 1:56.
[92] Brandenburg, "Beethovens Oratorium *Christus am Ölberg*," 203–5.

almost gratuitous, sensuality and physicality of the text, especially in the words Christ uses to describe his own suffering, were seen as reflecting Baroque sensibilities.[93] Tellingly, this aspect of the work also led other contemporary reviewers to label *Christus* specifically as a Catholic oratorio.[94] The unusually theatrical approach Beethoven adopted in *Christus* might be related to some degree to a genre called the *sepolcro*: a fully staged Passion oratorio intended for performance on Good Friday that had been popular in Vienna.[95] This genre had emerged at the beginning of the seventeenth century, in the context of Baroque Catholicism.[96] Though, strictly speaking, the *sepolcro* was no longer performed during Beethoven's time, its legacy remained in the popularity in Vienna of other types of staged musical works on religious subjects.[97]

The fact that, as has been discussed, Beethoven knew about the Protestant lyric oratorio model from Sulzer's writings and adopted some aspects of that model in *Christus am Ölberge* indicates that the decision to go against the model in other respects was quite conscious and deliberate. Further evidence in this regard is provided by the convoluted saga surrounding revisions made to the libretto between the premiere in April 1803 and the eventual publication of the first edition (*Originalausgabe*) much later, in 1811. Between the 1803 premiere and the second performance in 1804, Beethoven and Huber made only minor alterations to the libretto.[98] Beethoven's publisher Breitkopf & Härtel apparently disliked the 1804 libretto so much that the company commissioned a new text, which Mühlenweg has labeled the *Neutextierung*, by Christian Schreiber, the same person who produced the German text for the Mass in C.[99] For reasons that are unclear, when the first edition (*Originalausgabe*) was ultimately published, the text employed was not Schreiber's *Neutextierung* (which was never used), but one that melded the 1804 Huber/Beethoven libretto with revisions by Breitkopf and Friedrich Rochlitz, editor of the *AmZ*.[100]

---

[93] Brandenburg, 207–8.
[94] See Jung, "'Wahr' Mensch und wahrer Gott,'" 59; and Lodes, "Probing the Sacred Genres," 223.
[95] Jung, "'Wahr' Mensch und wahrer Gott,'" 51–52.
[96] Jung, 50, 52. See also Massenkeil, "Katholischer deutscher Passionsgesang"; and Petersen, "*Sepolcro*."
[97] Biermann, "*Christus am Ölberge*," 276–77.
[98] See Brandenburg, "Beethovens Oratorium *Christus am Ölberg*," 208. The *musical* revisions made between the first and second performance were, however, quite extensive: see Mühlenweg, "Ludwig van Beethoven," 1:32. From the second performance to the 1811 first edition, the situation would be reversed: the textual revisions were significant, but the musical ones minor; see Brandenburg, "Beethovens Oratorium *Christus am Ölberg*," 208.
[99] Mühlenweg, "Ludwig van Beethoven," 1:32–33, 43–46, 51–54.
[100] Mühlenweg, 38–43.

What is significant is that many of the revisions made to produce the *Originalausgabe* libretto occurred in violation of Beethoven's wishes, or in some cases even without consulting him at all.[101] Though the *Originalausgabe* text makes fewer changes to the Huber/Beethoven text than does Schreiber's *Neutextierung*, the changes that it does make are in most cases identical to what the *Neutextierung* suggests for the same points in the libretto. Moreover, the changes for the *Originalausgabe* libretto seem to have been made in the same spirit as the *Neutextierung*, which, as Sieghard Brandenburg has argued, greatly curtails the dramatic nature of the original Huber/Beethoven libretto in order to bring the work more into line with the lyric conception of oratorio discussed above.[102] Both the *Neutextierung* and the *Originalausgabe* versions of the libretto are thus useful representations of an approach to the oratorio genre that Beethoven *rejected*.

The portrayal of Christ in the *Neutextierung* is also less emotionally vivid than in the Huber/Beethoven libretto. Christ actually seems to suffer less, to struggle less.[103] For example, in the Huber/Beethoven version of Christ's opening recitative, Christ hears himself being asked a question by the Seraph: "Who instead of mankind / now wishes to give himself up before your judgment?" (*Wer statt der Menschen sich / vor dein Gericht jetzt stellen will?*). It is as if the Seraph is trying to convince him by saying, "If you won't undergo suffering, who will?" In the *Neutextierung*, Christ is much more emphatic and there is no questioning whether he will do what he knows he must do: "I hear your Seraph's grave voice / which calls anxious humanity to judgment, / bound by shame of sin!" (*Ich höre deines Seraphs ernste Stimme / die zum Gericht die bange Menschheit ruft, / gefeßelt von der Sünde Schmach!*). In the aria that follows, overly graphic or sentimental language is removed from Huber and Beethoven's original. Gone are the vivid descriptions of "horrible shuddering" (*gräßlich schaudernd*) and "feverish shivering" (*Fieberfrost*). Instead of "from my countenance trickles down / blood instead of sweat" (*von meinem Antlitz träufet, / statt des Schweißes Blut herab*), we have something more matter-of-fact: "can the cup of pain / not pass by before me" (*kan[n] der Kelch der Schmerzen / nicht vorüber vor mir gehn*).

---

[101] See Mühlenweg, 38–43; and Brandenburg, "Beethovens Oratorium *Christus am Ölberg*," 214–15. Mühlenweg's 2008 Urtext edition of the oratorio, published by Henle, uses the Huber/Beethoven 1804 libretto, regarding it as the most faithful to the composer's intentions.
[102] Brandenburg, "Beethovens Oratorium *Christus am Ölberg*," 213.
[103] Brandenburg, 213.

Additionally, Schreiber's revised text removes the most explicit Christian references. This is especially apparent in the Seraph's aria (No. 2). For instance, the *Neutextierung* has "if you are true in love / in faith and hope" (*wenn ihr getreu in liebe / in Glaub' und Hoffnung seyd*), instead of "if you are true to the teaching / of God's mediator" (*wenn ihr getreu der Lehre / des Gottvermittlers seid*). This change also occurs in the *Originalausgabe*. Huber and Beethoven's original stresses faithfulness and obedience (*getreu*) to Christ, who is specifically defined as *Gottvermittler*, the mediator between God and humanity. Schreiber's version tilts the emphasis toward ethical conduct, rather than obedience to God. God is similarly depersonalized just two lines later, as Schreiber's "Fluch der Sünde" (curse of sin) replaces "Fluch des Richters" (curse of the Judge). Once again, the stress is on human conduct instead of a specific divine person ("the Judge"). Moreover, Schreiber follows this up by removing entirely an explicit reference to damnation ("Verdammung"). Instead, his text stresses the more immediate suffering that sin brings upon the sinner, rather than the divine punishment that sin ultimately incurs. In the last number, Huber and Beethoven have Christ, Peter, and the Seraph sing the Gospel exhortation to love one's enemies ("liebt jenen, der euch hasset"). Schreiber replaces this classic Christian dictum with "das Reich der Tugend blühe" (may the kingdom of virtue prosper), and precedes this line with the anthropocentric phrase "aus edler Menschlichkeit" (from noble humanity).[104]

Beethoven's resistance to the textual changes that Breitkopf tried to force on him suggests a sincere and deliberate commitment on his part to a conception of the oratorio that was out of favor, at least from the point of view of many prominent critics of his time, along with a graphic and highly sentimental portrayal of Christ. The intense focus on the person of Christ in *Christus* is also apparent in the musical devices Beethoven uses to depict Christ's emotional development. In the opening aria, for instance, Christ's apparent fear of going through with his divine mission is vividly depicted by Beethoven's use of a kind of sonata form.[105] Within this structure, Beethoven cycles through the text twice, but, as we shall see, with some noteworthy changes when the text is repeated. The exposition, which moves from the tonic C minor to E-flat major, has the following structure:

---

[104] Brandenburg, 213.
[105] See Biermann, "*Christus am Ölberge*," 287.

mm. 105–24: Primary theme, C minor
mm. 125–43: Transition, E-flat major → E-flat minor → E-flat major
mm. 144–57: Secondary theme, E-flat major

An eleven-measure interlude (mm. 158–68) then substitutes for a proper development section before the recapitulation begins at measure 169, in C minor, as expected, along with a return of the opening line of text, "Meine Seele ist erschüttert" (My soul is shaken). But there is a striking change in comparison to the exposition. On these words, Christ sings an E-*natural* instead of E-flat (m. 171). Briefly, then, we have a promising glimmer of C major. Moreover, in conjunction with a shortening of the primary theme area and transition section in the recapitulation, Beethoven also removes four lines of text that had appeared in the exposition—text that had been especially vivid in its portrayal of Christ's mental anguish:

Schrecken faßt mich und es zittert gräßlich schaudernd mein Gebein.	Terror grips me and my bones tremble, shuddering horribly.
Wie ein Fieberfrost ergreifet mich die Angst beim nahen Grab.	Like a feverish shivering fear seizes me as I approach the grave.

Having just prayed to his Father, might Christ be a little more hopeful that his cup of suffering will be taken away? Or, alternatively, is he starting ever so slightly to find the courage to accept that suffering? As with any minor-key sonata form, Beethoven then had a choice to make between recapitulating the secondary theme in the actual—minor—tonic, or "redeeming" the minor mode by having the secondary theme in the *major* tonic. Here, he opts for the second option (see m. 197). For a moment, we are given hope that the aria might end in the major, and thus signal either that the Father has agreed to take Christ's cup of suffering away, or that Christ has come to accept his suffering mission. This is not to be. At measure 212, the music turns back to C *minor* for the last two lines of text ("Deiner Macht ist alles möglich, / nimm den Leidenkelch von mir!"). The aria seems to conclude with Christ feeling the way he felt at the beginning, fearful and terrified. Indeed, his fear may even have increased. In a coda section (m. 219ff.) that Beethoven added only when revising the score after the oratorio's first performance in 1803, Christ sings repeatedly and desperately, "Nimm den Leidenkelch von mir!" (Take the cup of suffering from me!).[106]

The tonal strategy of thwarting the major-mode "redemption" of a minor-key sonata form should be familiar to many from the first movement of Beethoven's Fifth Symphony, also in C minor, where the coda section snatches defeat from the jaws of victory by plunging the music back into C minor after a C-major secondary theme. Beethoven's employment of this strategy in Christ's aria illustrates the depths of Christ's anguish and his fear of his impending suffering and death, a fear he eventually overcomes as the oratorio progresses. It serves as a striking example of the unusual emphasis that the oratorio as a whole places on the inner psychology of Christ, especially on his struggle to accept his salvific mission.

The emotionally intense focus on the person of Christ in *Christus* represents, I would suggest, a outlook at odds with the German Catholic Enlightenment, and more in line with the Catholic Restoration which, as discussed in chapter 1, involved a return to many aspects of Baroque Catholicism. There are parallels in this regard between the oratorio and what can be described as the Christocentric outlook of the theologian Johann Michael Sailer, whose connection to Beethoven will be explored in detail in chapter 5.

Beethoven and Christ

Beethoven's unfashionably sentimental portrayal of Christ in *Christus am Ölberge* can be interpreted as a subtle departure from the Catholic Enlightenment outlook that otherwise characterized his religious views. Christ is depicted not just as a model for virtuous conduct, but as a person with whom the believer should connect in an intimate manner. As will become apparent in later chapters, the oratorio thus foreshadows Beethoven's engagement with the writings of Johann Michael Sailer as well as certain aspects of the *Missa solemnis*, which point to an openness to the ideas of the Catholic Restoration. Given the historical context discussed previously, it is possible that even at this relatively early stage of his career, more conservative religious approaches were already beginning to appeal to Beethoven, as they did to so many others in his culture as a reaction to the upheavals of

---

[106] Mühlenweg, "Ludwig van Beethoven," 1:74–75.

war and revolution. Just as likely, however, personal factors were at work in drawing Beethoven to the figure of Christ.

The thematic links connecting the Heiligenstadt Testament, Gellert Lieder, and *Christus am Ölberge* provide some clues in this regard. Most obviously, Christ could have served as a model of stoicism and courage in the face of suffering and death: these themes are prominent in both the Testament and in *Christus*, given the oratorio's emphasis on Christ's ultimately successful struggle to accept the mission his Father has given him. But stoicism is also a theme in the Gellert Lieder, in the text of the third song, "Vom Tode":

Daß du dieses Herz erwirbst,	So that you acquire this heart,
Fürchte Gott und bet und wache.	Fear God and pray and watch.
Sorge nicht, wie früh du stirbst;	Do not care about how early you die;
Deine Zeit ist Gottes Sache.	Your lifetime is a thing for God.
Lern nicht nur den Tod nicht scheun,	Learn not only not to fear death
Lern auch seiner dich erfreun.	But also learn to delight in it.
Überwind ihn durch Vertraun;	Overcome it through trust;
Sprich: Ich weiß, an wen ich gläube,	Say: I know in whom I believe,
Und ich weiß, ich werd' ihn schaun	And I know, I shall behold him
Einst in diesem, meinem Leibe.	One day in this, my body.
Er, der rief: Es ist vollbracht!	He, he who cried out: It is finished!
Nahm dem Tode seine Macht.	Took from death its power.

As in the oratorio, Christ is described here as a victor over death, and his words "Es ist vollbracht!" are alluded to near the end of *Christus* as well: "Meine Qual ist bald verschwunden, / der Erlösung Werk vollbracht" (My agony will soon disappear, / the work of redemption will be completed). Just like Christ in the oratorio, the Beethoven of the Heiligenstadt Testament stoically overcomes his suffering out of a sense of duty to others.

Another possible reason for Beethoven's interest in Christ may have been the personal relevance to him of the idea of healing, which can easily be linked to Christ's role as Savior and Redeemer. In the Heiligenstadt Testament, Beethoven turns to the divine for healing, in both a physical sense because of his deafness, and an emotional one because of the anguish that his deafness has produced.[107] Understood in broader terms, healing can also be considered an important theme in both the Gellert Lieder and *Christus am Ölberge*. These works foreground the idea of Christ's redemptive work, his healing of human sinfulness. In *Christus*, the opening lines of the Seraph's aria neatly sum up the oratorio's central point:

Preist des Erlösers Güte,	Praise the goodness of the Redeemer,
preist Menschen, seine Huld.	praise, O people, his grace.
Er stirbt für euch aus Liebe,	He dies for you out of love,
sein Blut tilgt eure Schuld.	his blood erases your guilt.

In the Gellert Lieder, an interest in the forgiveness of sins is detectable in the final song, "Bußlied" (Penitential song). This song is the only one of the six that is through-composed, and its distinctive structure in the context of the collection makes it come across as a kind of finale. As Rumph has written, the design of the whole cycle culminating in "Bußlied" creates an "overall plot"— "a quest for forgiveness and salvation."[108] This design appears to have been very deliberate: just before publication by Artaria, Beethoven changed the order of the songs so that the cycle ended with "Bußlied" instead of "Gottes Macht."[109] Ending the cycle with "Bußlied" also makes sense given that the cycle began with a poem in which the speaker prays for mercy: "Laß du mich nur Barmherzigkeit / Vor dir im Tode finden" (Allow me only to find mercy / Before you [God] in death). Mercy and forgiveness—forms of spiritual healing—are thus brought to the fore in a song cycle that begins with a plea for mercy and ends with an expression of confidence in that mercy.

That Christ had assumed a special significance for Beethoven during the personal crisis surrounding the onset of his deafness may explain why, a few years later, when he completed his first mass, he gave parts of the liturgical text referring to Christ especially vivid musical treatment. In the Mass in C, the Christe section of the Kyrie puts a pronounced rhythmic emphasis on the name of Christ (see example 3.13).

---

[107] Solomon has discussed the importance of healing as an idea for understanding Beethoven's late works, including the "Heiliger Dankgesang": see "Healing Power of Music." I shall return to the topic of healing in later chapters, including in my discussion of the *Missa solemnis*.

[108] Rumph, *Beethoven after Napoleon*, 38. Joanna Biermann has made a similar argument: see "Cyclical Ordering," 174-76.

[109] Biermann, "Cyclical Ordering," 170-74. Biermann adds that "Bußlied" is the final song in both of the two editions (from Artaria and Hoffmeister & Kühnel) that were published in 1803, even though for the Hoffmeister edition, Beethoven altered the order of the earlier songs.

RELIGIOUS WORKS BEFORE THE *MISSA SOLEMNIS* 123

At the beginning of this section, the soprano, alto, and tenor soloists sing "Christe eleison" (Christ, have mercy) in measures 37–40, imitated by the chorus in measures 41–44. At measure 45, the alto soloist sings just the word "eleison," imitated immediately by the tenor soloist. In all these instances, the word "eleison" is sung with the syllable "-son" falling on a downbeat. This follows the practice in the preceding Kyrie section, with the single exception of measure 25 (in the solo tenor). In measure 49, the chorus replies to the alto and tenor soloists with its own statement of "eleison." Beethoven's previous rhythmic treatment of the word leads the listener to expect that "-son" will once again fall on a downbeat here. Instead, Beethoven "compresses" the

Example 3.13 Mass in C major, op. 86, Kyrie, mm. 37–56 (vocal parts only)

Example 3.13 Continued

rhythm, such that "-son" comes early on the last eighth note of the measure, followed immediately by the word "Christe," which itself seems premature as a result (mm. 49–50). A kind of run-on effect is produced, as the text here sounds like the syntactically irregular "eleison Christe" (instead of the usual "Christe eleison"). As with the anticipated choral entries described in a previous section, "Christe" comes across like a spontaneous cry, exclaimed ahead of when we expect it.

Beethoven also uses a variety of musical devices either to stress important theological points about Christ's identity and divine mission, or to evoke religious ideas about Christ that are not literally in the liturgical text but might be associated with it. For instance, the Kyrie and Christe sections of the Kyrie movement are not as contrasting as one might expect from a Mass setting. Instead, the sections are tied together by close motivic similarities, an observation that is supported by evidence of Beethoven's compositional process from his sketchbooks.[110] Most notably, the pitch e^2 is used as a unifying element that Beethoven returns to repeatedly throughout the entire movement. This close tie between the Kyrie and Christe sections is reinforced by the early return of the text "Kyrie eleison" (Lord, have mercy) after the Christe section (m. 70). Textually, the Kyrie section comes back at this point. However, the music still remains in E major, the key of the Christe section,

---

[110] This topic is discussed in exhaustive detail in McGrann, "Beethoven's Mass in C," 1:135–204. McGrann stresses that Beethoven's approach to setting the Kyrie differed substantially from the models provided by Haydn's masses (ibid., 199–200).

and does not return to C major until measure 84. There is thus a disjunction between textual and musical structure that further blurs the lines between the two sections. What results is a closer connection between "Kyrie" and "Christe": "Kyrie eleison" and "Christe eleison" do not refer to separate entities, but to the same Christ who is Lord.

In a striking passage from the Credo movement (mm. 54–73), Beethoven musically highlights the words "Deum verum de Deo vero / genitum, non factum" (true God from true God / begotten, not made), an important theological description of Christ's nature. First comes a sudden fortissimo dynamic for "Deum verum de Deo vero," sung on a pitch-class-unison G in both chorus and accompanying strings (mm. 65–68), the only time Beethoven employs such a texture in the Credo. There is then a sudden harmonic shift to V7 of F for "genitum," which is sung on exactly the same notes twice, with both iterations preceded by fanfare-like chords in the winds (mm. 68–70). The orchestra accompaniment then cuts out entirely for two whole measures (mm. 70–71), and the chorus declares bluntly, in unison: "non factum," which emphasizes Christ's eternal nature. Later in the same movement, Beethoven sets the text "Qui propter nos homines et propter nostram salutem" (Who for us human beings and for our salvation), referring to Christ's descent to earth, with exceptional tenderness (mm. 95–102). As McGrann points out, this passage is the only time in the movement that a duet texture is used, generating "a more intimate mood which makes clear the personal nature of Christ's mission as stated in the text."[111] These words are then repeated (mm. 111–18), though this time in C minor instead of C major. The move to C minor here smoothens the transition from C major to E-flat major, the key of the next section, beginning with "Et incarnatus" at measure 133. However, the major–minor duality may also suggest the emotionally ambivalent nature of Christ's coming to earth. On the one hand, it is a moment of happiness because it wins humanity's salvation; on the other, Christ's coming also entails his violent death on the cross. One final example of Beethoven's attention to Christ-related portions of the Credo comes nearer the end of the movement, when Beethoven sets the line "et exspecto resurrectionem mortuorum" (and I look forward to the resurrection of the dead; mm. 183–84) to a similar melodic contour as the earlier lines "et resurrexit tertia die" (and he rose again on the third day; mm. 190–91) and "et ascendit in coelum" (and he ascended

---

[111] McGrann, 2:537–38.

126   THE CATHOLIC BEETHOVEN

into heaven; mm. 269–70). This correspondence connects the hoped-for resurrection of the individual believer to the actual resurrection of Christ.[112]

Beethoven draws further connections *across* movements between different Christ-related texts. The words "Jesum Christum" in the Credo (mm. 36–37) occur at the first significant moment of tonal instability in that movement. Prior to this point, accidentals do appear within the C-major tonal context. B-flats and F-sharps enable local tonicizations of IV and V respectively, and A-flat occurs once, in measure 8, as part of a minor IV chord. At "Jesum Christum," however, V7 of F is reinterpreted as a German sixth chord, resolving to B major. This tonal surprise by itself places special emphasis on the word "Christum," but, as McGrann has argued, the B-major chord can also be understood as V of E major, a key that previously became associated with Christ as the key of the Christe section in the Kyrie.[113] E major is also alluded to later in the Credo for another Christ-related line: "qui cum [ex] Patre filioque procedit" (who proceeds from the Father and the son).[114]

A similar example is found by noticing the parallels between the Et incarnatus section of the Credo and the Benedictus section of the Sanctus movement. These sections, though temporally disconnected, share a slowing of the tempo within the immediate musical context, exclusive use of vocal soloists (instead of the chorus), and an arpeggiated figure in the orchestral accompaniment.[115] These similarities may be intended to stress the fact that both these moments in the Mass refer to Christ's physical presence on earth: first at the Incarnation itself, and then during the liturgy through the mystery of transubstantiation, the traditional Catholic belief that Christ becomes really present in the Eucharistic bread and wine consecrated by the priest. Such an interpretation is reinforced by the use of solo instruments in both places. The Et incarnatus begins with the sudden interjection of a solo clarinet playing a downward arpeggio, a rather graphic depiction of Christ's descent to earth (mm. 131–33). In the Benedictus, the first edition of the Mass in C includes a direction for a solo cello, though it is unclear why Beethoven's direction for the solo cello was removed from later editions of the Mass in C,

---

[112] McGrann, 2:544.
[113] McGrann, 2:498.
[114] The word "cum" instead of the liturgically prescribed "ex" here is a mistake, most likely attributable to the publisher rather than Beethoven. The error also appears in some early editions of the *Missa solemnis*. See Skwara, "Cum versus ex," 46–47.
[115] McGrann, "Beethoven's Mass in C," 2:546–47. McGrann has identified further affective similarities between the Crucifixus section in the Credo and the opening of the Agnus Dei, similarities that serve to highlight the common reference to Christ's death that unites both texts.

so far as we know without Beethoven's approval.[116] The solo cello here recalls Beethoven's employment of the same instrument during a crucial moment in *Christus am Ölberge*: the duet between Christ and the Seraph (No. 3), when, for the first time in the oratorio, Christ accepts his suffering mission. Beethoven's decision to use the same solo instrument in both contexts makes theological sense. Despite its laudatory tone—"Blessed is he who comes in the name of the Lord"—the text of the Benedictus is actually associated with Christ's Passion. Not only does it occur during the Eucharistic rite, which is meant to recall Christ's death, but the words are derived originally from Matthew 21:9, describing Jesus's entry into Jerusalem before his Passion.

To highlight Beethoven's attention to the meaning of Christ-related lines of the Mass might seem merely to extend my earlier discussion of the composer's efforts at performing a musical exegesis of the liturgical text. But, as we shall see in chapter 6, a special focus on Christ can be detected again in the *Missa solemnis*. The commonality in this regard between his two completed masses, along with the characteristics of the oratorio *Christus am Ölberge* described above, point to a particular fascination with the figure of Christ that manifested itself over multiple periods of the composer's adult life.

Considered as a group, Beethoven's major religious works before the *Missa solemnis*—the Gellert Lieder, *Christus am Ölberge*, and the Mass in C— reflect important ideas that were associated with the German Catholic Enlightenment, in particular ecumenism, the presence of God in the natural world, ethical conduct, and active engagement with the liturgy. In the next chapter, we shall see how similar ideas appear in books with religious themes in Beethoven's library that he most likely read during the 1810s. It thus appears that the German Catholic Enlightenment that was a prominent part of his upbringing in Bonn continued to exert an impact on the composer's outlook well into his later years. That said, the portrayal of Christ in *Christus am Ölberge* provides an early hint that Beethoven may also have been open to more conservative approaches to Catholicism. In exploring Beethoven's connection to Johann Michael Sailer and various compositional choices he would make in the *Missa solemnis*, chapters 5 and 6 will consider the possibility that this aspect of his outlook became more prominent in the final decade of his life.

---

[116] As indicated previously, the edition is available at https://www.beethoven.de/en/media/view/6740031603474432/, accessed August 1, 2024. Jeremiah McGrann's Urtext edition for the *Neue Beethoven-Gesamtausgabe* (Munich: G. Henle, 2003) restores the "solo" designation for the cello part that is omitted in many other editions.

4
Religion in Beethoven's Library
Christoph Christian Sturm and Ignaz Aurelius Feßler

The posthumous inventory of Beethoven's possessions lists several books with explicitly Christian content. These include the classic medieval devotional text *The Imitation of Christ* by Thomas à Kempis, *Ansichten von Religion und Kirchenthum* (Views on religion and the church) by Ignaz Aurelius Feßler, and three works by Johann Michael Sailer.[1] In addition, though the work is not listed in the inventory, Beethoven's own copy of Christoph Christian Sturm's *Betrachtungen über die Werke Gottes im Reiche der Natur und der Vorsehung* (Reflections on the works of God in the realm of nature and of Providence) has survived.[2] Based on publication dates as well as other documentary evidence, we know that Beethoven engaged with all of these books in the 1810s or early 1820s, in the decade or so leading up to his composition of the *Missa solemnis* (and after he had completed the Mass in C). This chronology raises the question of what might have motivated these actions. As with the composition of his first mature religious pieces in 1802–1803, personal difficulties probably played an important role. During the 1810s, the composer was confronted with a series of crises in his private and family life, a fact that has been much discussed in Beethoven scholarship. First, in the summer of 1812, came Beethoven's unrequited obsession with his "Immortal Beloved."[3] The composer's brother Kaspar Karl fell ill during the same year, and eventually died in late 1815.[4] Kaspar Karl's passing triggered a lengthy legal battle between Beethoven and his brother's widow

---

[1] The relevant items in the *Schätzungsprotokoll* are no. 23 (Thomas à Kempis), no. 16 (Feßler, spelled "Fessler" in the inventory), and nos. 1 and 11 (Sailer). Albrecht's transcription of the *Schätzungsprotokoll* is missing one of the three books by Sailer, *Friedrich Christians Vermächtniß*, but this is an error, as will be discussed in the next chapter.

[2] Berlin, Staatsbibliothek, Mus.ms.autogr. Beethoven, L.v. 40,2.

[3] The identity of this "Immortal Beloved" has been the subject of lengthy debate among Beethoven scholars. See Caeyers, *Beethoven*, 337–43; and Walden, *Beethoven's Immortal Beloved*. Maynard Solomon has argued in favor of Antonie Brentano as the mystery woman: see *Beethoven*, 207–46. We shall return to Antonie in the next chapter in connection with Johann Michael Sailer.

[4] Solomon, *Beethoven*, 283, 297, 302–3.

The Catholic Beethoven. Nicholas Chong, Oxford University Press. © Oxford University Press 2024.
DOI: 10.1093/9780197752951.003.0005

Johanna over custody of their son Karl (Beethoven's nephew).[5] Johanna had a history of criminal conduct, and Beethoven did not think her morally fit to raise Karl. Throughout this whole period, Beethoven's own physical health was also deteriorating.[6] As various commentators have suggested, all of these challenging events in Beethoven's life may have prompted a second period of heightened interest in religious issues, similar to what had occurred around the time of the Heiligenstadt Testament.[7]

In the case of the writings by Johann Michael Sailer, a personal connection can actually be established between Beethoven and the author, even if that connection was somewhat indirect. Beethoven's copy of Thomas à Kempis's *Imitation* was also most likely in a translation by Sailer.[8] For these reasons, and because Beethoven had multiple titles by Sailer in his library, both the books by Sailer and *Imitation of Christ* will be discussed separately in the next chapter. For the moment, this chapter will focus primarily on Sturm's *Betrachtungen* and Feßler's *Ansichten*. Though, as we shall see, Sturm's and Feßler's biographies can both be connected to German Catholicism of the time, neither of them was Catholic; in Feßler's case he actually converted from Catholicism to Protestantism. Nevertheless, important themes of these books overlap obviously with ideas prominent in the Catholic Enlightenment, especially ecumenism and religious tolerance, the importance of ethical conduct, an emphasis on learning about God through physical nature, and active engagement with the liturgy. These same ideas were discussed in the previous chapter in connection with Beethoven's religious works before the *Missa solemnis*. Beethoven copied down a passage from Sturm's *Betrachtungen* into his *Tagebuch*, a combination of a diary and a commonplace book that he maintained between 1812 and 1818. This chapter will thus also devote a section to discussing the eclecticism of the religious references in that document, especially the high number of non-Christian quotations. I shall argue that within the framework of the German Catholic Enlightenment, this situation need not, as has often been the case in previous scholarship, be interpreted as evidence of Beethoven's estrangement from traditional Christian belief.

---

[5] See Solomon, 297–330; and Caeyers, *Beethoven*, 390–400.
[6] Solomon, *Beethoven*, 333–35.
[7] See Solomon, 340–42; Lodes, "'So träumte mir,'" 185–87; and Herttrich, "Beethoven und die Religion," 35–37.
[8] See Ito, "Johann Michael Sailer and Beethoven," 90–91.

Sturm's *Betrachtungen über die Werke Gottes*

Christoph Christian Sturm's *Betrachtungen über die Werke Gottes im Reiche der Natur und der Vorsehung* is a series of religious meditations for each day of the year, united by the common theme of showing the signs of God's presence in the natural world. It was an extremely popular book.[9] First published in 1773, it later went through multiple editions and translations. As late as 1823, the translator of an English edition published in London that year reports that "several translations of [*Betrachtungen*] have already appeared," and also that "the continued and increasing demand for the works of Sturm has occasioned the present edition."[10] Sturm himself, who lived from 1740 to 1786, has become an obscure figure. The only biography of him that exists was written in the year of his death by one Jacob Friedrich Feddersen.[11] During his lifetime, however, Sturm was a prominent Lutheran priest. He studied in Jena, then held posts in Magdeburg and Hamburg, where he was the main pastor of the city's most important church. C. P. E. Bach, who also lived in Hamburg, set much of Sturm's religious poetry to music, and his songs on Sturm's texts greatly aided in their broad dissemination.[12] In terms of his theological views, Sturm was known for his advocacy of religious tolerance.[13] And, not surprisingly given the content of *Betrachtungen*, he was a follower of the physico-theology that was also prominent in the Catholic Enlightenment during the eighteenth century, stressing the role of nature in religious understanding.[14]

In contrast to the other religious texts discussed in this book, Christoph Christian Sturm's *Betrachtungen* is unusual in that the actual copy Beethoven owned has survived: it is currently held in the Berlin State Library.[15] This copy also contains annotations that Beethoven made, though Lewis

---

[9] See Witcombe, "Beethoven's Markings," 10–11; and Leisinger, "C. P. E. Bach and C. C. Sturm," 120.

[10] Sturm, *Reflections*, 1:v.

[11] Witcombe, "Beethoven's Markings," 10–11; and Leisinger, "C. P. E. Bach and C. C. Sturm," 119–20.

[12] Leisinger, "C. P. E. Bach and C. C. Sturm," 116–21.

[13] Witcombe, "Beethoven's Markings," 11.

[14] Leisinger, "C. P. E. Bach and C. C. Sturm," 120.

[15] Berlin, Staatsbibliothek, Mus.ms.autogr. Beethoven, L.v. 40,2. Beethoven's copy, along with his annotations therein, have been studied in detail in a master's thesis by Charles Witcombe, which includes a transcription of all the passages from Sturm's book marked by Beethoven, along with an English translation of the same: see "Beethoven's Private God," 98–217. In what follows, I shall use Witcombe's translations unless otherwise stated. The findings of Witcombe's thesis also appear in a much more concise form in "Beethoven's Markings."

Lockwood's description of these annotations as "extensive" seems a little exaggerated.[16] Beethoven marked a total of 117 passages, covering seventy-two different meditations.[17] But instances where Beethoven wrote his own words in response to particular passages are rare, occurring just four times. As will become evident in examples to be cited below, Beethoven's words are extremely brief and cryptic, and do not lend themselves to conclusive interpretation. In the overwhelming majority of cases, Beethoven simply marked passages with vertical lines in the margin—either one, two, or three parallel lines are used depending on the passage—or by underlining sections of text, sometimes just the title of a meditation. Beethoven's annotations, though vague in the way I have just described, have enabled Charles Witcombe to conclude that the composer most likely read Sturm's book in the year 1816.[18] For the first seven daily meditations, Beethoven marked the days of the week, so we know that in the year he read the book, January 1 was a Monday. Beethoven's copy was published in 1811, in Reutlingen.[19] Between this year and the composer's death, January 1 fell on a Monday in 1816, 1821, and 1827. Since Beethoven copied a passage from Sturm's text into his *Tagebuch* in 1818 (a point to which I shall return below), 1816 seems the likeliest of these three possibilities, since it is reasonable to assume that he would have read the book before deciding what to note down from it.

In any event, Beethoven's annotations make it undeniable that he read Sturm's *Betrachtungen* rather closely. In doing so, he would have been returning to religious ideas that he had previously engaged with in the Gellert Lieder and *Der Wachtelschlag*—ideas that were typical of the German Catholic Enlightenment. The main theme of Sturm's book is that nature should be regarded as an important source of knowledge about God. The meditation for May 4 concisely encapsulates this overall point. Its title, which Beethoven marked with three lines in the margin, reads: "An Invitation to Seek God in the Works of Nature."[20] Sturm writes, "When you look at the

---

[16] See Lockwood, *Beethoven's Symphonies*, 125.
[17] Witcombe, "Beethoven's Markings," 13.
[18] Witcombe, 12.
[19] Sturm, *Betrachtungen* (1811). A digitization of Sturm's book in this precise edition is available online at https://onb.digital/result/1029165E (vol. 1) and https://onb.digital/result/10291667 (vol. 2), accessed August 1, 2024. That the publication year of Beethoven's copy postdates the composition of the *Pastoral* Symphony (1808) calls into doubt David Wyn Jones's suggestion that Sturm's book influenced the symphony: see *Beethoven: Pastoral Symphony*, 20–22. But Anton Schindler, who likewise linked the book to the symphony, claimed that Beethoven owned an older edition of Sturm's text in addition to the 1811 one: see *Beethoven as I Knew Him*, 143n; and *Biographie*, 3rd ed., 1:152n.
[20] See Witcombe, "Beethoven's Private God," 155–59; and Sturm, *Betrachtungen* (1811), 1:341: "Ermunterung, Gott in der Natur zu suchen."

sky's beautiful colors, the stars which shine there in the light which makes things around you visible, ask yourself where all of this must come from? ... Thus it must become my most precious duty to seek you, Eternal One, in all of your works."[21] Similar sentiments are expressed in the meditation for September 19. In a passage Beethoven marked with one broken line in the margin, Sturm addresses his reader, "Christian! You witness of God's wonders."[22] Elsewhere, in the meditation for December 8, entitled "Nature as a School for the Heart" (*Die Natur als eine Schule für das Herz*), Beethoven marked with one vertical line Sturm's contention that in nature the believer will "meet God and find a taste of heaven in his wisdom."[23] Some of the descriptions of nature in *Betrachtungen* are so detailed as to recall a scientific treatise. The meditation for January 21, for instance, describes the anatomical basis for human vocal production; Beethoven marked three excerpts from this meditation.[24] Similar meditations among those marked by Beethoven deal with geology (February 24), zoology (May 15 and May 22), and magnetism (June 13).[25] Unsurprisingly given his special interest in the subject, Beethoven marked three passages in Sturm's *Betrachtungen* that concern astronomy. In the meditation for April 2, for instance, the reader is exhorted to trust in a God who reliably governs the order of the solar system.[26] The meditations for January 12 and June 10 refer more specifically to the stars. Entitled respectively "Betrachtung des gestirnten Himmels" (Contemplation of the starry heavens) and "Unermesslichkeit des Sternenhimmels" (The immensity of the starry heavens), both emphasize the seeming infinitude of the universe.[27] In the first of these two meditations, this infinitude is explicitly linked to the infinitude of God:

> Yet all these observations, as astounding as they are, lead us barely to the furthest frontier of the works of God. If we are able to swing over the Moon, and approach the planets; if we could climb up to the highest stars, then we

---

[21] See Witcombe, 155–59; and Sturm, 1:341–43: "Denke bei dir selbst, wenn du den Himmel dessen schöne Farben, die Gestirne, die daran leuchten, das Licht, welches die Gegenstände um dich her sichtbar macht, stehest denke, woher muß doch alles diese kommen? ... O so müsse es denn meine theuerest Pflicht bleiben, dich, Unendlicher, in allen deinen Werken zu suchen."

[22] See Witcombe, 210–11; and Sturm, 2:241: "Christ! du Zeuge der Wunder Gottes."

[23] See Witcombe, 215–16; and Sturm, 2:493, 497: "Hier werde ich Gott kennen lernen und in seiner Erkenntniß einen Vorgeschmack des Himmels finden."

[24] See Witcombe, 114–19; and Sturm, 1:58–61.

[25] See Witcombe, 125–27, 162–64, 168–69, 183–85; and Sturm, 1:152–55, 372–74, 391–94, 458–61.

[26] See Witcombe, 145–52; and Sturm, 1:255–58.

[27] See Witcombe, 103–7, 176–77; and Sturm, 1:31–36, 448–51.

would discover new unfolding heavens, new stars, new and perhaps even more exalted planetary systems. Yet there would our great Creator's territories still not end; rather, we would with astonishment observe that we have not come to the border of outer space.[28]

This passage resonates strikingly with the multiple instances where Beethoven associated the stars with the divine in his music, as discussed in the previous chapter.[29]

As in the texts of the Gellert Lieder, the connection between nature and the divine is expressed not only in the beauty and majesty of the created order but through the concept of divine providence. The very word "providence" (*Vorsehung*) is, of course, part of the title of Sturm's work. But throughout the book itself, Sturm repeatedly stresses the purposeful aspect of nature, a sign of God's constant care for his creation and especially for human beings. References to agriculture thus occur frequently, including in meditations that Beethoven himself marked. The meditation for January 11, for instance, reflects on the fertilizing effects that snow brings to the soil: "God has covered the earth with snow not only to warm the earth, but also to fertilize it. How much trouble it costs us to give the fields the necessary manure! And how easy it is for nature to achieve many goals!"[30] And to cite another

---

[28] See Witcombe, 103–7; and Sturm, 1:34–35: "Doch alle diese Bemerkungen, so erstaunenswürdig sie sind, führen uns kaum zu den alleräußersten Grenzen der Werke Gottes. Könnten wir uns über den Mond hinweg schwingen, und uns den Planeten nähern; könnten wir zu dem höchsten Sterne hinansteigen, so würden wir neue Himmel ausgebreitet, neue Sonnen, neue Sterne, neue, und vielleicht noch edlere Weltgebäude entdecken. Allein auch da würde sich noch nicht das Gebieth unsers großen Schöpfers endigen: sondern wir würden mit Erstaunen bemerken, daß wir nicht weiter als bis zu den Grenzen des Weltraums gekommen sind." I have slightly amended Witcombe's translation.

[29] As I argue elsewhere ("Beethoven and Kant's *Allgemeine Naturgeschichte*"), this passage is strikingly similar to one found in another book in Beethoven's library, Immanuel Kant's *Universal Natural History and Theory of the Heavens*: "The theory we have put forward opens a perspective onto the infinite field of creation for us and presents some inkling of God's work that is appropriate to the infinitude of the great architect.... There is no end here but rather an abyss of a true immeasurability into which all capacity of human concepts sinks even if it is raised with the help of mathematics. The wisdom, the goodness, the power that has revealed itself, is infinite and in the same measure fruitful and industrious; the plan of its revelation must for that reason be as infinite and without limits as it is" (Kant, *Natural Science*, 222; translation by Olaf Reinhardt). Kant's original German is as follows: "Der Lehrbegriff, den wir vorgetragen haben, eröffnet uns eine Aussicht in das unendliche Feld der Schöpfung und bietet eine Vorstellung von dem Werke Gottes dar, die der Unendlichkeit des großen Werkmeisters gemäß ist.... Es ist hier kein Ende, sondern ein Abgrund einer wahren Unermeßlichkeit, worin alle Fähigkeit der menschlichen Begriffe sinkt, wenn sie gleich durch die Hülfe der Zahlwissenschaft erhoben wird. Die Weisheit, die Güte, die Macht, die sich offenbart hat, ist unendlich und in eben der Maße fruchtbar und geschäftig; der Plan ihrer Offenbarung muß daher eben wie sie unendlich und ohne Grenzen sein" (*Kants gesammelte Schriften*, 1:255–56).

[30] See Witcombe, "Beethoven's Private God," 101–3; and Sturm, *Betrachtungen* (1811), 1:30: "Jedoch nicht bloß zur Erwärmung, sondern auch zur Befruchtung hat Gott die Erde mit

example, the meditation for February 1, entitled "The Arrangement of all of Nature for the Benefit of Mankind" (*Einrichtung der ganzen Natur zum Nutzen der Menschen*), describes how horses were made by God to assist humans in the pulling of loads.[31]

Beyond teaching people about God, Sturm also shows how nature can provide instruction concerning God's moral laws. As in the Gellert Lieder (see chapter 3), Sturm's book thematizes the importance of ethical conduct in addition to the presence of God in nature, and both of these ideas were key aspects of the German Catholic Enlightenment. The meditation (for January 21) concerning human vocal production, cited above, includes the following passage that Beethoven marked:

> These observations, my Christian, give you a new occasion to reflect and to be astonished over the ineffable wisdom and goodness of God, which is manifested in the arrangement of every part of your body. May you also be aroused through this mental image to value speech for its worth through which you have been raised above all animals. . . . Use it as your creator intended. You should primarily use it for beneficial effects to proclaim the glory of God and for those activities which would either help, or instruct, or console your brother.[32]

Sturm connects what comes across initially as an empirical description of human voices to God's goodness, and in turn to the duty of human beings to serve God and neighbor. The meditation for March 11 contains a prayer to God for help in performing good works. Here Beethoven underlined the words "do not stop working on my improvement," as well as "Let me only return to you, in whatever way it may be, and become fruitful through good

---

Schnee bedeckt. Wie viele Mühe kostet es uns, dem Acker die nöthige Düngung zu geben! Und wie leicht ist es der Natur, diesen Endzweck zu erhalten!"

[31] See Witcombe, 123–25; and Sturm, 1:88–91.

[32] See Witcombe, 114–19; and Sturm, 1:61: "Diese Betrachtungen, mein Christ, geben dir eine neue Veranlassung, über die Wunder der Weisheit und Güte Gottes, die er bey der Einrichtung eines jeden Theils deines Körpers geoffenbaret hat, nachzudenken und zu erstaunen. Möchtest du doch durch diese Vorstellung ermuntert werden, auch die Sprache, durch welche du über alle Thiere erhaben bist, nach ihrem Werthe zu schätzen! . . . Gebrauche sie nach der Absicht deines Schöpfers. Du wirst sie aber alsdann erst heilsam gebrauchen, wenn du sie zur Verkündigung der Ehre Gottes, und zu solchen Beschäftigung anwendest, durch welche dein Mitbruder erbaut, oder unterrichtet, oder getröstet wird." I have slightly amended Witcombe's translation.

works."[33] In the meditation for September 5, Beethoven marked a passage that clearly emphasizes the link between ethical duty and service to God:

> Servile unto God, but free
> According to wise duties, act,
> Praise him and be forever happy.[34]

The meditation for September 18 bemoans the moral decline of the age:

> You authorities, you preachers, you school teachers, how much you could contribute to the betterment of the world and to the salvation of the descendants if you wished to lead a savage country, a salted city or an evil village to wisdom, religion and all social virtues by means of rewards, encouragement and other obligatory tasks.[35]

Beethoven not only marked this passage, but it provoked him to such a degree that he wrote in the margin, "Wo seid ihr? Doch nicht hier!!" (Where are you? Not here!!), perhaps meaning that he felt his own society to be lacking in the good people necessary to encourage ethical improvement. To point to one final example, in the meditation for June 22, which Beethoven marked with a vertical line in the margin, Sturm encourages the reader to learn wisdom from observing a nightingale. Though the nightingale lacks physical beauty, Sturm contends, it sings beautifully. Christians should thus refrain from judging others based solely on their outward appearance.[36] The literary conceit of a bird teaching lessons about God clearly recalls the text of Beethoven's own song *Der Wachtelschlag*, discussed in the previous chapter, in which the poetic speaker hears in the call of a quail exhortations to fear, love, praise, thank, seek, and trust God.

---

[33] See Witcombe, 131–34; and Sturm, 1:197: "höre nicht auf an meiner Besserung zu arbeiten"; "Laß mich nur, auf welche Weise es wolle, zu dir kehren, und an guten Werken fruchtbar werden." I have slightly amended Witcombe's translation.

[34] See Witcombe, 202–4; and Sturm, 2:195: "Gott unterwürsig, aber frei. / Nach weisen Pflichten, handle, / Ihn lob' und ewig glücklich sey."

[35] See Witcombe, 206–9; and Sturm, 2:238: "Ihr Obrigkeiten, ihr Prediger, ihr Schullehrer; wie viel konntet ihr zum Besten der Welt und zum Heile der Nachkommen beytragen, wenn ihr durch Belohnungen, Ermunterungen und andere Pflichtmatzige Arbeiten ein verwilderies Land, ein versalzene Stadt oder ein schlectes Dorf zur Weisheit, Religion und allen gesellschaftlichen Tugenden führen wolltet!"

[36] See Witcombe, 185–89; and Sturm, 1:486–88.

Beethoven's reading of Sturm's *Betrachtungen* has frequently been cited as proof that the composer did not adhere to a traditionally Christian concept of God. Lewis Lockwood, for instance, argues that the composer's engagement with Sturm's book reflects his "pantheistic belief in the presence of God in natural things."[37] But pantheism refers specifically to a belief in a God who is *identical* with the natural world, who is immanent in all things. And it is not the same as the idea that God reveals his glory in nature and is present in the natural world—an idea perfectly compatible with orthodox Christian belief. The latter idea is fundamental to Sturm's book, but, as Leon Plantinga has argued, there is simply nothing in Sturm's book that points to pantheism, that is, the notion that natural objects are themselves divine rather than created by God.[38]

One of the meditations in Sturm's book that seems to have particularly captured Beethoven's attention is the meditation for September 1, which refers to "Gottes Allgegenwart" (God's omnipresence).[39] (The phrase "Gottes Allgegenwart" also appears in Christian Schreiber's German text for Beethoven's Mass in C, discussed in the previous chapter.) Beethoven was so taken by this meditation that he wrote in the margin, "poetic material for music" (*poetischer Stoff zu einer Musik*). But divine omnipresence is not the same as pantheism: God can be everywhere but still be distinct from the created order.

Regardless of whether they explicitly advance a pantheist interpretation of the text, attempts to de-Christianize Sturm's *Betrachtungen* are particularly puzzling given that the book contains explicit, unambiguous references to Jesus. To cite just one example, the meditation for September 18, which I have quoted above as an example of Sturm's concern for ethical conduct, encourages the reader to turn specifically to the person of Jesus as the solution to the moral deficiencies of society. The title of the meditation, "Der Weinstock" (The grapevine), is a clear reference to John 15:1, where Jesus describes himself as the "true vine." Within this meditation, Beethoven marked a passage suggesting that it is Jesus whom people should follow in order to make society better: "Jesus, who was transplanted as a lean grain of rice to an unfruitful land, brought those fruits which proved a blessing

---

[37] Lockwood, *Beethoven*, 403.
[38] Plantinga, "Beethoven, Napoleon, and Political Romanticism," 495: "While we may detect a certain pantheistic tinge in some of Sturm's exultations [about nature], in the end he urges an orthodox theist response to natural wonders."
[39] See Witcombe, "Beethoven's Private God," 199–201; and Sturm, *Betrachtungen* (1811), 2:182.

for the whole world. And through his example he showed us that one could live poorly, despised and miserable in the world, but can nevertheless foster God's honor and the best in men."[40] As we shall see in the next chapter, Sturm's insistence here on a close connection between ethical conduct and belief in Jesus resonates with the theology of Johann Michael Sailer.

Elsewhere in Sturm's text, the figure of Jesus is also closely linked to stoicism in the face of suffering and to spiritual preparation for a Christian death. As discussed in the previous chapter, this is a theme prominent in Beethoven's Gellert Lieder and *Christus am Ölberge*, as well as the Heiligenstadt Testament, and one that would have been of special personal relevance for him given his physical ailments. Among the passages Beethoven marked in the book are these three:

> Who knows whether your name is on the list of those whom death will take from the world? And now I leave it to the decision of your own heart. What would you wish you had done if in sleep you were put before the judgment seat of Jesus?[41]

> From now on, let nothing terrify you, but rather conquer every fear and all mistrust through faith in the almighty Father of heaven and of earth, who has become your consoling father through Jesus.[42]

> Would that the whole world of bodies be able to be destroyed, than that my soul, which is redeemed by Jesus, should perish.[43]

Next to the last of these passages, Beethoven wrote in the margin, "Zülln," an Austrian dialectical variant of "Zille," meaning a barge or small boat. One

---

[40] See Witcombe, 206–9; and Sturm, 2:239: "Jesus, der als ein dürres Reis in ein unfruchtbares Land verpflanzt war, brachte solche Früchte, die der ganzen Welt zum Segen gereichten. Und er zeigte uns mit seinem Beyspiele, daß man arm, verachtet und elend in der Welt leben, aber dennoch die Ehre Gottes und das Beste der Menschen befördern könne."

[41] Meditation for January 30. See Witcombe, 121–22, and Sturm, 1:34: "Wer weiß? steht nicht auch dein Name auf der Liste derjenigen, welche der Tod aus der Welt nehmen wird? Und nun überlasse ich es der Entscheidung deines eigenen Herzens. Was wünschtest du gethan zu haben, wenn du im Schlafe vor den Richterstuhl Jesu gerückt würdest?" I have amended Witcombe's translation here.

[42] Meditation for April 2. See Witcombe, 149–52; and Sturm, 1:258: "Von nun an laß dir vor nichts grauen, sondern besiege jede Furcht und jedes Mißtrauen durch den Glauben an den allmächtigen Vater des Himmels und der Erden, welcher durch Jesum dein versöhnter Vater worden ist."

[43] Meditation for April 16. See Witcombe, 153–54; and Sturm, 1:294: "Eher wird die ganze Körperwelt vernichtet werden können, als daß meine Seele, die durch Jesum erlöset worden, zu Grunde gehe sollte." I have amended Witcombe's translation here. This quotation comes from a larger passage that presents an argument for the immortality of the soul.

wonders if this cryptic word might refer to the gospel story of Jesus calming a storm while sailing on a small boat with his disciples, a story that is meant to teach the believer to trust in Jesus even when one's life is threatened.[44] Beethoven marked many other passages in Sturm's book concerning the importance of maintaining one's faith when faced with suffering. The very first meditation, for January 1, is about trusting that God will provide one with friends even in times of suffering.[45] (In response to this meditation, Beethoven wrote "Ach, Ich habe zu ...," though this utterance is too fragmentary for its meaning even to be guessed at.) The meditations for January 27 and May 17 both ask the reader to reflect on the brevity of life.[46] The latter emphasizes, too, the Christian belief in resurrection: "You must die, / In order to live."[47] The meditation for March 27 speaks of embracing God's will when it comes to death:

> I have surrendered myself unto him
> To die and to live:
> How and when he desire
> I live or die.[48]

Death features prominently, too, in the meditation for May 24.[49] Here, Sturm's phrase "Dann eil ich dir entgegen" (Then I hasten toward you [God]) bears a striking resemblance to the line "Stündlich eil' ich zu dem Grabe" (With each hour I hasten toward the grave) in "Vom Tode," the fourth song in the Gellert Lieder, and also to "Mit Freuden eil ich dem Tode entgegen" (Joyfully I go to meet Death) in the Heiligenstadt Testament.[50] In the same meditation, Sturm writes, "Des Lebens frische Blüthe / Vermodre nur im Staub" (Life's fresh blossoms / Only rot in the dust). This metaphorical use of dust to evoke death recalls its use in Schreiber's German text for Beethoven's Mass in C, discussed in the previous chapter, where dust is employed as a symbol for human lowliness and sinfulness, of which death is the ultimate sign. Dust is also evoked in two of the songs in the Gellert Lieder. In "Die

---

[44] See Matthew 8:23–27, Mark 4:35–41, and Luke 8:22–25.
[45] See Witcombe, "Beethoven's Private God," 98; and Sturm, *Betrachtungen* (1811), 1:1–4.
[46] See Witcombe, 119–20, 164–66; and Sturm, 1:75–77, 376–79.
[47] See Witcombe, 164–66; and Sturm, 1:379: "Du müssest sterben, / Also zu leben."
[48] See Witcombe, 139–45; and Sturm, 1:242: "Ihm hab ich mich ergeben, / Zu sterben und zu leben: / Wie und wann er gebeut / Ich lebe oder sterbe."
[49] See Witcombe, 167–71; and Sturm, 1:397–400.
[50] "The Heiligenstadt Testament," in Anderson, *Letters to Beethoven*, 1351–54, at 1353 (*BGA* no. 106, p. 123).

Ehre Gottes," the poem asks, "Kannst du der Wesen unzählbare Heere, / Den kleinsten Staub fühllos beschaun?" (Can you contemplate without feeling the innumerable armies of beings, / The tiniest dust?). And "Gottes Macht" contains the lines "Ein jeder Staub, den du hast werden lassen, / Verkündigt seines Schöpfers Macht" (Each piece of dust that you have allowed to come into being / Proclaims the power of its creator).

Beethoven's reading of Sturm's *Betrachtungen* thus should not be taken as proof that his worldview was distant from Christianity. Moreover, Sturm's central preoccupation—that the natural world reflects God's glory—overlapped with one of the key concerns of the German Catholic Enlightenment. Though Sturm himself was a Protestant rather than a Catholic, his work was hardly unknown among German Catholics. I have found at least one edition of the book that includes on its title page a note that it was published specifically for Catholic consumption ("für katholische Christen herausgegeben") by one Bernard Galura: see figure 4.1. The edition even includes an official statement of approval, or imprimatur, from the very important German electoral archdiocese of Trier (see figure 4.2):

> The excellent work, Sturm's *Betrachtungen*, is produced in this edition also for reliable use by Catholics, and not only contains nothing against Catholic dogmatic or moral teachings, but in general it merits promotion especially by pastors, as a schoolbook, a reader, an educational book to be recommended to the people for their enlightenment.

Though the cover indicates that this edition was printed in Augsburg in 1813, the imprimatur is dated 1803, suggesting that the edition was a reprint. The existence of this edition, especially with its enthusiastic imprimatur, indicates that Sturm's *Betrachtungen* was not only considered entirely compatible with Catholicism at the time, but might even have been widely read among German Catholics—an unsurprising fact given the ecumenical outlook of the Catholic Enlightenment and its openness to Protestant writings.

Quotations from Non-Christian Sources in Beethoven's *Tagebuch*

In addition to the annotations he made in his copy of Sturm's *Betrachtungen*, Beethoven's engagement with the text is demonstrated by the fact that he

Figure 4.1 Cover of an edition for Catholic readers of Christoph Christian Sturm's *Betrachtungen über die Werke Gottes*, edited by Bernard Galura (Augsburg, 1813). Reproduced from the original held by the Department of Special Collections of the Hesburgh Libraries of the University of Notre Dame.

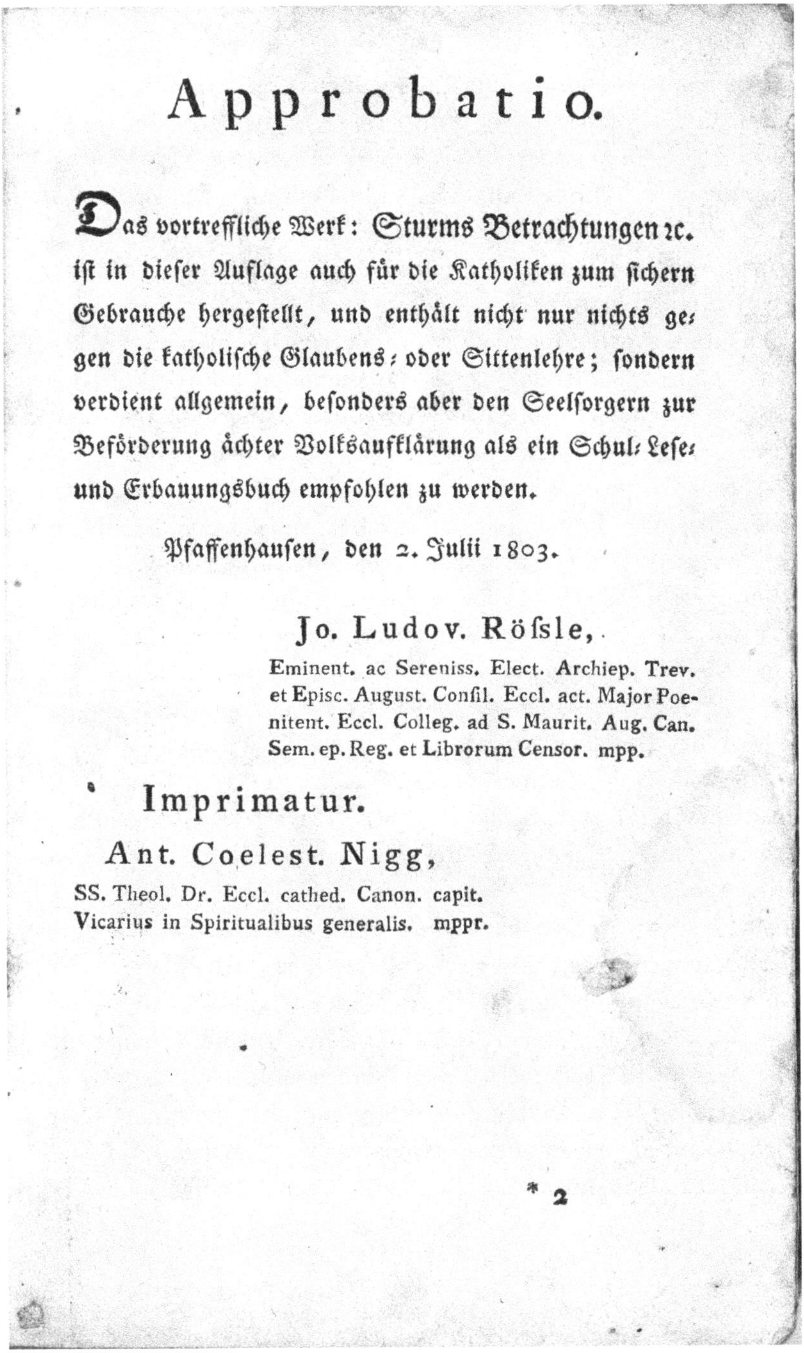

Approbatio.

Das vortreffliche Werk: Sturms Betrachtungen ꝛc. ist in dieser Auflage auch für die Katholiken zum sichern Gebrauche hergestellt, und enthält nicht nur nichts gegen die katholische Glaubens- oder Sittenlehre; sondern verdient allgemein, besonders aber den Seelsorgern zur Beförderung ächter Volksaufklärung als ein Schul- Lese- und Erbauungsbuch empfohlen zu werden.

Pfaffenhausen, den 2. Julii 1803.

Jo. Ludov. Rößle,

Eminent. ac Sereniss. Elect. Archiep. Trev. et Episc. August. Consil. Eccl. act. Major Poenitent. Eccl. Colleg. ad S. Maurit. Aug. Can. Sem. ep. Reg. et Librorum Censor. mpp.

Imprimatur.

Ant. Coelest. Nigg,

SS. Theol. Dr. Eccl. cathed. Canon. capit. Vicarius in Spiritualibus generalis. mppr.

Figure 4.2 Statement of ecclesiastical approval in a Catholic edition of Christoph Christian Sturm's *Betrachtungen über die Werke Gottes*, edited by Bernard Galura (Augsburg, 1813). Reproduced from the original held by the Department of Special Collections of the Hesburgh Libraries of the University of Notre Dame.

wrote out a quotation from Sturm's book in his *Tagebuch*. (Indeed, the quotation is the very last entry in the *Tagebuch*.) This quotation comes from the meditation for December 29, which Beethoven also marked in his copy of Sturm's book: "Thus I want to calmly submit myself to all changes, and to place my trust only in your unchangeable goodness, oh God! / In you, Unchangeable One! In you / My soul shall rejoice. / Be my rock, God! Be my light, / Eternally my trust!"[51]

In the context of the *Tagebuch* as a whole, which contains material copied down from many different sources, the quotation from Sturm is unusual in coming from an ostensibly Christian source. Otherwise, the *Tagebuch* is noteworthy for drawing from a diverse variety of sources of a religious or at least broadly spiritual nature, mainly from non-Christian texts. For this reason, it has often been used to stress Beethoven's distance from Christian belief, never mind Catholicism specifically. Maynard Solomon, for instance, describes the *Tagebuch* as representing a "complex, apparently random search for religious meaning in Eastern and Egyptian ritual, Classical mythology, and Christian theology."[52] And he takes pains to stress that the diversity of religious sources in the *Tagebuch* is indicative of Beethoven's rejection of traditional Christianity: "His even-handed acceptance of Christian, Eastern, and Greco-Roman religious conceptions is typical of both Romantic and Enlightenment viewpoints, which rejected the authority of the church while postulating that religious truth is independent of its formal manifestations."[53]

In the context of the complex cultural-historical period shaped by the Catholic Enlightenment, however, an interest in non-Christian religions was not at all unusual among self-identifying German Catholics. As an illustration of this phenomenon, we shall discuss in the next chapter a book by Johann Michael Sailer that Beethoven owned, *Goldkörner der Weisheit und Tugend*. But it should be pointed out that at the time engagement with non-Christian thought occurred even among more conservative Catholics not aligned with the Catholic Enlightenment. The Romantic writer and philosopher Friedrich

---

[51] See Witcombe, "Beethoven's Private God," 217; and Sturm, *Betrachtungen* (1811), 2:565: "Gelassen will ich mich also allen Veränderungen unterwerfen, und nur auf deine unwandelbare Güte, o Gott! mein ganzes Vertrauen setzen. / Dein, Unwandelbarer! dein / Soll sich meine Seele freun. / Sey mein Fels, Gott! sey mein Licht, / Ewig meine Zuversicht!" The entry in the *Tagebuch* is no. 171, c. 1818.
[52] Solomon, "Quest for Faith," 223.
[53] Solomon, "Beethoven's Tagebuch," 236. For similar views, see Lodes, "'So träumte mir,'" 185–86; and Lockwood, *Beethoven*, 403.

Schlegel (1772–1829), whose prominence in the Catholic Restoration will be discussed in greater detail below, published in April 1808 a highly influential study of ancient Indian religion entitled *Über die Sprache und Weisheit der Indier* (On the language and wisdom of the Indians).[54] He did so during the same week that he converted to Catholicism.[55] Evidence from the conversation books suggests that Beethoven himself was very likely aware of the existence of Schlegel's book, though this evidence comes from 1823, several years after the composer made his last entry in his *Tagebuch*.[56] As Robert Bruce Cowan has pointed out, despite Schlegel's fascination with and apparent respect for the traditional Indian religions of Hinduism and Buddhism, he ultimately regarded them as imperfect versions of Christianity, for which they paved the way.[57] In this regard, Schlegel's attitude was shared by other German Romantics such as Novalis and Schelling.[58] Cowan's reading of Schlegel's text accords with the views of Schlegel's contemporaries. In his essay "The Romantic School," Heinrich Heine remarked of the work: "My only criticism is the ulterior motive behind the book. It was written in the interests of Catholicism. These people had rediscovered in the Indian poems not merely the mysteries of Catholicism, but the whole Catholic hierarchy as well and its struggles with secular authority."[59] Earlier in the same essay, Heine claimed that Goethe, too, "suspected Catholic wile" in the efforts of Schlegel and his associates to study Sanskrit.[60]

Might Beethoven's interest in non-Christian religions in the *Tagebuch* have been motivated by a similar spirit, at least in the superficial sense of a desire to find common ground between Catholicism and more culturally remote religious traditions? It is noteworthy that few, if any, of the ostensibly non-Christian quotations in the *Tagebuch* contain religious messages that conflict with traditional Christian teaching.[61] This is true even of the quotations drawn from Hindu texts, a sampling of which I quote here:

---

[54] On the impact of Schlegel's work, see Cowan, "Fear of Infinity," 333–35.
[55] Cowan, 322.
[56] *BCB* 3:85–86 (*BKh* 2:348), January 30–February 6, 1823; and *BCB* 3:114 (*BKh* 3:23), c. February 6/7–12, 1823. See also *BCB* 3:85n22, 114n33.
[57] Cowan, "Fear of Infinity," esp. 322–25, 333–36.
[58] Cowan, 322.
[59] Heine, "Romantic School," 49.
[60] Heine, 43.
[61] The same might be said of the purportedly Egyptian quotations discussed in this book's introduction, which Schindler claimed Beethoven kept on his desk.

144 THE CATHOLIC BEETHOVEN

Free from all passion and desire, that is the Mighty One. He alone. No one is greater than He.[62]

O God [*Gottheit*] ... You are the true, eternally blessed, unchangeable light of all times and spaces.[63]

All things flowed clear and pure from God [*Gott*]. If afterwards I become darkened through passion for evil, I returned, after manifold repentance and purification, to the elevated and pure source, to the Godhead [*Gottheit*].[64]

God [Gott] *is immaterial, He is above all conception; as He is invisible, He can have no form; but from what we behold of His works, we may conclude that He is eternal, omnipotent, knowing all things, present everywhere.*[65]

For God [*Gott*], time absolutely does not exist.[66]

That the Christian God is eternal, infinite, noncorporeal, not bound by space and time, are facts taken for granted in traditional Christian theology. Solomon has argued that the concept of timelessness emphasized in such quotations is more compatible with Eastern religion than with Christianity, and connects this idea, in turn, to the sense of timelessness he perceives in some of the transcendent music in Beethoven's late style.[67] Birgit Lodes has applied Solomon's view to an analysis of the op. 127 quartet, arguing that this work creates a sense of "mythic" time at odds with traditional Christian conceptions of time.[68] But there is nothing about divine timelessness that

---

[62] *Tagebuch* no. 61a, c. 1815, quotation from a commentary on the *Rig-Veda* (Beethoven's emphasis): "Was frey ist von aller Lust und Begier[,] das ist der Mächtige[.] Er allein. Kein Größerer ist, als Er."
[63] *Tagebuch* no. 61b, c. 1815, quotation from a Brahman hymn: "O Gottheit[,] du bist das wahre[,] ewig selige[,] unwandelbare Licht aller Zeiten und Räume."
[64] *Tagebuch* no. 63a, c. 1815, possibly Beethoven's paraphrase of Brahman texts, including the *Bhagavad Gita*: "Aus Gott floß alles rein und lauter aus. Werd' ich nochmals durch Leidenschaft zum Bösen verdunkelt[,] kehrte ich nach vielfacher Büßung und Reinigung zur ersten erhabenen[,] reinen Quelle, zur Gottheit zurück."
[65] *Tagebuch* no. 93b, c. 1816, quotation of spurious Indian origin (Beethoven's emphasis): "Gott ist immateriel[,] deßwegen geht er über jeden Begriff; da er unsichtbar ist, so kann er keine Gestalt haben. Aber aus dem, was wir von seinem Werken gewahr werden, können wir schließen, daß er ewig, allmächtig, allwissend, allgegenwärtig ist."
[66] *Tagebuch* no. 94d, c. 1816, quotation from an anthology of Hindu sayings compiled by Sir William Jones: "Zeit findet durchaus bey Gott nicht statt."
[67] Solomon, "Intimations of the Sacred," 207.
[68] Lodes, "'So träumte mir.'"

conflicts with traditional Christian ideas of God. A Hindu text about reincarnation, for instance, might have been incompatible with Christianity, but Beethoven does not seem to have copied one down. Indeed, the one reference to life after death in the *Tagebuch* is in a quotation from a tragedy by Amandus Müllner that seems to refer to the *resurrection* of the dead: "Dost thou ask the cause when stars rise and set? / Only *what* happens is clear / The *why* will become apparent / When the dead arise!"[69] In any event, as Ernst Herttrich has suggested, one should not be surprised that the *Tagebuch* quotes more from other religions than it does from Christianity, given that Christianity would have been the default religion of Beethoven's culture, and the religion in which he was raised.[70]

More problematic for my attempt here to show the *Tagebuch*'s compatibility with Christian belief might be the appearance of the German term "Gottheit," which Solomon translates variously as "God" or "Godhead," in the Hindu quotations cited above. Beethoven himself uses the word "Gottheit" to address God twice in the Heiligenstadt Testament (in Emily Anderson's translation below, the word is rendered as "Almighty God"):

> Almighty God [*Gottheit*], who look down into my innermost soul, you see into my heart and you know that it is filled with love for humanity and a desire to do good.[71]

> For so long now the inner echo of real joy has been unknown to me—Oh when—oh when, Almighty God [*Gottheit*]—shall I be able to hear and feel this echo again in the temple of Nature and in contact with humanity.[72]

"Gottheit" also occurs in the famous programmatic title of the third movement of Beethoven's op. 132 string quartet: "Heiliger Dankgesang eines Genesenen an die Gottheit" (Holy song of thanksgiving of a convalescent to God).[73]

---

[69] *Tagebuch* no. 7d, c. 1813 (Beethoven's emphasis): "Fragst du nach der Ursach[,] wenn / Sterne auf und unter gehn? / Hier ist das geschieht nur klar / Das Warum wird offenbar[,] / Wenn die Todten auferstehn!"

[70] Herttrich, "Beethoven und die Religion," 36.

[71] "The Heiligenstadt Testament," in Anderson, *Letters to Beethoven*, 1351–54, at 1353 (*BGA* no. 106, p. 122). "Gottheit du siehst herab auf mein inneres, du kennst es, du weist daß menschenliebe und neigung zum Wohltun drin Hausen."

[72] "Heiligenstadt Testament," 1354 (*BGA* no. 106, p. 123). "So lange schon ist der wahren Freude inniger widerhall mir fremd—o wann—o Wann o Gottheit—kann ich im Tempel der Natur und der Menschen ihn [den Widerhall] wider fühlen."

[73] The translation of "Gottheit" in this title as "Godhead" is the most common in the Beethoven literature, though "Divinity" is sometimes used as an alternative.

The ambiguity of this term might be suggestive of a desire on Beethoven's part to distance himself from Christian tradition. However, the definition of the word provided by the mid-nineteenth-century *Deutsches Wörterbuch*, published by the Grimm brothers, points to a more nuanced meaning.[74] The *Wörterbuch* identifies "Gottheit" as a common substitute for "God" during the Enlightenment and in subsequent periods. Though the word did imply a more general and abstract idea of the divine that transcended particular dogmas and religious confessions, it did not necessarily exclude the concept of God rooted in Christian revelation. (Indeed, in the next chapter, I shall demonstrate an occurrence of the word in Johann Michael Sailer's writings.) Within the complicated historical context of the Catholic Enlightenment, this situation makes perfect sense, for we recall that the boundaries between the secular Enlightenment and the Catholic Enlightenment were quite porous, and that openness to non-Catholic religious beliefs and general religious tolerance were important ideas associated with the Catholic Enlightenment.

The eclecticism of Beethoven's religious interests in his *Tagebuch* thus cannot be regarded as a sign that he had separated himself from Catholicism. His youthful exposure to Catholic Enlightenment ideas might well have taught him that being a Catholic need not preclude being open to ideas from outside Catholicism.

Feßler's *Ansichten von Religion und Kirchenthum*

In a more extreme manner, an openness to different religious perspectives was also the distinctive feature of the life of Ignaz Aurelius Feßler (1756–1839), the second of the two religious writers we are focusing on in this chapter. Feßler's life story involved a complicated journey that was emblematic of—perhaps even a caricature of—the cultural and religious upheaval of the period.[75] Feßler was born in the small Austrian town of Zurndorf, in Burgenland, near the Hungarian border. His mother was a devout Baroque Catholic, yet was open to Lutheran, especially Pietist, spiritual influences. Feßler was educated by the Jesuits and nearly joined that order before

---

[74] The Grimm *Wörterbuch* is available online at woerterbuchnetz.de/DWB/, accessed August 1, 2024.
[75] My overview of Feßler's life is based on Barton, "Ignatius Aurelius Feßler."

changing his mind and becoming a Capuchin priest. After being exposed to reformist writings associated with the German Catholic Enlightenment, Feßler became disillusioned with monastic life and with the Baroque Catholicism in which he had been raised. He began to express public support for Jansenist and Febronian ideas, as well as the Josephinist reforms that his order officially opposed. Expelled by the Capuchins for his perceived radical leanings, Feßler eventually moved to Berlin, where, around 1791, he began to identify as a Lutheran, though he did not officially convert until many years later. In the meantime, he became an active Freemason, and was considered an important figure in Berlin intellectual circles. Feßler was attracted to Kant's philosophy, and even exchanged correspondence with Kant. Later, however, his reading of Herder's works led him away from Kantian thought, and, in 1816, the death of his daughter Angelica Maria provoked in him a profound conversion experience. He finally converted to Lutheranism and became a pastor in that confession, while moving away from Freemasonry, as well as many of the unorthodox theological positions that he had previously espoused. In 1819, Feßler became the Lutheran bishop of the missionary diocese of Saratov, a city in Russia with a significant population of ethnic Germans, and remained in this position for the rest of his life.

Given the evolving and eclectic nature of Feßler's religious allegiances, it is important for our purposes to focus specifically on the content of the specific book by him that Beethoven owned: the three-volume *Ansichten von Religion und Kirchenthum*. Beethoven's copy of Feßler's *Ansichten* was a first edition, published in 1805.[76] It is unclear when the composer actually purchased the book, but we know he probably made use of it in 1819. In a manuscript now at the Berlin State Library, Beethoven copied out the Latin text of three parts of the Mass—the Credo, Sanctus, and Agnus Dei—alongside a German translation.[77] Two of the manuscript's six folios (2^v and 3^r) also contain fragmentary musical sketches for the *Missa solemnis*. As Birgit Lodes has recently demonstrated, the translation of the Mass text in this manuscript comes straight from Feßler's book, the second volume of which contains a

---

[76] A digitization of Feßler's book in this 1805 edition is available online at https://onb.digital/result/107B3416 (vol. 1), https://onb.digital/result/107B340D (vol. 2), and https://onb.digital/result/107B33F0 (vol. 3), accessed August 1, 2024.

[77] Berlin, Staatsbibliothek, Mus.ms.autogr. Beethoven, L.v. 35,25. On the very first page of the manuscript, a description of its contents appears in Anton Schindler's hand that dates the document to the year 1818. As Birgit Lodes argues, however, Schindler was likely to have been mistaken, since Beethoven could not have started work on the *Missa* before 1819, when he learned about Rudolph's appointment in Olmütz: see Lodes, "Composing with a Dictionary," 190.

full German translation of the Mass as an appendix.[78] There are hardly any differences between the texts except for occasional spelling differences, and one or two missing words—minor discrepancies that can easily occur when copying by hand. The manuscript even shows that Beethoven reproduced an authorial or typographical error in Feßler's translation. For the Latin "Deum verum de Deo vero" (true God from true God), which would be translated literally into German as "wahrer Gott vom wahren Gott," Feßler simply has "wahren Gott," which makes no grammatical sense. Lodes also notes that full German translations of the Mass Ordinary were rare in prayer books during Beethoven's time.[79] More common were books containing prayers to be said by the laity while the priest and choir recited or sang the actual Mass text. There did exist translations of the Mass that were comparatively easier to obtain than Feßler's, but none of these was used by Beethoven.

Aside from establishing Beethoven's engagement with Feßler's *Ansichten*, the manuscript just described provides important insights into Beethoven's compositional approach to the *Missa solemnis*, and I shall return to it in chapter 6. It should also be noted in passing that Beethoven's interest in Feßler seems to have been rekindled during the last years of his life. The conversation books indicate that in February 1823 Beethoven sought to purchase two historical novels by Feßler: *Marc-Aurel* and *Aristides und Themistocles*.[80] Unlike *Ansichten*, these books were not explicitly religious in nature. Both in genre and content, however, they do evoke political and religious ideas associated with the German Catholic Enlightenment, and will be discussed further in the conclusion.

The inventory of Beethoven's library made after his death indicates that the Viennese authorities confiscated his copy of Feßler's book, presumably because it was banned by the censors.[81] This fact gives the impression that the work was extremely radical for its time, but a close examination of its content reveals a more complicated picture. Despite leaving the Catholic Church for Lutheranism, Feßler's thought, as has been hinted at above, was heavily influenced by the German Catholic Enlightenment. In *Ansichten*, however, this influence is balanced by important departures from Catholic Enlightenment ideas, especially those associated with Josephinism. Feßler,

---

[78] Lodes, "Composing with a Dictionary," 190–201, esp. 191–93. See also Feßler, *Ansichten*, 2:409–49; the translation of the Credo begins on p. 424.
[79] Lodes, "Composing with a Dictionary," 191.
[80] *BCB* 3:147 (*BKh* 3:56), February 12–21/22, 1823.
[81] See *Schätzungsprotokoll* no. 16; and Albrecht, *Letters to Beethoven*, 3:233.

as we shall see, objected to excessively rationalist approaches to religion. And though he had earlier in his life been outspoken in his support for Josephinism, *Ansichten* hints at a more ambivalent attitude toward state involvement in church government. The fact that *Ansichten* was written during Feßler's Masonic period creates an additional temptation to overstate the book's radicalism. But to return to a point made previously, Masonic beliefs and Christianity were by no means mutually exclusive during this era. In Feßler's case, the compatibility of Christianity with Freemasonry attains even greater importance given his particular approach to Masonic thought, for Feßler devoted himself to reforming Freemasonry specifically so that it would become more closely aligned with Christian belief. These efforts to Christianize Masonry did not go down well with his fellow Masons, and as a result Feßler was forced to step down from leadership roles within Masonic circles in Berlin.[82] It is noteworthy also that Feßler does not seem to have shared the progressive *political* views held by many prominent Masons. Indeed, *Ansichten* does not contain any explicit political content. The confiscation of Beethoven's copy seems likely to have been prompted by the perceived unorthodoxy of its theological views rather than any kind of political subversiveness.

The fundamental goal of Feßler's *Ansichten* is to present an ecumenical and irenic vision of Christianity as a whole. Though written ostensibly from a Protestant perspective for a Protestant audience, in this regard Feßler's book can also be tied to the ecumenism of the Catholic Enlightenment, especially given its author's own formation within that context. Peter Barton, a scholar of Feßler's thought, has described the book as a strange blend of a number of disparate theological and philosophical influences, befitting Feßler's itinerant spiritual journey. These influences include Baroque Catholicism, Jansenism and Josephinism, and Freemasonry, as well as Kant, Spinoza, Lessing, Herder, Schelling, and Schleiermacher.[83] *Ansichten* presents a complex, and in many respects startlingly modern, theory of Christian confessions. Feßler's ultimate point is that Christianity is not equivalent to its religious institutions, to any one of its different denominational or confessional traditions. To explain this idea, he makes a distinction

---

[82] Barton, "Ignatius Aurelius Feßler," 122.
[83] Barton, "Ignatius Aurelius Feßlers Wertung," 134–35. This article provides an insightful and detailed overview of Feßler's *Ansichten*, and has been of great assistance to me in understanding the book's contents. In the remainder of this section, citations for Feßler's book (volume and page numbers) will be provided in the main text rather than in the footnotes.

between *Religion*, religion in its essential form, and *Religiosität* (religiosity), or religious practice (1:128–42). *Religion* is presented as an individual and interior act of belief, while *Religiosität* refers to social, communal, and exterior manifestations of *Religion* in religious practices, rituals, and institutions. While *Religion* is necessarily prior to *Religiosität*, Feßler constantly insists that *Religiosität* remains important and useful, as well as unavoidable.[84]

Feßler spends the first of *Ansichten*'s three volumes providing a very thorough history of Christianity from the earliest Christian communities up to the Reformation. His aim is to show that Christianity in its most fundamental and essential sense—Christianity as *Religion*—is an "invisible community of God" (1:viii; *unsichtbare Gemeinde Gottes*). This community endures regardless of the institutional forms and external practices through which Christianity is lived out in the world. In other words, *Religion* always stays the same even as *Religiosität* changes. In the second and third volumes of the book, Feßler then proceeds to explore in detail four varieties of Christianity: Catholicism, Lutheranism, Calvinism, and the Moravian Church (also known as the Moravian Brethren), a small Protestant group that traces its roots to the fifteenth-century followers of Jan Hus in the Czech lands.[85] Barton provides a useful summary of Feßler's overall point in investigating each of these confessions: "Since each confession can only provide a section and partial aspect of the universe of religious insights, the truly religious Christian is justified in and obligated to adopt the religious insights

---

[84] Birgit Lodes has characterized Feßler's book as "argu[ing] that God's spiritual realm exists apart from and above the dogmatic Church or other religious institutions" ("'When I Try,'" 145). But this description is misleading if it is meant to imply that Feßler believed institutional religion was unimportant.

[85] Beethoven himself can be linked to the Moravian Church, but in only tenuous and indirect ways. In July 1810, Breitkopf & Härtel wrote a brief letter to a member of the Moravian Church community in Fulneck, near Leeds, in England (Albrecht no. 151). The letter announces that several new Beethoven works published by Breitkopf would soon be available in England. Another letter by George Thomson to Beethoven, from October 1814, requested that Beethoven compose a set of religious songs in a "simple and natural style" (Albrecht no. 190 / *BGA* 752). Thomson enclosed an example of a work taken from a collection by Christian Ignatius Latrobe, a prominent clergyman of the Moravian Church in England, and an important figure in the dissemination of Continental religious music in that country. (Latrobe had a more famous brother, Benjamin Henry Latrobe, the architect who designed the United States Capitol.) In its modern form, dating back to the 1720s, the Moravian Church was founded by Nikolaus von Zinzendorf (1700–1760), whose nephew Karl von Zinzendorf (1739–1813) left behind a diary that has been cited as a source about musical life in Vienna in the late eighteenth and early nineteenth centuries. See Link, "Zinzendorf, Count Karl Zinzendorf und Pottendorf"; and Link, *National Court Theatre*, 191–398. Sarah Eyerly has recently written about the role of Moravian Church music in North America, especially within the context of missions to indigenous peoples: see *Moravian Soundscapes*, and "Mozart and the Moravians."

of all 'confessions' and to participate in all religious acts and sacraments."[86] Each confession reflects a different side of Christianity, and no one confession exhausts the fullness of the Christian message. At the same time, Feßler believes it is unavoidable that Christians will live out their faith through external institutions—that is, through their respective confessions. Indeed, individual confessions are indispensable as vehicles through which they should nurture and cultivate their faith. Nevertheless, Christians must ultimately see past confessional differences to the one true *Religion* that unites them all. Feßler allows that individuals should join the confession that speaks best to their religious leanings (2:7). In this sense, his conception of religion does have a subjective emphasis. However, his stress on the continued importance of institutional churches suggests that he does not believe religion should be *purely* subjective. Belief matters more than worship in an external sense, but this does not mean that worship is unimportant. *Religion* takes priority over *Religiosität*, but it still requires *Religiosität*.

Feßler's ecumenical recognition of the value of different forms of Christianity reflects the influence of Catholic Enlightenment ideas to which he was exposed in his youth, and can also be seen to represent a more general belief in religious tolerance often associated with the secular Enlightenment. Yet Feßler is explicit in opposing any conception of Enlightenment that threatens Christian belief. This is apparent in his discussion of an idea he calls "wahrer Protestantismus" (3:226–34; true Protestantism).[87] Feßler uses this term to describe the common goal to which all Christian confessions are journeying, in a kind of quasi-Hegelian theory of ecclesiastical history. "Wahrer Protestantismus" does not, however, refer to any institutional Protestant church, not even the Lutheranism that Feßler personally identified with at the time he wrote *Ansichten*. Rather, true Protestantism is

> an interior Protestantism, that expresses itself through no fight against the dogmas of the church, through no contempt for the forms of individual religious cults, through no resistance against [the church as] a social authority.... True and interior Protestantism does not lead the righteous and powerful man away from the church into the cold darkness of a so-called

---

[86] Barton, "Ignatius Aurelius Feßlers Wertung," 135: "Da jedes Kirchentum nur einen Ausschnitt und Teilaspekt des Universums der religiösen Erkenntnisse bieten könne, sei der wahrhaft religiöse Christ berechtigt und verpflichtet, sich die religiösen Erkenntnisse aller „Kirchentümer" anzueignen und an allen religiösen Akten und Sakramenten teilzunehmen." See also Feßler, *Ansichten*, 1:329–75.
[87] See also Feßler, *Ansichten*, 2:6.

religious enlightenment [*Aufklärung*], or into the land of fairies that is a supposed natural religion. But it raises him up above the church, to the bright heights of the infinite, to the view of a religion revealed by the whole universe (3:232).[88]

What Feßler means is that true Protestantism is something that enables Christianity to transcend confessional differences. But he is not simply advocating interconfessional tolerance for its own sake. Instead, Feßler implies that Christians must come together to combat what he perceives as attacks on Christianity from the secular Enlightenment and so-called natural religion. Feßler seeks a kind of "nonpartisan" Christianity (*ohne Partheylichkeit*), focused on unity in fundamental truths (*Religion*) rather than on disagreements over less fundamental issues governing religious practice (*Religiosität*; 3:226). Underlying his whole book is the argument that interconfessional disagreement must give way to a common fight by a unified Christianity against the scourge of irreligion.[89]

Feßler arrives at his discussion of "wahrer Protestantismus" only after a very extended exploration of Catholicism. Indeed, Catholicism occupies the entirety of Feßler's second volume, with discussion of Feßler's three other exemplary confessions—Lutheranism, Calvinism, and the Moravian Church—all squeezed into the third volume. With regard to Catholicism, Feßler makes a distinction between the "essence" or *Wesen* of Catholicism and the "cult" or *Cultus* of Catholicism. This distinction, which is the underlying topic of the entirety of the second volume, seems to parallel his more fundamental distinction between *Religion* and *Religiosität* with regard to Christianity in general. For Feßler, the only doctrines that are part of the *Wesen* of Catholicism are those that have been decided on by an ecumenical council of bishops. Such a position on the nature of church authority, known as episcopalism or conciliarism, was popular during the German Catholic Enlightenment, and it makes sense given Feßler's Jansenist leanings. Neither the Roman Curia nor the pope alone has the authority to make doctrinal

---

[88] "Einen innern Protestantismus, der durch keinen Streit gegen kirchliche Dogmen, durch keine Verachtung gegen Formen des Cultus, durch keinen Widerstand gegen die Social-Autorität [*sic*] sich äußert.... Der wahre und innere Protestantismus den rechtschaffenen und kraftvollen Mann nicht aus der Kirche hinaus, in das kalte Blaue einer sogenannten religiösen Aufklärung, oder in das Feengebiet einer vorgeblichen Naturreligion führ[t], sondern ihn über die Kirche hinauf, zur lichtvollen Höhe des Unendlichen, in der Anschauung des Universums sich offenbarenden Religion erheb[t]."

[89] See Barton, "Ignatius Aurelius Feßlers Wertung," 135, 175–76.

decisions for the universal Church (2:7-12). Feßler unequivocally rejects the idea of papal infallibility, which he describes as an "evil spirit" (*bösen Geist*) and a specter (*Schreckgespenst*), and indeed any grant of excessive authority to the papacy (2:16-21).[90] He also argues that much of traditional Catholic theology, especially of the Thomistic or Augustinian varieties, is not essential to Catholicism (2:9).

Whatever does not belong to the *Wesen* of Catholicism is only part of the *Cultus* of Catholicism (2:184). It is incidental to Catholicism, but not essential to it. Yet Feßler also insists that the things constituting Catholicism's *Cultus* are not therefore invalid, as many Protestants would claim. Nonessential practices should be permitted and encouraged. These include such fundamental Catholic religious beliefs and practices as transubstantiation, the adoration of the Eucharist, and the use of Latin in the liturgy. These practices may not be necessary for salvation, but they are still helpful for cultivating the believer's faith and for binding together a community of believers (2:221-22, 232-33). Feßler even specifically rejects the familiar Protestant (and Enlightenment) critique of such practices as superstitious (2:269-70). One must recognize on the one hand that "all external cults [*Cultus*] are by their very nature anthropomorphic" (2:183).[91] But on the other hand, "all confessions must limit themselves plainly and necessarily to [their respective cults], and without [cults] no church can exist" (2:183).[92] *Cultus* is subordinate to *Wesen* just as *Religion* is subordinate to *Religiosität*. But no external church community can possibly exist without *Religiosität*, and thus Catholicism as *Wesen* also needs Catholicism as *Cultus*. Feßler may hold that the religious beliefs lying behind religious practice take priority over the practice itself. However, this also means, conversely, that religious practice, if inspired by correct beliefs, cannot be condemned outright, even if not *essential* to religion (2:185). This nuanced attitude toward Catholicism as *Cultus* is further apparent in Feßler's defense of clerical celibacy. Though this practice undeniably arose out of particular and contingent historical circumstances, that does not mean it is not useful in preventing a priest's energies from being divided between his congregation and his own family (2:345-47). In addition, despite his rejection of papal infallibility, Feßler defends the papacy as an important bulwark for the Church against secular

---

[90] Feßler goes through a whole catalog of abuses of papal power: see *Ansichten*, 2:175-76.
[91] "Aller äußere Cultus ist seiner Natur nach anthropomorphistisch."
[92] "Auf ihn muß sich alles Kirchenthum schlechthin und unbedingt beschränken, und ohne ihn kann nie eine Kirche bestehen."

political power, especially when that power threatens to corrupt individual bishops (2:302–4). In this regard, Feßler's *Ansichten* seems to depart from Josephinism in its suspicion of excessive state interference in church governance, even if isolated Josephinist influences are still apparent, for instance in Feßler's belief that the number of Catholic holy days should be reduced (2:264–66).

Feßler wants those who reject Catholicism's external practices—Lutherans and Calvinists, for instance—to recognize that those practices are grounded in perfectly good Christian beliefs: "A fair-minded, nonpartisan judge would pay attention not to the sensual forms of the cult [*Cultus*], but to the [religious] disposition which the church through the use of the same cult has expressed in its ancient prayers for so many centuries" (2:270).[93] But a more important reason for Protestants to respect their Catholic counterparts emerges when Feßler engages in somewhat surprising critiques of both Lutheranism and Calvinism.[94] In Feßler's view, Luther, along with his follower Philipp Melancthon, had unintentionally turned subjective freedom into a fundamental religious principle. Feßler approves of Luther's respect for the freedom of individual conscience. But where Luther had erred was in his failure to articulate a coherent concept of church unity. Christian ministers inevitably disagreed about the interpretation of Scripture, and Luther provided no guidance as to how such disputes should be resolved (3:70–71). Lutheranism thus possesses no unified teaching authority, and this is what made it especially susceptible to corruption by Enlightenment rationalism, which Feßler believes had turned Lutheran Christianity into merely a school for ethics, rather than a vehicle for faith in Christ (3:100). While acknowledging Luther's personal sanctity, Feßler, supposedly a Lutheran himself, even goes so far as to declare Luther a dogmatic heretic (3:86). Feßler is less scathing in his critique of Calvinism but takes issue with it on similar grounds. While Calvinism's greater emphasis on the authority of national synods means it does not have problems with church unity to the same extent as Lutheranism, differences among those national synods persist, including on issues as fundamental to Calvinist teaching as predestination (3:107).

---

[93] "Nicht an die sinnlichen Formen des Cultus, sondern an die Gesinnung, welche die Kirche bey dem Gebrauche derselben in ihren so viele Jahrhunderte alten Gebeten ausspricht, und in ihrem Geboten offenbaret, muß sich der gerechte, partheylose Richter halten."
[94] Feßler's characterizations of Lutheranism and Calvinism might strike some readers as inaccurate. Their validity is, however, not our concern here, but rather what they demonstrate about Feßler's ecclesiology.

More importantly for Feßler, Calvin had made the mistake of neglecting the external aspects of religion, and this had also reduced the church to a mere society for ethical instruction (3:110–43).[95]

What Feßler is trying to show is that Lutheranism and Calvinism need to recover some sense of the ecclesiastical unity that he believes is exemplified by Catholicism as *Wesen*. In this regard, these Protestant groups should become more Catholic. This view explains Feßler's insistence that the Reformation should be regarded not as a movement opposed to Catholicism, but one within Catholicism itself (3:7–11). During the Reformation, Lutheranism and Calvinism went too far in distancing themselves from the Catholic Church because they failed to distinguish between Catholicism as *Cultus* and Catholicism as *Wesen*. Even if they wished to depart from the external practices and structures of Catholicism, including papal authority, they ought not to have rejected Catholicism as *Wesen*, especially the idea that there must be some universally recognized council of church leaders possessing the authority to make definitive pronouncements on doctrinal matters (2:105–10, esp. 109).[96] Feßler thus makes the paradoxical argument that in order for Lutheranism and Calvinism to become truly Protestant in the sense of his *wahrer Protestantismus*, they must also aspire to "true Catholicism" (*wahrer Katholicismus*), a term Feßler goes on to use in the same sense as Catholicism as *Wesen* (3:226–24). Feßler's idiosyncratic conception of Catholicism, along with his apparent desire to re-Catholicize Lutheranism and Calvinism according to this conception, explains his praise of both Jansenists within the Catholic Church and the Moravian Church. According to Feßler, in both these communities, the *Wesen* of Catholicism is preserved without rigidity about *Cultus*, or the external aspects of religious practice. The Jansenists and the Moravians both unite true Catholicism with true Protestantism (1:321–24).

Though Feßler had officially left the Catholic Church by the time he wrote the *Ansichten*, both his Jansenist sympathies and his ecumenism were probably rooted in his earlier support for the ideas of the Catholic Enlightenment, especially in its Josephinist form. However, his rejection of a Christianity that emphasized ethics over dogma to an excessive degree, along with his belief in the indispensable role of the Catholic liturgy as an expression of

---

[95] For a useful summary of Feßler's ambivalent views of Calvinism, see Barton, "Ignatius Aurelius Feßlers Wertung," 167–71.
[96] See also Feßler, *Ansichten*, 3:103.

dogma (Catholicism as *Cultus*), appears to diverge to some degree from the Catholic Enlightenment. (Although he was writing as a Lutheran in the *Ansichten*, these views might ironically have found a degree of favor in the eyes of the Catholic Restoration.) Feßler's nuanced views in this regard recall Sturm's explicit view that following Jesus is the starting point for moral conduct. As we shall see in the next chapter, the importance of not separating ethics and dogma was also a central preoccupation of the theology of Johann Michael Sailer. Feßler's conception of Christian unity across denominations as a means of defending Christianity from its secular opponents constitutes an additional point of overlap with Sailer's thought.

Beethoven and the Ascendancy of the Catholic Restoration in Vienna

Though their authors were Protestant rather than Catholic, the main themes in Sturm's *Betrachtungen* and Feßler's *Ansichten* reflect important concerns of the German Catholic Enlightenment: the presence of God in nature, ethical conduct, and ecumenism. These issues, we recall, were also thematized by Beethoven's religious works discussed in the previous chapter. At the same time, some aspects of these texts, especially their emphasis on dogma and a relationship with Christ over ethics, can be read as departing from the Catholic Enlightenment to a certain degree. This situation creates a parallel with Beethoven's depiction of Christ in *Christus am Ölberge*, which I characterized as signaling an openness to more conservative approaches to Catholicism, even if the ideas of the Catholic Enlightenment remained dominant in his outlook. As we shall see in the next chapter, such a nuanced and ultimately partial commitment to the Catholic Enlightenment was also a key feature of the thought of Johann Michael Sailer, whose theology blended elements of the Catholic Enlightenment and Restoration.

The complexity of Beethoven's religious views in the 1800s and 1810s accords with the broader context of the state of religion in Vienna during this period of time. The rise of the Catholic Restoration that had begun in the 1790s, in response to the French Revolution and subsequent military conflicts, became more pronounced in the second half of the 1800s, especially as a result of Napoleon's invasions of Vienna in 1805 and 1809. The reputation of the Church among ordinary people improved significantly because of the active role it played in uniting society against the French threat.[97] When Napoleon invaded, for instance, it was the Catholic clergy who negotiated with the French emperor after the Habsburg court had fled.[98] French troops also angered the local Viennese population by seizing church property and disrupting religious services during their occupation.[99] The Habsburgs, for their part, were happy to play up the centrality of Catholicism to the cultural identity of the Austrian Empire—a new entity created after the dissolution of the Holy Roman Empire—and to stress the contrast between the Austrians and the apparently "godless" French aggressors.[100]

A pivotal moment in the advance of the Catholic Restoration in Vienna was the arrival in 1808 of a Redemptorist priest named Klemens Maria Hofbauer (1751–1820), who came to the city after previously serving as a missionary in Poland. Hofbauer, who would be made a patron saint of Vienna after his death, was perhaps the most important Catholic Restoration figure in Vienna during Beethoven's time.[101] His preaching attracted a number of prominent Romantic artists, most notably Friedrich Schlegel (1772–1829), whose writings on Indian religion I have discussed above. Schlegel, a member of the original Jena Romantic circle, had converted to Catholicism and moved to Vienna shortly before Hofbauer's arrival. His wife Dorothea (1764–1839) was similarly attracted to Hofbauer. A writer herself, she was the daughter of Moses Mendelssohn and had converted to Catholicism with her husband (in her case from Judaism rather than from Protestantism).[102] Other members of the group included Zacharias Werner (1768–1823), another writer, and the painter Philipp Veit (1793–1877), who founded the Nazarene movement in the visual arts, later to become an important influence on the pre-Raphaelites in England.[103] (Veit was Dorothea's son from a previous marriage.) Another artistic figure associated with Hofbauer was the poet Clemens Brentano (1778–1842). Brentano's obsession with religious mysticism was reflected most clearly in his role as secretary to a stigmatic nun

---

[97] Loidl, *Geschichte des Erzbistums Wien*, 203. See also Hänsel, *Geistliche Restauration*, 20.
[98] Loidl, *Geschichte des Erzbistums Wien*, 203–6.
[99] Loidl, 204–6.
[100] See Loidl, 207; and Coreth, *Pietas Austriaca*, 26.
[101] On Hofbauer's role in Vienna, see Walker, "Zacharias Werner"; Bunnell, *Before Infallibility*, 44–50; and Loidl, *Geschichte des Erzbistums Wien*, 211–16. For a book-length biography of Hofbauer, see Weiss, *Begegnungen mit Klemens Maria Hofbauer*.
[102] On Dorothea Schlegel, see Meyer, "Judaism and Christianity," 179–80.
[103] See Loidl, *Geschichte des Erzbistums Wien*, 211–16; and Walker, "Zacharias Werner," 35. On the Nazarene painters, see Grewe, *Nazarenes* and *Painting the Sacred*; and Frank, *German Romantic Painting Redefined*.

named Anna Katharina Emmerich (1774–1824), whose spiritual visions he noted down and published.[104] Beethoven corresponded with Brentano in 1813 and 1814, and may have met him in person at least once, in 1811.[105] And as will be discussed further in the conclusion, Beethoven also sought out writings by Zacharias Werner. Along with the highly sentimental portrayal of Christ in *Christus am Ölberge* described in the previous chapter, these engagements with Brentano and Werner might be small signs of an openness to the Catholic Restoration on the composer's part, even if on the whole the characteristics of his religious music and the content of religious books in his library suggest that his outlook was still shaped predominantly by the Catholic Enlightenment.

At least initially, the appeal of Hofbauer's preaching was largely limited to the educated middle and upper classes, though by the 1820s, the conservative vision of the Church that he represented would become more widespread.[106] Despite the growing political and cultural conservatism associated with the response to the French Revolution, Josephinism continued to be very influential in Vienna into the first few decades of the nineteenth century. The strength of the Habsburg bureaucracy, which had gained a lot of power because of Josephinism, was the main reason for this.[107] Moreover, even more religiously conservative emperors were reluctant to cede whatever powers Josephinism had won them over the Church in their domains.[108] Though one would expect a conservative cleric to have been politically useful for an authoritarian regime seeking legitimacy from the Church, Hofbauer actually had a tense relationship with the government.[109] Notwithstanding his authoritarian reputation, Metternich was actually highly suspicious of religion because of its potential for encouraging social instability.[110] The Viennese police placed Hofbauer under surveillance, fearing that his preaching would cause public disorder.[111] The authorities were also suspicious of his repeated

---

[104] Hänsel, *Geistliche Restauration*, 76–82. See also M. L. Anderson, "Limits of Secularization," 664.
[105] See Albrecht nos. 175, 179 (*BGA* nos. 683, 689); Anderson no. 296 (*BGA* no. 485); and E. Anderson, *Letters of Beethoven*, 1:313n3. Clemens's name also appears in an entry in Beethoven's conversation books from early 1819; see *BCB* 1:33 (*BKh* 1:53).
[106] See Bunnell, *Before Infallibility*, 48; and Loidl, *Geschichte des Erzbistums Wien*, 211.
[107] Beales, *Enlightenment and Reform*, 291.
[108] Beales, *Joseph II*, 2:680–81. After Cardinal Migazzi's death in 1803, the next three archbishops of Vienna were all to varying degrees still adherents of Josephinism: Sigismund Anton Graf von Hohenwart (1803–1820), Leopold Maximilian Graf von Firmian (1822–1831), and Vincenz Eduard Milde (1832–1853). See Loidl, *Geschichte des Erzbistums Wien*, 200–1, 219, 222.
[109] See Loidl, *Geschichte des Erzbistums Wien*, 44–50.
[110] Beller, *Habsburg Monarchy*, 36.
[111] Walker, "Zacharias Werner," 40.

attacks on the Josephine church reforms, which he derided for their subversion of papal authority and their suppression of popular devotions that had flourished under Baroque Catholicism.[112] His follower Schlegel, on the other hand, served as a high-ranking official in Metternich's government. In this regard, the contrast between Hofbauer and Schlegel in terms of their relationship with the Habsburg authorities provides a useful illustration of the complexities of the Catholic Restoration discussed in chapter 1.

In both Vienna and elsewhere in the German Catholic lands, conservatives like Hofbauer competed with more progressive figures in a fight for Catholicism's identity in an age of political and cultural turmoil. In addition to churchmen still loyal to the Josephine reforms were some who thought the Catholic Enlightenment had actually not gone far enough. Georg Hermes (1775–1831), for instance, taught at the University of Bonn in the 1820s, and focused on reconciling Catholicism with Kantian philosophy, an approach that was later condemned by the Vatican.[113] Ignaz Heinrich von Wessenberg (1774–1860), vicar-general of the Diocese of Constance, led an unsuccessful movement to establish a German national Church with even greater autonomy from Rome than existed under Josephinism.[114] The contested nature of German Catholicism during this period helps us make sense of Beethoven's religious outlook: largely sympathetic to the Catholic Enlightenment, but not fully embracing it either. It also provides an important background for understanding the ideas of Johann Michael Sailer, a centrist caught between conservative and progressive currents whose particular importance for Beethoven will be explored in detail in the next chapter.

---

[112] Walker, 32.
[113] Holzem, *Christianity in Germany*, 2:1061–63.
[114] See Holzem, 2:1026–30; and Printy, *Enlightenment*, 213. Beethoven's familiarity with at least the secular writings of Wessenberg will be discussed in chapter 6.

5
Beethoven and Johann Michael Sailer

In February 1819, as Beethoven's legal battle for custody of his nephew Karl dragged on, his friend Antonie Brentano wrote a letter on his behalf to Johann Michael Sailer (1751–1832), a Catholic theologian in Bavaria who was a friend of the Brentano family.[1] According to Antonie, Beethoven had been an admirer of Sailer's for some time, and, believing Sailer well suited to the task, he wished to know if the theologian would be willing to educate his nephew:

> May it not unpleasantly surprise you that I bother you again so soon with a letter, but having been selected as a go-between in order to ask a favor of you (in fact, a good deed because the question concerns the welfare—even the salvation, I believe—of a human being), I do not hesitate, with all the confidence *you* inspire so sincerely, to call upon you for your counsel and action.... [Beethoven] wishes to send this talented, lighthearted boy to a Catholic university that is not too expensive, where, besides the Invisible Spirit to protect him, a visible spirit would lovingly care for his salvation and preservation. Heaven has suggested Landshut to him, and since he learned through one of my relatives that I was fortunate enough to know you personally—you, whom he has already venerated in spirit for a long time—he very ardently desired that I would introduce the matter to you.[2]

---

[1] Antonie Brentano has been proposed, most notably by Maynard Solomon, as one of several candidates in the still ongoing debate on the identity of Beethoven's "Immortal Beloved": Solomon, *Beethoven*, 207–46. For an overview of the debate, see Walden, *Beethoven's Immortal Beloved*, 7–26.

[2] Albrecht no. 256, February 22, 1819, translation slightly amended. For the German original, see *BGA* no. 1289: "Möge es Sie nicht unangenehm befremden, daß ich Sie schon wieder mit einem Brief belästige; aber als Vermittler gewählt, Sie um eine Gefälligkeit, ja um ein gutes Werk anzusprechen—denn es handelt sich um die Wohlfahrt, ja, ich glaube sogar um die Rettung eines Menschen—zögere ich nicht, mit allem Vertrauen, das Sie so herzlich einflößen, zu Rat und Tat Sie aufzufordern.... [Beethoven] wünscht, diesen talentvollen, leichtsinnigen Knaben nach einer katholischen, nicht zu kostspieligen *Universität* zu schicken, wo nebst dem unsichtbaren Schutzgeist ihm noch ein sichtbarer, für seine Rettung und Erhaltung liebreich besorgter, beygegeben wäre, der Himmel hat ihm *Landshut* eingegeben, und da er durch eine meiner Verwandten erfahren hat daß ich so glücklich bin, Sie persönlich zu kennen, Sie den er schon lange im Geiste verehrt, hat er sehr eifrig gewünscht daß ich Ihnen die Sache vorstelle" (Beethoven's emphasis). The same letter is also transcribed in Schiel, *Johann Michael Sailer*, 1:574–75.

The Catholic Beethoven. Nicholas Chong, Oxford University Press. © Oxford University Press 2024.
DOI: 10.1093/9780197752951.003.0006

In biographical Beethoven sources from 1819 and 1820, Sailer's name appears with unusual frequency for a public figure who was neither a musician nor a close personal associate of the composer. Beethoven himself expressed his esteem for the theologian in a letter dating from late April or early May 1819 to the Archduke Rudolph, later the dedicatee of the *Missa solemnis*: "At Landshut everything is very well arranged for the training of my nephew, because the worthy and celebrated Professor Sailer would superintend everything pertaining to his education."[3]

Beethoven's opinion of Sailer was shared by Karl Joseph Bernard, editor of the *Wiener Zeitung* and one of the composer's closest friends. In a statement addressed to Beethoven in the conversation books of early 1819, Bernard advised, "If you want to achieve some degree of peace, I believe that it would be good for you to appoint a guardian, as you were willing to do yesterday. If it should work out, however, that the boy can be taken to Sailer in Landshut, it would of course be even better, since you could have all reassurance to that extent, because you would know that he was in the best hands."[4] Shortly afterward, Bernard also reported to Beethoven the high regard in which the theologian was held by one Father Ignatius, prior of the Michaelskirche in Vienna: "[Father Ignatius] cannot praise Professor Sailer enough, and says that no greater salvation could befall the boy than to spend a couple of years under his supervision"; "[Father Ignatius] is enthusiastic about him [Sailer?]. If I were to reflect for 100 years, he said, I would not be able to conceive anything better than to entrust the boy to Prof[essor] Sailer."[5] Bernard had cautioned Beethoven against making specific mention to the Viennese authorities of his plan to send Karl to Sailer.[6] But Beethoven ultimately

---

[3] Anderson no. 946 (*BGA* no. 1300): "Auch ist alles für Die ausbildung meines Neffen in *landshut* so gut berathen, indem der würdige berühmte Professor Sailer darüber die Oberaufsicht führt, was die Erziehung meines Neffen betrifft" (Beethoven's emphasis).

[4] *BCB* 1:16 (*BKh* 1:39): "Wenn Sie zu einiger Ruhe gelangen wollen, so halte ich für gut, daß Sie einen Vormund ernenn[en], so wie Sie gestern Willens waren. Sollte es aber angehen, daß der Knabe zum Seiler [sic] nach Landshut kann gebracht werden, so wäre es freylich noch besser, da Sie insofern alle Beruhigung haben könnten, in dem Sie ihn in den besten Händen wüßten."

[5] *BCB* 1:53, 57 (*BKh* 1:68–69, 72): "Uibrigens kann [Pater Ignatius] den Prof[essor] Seiler [sic] nicht genug erheben, und sagt, daß dem Knaben kein größeres Heil widerfahren könne, als wenn er ein paar Jahre unter seine Aufsicht kommt"; "[Pater Ignatius] ist für ihn begeistert. Wenn ich 100 Jahre nachsinnen sollte, sagte so, so würde ich nichts bessres ersinnen können, als den Knaben zum Prof[essor] Seiler [sic] zu geben."

[6] *BCB* 1:29 (*BKh* 1:48–49): "Court councillor Ohms says it is not necessary to name Professor Sailer, and one simply ought to state that the boy will be taken to [stay with] relatives for one or two years" (*Der Hofr[at] O[hms] sagt, es sey nicht nöthig den Professor Seiler [sic] zu nennen, und man soll nur angeben, daß der Knabe zu Verwandten auf ein oder zwey Jahre gebracht wird*).

ignored this advice. In February 1820, he made the following declaration in a draft of a legal memorandum to the Viennese Court of Appeal:

> Meanwhile I had received an offer from the renowned and worthy scholar and clergyman J. M. Sailer to take my nephew into his home at Landshut and to supervise his education. The worthy Abbot of St. Michael [Father Ignatius of the Michaelskirche] described this as *the greatest stroke of luck* which could befall my nephew; and other *enlightened people* expressed the *same opinion*. Even His Imperial Highness, the present Archbishop of Olmütz [Archduke Rudolph], endorsed this view and used his influence for this very purpose.[7]

The statement suggests that Sailer had agreed to accept Karl as a student, although no letter from Sailer to either Antonie Brentano or Beethoven has survived. A reference in the conversation books by Beethoven's secretary Franz Oliva to a planned "journey to Bavaria" provides an additional clue as to the seriousness of Beethoven's intentions regarding Karl and Sailer.[8] In the end, however, the court denied Beethoven permission to send Karl out of Vienna, despite granting him the legal custody he had sought.[9] A letter from the composer to the publisher Nikolaus Simrock hints at his disappointment: "As for Karl, I have not been able to send him even to Landshut to the celebrated and worthy Professor Sailer."[10]

Beethoven's interest in Sailer went beyond identifying him as a suitable teacher for his nephew. The posthumous inventory of the composer's possessions includes three books by the theologian:

---

[7] E. Anderson, *Letters of Beethoven*, 3:1394 (Beethoven's emphasis). The German original is in Weise, *Beethoven: Entwurf einer Denkschrift*, 1:45: "Indessen war mir der Antrag von dem berühmten würdigen Gelehrten u[nd] Geistlichen *J. M. Sailer* zugekommen, meinen Neffen zu sich nach Landshuth zu nehmen, u[nd] die Oberaufsicht über seine Erziehung zu führen, der würdige Abt von St: *Michael* erklärte dieses für das größte Glück, was meinem Neffen begegnen könnte, so wie andere erleuchtete Männer dasselbe, selbst Se[ine] Kaiserliche Hoheit der jezige Erzbischof von *Ollmüz* erklärten u[nd] verwendeten sich dafür."
[8] *BCB* 1:24 (*BKh* 1:44): "Reise nach Bayern."
[9] See Solomon, *Beethoven*, 316.
[10] Anderson no. 1005 (*BGA* no. 1365), February 10, 1820: "Was Ka[rl] betrifft, so konnte ich ihn nicht einmal nach *Landsh[ut]* zu dem berühmten u[nd] würdigen Profeßor Sailer b[ringen]." Two conversation book entries referring to Sailer date from after the plan to send Karl to the theologian had fallen through. In March 1820, Friedrich Wähner called Sailer "a fine man" ("ein tüchtiger Mann"), and in July or August of that year, Josef Köferle described Joseph Weber, another Catholic theologian, as a close friend of Sailer: *BCB* 2:42, 2:277 (*BKh* 1:364, 2:187–89).

Goldkörner der Weisheit und Tugend [Golden grains of wisdom and virtue]. 3rd improved and expanded printing ["3te verbesserte und vermehrte Auflage"]. Grätz, 1819.

Friedrich Christians Vermächtniß an seine lieben Söhne [Friedrich Christian's bequest to his beloved sons]. 2nd improved and expanded printing ["2te verbesserte und vermehrte Auflage"]. Grätz, 1819.

Kleine Bibel für Kranke und Sterbende und ihre Freunde [Little Bible for the sick and dying and their friends]. 3rd improved and expanded printing ["3te verbesserte und vermehrte Auflage"]. Grätz, 1819.[11]

(Beethoven's own copies of these books by Sailer are no longer extant.) The conversation books show that Beethoven himself noted down in early 1819 the titles of these three books, as well as that of another work by Sailer, *Von der Priesterweihung: Eine Rede* (On the ordination of priests: A speech), not listed in the inventory. He also copied down prices and publication information for each title:

At Wimmer's across from the Jägerhorn [Hunter's Horn], J. M. Sailer's *Rede von der Priesterweihung*, 8vo, Landshut, 1817; 40 kr.

---

[11] Theodore Albrecht's English translation of this inventory, cited elsewhere in this book using the abbreviation *Schätzungsprotokoll*, lists *Goldkörner* and the *Kleine Bibel* as item numbers 1 and 11 respectively, but omits *Friedrich Christians Vermächtniß*. Albrecht's version is based on the inventory provided, in German, by Hanns Jäger-Sunstenau in 1970 ("Beethoven-Akten im Wiener Landesarchiv," 22–23), which also omits this title. However, an older German transcription of the inventory from 1921, made by Albert Leitzmann, does include *Friedrich Christians Vermächtniß*, listing it as item no. 1 on the same line as *Goldkörner*: see Leitzmann, "Beethovens Bibliothek," 381. (Leitzmann gives the title as *Christians Vermächtnis an seine lieben Söhne*.) Leitzmann has modernized the spelling of the word "Vermächtniß" to "Vermächtnis," but otherwise his transcription matches what appears in the original inventory document, and is thus more accurate than the versions by Albrecht and Jäger-Sunstenau: see the facsimile of the document's first page in Bory, *Ludwig van Beethoven*, 222. I have found one copy of *Friedrich Christians Vermächtniß* published in Grätz in 1819 (as Beethoven's copy was) whose second of two volumes reproduces the text of *Goldkörner* in its entirety, though under the different title of *Sprüche der Weisen, latein und deutsch* (Sayings of the wise, Latin and English). Compare vol. 2 of this copy—https://onb.digital/result/109E34A5—with a copy of *Goldkörner* also published in Grätz in 1819, though unattached to *Friedrich Christians Vermächtniß*: https://onb.digital/result/105E5101 (start on p. 209 of the digitization). (For vol. 1 of the copy of *Friedrich Christian Vermächtniß* just mentioned, see https://onb.digital/result/103770CF; all weblinks just provided accessed August 1, 2024.) I have not ascertained whether all copies of *Friedrich Christians Vermächtniß* that appeared in Grätz in 1819 were published in this manner, but the possibility that this text was combined with the text of *Goldkörner* in Beethoven's own copy may explain the conflation of these titles in the *Schätzungsprotokoll*.

In all bookshops: *Friedrich Christians Vermächtniss an seine Söhne*, etc., etc. by J. M. Sailer; 2 parts with the author's portrait; 2nd improved and expanded edition; 1 fl. 30 kr. W.W.

By the same author: *Goldkörner der Weissheit u[nd] Tugend zur Unterhaltung für edle Seelen*, in 2 parts, 3rd improved and expanded edition, 1 fl. 12 kr. W.W.

By the same author: *Krankenbibel*, 3rd expanded and improved edition, 1 fl. 30 kr. W.W.[12]

Whether these conversation book entries were meant as reminders to himself or as instructions to one of his associates to purchase these books for him, Beethoven seems to have made a specific effort to seek out books by Sailer, suggesting that his interest in the theologian's writings was both sincere and active. The contents of his personal library may contain one additional link to Sailer: a copy of *The Imitation of Christ* (*Von der Nachfolge Christi*) by the medieval monk Thomas à Kempis (Thomas von Kempen, ca. 1380–1471), in a German translation probably by Sailer, published in 1821.[13] Originally in Latin, this well-known Christian devotional text was one of Sailer's favorite books, and his translation helped to popularize it among both Catholics and Protestants throughout the German-speaking lands.[14] In a conversation book entry of late 1819, Beethoven's friend Bernard, whose regard for Sailer was noted above, told Beethoven that he had received a copy of this text as a gift, which may have prompted the composer to obtain one for himself.[15]

As John Paul Ito has pointed out, moreover, Beethoven went so far as to use a number of Latin quotations from Sailer's *Goldkörner der Weisheit und Tugend*—the first of the three books by Sailer listed in the posthumous inventory—in documents associated with the legal dispute over the guardianship of his nephew Karl.[16] Sailer's *Goldkörner* is actually an anthology of

---

[12] *BCB* 1:18, 1:63 (*BKh* 1:41, 1:77). The abbreviations "fl" (florin) and "kr" (kreuzer) refer to units of Viennese currency (*Wiener Währung*, abbreviated "W.W." as in the quotation); see *BCB* 1:xxx.

[13] See Ito, "Johann Michael Sailer and Beethoven," 90–91. Beethoven's copy is listed as item no. 23 in the *Schätzungsprotokoll*.

[14] See Heim, "Nachwort," 122–23. See also Gajek, "Dichtung und Religion," 74–75. Sailer's translation remains widely available today in German-speaking countries, most readily in a pocket-sized edition published by Reclam in its Universal-Bibliothek series of classic texts: Thomas von Kempen, *Das Buch*.

[15] *BCB* 1:161 (*BKh* 1:169).

[16] Ito, "Johann Michael Sailer and Beethoven," 88.

Latin aphorisms he compiled from three historical figures: Janus Anysius, a fifteenth-century Neapolitan abbot with humanist leanings; Juan Luis Vives (Ludovicus Vivis), a humanist contemporary and friend of Erasmus; and St. Martin of Braga, a sixth-century Portuguese bishop. Sailer appends German translations and commentary to these sayings, in certain cases reinterpreting them in accordance with Christian doctrine. One quotation from *Goldkörner*, a saying originally from Vives, appears in Beethoven's letter to Franz Xaver Piuk, a local legal official, dated July 19, 1819: "Solum humanae faciei tegumentum decorum, modestia et verecundia" (Modesty and a sense of shame are the only fitting covering of the human face).[17] Four other quotations appear in the 1820 legal memorandum mentioned above:

1. "Lite abstine, nam vincens, multum amiseris" (Refrain from litigation, for even if you win you will have lost a great deal)
2. "Mendacio comites tenebrae" (Darkness is companion to falsehood)
3. "Sapienti honestas lex est, libido lex est malis" (Decency is a law to the wise, lust is a law to the wicked)
4. "Convitia hominum turpium, laudes puta" (Treat the abuse of odious people as praise)[18]

The first, third, and fourth quotations are taken from Janus Anysius, the second from Juan Luis Vives. In addition to these five cited by Ito, I have found three further quotations from Sailer's *Goldkörner* in a conversation book entry of early 1820, written in Beethoven's hand:

1. "Cui credere debeas, quid et quantum vide" (What you should believe, what and how much, examine that)
2. "Hospes, ne curiosus" (As a guest, do not be curious)
3. "Populo cede, non pare" (Yield to the people, but do not obey them)[19]

---

[17] Anderson no. 953 (*BGA* no. 1313), translation by Anderson. Cf. Sailer, *Sprüche-Buch: Goldkörner*, 54.

[18] E. Anderson, *Letters of Beethoven*, 3:1389, 1392, 1405, 1408; cf. Sailer, *Sprüche-Buch: Goldkörner*, 21, 36, 12, 15. The translations of the Latin quotations here are by Anderson, slightly amended. (Anderson was unaware that Beethoven had taken these quotations from Sailer's *Goldkörner*: ibid., 3:1389n1.)

[19] *BCB* 1:226 (*BKh* 1:228); Sailer, *Sprüche-Buch: Goldkörner*, 16, 36, 37. The translations of the Latin here are by Albrecht.

16

80. Sine mente dives, aureo aries est velere.
Viel Geld und kein Verstand dazu —
Ein Schaf in goldner Wolle.

81. Infirmo eunt pede consilia hominis inopis.
Auf schwachen Beinen geht der Rath des Dürftigen;
Ein leises Windchen weht ihn um.

82. Tanti aestima te, quantus es, nisi desipis.
Sich mißt der Weise nach dem Seyn:
Das Narren-Maß ist Schein vom Schein.

83. Beneficii cito senescunt gratiae.
Oft wächset schon im ersten Jahr'
Dem Danke — graues Haar.

84. **Cui credere debeas, quid et quantum vide.**
Schau siebenmahl, und öfters noch,
Wem, was, wie viel zu trauen sey!

85. Non laede quemquam; nam ira senescit tardius.
Verwunde nicht:
Gereitzter Zorn stirbt lange nicht.

86. In animo egestas atque opes hominum sedent.
Nicht außer dir, nicht um dich her,
In dir, in dir darin —
Wohnt Reichthum oder Durft.

87. Armatur sero galea saucium caput.
Vor Wunde schützen — kann der Helm:
Die Wunde heilen — kann er nicht.

88. Infestius nihil alteri est, quam homini homo.
Des Menschen erster Feind — der Mensch.

89. Injuriam inferre est ferae, ferre est viri.
Verwunden kann das Thier:
Der Mann den Schmerz der Wunde dulden.

90. Diversa studia odere cuncti, amant sua.
Der Künstler liebt nur seine Kunst —
Und sich in ihr.

91. Aerugo ut aes, ita invidia est praecordia.
Am Eisen frißt der Rost,
Der Neid am Herzen.

92

Figure 5.1 Latin quotation used by Beethoven as it appears in Sailer's *Goldkörner der Weisheit und Tugend* (Grätz, 1819). Image courtesy of the University Libraries, University of North Carolina at Chapel Hill.

Anysius is the author of the first quotation, Vives of the second and third. Figure 5.1 shows the first quotation as it appears in a copy of *Goldkörner* in the same edition as Beethoven had. Beethoven's use of the *Goldkörner* quotations in three different places—his correspondence, the legal memorandum, and the conversation books—suggests that Sailer's books did not just sit idly on his bookshelf.

Beethoven's connection to Sailer has been acknowledged in the Beethoven literature both because of its relevance for understanding the composer's religious outlook, and because it coincides chronologically with the start of his work on the *Missa solemnis*, traditionally considered his most significant piece of religious music. Indeed, Beethoven's noting down of various book titles by Sailer, described above, occurs in the same conversation book (Heft 2) as the earliest documentary evidence relating to the *Missa*, a cryptic comment by Beethoven about an organ prelude preceding a Kyrie.[20] Sailer and his ideas have, nevertheless, seldom been discussed in detail.[21] It is even quite common for biographical accounts or commentaries on the *Missa solemnis* to make no reference to Sailer at all.[22] When he has been mentioned, descriptions of Sailer's ideas have tended to be vague, and occasionally even of suspect accuracy. Maynard Solomon, for example, claims that Sailer espoused a "religion of the heart," without going into exactly what is meant by this expression.[23] Lewis Lockwood writes that Sailer stressed the primacy of the individual believer's interior religious experience against "mechanical" and "scholastic" modes of observance, but does not elaborate further.[24] Both Solomon and Lockwood also claim inaccurately that Sailer was a fideist—a person who believes, against traditional Catholic doctrine, that reason is independent of faith. Sailer merely argued against the abuse of reason to separate religion from morality—a view he attributed to Immanuel Kant, among other thinkers of his time.[25] (This issue will be discussed in more detail below.)

---

[20] *BCB* 1:18 (*BKh* 1:42): "The organist plays the Kyrie prelude loudly, and then comes down to *piano* [just] before the Kyrie" ("Preludieren des Kyrie vom organisten stark u[nd] abnehmend bis vor dem Kyrie piano"). This statement occurs on folio 10ʳ in the original document, only a few pages after Beethoven inscribed the title of Sailer's *Von der Priesterweihung* (see above) on folio 8ʳ. The three other Sailer titles appear later, on folio 97ʳ of the same conversation book.
[21] For two examples of relatively brief discussions of Sailer, see Lockwood, *Beethoven*, 403–5, and Solomon, "Quest for Faith," 222–23.
[22] A notable example is William Kinderman's *Beethoven*, usually counted among the most important English-language biographies of the composer.
[23] Solomon, "Quest for Faith," 222.
[24] Lockwood, *Beethoven*, 403.
[25] See Schwaiger, *Johann Michael Sailer*, 95–97.

Lockwood's discussion of Sailer further adds that the theologian was part of the "anti-establishment wing" of German Catholicism.[26] This label, along with the notion that Sailer's fideism made him a less-than-orthodox Catholic thinker, harmonizes well with the long-standing tradition of distancing Beethoven from the Catholic religion that I have been seeking to question throughout this book. If one accepts the received wisdom regarding Beethoven the religious nonconformist, then it makes sense for him to have been attracted by a purportedly nonconformist theologian like Sailer.

The article by Ito cited above reverses this usual view, albeit in a less than straightforward sense.[27] Ito points out—correctly, as we shall see—that Sailer was a more conservative theologian than has been suggested, but takes for granted the composer's estrangement from the Catholic Church that I have described as a mainstay of Beethoven scholarship. He thus concludes that Sailer did not exert a significant influence on Beethoven, precisely because of the theologian's conservatism.[28] Ito offers a number of arguments for his position that seem quite problematic. For instance, he speculates that Antonie Brentano may not have been truthful when she told Sailer, in the letter quoted at the beginning of this chapter, that Beethoven had learned about him from one of her relatives.[29] He points out that Beethoven was on close terms with no members of the extended Brentano family other than Antonie and her husband Franz, and argues that it was most likely Antonie herself who first told Beethoven about Sailer. Ito fails to consider the possibility that the relative to which Antonie refers is the poet Clemens Brentano, with whom Beethoven corresponded (see chapter 4). Clemens is a credible candidate given that he was the half-brother of Antonie's husband Franz, to whom Sailer was an important spiritual advisor.[30] But even if this were not the case, and Ito's theory about Antonie's dishonesty were correct, the question of who actually told Beethoven about Sailer seems of little relevance to the issue of Beethoven's own attitudes toward the theologian.

---

[26] Lockwood, *Beethoven*, 403.

[27] Ito, "Johann Michael Sailer and Beethoven." Ito's article constitutes a notable exception to the general neglect of Sailer in the Beethoven literature.

[28] Ito, 91. In another recent essay, Alexander Wolfshohl discusses Sailer more briefly than Ito, but makes a similar argument ("Beethoven liest Autoren und Texte," 115–17). Wolfshohl acknowledges that in the explicitness of their Christian content, the books by Sailer in Beethoven's library seem anomalous when compared with other books with religious themes that the composer owned. Wolfshohl thus asserts that Beethoven's interest in Sailer's work was not sincere but motivated only by his desire to learn more about the teacher he was considering for his nephew Karl.

[29] Ito, 90.

[30] See Hänsel, *Geistliche Restauration*, 76–82.

Above all, however, Ito too easily dismisses the question of why Beethoven was so keen on Sailer in the first place, especially given that Sailer lived so far from Vienna. Beethoven could have sent Karl to a different teacher: that he was interested in Sailer in particular suggests that the theologian's views appealed to him personally in some way. That Beethoven's interest in Sailer was linked to his relationship with his nephew points to a still more important fact: though, as we have seen in the previous chapter, Beethoven engaged with writings by other religious thinkers, Sailer is the one such figure for whom some kind of personal connection can be established, even if only indirectly, through Antonie Brentano's assistance as a go-between. The importance of this fact cannot be overstated, and speaks further against any casual dismissal of Sailer's significance for Beethoven's own religious outlook.[31]

Ito's article also does not consider potential links between Sailer's ideas and Beethoven's *Missa solemnis*, whose composition roughly coincided with Beethoven's exposure to Sailer and his writings. I shall take up this subject in detail in the next and final chapter, but before doing so, I shall use the remainder of this chapter to provide a broad overview of Sailer's life and thought, and to explore in detail the content of the three books by Sailer that Beethoven had in his library. For reasons that will become apparent, my discussion of Sailer's *Kleine Bibel* will also address Thomas à Kempis's

---

[31] I can offer two further points of rebuttal to Ito. First, Ito argues that "many of the entries about Sailer in the conversation books show Beethoven asking very simple questions about Sailer without any follow up; this suggests that he had only minimal familiarity with him, as those short assessments would hardly have been helpful to someone with a deeper knowledge" ("Johann Michael Sailer and Beethoven," 89). Ito does not cite precisely which conversation-book entries he is referring to but probably means those that I have discussed earlier in this chapter. The statements in the conversation books are by Beethoven's interlocutors, rather than by Beethoven himself, and are presumably replies to questions that Beethoven asked verbally. Even if one ignores the obvious difficulty of guessing what Beethoven's questions actually were, Ito's argument is rather weak. Beethoven's interlocutors express their own opinions about Sailer's reputation and Beethoven's plan to send Karl to him; that they do not go into any detail about Sailer's theological views says absolutely nothing about what *Beethoven* may or may not have known about Sailer. Second, Ito, while acknowledging the possibility that Beethoven's use of quotations from Sailer's *Goldkörner* may be a sign of his "deep engagement" with the book, writes: "The fact that he did not continue to quote from it following the conclusion of the guardianship struggle suggests that it did not hold his interest and attention beyond that time" (ibid., 88–89). This argument seems highly speculative. If Beethoven did move on to other interests or other books after his engagement with Sailer's, that hardly means what he read earlier automatically ceased to resonate with him in some way. To make such a claim requires the unjustified assumption that Beethoven's views changed fickly with each thinker or writer he encountered. Ito adds that "a cynic might also observe that he drew on [Sailer's *Goldkörner*] only in correspondence with powerful officials, presumably with the intention of appearing more highly erudite" (ibid., 89). But this argument would only apply to the quotations in the 1820 legal memorandum and the letter to Piuk, and not to the quotations that Beethoven employs in the conversation books, which I pointed out above.

Imitation of Christ, whose connection to Beethoven's engagement with Sailer has been described above. As we shall see, Sailer's overall theological outlook, which is reflected in the books by him Beethoven owned, attempted to forge a middle way between the Catholic Enlightenment and the Catholic Restoration.[32] More importantly for our purposes, his views resonate with Beethoven's religious concerns as described in previous chapters. In light of these parallels, it would be misleading to claim that Beethoven's encounter with Sailer's thought precipitated some kind of sudden or dramatic change in the composer's religious views. The more credible scenario is that he found Sailer appealing because the theologian's approach to Catholicism was one toward which he had already been leaning. Even so, it is noteworthy that in the context of the time, Sailer's thought was more conservative, more tilted toward the Catholic Restoration, than other religious thinkers with whose writings Beethoven engaged. This fact, when combined with the personal connection to Sailer discussed at the beginning of this chapter, raises the possibility that Beethoven himself was, in the last decade of his life, becoming more open to religious views less clearly aligned with the Enlightenment, whether in its Catholic or secular strands.

Johann Michael Sailer in Historical Context

Though his name is obscure today, Johann Michael Sailer was, during Beethoven's lifetime, quite simply the best-known Catholic theologian in the German-speaking world.[33] Throughout his long career, he was in contact with numerous intellectual and artistic figures, Catholic and non-Catholic alike, including individuals as prominent as Goethe, with whom

---

[32] This characterization of Sailer as a centrist or moderate figure is the most common one in commentary on his work and is the one I shall assume here. However, because of continued debates on how broadly to define the Catholic Enlightenment as a concept, some scholars have treated Sailer nominally as a representative of the Catholic Enlightenment, albeit a conservative one. For examples, see Chadwick, *Popes and European Revolution*, 611; and Printy, *Enlightenment*, 172, 184n69, 215. Recently, Wilhelm Schmidt-Biggemann has described Sailer as evolving from being an Enlightenment figure of a "sentimental" (*empfindsamer*) variety to being a Romantic: see "Johann Michael Sailer als Aufklärer," esp. 116. Andreas Holzem characterizes Sailer similarly as bridging the Enlightenment and Romanticism: see *Christianity in Germany*, 2:880–82. (For a recent discussion of persistent disagreements concerning the definition of the Catholic Enlightenment, see also Printy, "History and Church History.") Ultimately, the precise nature of Sailer's ideas matters more for our purposes than the labels chosen to describe them.

[33] See Baumgartner, *Johann Michael Sailer*, 27.

he corresponded in May 1810.[34] Sailer was especially well known as a "Brief-Seelsorger," a clergyman who offered pastoral advice to individuals by correspondence.[35]

Born in 1751 in the small town of Aresing bei Schrobenhausen in Bavaria, Sailer grew up in a culture permeated with the spirit of Baroque Catholicism, even if this culture was gradually being eroded by the reformist agenda of the Catholic Enlightenment.[36] At age twenty-one, Sailer decided to become a Jesuit and undertook studies at the University of Ingolstadt, where he was mentored by a dogmatic theologian named Benedikt Stattler (1728–1797). Stattler was among a significant minority of Jesuits sympathetic to church reform and open to some Enlightenment ideas, especially the philosophical rationalism of Christian Wolff.[37] At the same time, he opposed strands of Enlightenment thought he believed to be too extreme and later in his career became well known for doing everything in his power to stop the influence of Kantian metaphysics on Catholic theology.[38] As we shall see, Stattler's nuanced stance toward the Catholic Enlightenment, and his specific opposition to Kant, would exert a lifelong influence on his student Sailer.

Sailer's formation as a Jesuit was ended by the suppression of the order in 1773 (an event discussed in chapter 1), which compelled him to seek ordination instead as a secular priest. Sailer then stayed on at Ingolstadt to teach theology, assisting his teacher Stattler. In 1781, however, both he and Stattler were dismissed from their positions for being ex-Jesuits, association with the Jesuits being regarded in the intellectual climate of the time as betokening insufficient support of Catholic Enlightenment reforms. After several years without a position, Sailer secured a new appointment at the University of Dillingen but would be dismissed again after ten years, this time because his

---

[34] The letter is now lost, but we know about it from a different letter to Goethe from Bettina Brentano (Bettina von Arnim), in which she mentions having received a message that Sailer had asked Goethe to pass on to her; see Schiel, *Johann Michael Sailer*, 1:429; and Baumgartner, *Johann Michael Sailer*, 144–45. Bettina also sent several other letters to Goethe in which she praised Sailer; see Schiel, *Johann Michael Sailer*, 1:410, 422, 427. Bettina, who was married to the poet Achim von Arnim, was the sister of Clemens Brentano, as well as the half-sister of Franz Brentano, husband of Antonie Brentano. Like Antonie, she has been proposed as a candidate for Beethoven's "Immortal Beloved"; see Walden, *Beethoven's Immortal Beloved*.

[35] See Baumgartner, *Johann Michael Sailer*, 21.

[36] My overview of Sailer's biography is based on Baumgartner, *Johann Michael Sailer*, 9–36. Additional citations will be provided where I have supplemented information from this section of Baumgartner's book with material from other sources. On Sailer and Baroque Catholicism, see ibid., 37–38. As in the Habsburg territories (see chapter 1), Baroque Catholicism was especially strong in Bavaria: see Forster, *Catholic Germany*, 182; and Chadwick, *Popes and European Revolution*, 80.

[37] Lehner, "Benedict Stattler."

[38] Lehner, 186–87. Lehner's labeling of Stattler as an "enlightened conservative" might be equally appropriate for Sailer, as we shall see.

ideas were considered too *progressive*. The academic climate had changed; since around 1790, conservative opposition to the Catholic Enlightenment had been growing, and Sailer now became a victim of efforts to roll back the reformist tide. For the next five years, Sailer once again lived without a position, but in 1799, the Bavarian government appointed him to a chair back in Ingolstadt. The government, which continued to be partial to the ideas of the Catholic Enlightenment, found him attractive because it believed him, not entirely accurately, to be a reliable progressive. The following year, the upheaval created by the Napoleonic Wars forced the University of Ingolstadt to move to Landshut, where Sailer found himself at the time of Antonie Brentano's letter to him on Beethoven's behalf.[39]

For the remainder of his career, Sailer continued to be attacked by both sides of the progressive–conservative divide in the German Church of his time: by figures more partial to the Catholic Enlightenment and those associated with the emerging Catholic Restoration. As the Catholic Restoration gained ground, however, it was more conservative churchmen who increasingly sought to thwart the advancement of his ecclesiastical career. In 1818, Sailer was passed over as a candidate for the important position of Archbishop of Cologne.[40] As a native of Bonn, Beethoven had grown up in the Archdiocese of Cologne, and it is worth speculating whether he would have known about Sailer's failure to attain that appointment, given that his plan to send his nephew to Sailer was formulated just the following year, in 1819. Sailer was also rejected by the Holy See as a candidate for Bishop of Augsburg. Despite conservative opposition, however, Sailer retained powerful political allies, most notably Crown Prince Ludwig (later King Ludwig I) of Bavaria, who had once been his student.[41] As a result of Ludwig's intercessions on his behalf with the Roman Curia, Sailer became Bishop of Regensburg in 1829, serving until his death in 1832. After Sailer's passing, the turn against Catholic Enlightenment ideas in the Catholic Church (see chapter 1) created a climate in which the more progressive aspects of his theology became increasingly suspect. At one point, his books were even investigated by the Roman Inquisition, and conservative

---

[39] In Landshut, the University of Ingolstadt was refounded as the Ludwig-Maximilians-Universität, which later relocated to Munich, where it remains today.

[40] In the aftermath of the secularization and "mediatization" of individual German states precipitated by the Napoleonic Wars, this position no longer fused spiritual and temporal authority as a prince-archbishopric, unlike the situation during Beethoven's youth in Bonn (see chapter 2). For a general source on German mediatization, see Holzem, *Christianity in Germany*, 2:981–88.

[41] Baumgartner, *Johann Michael Sailer*, 27.

antipathy toward his views encouraged the scholarly neglect of his works, at least until his reputation was rehabilitated in the second half of the twentieth century, in no small part because his ideas exerted a significant influence on the reforms of the Second Vatican Council.[42] (Sailer's writings have been cited by two post-conciliar popes, John Paul II and Benedict XVI.[43])

The centrist or moderate nature of Sailer's outlook combined cautious advocacy for some of the Catholic Enlightenment's most important ideas with opposition to what Sailer considered its excesses. For instance, in line with the Catholic Enlightenment, Sailer displayed an irenic and ecumenical attitude in engaging with Protestants. He regularly stressed the importance of Christian unity, recognizing that, in his time, unbelief had become a graver threat to Catholicism than Protestantism.[44] Throughout his career, he remained in close contact with numerous Protestant figures, most notably the philosophers Johann Georg Hamann (1730–1788) and Friedrich Heinrich Jacobi (1743–1819) and the Swiss theologian Johann Kaspar Lavater (1741–1801).[45] This interaction went beyond a simple, diplomatic desire for cordial interdenominational relations. Sailer's reading of Lavater's work, for instance, influenced his own distaste for overly rationalistic approaches to religion, a point to which I shall return to below.[46] Sailer's works were in turn very popular among Protestant readers.[47] His openness to non-Catholic thought extended to non-Christian writers too, and in this respect he reflected the broader encouragement of religious tolerance that characterized the Catholic Enlightenment. In addition to reminding Catholics of their duty to love nonbelievers, Sailer himself established friendships with figures such as the atheist philosopher Ludwig Feuerbach (1804–1872), and he was keen on exploring relationships between non-Christian and Christian texts; in this regard, he was inspired by Novalis and Hamann, both of whom dedicated themselves to the Christianization of non-Christian, especially classical, writings.[48]

---

[42] Schwaiger, *Johann Michael Sailer*, 97–98, 166–68. See also Hofmeier, "Gott in Christus," 27–28; and Donakowski, "Age of Revolutions," 385.

[43] Baumgartner, *Johann Michael Sailer*, 167. See also Wolf, *Johann Michael Sailer*, 7; and Nichols, *Thought of Pope Benedict XVI*, 142. One discussion of Sailer's thought in the writings of Pope Benedict XVI (then Joseph Ratzinger) can be found in "What Will the Future Church," 109–13.

[44] See Schuh, *Johann Michael Sailer*, 26; and Printy, *Enlightenment*, 215.

[45] Schuh, *Johann Michael Sailer*, 15.

[46] Dietrich, *The Goethezeit*, 120–21.

[47] See Schmidt-Biggemann, "Johann Michael Sailer als Aufklärer," 86–87.

[48] See Schuh, *Johann Michael Sailer*, 15, 64, 71–73.

Connected to Sailer's ecumenical attitudes was his promotion of private Bible-reading among the laity. During his time as Bishop of Regensburg, for instance, he sponsored two new German translations of the Scriptures.[49] As discussed in chapter 1, a new emphasis on the Bible among Catholics had been a significant Protestant-influenced feature of the German Catholic Enlightenment, though Sailer's attention to Scripture may also have been influenced by Jesuit meditation practices.[50] Sailer's encouragement of vernacular Bible-reading was part of a larger interest in the religious education of lay Catholics and the cultivation of individual piety separate from the church's official liturgy—measures that he believed were necessary for the renewal of Christianity in society.[51] Sailer constantly emphasized the importance of individual families for the propagation of the faith, believing that the smallest church community was to be found in the home.[52]

Both Sailer's ecumenical outlook and his encouragement of individual piety constituted the most progressive elements of his theological outlook, those elements most in line with the German Catholic Enlightenment.[53] Indeed, Sailer's ecumenical efforts were the main reason for the criticism he received from his most forceful opponent: the Viennese Redemptorist priest Klemens Maria Hofbauer, whom we have met in the previous chapter. Despite their theological disagreements, Sailer expressed admiration for Hofbauer, especially for the latter's efforts at encouraging a revival of traditional Catholic devotional practices.[54] This charitable attitude toward Hofbauer was, to put it mildly, not reciprocated. In 1817, Hofbauer wrote an infamous report of a visit he had paid to Sailer, in which he claimed that Sailer was a member of the Illuminati and hostile to religious belief.[55] Hofbauer even went so far as to say that he had felt it necessary to flee Sailer's home, fearing for his own faith.

Hofbauer's attacks notwithstanding, the apparently progressive aspects of Sailer's theology were sprinkled with more conservative elements deviating from Catholic Enlightenment tendencies. Despite his outreach to Protestants and nonbelievers, Sailer held firmly to the notion that salvation

---

[49] Schuh, 44. See also Chadwick, *Popes and European Revolution*, 77.
[50] Baumgartner, *Johann Michael Sailer*, 42.
[51] See Baumgartner, 24.
[52] Probst, *Gottesdienst in Geist und Wahrheit*, 136.
[53] See Schmidt-Biggemann, "Johann Michael Sailer als Aufklärer," esp. 86–92, 109–14.
[54] Baumgartner, *Johann Michael Sailer*, 98–101.
[55] Baumgartner, 99.

could be attained only through the Catholic Church: his dialogue with non-Catholics was motivated at least to some degree by a desire to make arguments on Catholicism's behalf.[56] To cite one notable example, Sailer developed late in his career an interest in Romantic thought, especially that of Friedrich Schelling, whose works he encouraged his students to read.[57] Sailer was much taken by Schelling's anti-Enlightenment emphasis on the importance of the imagination in religious experience, but he eventually argued that Schelling's thought was too pantheistic and denigrating of human reason to be entirely compatible with Catholic belief.[58] With regard to Protestantism, even if Sailer did prefer to emphasize the positive rather than the negative, he still considered Protestant churches deficient in not having the pope as a symbol of unity.[59] And though he was uncomfortable with ultramontane views of the papacy, he never came anywhere close to questioning papal primacy.[60] Finally, Sailer's encouragement of extra-liturgical devotional practices was counterbalanced by his insistence that such private acts of worship were not meant to replace participation in the church's public liturgy, especially the sacraments of Confession and the Eucharist.[61] To borrow Manfred Probst's formulation, for Sailer "devotion of the heart" and "devotion of the home" must lead to "devotion of the church."[62]

Sailer's nuanced attitude toward the German Catholic Enlightenment is also evident in his views on how the Church should engage with the secular world. Sailer, as has been discussed, was open to engaging with ideas proposed by nonbelievers, but he cautioned his fellow Catholics against skirting too close to positions advocated by secular Enlightenment thinkers that, in his view, threatened the Christian faith. He was particularly suspicious of any concessions by Catholics to deism, philosophical materialism, or excessive individualism.[63]

Sailer notably objected to the influence that Kantian metaphysics was beginning to exert on German Catholic theologians of more progressive

---

[56] Schaefer, "Program," 439.
[57] O'Meara, *Romantic Idealism and Roman Catholicism*, 42–46.
[58] O'Meara, 43, 113–14. See also Schuh, *Johann Michael Sailer*, 30.
[59] See Baumgartner, *Johann Michael Sailer*, 53–54.
[60] Dietrich, *The Goethezeit*, 128.
[61] See Dietrich, 70; and Schmidt-Biggemann, "Johann Michael Sailer als Aufklärer," 109–14.
[62] Probst, *Gottesdienst in Geist und Wahrheit*, 37: "Andacht des Herzens"; "Andacht des Hauses"; "Andacht der Kirche."
[63] See Baumgartner, *Johann Michael Sailer*, 40. See also Hofmeier, "Gott in Christus," 35.

persuasions.[64] (As discussed in chapter 2, the university at Bonn was an important center for such theologians, many of whom were influenced by Kant.) In 1785, following in the footsteps of his teacher Stattler, he published a forceful critique of Kantian philosophy entitled *Vernunftlehre für Menschen, wie sie sind* (Lessons on reason for human beings, as they are).[65] While he appreciated Kant's recognition of the limits of human reason, he disagreed with what he regarded as Kant's abstract, theoretical treatment of God, defending instead the traditional Judeo-Christian view that God acts in history and in time.[66] Sailer was further perturbed by Kant's separation of religious dogma and morality, which he believed led to an overly anthropocentric view of religion. Reason (*Vernunft*), in his view, should not be separated from knowledge of God; revelation (*Offenbarung*) is needed for reason to understand itself and its own limits.[67] In a similar vein, Sailer had a highly nuanced view of the role of ethics in Christian belief. While sharing their concern with ethical conduct, he criticized many Catholic Enlightenment thinkers for encouraging an excessive emphasis on ethics over dogma.[68] There was obviously nothing wrong with stressing the importance of loving one's neighbor; indeed, Sailer regarded the secular Enlightenment's emphasis on ethical conduct as a tool that could be carefully harnessed to revive Christian culture.[69] But true love of neighbor, in Sailer's view, must be rooted first in love of God. Simply put, religion in its dogmatic sense is more important than morality. Since the reason that allowed a philosopher like Kant to discern moral truths comes from God in the first place, God is necessarily prior to morality.[70] Because of the inherent sinfulness of Man, one has no hope of loving others if one has not first been redeemed by God through Jesus Christ.[71] Ethics should thus be theocentric, rather than anthropocentric, and the unity of human beings with God is a prerequisite for the unity of human beings with each other. The Church, Sailer argued, was established precisely to create *both* these forms of unity.[72]

---

[64] Baumgartner, *Johann Michael Sailer*, 50.
[65] See Schmidt-Biggemann, "Johann Michael Sailer als Aufklärer," 96–103. For a broader discussion of Catholic reception of Kant, but with a specific focus on Sailer, see Schaefer, "Critique of Everyday Reason."
[66] Gajek, "Dichtung und Religion," 62. See also Schwaiger, *Johann Michael Sailer*, 95–97.
[67] Gajek, "Dichtung und Religion," 62.
[68] See Schmidt-Biggemann, "Johann Michael Sailer als Aufklärer," 103–8; and Schuh, *Johann Michael Sailer*, 21–25.
[69] Schuh, *Johann Michael Sailer*, 25.
[70] Baumgartner, *Johann Michael Sailer*, 71.
[71] See Baumgartner, 67–72.
[72] Baumgartner, 60.

Underlying Sailer's entire theological vision, in both its progressive and conservative aspects, was its Christocentrism—its particular concentration on the figure of Christ, and on an intimate relationship with Christ, as the foundation for all other religious ideas. This characteristic was encapsulated in his personal motto: "Gott in Christus—das Heil der Welt" (God in Christ—the salvation of the world).[73] Sailer's Christocentrism motivated his distaste for Josephinism: against what he perceived as Josephinism's excessive rationalism and emotional aridity, he sought to recover an emphasis on the believer's emotional experience and on God's supernatural work of salvation.[74] A focus on Christ also lay behind his nuanced views on ecumenism: the theologian presented his regard for Protestants not merely as a form of tolerance but as an act of love commanded by Christ for those who shared with Catholics the desire for Christ.[75] Above all, Christocentrism was fundamental to Sailer's placement of redemption and conversion at the heart of the Christian experience.[76] It is Christ who bridges the separation between God and human beings incurred by sin.[77] For Sailer, it made no sense to speak of ethics or morality without Christ. Anthropocentric views of religion, then, were a betrayal of the essence of Christianity.

Goldkörner der Weisheit und Tugend

Each of the three works by Sailer that Beethoven owned is quite different from the others. Collectively, however, they reflect key aspects of the theologian's outlook described in the previous section.

Goldkörner der Weisheit und Tugend (Golden grains of wisdom and virtue) is, as has been mentioned, a collection of Latin sayings selected by Sailer, for which he also provides German translations and commentary.[78] These sayings heavily emphasize the importance of ethical conduct, and the text as a whole comes across as a manual for upright living akin to the

---

[73] See Hofmeier, "Gott in Christus." See also Baumgartner, *Johann Michael Sailer*, 67.
[74] See Schmidt-Biggemann, "Johann Michael Sailer als Aufklärer," 114–15; Vilanova, *Histoire des théologies chrétiennes*, 3:278n1; and Dietrich, *The Goethezeit*, 126.
[75] See Baumgartner, *Johann Michael Sailer*, 53, 67.
[76] Baumgartner, 67.
[77] See Schuh, *Johann Michael Sailer*, 53.
[78] Throughout this section, page citations of Sailer's *Goldkörner* will be given in the main text rather than in footnotes. A digitization of Sailer's book, in the same 1819 Grätz edition owned by Beethoven, is available at https://onb.digital/result/105E5101 (accessed August 1, 2024), beginning on p. 209 of the digitization.

famous *Meditations* of Marcus Aurelius. This ethical focus is itself reflective of Catholic Enlightenment concerns. Recurring themes in *Goldkörner* are among those that have traditionally been held in common by the classical and Christian components of the Western intellectual tradition: virtue, wisdom, true friendship, the cultivation of a good conscience, stoicism in the face of death, mistrust toward the passions, the dangers of worldly wealth. Some of the quotations are strikingly pragmatic. For instance, one of the quotations from Janus Anysius reads: "Delibera tarde, perage quam ocissime" (21; Deliberate slowly, but act as quickly as possible). There is, too, a political aspect to the book. All of its source texts were intended by their authors to edify political leaders, and several quotations explicitly remark on the importance of good and wise governance. Among these is one of the quotations copied out by Beethoven (see above): "Populo cede, non pare" (Yield to the people but do not obey them), a quotation from Juan Luis Vives (37).

The importance of ethics in *Goldkörner* is, however, closely tied to the Christian religion and the worship of God. And in this regard, the book exemplifies Sailer's carefully considered openness to non-Christian thought. Two of its four sections, the first and last, have no Christian content at all. Sailer stresses in his introduction that much good can be learned from non-Christian sources, so long as they do not conflict with Christian teaching: "Some [of the sayings] are taken from our holy religion, the others from *healthy* reason" (5; my emphasis).[79] Sailer even writes a prayer asking God to bless the wisdom contained in the quotations he has selected, Christian and non-Christian alike (6–7). The fact that all four sections of the book have similar themes might be a way of pointing out to the reader the commonalities between Christian and non-Christian thought, but Sailer's ultimate point in drawing on non-Christian sayings is to show how they can be an aid and accompaniment to Christian spirituality. The non-Christian sayings in the first and fourth sections are thus not presented in an isolated way, but within an explicitly Christian context defined by Sailer's introduction and reinforced by the Christian content of the middle two sections.

In *Goldkörner*, not only is the content of the non-Christian sayings shown to be compatible with the Christian ones, but the German translations appended by Sailer sometimes emphasize this compatibility by alluding to Christian concepts not necessarily explicit in the Latin original. For instance, one of the quotations from Anysius, "Ut perfruare dulci, amari

---

[79] "Einige sind aus unserer heiligen Religion, die übrigen aus der gesunden Vernunft genommen."

aliquid feras" (To deserve sweet things, you would endure bitter things), is translated as "Vor Süss kommt Bitter, / Der Leidenskelch vor Himmelslust" (12; Before the sweet comes the bitter, / the cup of suffering before the joy of heaven). "Leidenskelch" clearly recalls the "cup of suffering" associated with Christ's Passion. (As pointed out in chapter 3, a variant of this word—"Leidenkelch"—appears in the libretto of Beethoven's *Christus am Ölberge*.) In a similarly elaborated manner, Sailer translates Martin of Braga's Latin "Nullum putaveris locum sine teste" (You will regard no place as being without witnesses) thus: "Ueberall wenigstens Ein Zeuge; denn Gottes Auge sieht überall, und zeuget überall, warnet und ermahnet überall, belohnet und strafet überall" (62; Everywhere there is at least one witness; for God's eye sees everywhere, and witnesses everywhere, warns and admonishes everywhere, rewards and punishes everywhere). Here, Sailer takes a simple moral injunction and links it much more explicitly to the idea that individuals are accountable to God.

These examples also illustrate the fact that Sailer's German translations in *Goldkörner* are often very free, and are far from literal renderings of the Latin. (In this regard, they recall Christian Schreiber's German text for Beethoven's Mass in C: see chapter 3.) In many cases, one might not describe them as translations at all. Rather, Sailer writes his own responses to the quotations, providing a kind of exegesis of each. This situation is more apparent in the latter three sections of *Goldkörner*, and some of the most extreme examples occur in the second section, containing quotations from Vives.[80] "Scopus vitae Christus" (Christ is the aim of life) receives the following German rendering from Sailer: "Die Eigenliebe bezieht Alles auf sich, der Christ Alles auf Christus. Er will ein Ebenbild Christi werden, wie Christus ein Ebenbild des Vaters war. Christus Reich—sein Zweck!" (28; Self-love refers everything to oneself, the love of Christ refers everything to Christ. He wants to become an image of Christ, as Christ was an image of the Father. Christ is the kingdom—his goal!). The equally terse "Pax Christi" (The peace of Christ) is elaborated as "Die wahre Friede ist eine

---

[80] Sailer indicates in the introduction that the edition he uses for the Anysius quotations itself included German translations (*Goldkörner*, 7). It is ambiguous whether Sailer has simply reproduced these translations from the original source or whether he has made his own German versions of the quotations, as he does for the quotations from Vives and Martin of Braga in the second, third, and fourth sections of *Goldkörner*. The former scenario would explain why the German renderings in the first section are on the whole less free than those in the other three sections. But even if Sailer did not make any of his own interventions in the Anysius quotations, this would not affect my earlier argument that the anthology as a whole has the effect of Christianizing non-Christian texts.

Gabe unsers Herrn: er beugt die Sinne unter die Vernunft, und die Vernunft unter seinen heiligen Geist. Der Wille des Menschen folgt dem Zuge seines Herrn" (28; True peace is a gift of our Lord: he subjects the senses under reason, and reason under his Holy Spirit. The will of the human being follows the way of his Lord). In teasing out the fuller implications of a brief text, Sailer invites the reader to meditate more deeply on its broader significance and associations.

The extreme freedom with which Sailer treats the act of translation also allows him to use the sayings in *Goldkörner* to highlight his favorite theological concerns. The inseparability of worshipping God and ethical conduct toward others is reflected not only in the structure of the anthology but also in Sailer's German versions of the Latin quotations. One example is: "Gott um seinetwillen, und den Menschen um Gotteswillen lieben—das ist die Tugend, und die ganze Tugend des Menschen" (To love God for His sake, and human beings for God's sake—that is virtue and the entire virtue of human beings). This is an elaboration of "Pietas in Deum et homines, omnis virtus" (Piety to God and to human beings is all of virtue), and more explicitly describes love of human beings as being rooted in love of God (45). "Eris in homines talis, qualem cupis Christum erga te" (You will be among human beings as you wish Christ to be toward you) is rendered in a manner that applies this saying more specifically to the concept of forgiveness: "Wie du wünschest, daß Christus dir verzeihen, dir geben soll: so gib und verzeih du Andern. Sey du Christus-Bild gegen Andere, wie Christus 'Bild des Vaters' gegen dich" (57; As you wish Christ to forgive you and to give to you, so give to and forgive others. Be an image of Christ toward others, as Christ is an image of the Father toward you). This elaboration of the Latin original exemplifies Sailer's preoccupation with the link between the need for a theocentric ethics and the human person's need for God's forgiveness. Finally, some of Sailer's German renderings in *Goldkörner* also point to his Christocentrism. One example is Sailer's treatment of "Probitas amorem eliciat, majestas cultum, sapientia fidem" (51; Honesty elicits love, majesty elicits worship, knowledge elicits faith). Sailer does translate this relatively literally as "Der Liebe gebührt Liebe, Anbetung der Majestät, Glaube der Weisheit." However, he also adds, "Es vereinigt sich in Christo die höchste Liebe, die höchste Majestät, und die höchste Weisheit" (The highest love, highest majesty, and highest truth are united in Christ). Sailer thus takes a statement of moral principles and links it more explicitly to the person of Christ.

Friedrich Christians Vermächtniß an seine lieben Söhne

In *Friedrich Christians Vermächtniß an seine lieben Söhne* (Friedrich Christian's bequest to his beloved sons), Sailer speaks through the persona of a father—the eponymous Friedrich Christian—who has written a letter to his sons that they read only after his death.[81] The allegorical meaning of Friedrich Christian's name is explained in an introduction: "Er in Christus, an den er glaubte, Heil und Friede gefunden hatte" (first unnumbered page of preface to volume 1; He had found in Christ, in whom he believed, salvation and peace). Friedrich's letter is a trenchant critique of contemporary culture, especially the decline of traditional Christian values, which he blames on anti-religious ideas encouraged by intellectuals and universities (1:54).

The bulk of Friedrich's letter is taken up by warnings to his sons not to be seduced by four "idols" (*Idolen*): false ideas that he believes have taken root in society. The first idol is the presumption that human reason is sufficient without Christian revelation (1:11–13). The second is unrestricted freedom of expression and the press (1:19–20). Friedrich's opposition to these bedrock ideas of political liberalism is very likely a reflection of Sailer's negative view of Josephinism, a key aspect of which was the relaxation of censorship laws (see chapter 1). Friedrich argues that such freedom of expression will lead to the dissemination of falsehoods and eventually to anarchy. He also makes the strikingly modern argument that greater individual freedom in this arena leads paradoxically to more power for the government, which alone decides how to limit such freedom—a possible reference to Josephinism's attempts to exert state control over the Church (1:23–24). Friedrich's third idol seems almost an outgrowth of the first. He criticizes what he terms "Räsonnirlust": the contemporary obsession with trying to understand everything, prompted by the fetishization of reason (1:24). Friedrich links this impulse in turn with an unhealthy materialism, which he describes as the "highest un-philosophy" (*höchstes Unphilosophie*) for reducing the human being to a mere animal (1:25). The belief that humans can come to know everything also leads to a kind of spiritual arrogance that

---

[81] Sailer, *Friedrich Christians Vermächtniß*. For a digitization of this book, see https://onb.digital/result/103770CF (vol. 1) and https://onb.digital/result/109E34A5 (vol. 2), accessed August 1, 2024. As discussed in a previous footnote, vol. 2 of this copy reproduces the text of *Goldkörner der Weisheit und Tugend*.

encourages excessive self-love, diminishing the humility necessary for religious faith (1:26–27, 29). Finally, the fourth idol is the tendency to insult religion in the public sphere (1:33):

> The new mint masters, I say, call a hypocrite a man who still attends a church, still worships in the church, and still visibly performs that worship with the gesture of devotion; a zealot a man who still believes in the Holy Spirit; a fanatic a man who with his entire family still cleaves to the Gospel of Christ, and to Christ himself, as a shipwrecked man cleaves to the piece of wood that saves him; a Capuchin a man who with his children prays from the heart before and after a meal (1:41).[82]

In this passage, Sailer rails against the negative labels used by those he perceives as enemies of the Catholic Church to ridicule those who remain faithful to it.

Friedrich's letter, for all of its polemics, cannot be reduced, however, to being merely an anti-Enlightenment screed. Rather than simply rejecting the Enlightenment, it attempts to reinterpret the idea of Enlightenment through a Christian lens—an argumentative move typical of Sailer's nuanced attitude toward secular thought.[83] A truly "enlightened" (*aufgeklärt*) society, Friedrich argues, is one illuminated "from the court down to the cottage by the light of Truth" (1:39; *von dem Hofe bis zur Hütte herab, von dem Lichte der Wahrheit*). This truth is found through reason—*Vernunft*—but the greatest form of reason is to serve God (1:39; *die Vernunft der allerhöchsten Vernunft—Gott dienete*). Elsewhere, Friedrich defines reason as God's "ray of light" (*Lichtstrahle Gottes*)—light that is to be found in Jesus Christ (1:17). God alone, Friedrich teaches his sons, is "the one source of all nature and all reason" (1:12; *Die Eine Quelle aller Natur und aller Vernunft*).

---

[82] "Die neuen Münzmeister, sage ich, nennen den, der noch eine Kirche besuchet, in der Kirche noch anbethet, und die Anbethung noch mit der Geberde der Andacht sichtbar machet, einen Heuchler; den, der noch an den heiligen Geist glaubet, einen Schwärmer; den, der mit seiner ganzen Familie noch an das Evangelium Christi, und an Christus selber so festhält, wie ein Schiffbrüchiger an dem rettenden Balken, einen Fanatiker; den, der mit seinen Kindern vor und nach Tische aus dem Herzen bethet, einen Kapuziner." Sailer's term "mint masters" (*Münzmeister*) may be a reference to the bureaucratic nature of the Josephine church.

[83] This kind of attempt to redefine "Enlightenment" in a manner more in harmony with a traditional Christian worldview appears elsewhere in Sailer's output: see Schmidt-Biggemann, "Johann Michael Sailer als Aufklärer," 114.

Sailer's *Kleine Bibel* and Thomas à Kempis's *Imitation of Christ*

If *Goldkörner der Weisheit und Tugend* comes across mainly as a kind of manual of ethical advice, and *Friedrich Christians Vermächtniß* as a work of social commentary, Sailer's *Kleine Bibel für Kranke und Sterbende und ihre Freunde* (Little Bible for the sick and dying and their friends) seems more clearly a book intended for actual devotional use.[84] As its title suggests, the *Kleine Bibel* is a collection of scriptural passages and prayers relevant to the sick, the dying, and their caregivers. Individual sections are intended specifically for each of these groups, and the book also includes detailed instructions on how one should prepare one's soul for death.

Taken as a whole, the *Kleine Bibel* illustrates Sailer's nuanced approach to ecumenism, as well as to individual piety. On the one hand, it is clear in stressing the importance of official Catholic liturgical practices in its detailed references to the Catholic sacraments, especially Confession, Eucharist, and Extreme Unction (131–36). Sailer even goes so far as to provide a vernacular translation of the text of the anointing rite associated with the last of these sacraments, seeking to explain its meaning to the reader (138). But much of the text avoids content that could be considered specifically Catholic, as opposed to more broadly Christian, making it especially suited to Protestant readers. This is in keeping with Sailer's ecumenical sensibilities, which were the part of his theological outlook most sympathetic to the Catholic Enlightenment. Though two non-biblical saints are mentioned in the *Kleine Bibel*, Polycarp and Ignatius (129–30), there are no prayers suggested to the saints themselves. There is also only the briefest of sections specifically on the Virgin Mary, who is described as the "mother of the Lord" (37; *Mutter unsers Herrn*).[85] One particularly evocative passage exemplifies the overall ecumenical tone: "All who sincerely seek the Lord, find the Lord, and all who have found the Lord, are One in faith, One in confidence, One in love,

---

[84] Sailer, *Kleine Bibel*. Throughout this section, page citations to this book will be given in the main text rather than in footnotes. A digitization of Sailer's text is available at https://onb.digital/result/10AFB934, accessed August 1, 2024.

[85] A similar de-emphasis of the veneration of Mary and the saints occurs in other books by Sailer intended to appeal to Protestant readers: see Schmidt-Biggemann, "Johann Michael Sailer als Aufklärer," 88–91. That said, Sailer far from discouraged such religious practices among lay Catholics (ibid., 109–14). As discussed in chapter 1, a reduced stress on devotion to Mary and the saints was typical of the Catholic Enlightenment.

and they who are One in love pray for each other, struggle unseen with each other.... One God. And all the children of God [are] One holy church of God" (65–66).[86]

The *Kleine Bibel* also reflects Sailer's interest in promoting Bible reading among ordinary Catholics. It quotes liberally from Scripture, and does so almost entirely in the German vernacular. The book is more than just a compendium of verses from the Bible. Rather, Sailer constantly provides the reader with exegesis, adopting a similar approach to what we have seen above in *Goldkörner der Weisheit und Tugend*, except that this time the exegesis is performed on words from the Bible rather than on sayings from ostensibly secular sources. In particular, Sailer concerns himself with making the meaning of individual passages specific to the situation of the sick and suffering. One example concerns 2 Corinthians 1:20: "For all the promises of God find their Yes in him. That is why we utter the Amen through him, to the glory of God." Sailer explains to the sick how this verse might apply to their own situation: "God in Christ brings to fulfillment through the apostles of Christ, and through a thousand other tools, the promises of the past. Christ is the center ...: from this center neither illness nor death, neither time nor eternity, should separate me" (63–64).[87] Sailer's exegesis of Scripture is at times extraordinarily detailed. At one point, he reflects at length on each and every line of the Lord's Prayer (106–7). With regard to John 10:28 ("And I give them eternal life, and they will never perish, and no one will snatch them out of my hand"), he spends almost two pages explaining the spiritual significance of just two words: "I give" (21–22; *Ich gebe*). The ultimate point of Sailer's exegesis seems always to encourage readers to respond actively—and personally—to each of the various texts, to internalize its meaning, to realize its significance for themselves as individuals.

This personalization of Scripture occurs in various other ways. In the fifth chapter of the book, Sailer quotes Romans 8:28: "We know that in everything God works for good with those who love him" (57). To this quotation, he adds: "Also auch diese Krankheit, auch der Tod selber" (Therefore also this illness, and death itself). Readers are here being encouraged to interpret

---

[86] "Alle, die den Herrn aufrichtig suchen, finden den Herrn, und alle die den Herrn gefunden haben, sind Eins in Glauben, Eins in der Zuversicht, Eins in der Liebe, und die Eines sind in der Liebe, beten für einander, kämpfen ungesehen miteinander.... Ein Gott. Und alle Kinder Gottes [sind] Eine heilige Kirche Gottes."

[87] "Gott in Christus bringt durch die Apostel Christi, und durch tausend andere Werkzeuge die Verheissungen der Vorzeit in Erfüllung. Christus ist der Mittelpunct ...: von diesem Mittelpuncte sollen mich weder Krankheit noch Tod, weder Zeit noch Ewigkeit trennen."

their own sufferings—their specific, personal situations—in light of this biblical verse. God will ensure that some good will indeed come out of their present hardships, and even out of their death. Elsewhere, Sailer discusses numerous characters from the Bible whose stories ought to inspire the suffering believer. The reader is encouraged to identify personally with these characters: "Abrahams Gott ist auch mein Gott," "Josephs Gott ist mein Gott," "Davids Gott ist mein Gott" (31–33). Throughout the book, Sailer's reflections on individual verses of Scripture also frequently take the form of pithy confessions of faith. For example, the exclamation "Christus, meine Zuversicht" (Christ, my assurance) accompanies Romans 9:33 (58): "See, I am laying in Zion a stone that will make men stumble, a rock that will make them fall; and he who believes in him will not be put to shame."[88] In such cases, it is almost as if Sailer is providing the reader with suggestions for how to respond verbally to the text. The reader is encouraged not only to learn the meaning of Scripture, but to *converse* with it.

Sailer's insistence that ethical concerns and worship of God cannot be separated is another theme that appears in the *Kleine Bibel*. In the book's opening paragraphs, addressed to caregivers, he points out that caring for the sick is a way of combating self-centeredness, as well as a form of evangelization (5). Christian charity in this regard is not simply ethically praiseworthy, but both strengthens the faith of believers and inspires those who do not believe (11–12). The clergy, especially, are reminded that in ministering to the sick, God appears in them (10). Sailer also uses scriptural examples to demonstrate the inextricable link between love of God and love of neighbor, including Christ's exhortation to St. John to care for the Virgin Mary (126). For Sailer, events, deeds, and actions are, moreover, vehicles through which God appears and intervenes in the world—an unequivocal rejection of deism. "God speaks through events," Sailer writes, "and almost always more clearly through unpleasant ones than pleasant ones. What God reveals to the sick person through illness is, like every word of God, Truth and Life" (77).[89] In addition, the suffering of individuals is meant as a spiritual lesson for those other than the sick themselves. Throughout the book, Sailer reminds the reader that living a truly Christian life before illness and death prepares

---

[88] Sailer mistakenly cites this verse as Romans 11:33.
[89] "Gott spricht durch Ereignisse, und fast immer vernehmlicher durch widerliche, als durch angenehme. Was Gott dem kranken durch Krankheit offenbart, ist, wie jedes Wort Gottes, lauter Wahrheit und Leben."

the believer to stay strong when suffering does eventually arrive (e.g., p. 84). From sharing in the experiences of others, then, one grows in one's own spirituality.

Above all, the *Kleine Bibel*, more than either of the other two books by Sailer in Beethoven's possession, serves as a striking example of Sailer's Christocentrism. In the very first pages, he stresses the absolute centrality of the figure of Christ to Christianity, which he defines as "nothing else but the seizing of eternal life in and through Christ, and a representation of eternal life in and through Christ" (12–13).[90] He bluntly describes Christ as "die ewige Gottheit" (the eternal God), who alone is capable of revealing God the Father (24). (Sailer's use of the term "Gottheit" to refer specifically to Jesus Christ suggests that Beethoven's use of the same word in the Heiligenstadt Testament, the *Tagebuch*, and the title of the "Heiliger Dankgesang" need not be understood as incompatible with Christian belief: see chapter 4.)

Throughout the *Kleine Bibel*, Sailer's constant emphasis is on the need for the suffering believer to become close to Christ, to draw comfort from him, a theme succinctly captured by the following passage:

> Dear suffering ones! Christ still lives, He is still your friend in dark hours as in happy days, He can help you to find light, comfort, strength, blessedness, even in this suffering, and wants you to do so. He is your teacher and your comforter, today as yesterday—always the same. Compose yourselves, learn to endure pain, collect your mind and heart, hear what He says—He has nothing but the words of eternal life, full of spirit and truth (14).[91]

Not only is Christ depicted as the ultimate healer of the body, but Sailer also connects the suffering believer's need for physical healing to their need for forgiveness, above all through the Catholic sacraments. In a section on Confession, he writes emphatically, "The sinner can only through a return to God (penance) and through faith in Christ be receptive to true consolation" (132).[92] The relevance of Christ for the sick and dying that the *Kleine*

---

[90] "nichts anders, als eine Ergreifung des ewigen Lebens in und durch Christus, und eine Darstellung des ewigen Lebens in und durch Christus."

[91] "Lieber Leidender! Christus lebet noch, ist noch in trüben Stunden dein Freund wie in frohen Tagen, kann und will dich auch in diesem Leiden Licht, Trost, Stärke, Seligkeit—finden lassen. Er ist dein Lehrer und dein Tröster, heut wie gestern—immer derselbe. Fasse dich nur, lerne dem Schmerzen gebieten, sammle Sinn und Herz, horche was Er spricht—Er hat lauter Worte des ewigen Lebens, voll Geist und Wahrheit."

[92] "Der Sünder kann nur durch Rückkehr zu Gott (Buße), und durch Glauben an Christus—eines wahren Trostes empfänglich werden."

Bibel foregrounds seems obvious enough given the importance of Christ's own suffering and death for Christian doctrine. But Christ in the *Kleine Bibel* is more than just an example to follow, more than just a person to be inspired by. Rather, he is presented repeatedly as someone to be encountered intimately, to become connected to in the deepest possible way. The name of Christ ("Christus" and its inflected forms) appears so frequently in the *Kleine Bibel* that it comes across as a kind of solemn mantra; Sailer is especially fond of short, slogan-like exclamations that invoke Christ's name (76): "Christus, meine Zuversicht" (Christ, my surety), "Gott in Christus—mein Heil" (God in Christ—my salvation).[93] The scriptural quotations he has selected from the New Testament more often than not include the name of Christ, and the meditations he has composed on such scriptural verses occasionally invite readers to imagine what Christ would say to them personally (e.g., p. 251).

In terms of its main thematic concerns and overall tone, Sailer's *Kleine Bibel* bears a striking resemblance to Thomas à Kempis's *Imitation of Christ*, which, as mentioned above, was a book that Sailer greatly admired, and also one that Beethoven had in his library in Sailer's own translation. Since Thomas's Latin original (*De imitatione Christi*) was completed in the early fifteenth century, the book has become one of the most beloved and influential Christian devotional books,[94] which makes it rather astonishing that its presence in Beethoven's library has occasioned so little comment in previous studies. As Jeffery Zalar has pointed out, it was a book commonly found in the homes of ordinary lay Catholics in Beethoven's home region of the Rhineland.[95] A specific discussion of Thomas's text here seems justified by the likely connection between Beethoven's ownership of a copy of *Imitation of Christ* and his interest in Sailer's writings.

On the whole, Thomas's *Imitation of Christ* shares with Sailer's *Kleine Bibel* an obvious Christocentrism. The title of the book's very first chapter places the reader's focus squarely on the person of Christ: "Imitate Christ and learn to despise what is fleeting."[96] Thomas's text then teaches that to emulate Christ's life is the fundamental requirement of the Christian, more

---

[93] "Gott in Christus—mein Heil" recalls Sailer's theological motto, "Gott in Christus—das Heil der Welt."
[94] See Leo Sherley-Price, introduction to *Imitation of Christ*, by Thomas à Kempis, 11–25.
[95] Zalar, Reading and Rebellion, 66–67.
[96] Thomas von Kempen, *Das Buch*, 9 (my translation): "Folge Christus nach und lerne verachten, was vergänglich ist." Sailer's German rendering follows the Latin original closely: "De imitatione Christi et contemptu mundi omniumque eius vanitatum." The entirety of Thomas's original Latin text can be found online at www.thelatinlibrary.com/kempis.html, accessed August 1, 2024. For convenience, in the remainder of my discussion of Thomas's book, I will cite and quote from the English

188 THE CATHOLIC BEETHOVEN

important than any theological knowledge: "Let the life of Jesus Christ, then, be our first consideration" (I.1).[97] Embedded in this intense emphasis on Christ is the irenic implication that the figure of Christ provides a kind of common ground for all Christians, transcending theological divisions:

> The teaching of Jesus far transcends all the teachings of the Saints. . . . Of what use is it to discourse learnedly on the Trinity, if you lack humility and therefore displease the Trinity? Lofty words do not make a man just or holy; but a good life makes him dear to God (I.1).[98]

> At the Day of Judgement, we shall not be asked what we have read, but what we have done; not what we have spoken but how holily we have lived (I.3).[99]

Such sentiments would probably have resonated with Sailer's, as well as Beethoven's, ecumenical outlook. *Imitation of Christ* is also akin to the *Kleine Bibel* in encouraging the believer to enter into an intimate, deeply personal relationship with Jesus. True peace, Thomas counsels, can only be found when one is "inwardly united to Christ" (II.1).[100] Using a technique that Sailer would emulate in the *Kleine Bibel*, Thomas further dramatizes the intimacy of the ideal relationship one should have with Jesus through passages that imagine Christ in a direct, one-on-one conversation with the individual believer (e.g., III.21).[101]

---

translation by Leo Sherley-Price (Thomas à Kempis, *Imitation of Christ*), while providing Sailer's German rendering in footnotes to facilitate comparison. I have made an exception to this rule in this instance, in order to provide the reader with a more literal sense of Sailer's German. Given the classic nature of this book and the wide availability of different versions and translations, I will also, in all cases, provide book and chapter numbers in the main text.

[97] Thomas à Kempis, *Imitation of Christ*, 27. See also Thomas von Kempen, *Das Buch*, 9: "Wir sollen also unsere höchste Aufgabe darin sehen, das Leben Jesu Christi zu erforschen."
[98] Thomas à Kempis, *Imitation of Christ*, 27. See also Thomas von Kempen, *Das Buch*, 9: "Die Lehre Christi übertrifft alles, was die Heiligen gelehrt haben. . . . Was nützt es dir, über die Dreieinigkeit hochgelert streiten zu können, wenn du die Demut nicht hast, ohne die du der Dreieinigkeit mißfällst? Wahrhaftig, hochgelehrte und tiefsinnige Worte machen den Menschen nicht heilig und nicht gerecht: ein Leben voll Tugend dagegen macht uns Gott genehm."
[99] Thomas à Kempis, *Imitation of Christ*, 31. See also Thomas von Kempen, *Das Buch*, 14: "Am Tage des Gerichtes wird man uns nicht fragen, was wir gelesen, sondern was wir getan haben; nicht fragen, wie schön wir gesprochen, sondern wie fromm wir gelebt haben."
[100] Thomas à Kempis, *Imitation of Christ*, 68. See also Thomas von Kempen, *Das Buch*, 57: "[du] wirst nirgends Ruhe finden, als in der innigsten Vereinigung mit Christus."
[101] Thomas à Kempis, *Imitation of Christ*, 120–22. See also Thomas von Kempen, *Das Buch*, 117–20.

Thomas's intense focus on Christ, as in Sailer's *Kleine Bibel*, is linked closely to the idea that Christ provides the believer with ultimate comfort in the midst of suffering, an idea that can be connected in turn to Beethoven's own personal suffering in body and soul, and to the composer's interest in healing. That Christ in his humanity has suffered as humans have—an idea highlighted in Beethoven's own *Christus am Ölberge*—makes him a perfect model for people to follow (II.12).[102] Hence, in one of the most moving passages in the whole book, Thomas tells his reader to pay attention always to that great symbol of Christ's suffering—the Cross—which will overcome all suffering:

> In the Cross is salvation; in the Cross is life; in the Cross is protection against our enemies; in the Cross is infusion of heavenly sweetness; in the Cross is strength of mind; in the Cross is joy of spirit; in the Cross is excellence of virtue; in the Cross is perfection of holiness. There is no salvation of soul, nor hope of eternal life, save in the Cross. Take up the Cross, therefore, and follow Jesus, and go forward into eternal life. Christ has gone before you, bearing His Cross; He died for you on the Cross, that you also may bear your cross, and desire to die on the cross with Him (II.12).[103]

The *Imitation* also emphasizes the spiritual value of suffering for the believer. Through suffering one learns that heaven is one's true home, not the earthly world (I.12).[104] In addition, like the *Kleine Bibel*, Thomas's text stresses the connection between suffering and human sinfulness. Meditating on the person of Christ enables the believer to realize that human nature is fallen and in need of salvation (I.25).[105] Another passage describes the fallen human being as "dust," a biblical image that we have already seen occurring in Beethoven's Gellert Lieder and in other sources associated with the

---

[102] Thomas à Kempis, *Imitation of Christ*, 84–89. See also Thomas von Kempen, *Das Buch*, 76–82.
[103] Thomas à Kempis, *Imitation of Christ*, 84–85. See also Thomas von Kempen, *Das Buch*, 77: "Im Kreuze ist Heil, im Kreuze ist Leben, im Kreuze ist Schutz vor den Feinden, im Kreuze ist Eingießung himmlischer Seligkeit, im Kreuze ist Stärke des Gemütes, im Kreuze ist Geistesfreude, im Kreuze ist höchste Tugend, im Kreuze ist vollendete Heiligung. Es ist kein Heil der Seele, keine Hoffnung des ewigen Lebens, außer im Kreuze. Nimm also dein Kreuz auf dich und folge Jesus nach, und du bist auf dem geraden Wege zum ewigen Leben. Sieh! er ging dir ja voraus und trug uns das Kreuz voran und starb sogar für dich am Kreuze, damit auch du dein Kreuz tragen lernen und Mut empfangen solltest, am Kreuze zu sterben."
[104] Thomas à Kempis, *Imitation of Christ*, 39. See also Thomas von Kempen, *Das Buch*, 23–24.
[105] Thomas à Kempis, *Imitation of Christ*, 64–65. See also Thomas von Kempen, *Das Buch*, 53.

composer: "I will presume to speak to my Lord, though I am but dust and ashes. If I esteem myself to be anything more, You confront me, and my sins bear a true witness against me, that I cannot contradict" (III.8).[106]

For Thomas as for Sailer, recognizing one's sinfulness should prompt one to prepare one's soul for death. *Imitation* does not shy away from warning its reader of the consequences of failing to repent before death: eternal punishment, hellfire, and damnation (I.22, 24–25).[107] Observing the deaths of others should always be a reminder to oneself that one will eventually face the same fate (I.23).[108] This idea also appears in Sailer's *Kleine Bibel*, as discussed above. The constant reminders in Thomas's text to keep death in mind, and to focus on the life to come, contribute greatly to the book's overall asceticism, its emphasis on abnegation and the separation of one's desires from those of the here-and-now. Thomas exhorts the reader to trust in God rather than in the things of this world (I.7).[109] Solitude, he proposes, is to be embraced as a helpful state for meditating on the divine (I.20).[110] In addition, Thomas's text stresses the theocentric conception of ethics that was so important to Sailer. Ethical conduct is to be connected always to love of God and Jesus: "Love all men for Jesus' sake, but Jesus for Himself" (II.8).[111] In another passage, Thomas defines virtue as "complete surrender of your heart to the will of God, not seeking to have your own way either in great matters or small, in time or eternity" (III.25).[112]

Sailer and Beethoven's Religious Interests

If we compare Sailer's outlook, especially as reflected in the books Beethoven owned, with prior evidence of Beethoven's religious interests presented in

---

[106] Thomas à Kempis, *Imitation of Christ*, 103. See also Thomas von Kempen, *Das Buch*, 97: "Ich will zu meinem Herrn sprechen, ob ich gleich Staub und Asche bin. Hielte ich mich für mehr, sieh! Herr, du stündest auf wider mich, und meine Sünden bezeugten die Wahrheit, und ich könnte nicht widersprechen."

[107] Thomas à Kempis, *Imitation of Christ*, 55–57, 60–66. See also Thomas von Kempen, *Das Buch*, 42–45, 48–55.

[108] Thomas à Kempis, *Imitation of Christ*, 57–60. See also Thomas von Kempen, *Das Buch*, 45–48.

[109] Thomas à Kempis, *Imitation of Christ*, 34–35. See also Thomas von Kempen, *Das Buch*, 17–18.

[110] Thomas à Kempis, *Imitation of Christ*, 50–53. See also Thomas von Kempen, *Das Buch*, 37–40.

[111] Thomas à Kempis, *Imitation of Christ*, 77. See also Thomas von Kempen, *Das Buch*, 68: "Du sollst alle Menschen um Jesu willen lieb haben, Jesus aber um seiner selbst willen."

[112] Thomas à Kempis, *Imitation of Christ*, 128. See also Thomas von Kempen, *Das Buch*, 126: "dass du dich von ganzem Herzen Gott und seinen Willen hingibst und nicht suchst, was dein ist, weder im Kleinen noch im Großen, weder in der Zeit, noch in der Ewigkeit." The original Latin text refers to "virtus" a little before the phrase I have quoted. Sherley-Price's English translation renders "virtus" as

previous chapters, it is easy to see why the theologian exerted such an appeal for Beethoven. Sailer's progressive side would have aligned well with Beethoven's sympathy for Catholic Enlightenment ideas, which had been cultivated by his upbringing in Bonn. The theologian's ecumenism parallels Beethoven's own engagement with Protestants, as reflected in the composer's decision to set poems by Christian Fürchtegott Gellert, and his preoccupation with ensuring the Mass in C was published with a high-quality German text (see chapter 3). Sailer's *Goldkörner* would also have been attractive to Beethoven as a collection of sayings of predominantly non-Christian origin from which a faithful Christian should still draw inspiration. The resemblance to Beethoven's own *Tagebuch* in this regard is striking and speaks against using the *Tagebuch* as evidence of the composer's distance from Catholicism (see chapter 4). It is worth noting, too, that Thomas à Kempis's *Imitation of Christ* draws on non-Christian sources alongside its heavy use of scriptural allusions. Ovid's *Remedia amoris* is quoted in a passage on resisting the temptation to do wrong, and Seneca's *Epistulae morales* in a section on the usefulness of solitude for the spiritual life.[113] These quotations not only parallel Sailer's own openness to non-Christian thought, but demonstrate that even in the Middle Ages, finding inspiration in non-Christian sources was by no means antithetical to being a Christian.

The moderate and nuanced nature of Sailer's views on ecumenism has similarities with arguments made by Ignaz Aurelius Feßler in his *Ansichten von Religion und Kirchenthum*, which Beethoven also consulted around the time he started working on the *Missa solemnis* (see chapter 4). Feßler's text, we recall, stresses that the external rituals of Catholicism (*Cultus*) should be distinguished from what he calls its "essence" (*Wesen*), which, he argues, is manifest even in non-Catholic churches.[114] The commonalities uniting different expressions of a more fundamental Christian faith should thus take precedence over the theological differences between them. Sailer would almost certainly have regarded Feßler's distinction between *Cultus* and *Wesen* as far too strict and have disagreed with his explicit rejection of the Catholic Church's monopoly on Christian truth. As described

---

"holiness," rather than "virtue." Sailer's translation uses the German "Tugend" ("virtue" in English) for "virtus."

[113] Thomas à Kempis, *Imitation of Christ*, 41, 50 (I.13, I.20). See also Thomas von Kempen, *Das Buch*, 26, 37.
[114] Feßler, *Ansichten*, esp. 2:7–10, 183–85.

above, for all of Sailer's openness to and engagement with non-Catholic Christians, he does not appear to have ever questioned the idea that the Roman Catholic Church was the one true Church through which salvation is to be attained, or that the Catholic sacraments play an indispensable role in the Christian life. Sailer, in other words, accorded the *Cultus* of Catholicism a more important role than Feßler did. Be that as it may, a broad interest in ecumenism provides a striking point of similarity between Sailer and Feßler—two religious thinkers whose writings Beethoven engaged with around the same time. Indeed, Feßler had a documented interest in Sailer's ideas, and it is possible that his own thinking was influenced by his engagement with them.[115]

The more conservative aspects of Sailer's outlook might at first appear to be in tension with Beethoven's Catholic Enlightenment leanings. But what is interesting is that even these aspects resonate with small hints of the composer's own openness to ideas that deviated to some degree from the Catholic Enlightenment. Sailer's belief in a specifically theocentric, rather than anthropocentric, conception of ethical conduct further recalls aspects of the musical works and religious texts discussed in the previous two chapters. Feßler's *Ansichten* and Sturm's *Betrachtungen* both emphasize that ethics should be inextricably tied to Christian dogma (see chapter 4). Feßler, for instance, argues that both the Lutheranism and Calvinism of his time have been reduced to mere ethical philosophies, stripped of the supernatural faith in the salvific nature of Christ, without which Christianity is meaningless. In Sturm's book, passages on nature and what nature can teach people about ethical conduct occur alongside those that stress the role of loving Jesus in enabling a believer to do good deeds. As we saw in chapter 3, Beethoven's oratorio *Christus am Ölberge* combines ethical and didactic characteristics with an intensely sentimental portrayal of Christ and an emphasis on his redemptive role in saving fallen humanity. And in the second song of the Gellert Lieder, "Die Liebe des Nächsten" (Love of neighbor), the text, while being the most ethically focused of the six poems Beethoven chose to set, also refers to Christ as "Erlöser" (Redeemer), and includes the following lines unambiguously linking ethics to Christ:

---

[115] During his time in Berlin, Feßler worked as a tutor to an aristocratic girl (who later became his wife) and assigned Sailer's works for her to read. Feßler also included prayers composed by Sailer in his own published writings. See Barton, *Ignatius Aurelius Feßler*, 306, 523.

Ich sollte Brüder hassen,	Should I hate my brothers,
Die Gott durch seines Sohnes Blut	Whom God has through the blood of his son
So hoch erkaufen lassen?	Purchased at so high a price?

Earlier in the same song, the text proclaims:

Wer zwar mit Rat, mit Trost und Schutz	Whoever with counsel, with comfort and protection
Den Nächsten unterstützet,	Supports his neighbor,
Doch nur aus Stolz, aus Eigennutz,	But only out of pride and self-interest,
Aus Weichlichkeit ihm nützet;	Uses him out of weakness;
Nicht aus Gehorsam, nicht aus Pflicht;	Not out of obedience, not out of duty;
Der liebt auch seinen Nächsten nicht.	He does not love his neighbor either.

These lines bear a striking similarity to an especially provocative moment in Sailer's *Kleine Bibel*, where the theologian encourages the reader to ask God's forgiveness not only for one's misdeeds but also for one's virtue (*Tugend*). If good deeds are done out of self-congratulatory pride, Sailer explains, they require God's pardon as much as obvious sins.[116]

The fundamental Christocentrism of Sailer's outlook, especially his emphasis on the need for the believer to cultivate an intimate relationship with Christ, brings to mind Beethoven's highly sentimental depiction of Christ in *Christus am Ölberge*. The specific connection in Sailer's *Kleine Bibel* between knowing Christ and experiencing suffering and death would have been of special relevance to Beethoven, given his own physical ailments and interest in the subject of healing. For instance, as discussed previously, in the course of reading Sturm's *Betrachtungen* Beethoven underlined several passages about the importance for a Christian of being ready for death and of trusting in Jesus during times of trial. Related ideas such as stoicism in the face of suffering and separating oneself from the cares of the present world, which are prominent in the *Kleine Bibel*, also appear in *Christus am Ölberge* and the Heiligenstadt Testament.

---

[116] Sailer, *Kleine Bibel*, 79.

Nevertheless, compared to other religious thinkers like Sturm and Feßler with whose writings Beethoven engaged previously, and compared to the progressive version of the German Catholic Enlightenment that Beethoven would have been exposed to during his youth in Bonn, Sailer's outlook is clearly more conservative, even if he was still far from aligned with the Catholic Restoration.[117] Given the frequent attempts to link Beethoven to the critical philosophy of Immanuel Kant (discussed in the introduction), Sailer's opposition to Kant's ideas is especially noteworthy. Though this aspect of Sailer's outlook is not explicit in the books Beethoven owned, it is implied in the scathing critique of liberal ideas in *Friedrich Christians Vermächtniß* and in the theocentric conception of ethics already discussed. That Beethoven was not only attracted to Sailer's writings, but also wanted his beloved nephew Karl to study with the theologian, suggests that he was becoming more open to conservative approaches to Catholicism in the last decade of his life. As we shall see in the remainder of this chapter as well as in the next one, this impression is reinforced by some of Beethoven's compositional choices in the *Missa solemnis* and the related possibility that Beethoven was familiar with Sailer's views on the Catholic liturgy.

Sailer's Views on Liturgy and Beethoven's Mass in C

In the overview I provided above of Sailer's theology, I briefly mentioned his approach to the liturgy, which emphasized the importance of individual piety and private devotional practices without neglecting the public liturgical life of the Church, especially the centrality of the Mass. A more detailed examination of Sailer's views on the liturgy reveals intriguing points of correspondence with Beethoven's treatment of the Mass text in his Mass in C, discussed in chapter 3. In this case, however, we are on less certain ground since liturgical issues do not feature as prominently in the books by Sailer in Beethoven's possession as the themes I have outlined above. Even so, as I shall explain, there is reason to believe that the composer might have had some familiarity with Sailer's liturgical views.

---

[117] As previously discussed, this conservatism was what led John Paul Ito to dismiss Sailer's importance for Beethoven: see "Johann Michael Sailer and Beethoven," esp. 91.

One of Sailer's most important works concerning the liturgy was entitled *Neue Beyträge zur Bildung des Geistlichen* (New contributions to the education of the clergy).[118] Here Sailer takes as his starting point a fundamental distinction between "inner" and "outer" religion (*innere und äußere Religion*).[119] Against those who would emphasize one of these over the other, Sailer argues that both are needed. Though faith begins with the revelation of Christ in the interior of each individual soul, it constantly seeks and requires externalization, a *physical* manifestation.[120] And it is in public worship—in the Church's liturgy, especially the Mass—that individual faith comes to life. Moreover, the liturgy is not merely a place for the believer to encounter Christ but a vehicle for the living out of Christian morality through good works performed for others. It is not enough to believe, but that belief must be brought to light, because each Christian is bound by Christ to bring the joy of the Gospel to the whole world. The Church and its liturgy, in being outer manifestations of inner religion, act as a vehicle for what Sailer calls the "unity of human beings" (*Vereinigung der Menschen*).[121] In this regard, Sailer's conception of the liturgy is intimately tied to the theocentric conception of ethics discussed above. Conversely, the external practice of public worship is meaningless if it does not cultivate and strengthen the faith and morals of each individual believer. As Sailer writes, "[The Church] is not just an institution of outward religion, she is also an institution of inward religion."[122] In Sailer's view, religion must be both individual and communal: one needs both inner, private spirituality, and outer, public worship. It is precisely in the public liturgy of the Church that inner and outer religion meet and animate each other. Both liturgical laxity *and* an excessively mechanistic attitude toward the liturgy are to be rejected.[123] The precise form of the liturgy really does matter, but at the same time, following the rubrics should never be an end in itself.[124]

---

[118] See Probst, *Gottesdienst in Geist und Wahrheit*, 150–205, 223–30. For a digitalization of Sailer's *Neue Beyträge*, see https://onb.digital/result/10292440, accessed August 1, 2024.

[119] Sailer, *Neue Beyträge*, 209.

[120] Sailer, 208–9.

[121] Sailer, 210. See also Probst, *Gottesdienst in Geist und Wahrheit*, 136–39.

[122] Sailer, 213: "Sie ist nicht bloß ein Organ der Religion nach Außen, sie ist auch ein Organ der Religion nach Innen."

[123] See Schuh, *Johann Michael Sailer*, 83–84.

[124] The distinction between inner and outer religion in Sailer's liturgical outlook bears a resemblance to that between the *Wesen* and *Cultus* of Catholicism in Feßler's *Ansichten*. As discussed in chapter 4, Feßler regarded the *Cultus* of Catholicism as important even if not essential to the faith, but the validity of *Cultus* depends on its ability to lead the believer to a deeper recognition of the *Wesen* of Catholicism. In the same way, Sailer insisted that liturgy, though central to the life of the Church, should never be an end in itself but rather a vehicle for cultivating a deeper and more active

196 THE CATHOLIC BEETHOVEN

There exists an edition of the *Neue Beyträge* that was published together with the *Kleine Bibel* in its 1819 Grätz edition—the edition of the *Kleine Bibel* that we are certain Beethoven owned—in a single combined volume: see figure 5.2. (This combined volume was itself published in Grätz in 1819.) It is thus not far-fetched to suggest that when Beethoven obtained his copy of the *Kleine Bibel*, the *Neue Beyträge* might have been included as well, and for whatever reason, the latter work was not subsequently listed in the posthumous inventory of Beethoven's possessions.[125] Either it was lost or was simply treated as part of the *Kleine Bibel* when it was recorded in the inventory. But even if it cannot be conclusively proven that Beethoven was familiar with this important representative of Sailer's liturgical views, the books by Sailer that Beethoven *did* have in his possession do contain a small number of references to liturgical issues, though such references are not always explicit.

In *Friedrich Christians Vermächtniß*, the eponymous Friedrich explicitly criticizes those who profess belief but do not worship publicly.[126] If one is truly religious, Friedrich argues, then one should want to share that faith with others. Conversely, those who find it difficult to believe might become inspired to do so through their participation in public worship. At the same time, however, Friedrich stresses that external religion, as symbolized by things like church buildings, exist not for their own sake, but to encourage the spiritual life of the individual.[127] "Do not separate yourselves from the holy place," he writes, "[But] do not forget, that the outer temples only stand there in order to strengthen the inner temples within you and within others."[128] Sailer's gloss on one of the Latin quotations in *Goldkörner* expresses similar sentiments: "May not only your body be in church; but may your understanding also be there... and may your heart, and above all things

faith in the individual believer. This similarity should not, however, obscure the fact that, as I have explained, Sailer hewed much closer to orthodox Catholic doctrine than Feßler did.

[125] Martin Cooper has claimed—tantalizingly for my purposes—that Beethoven mentioned the *Neue Beyträge* in the conversation books (*Beethoven*, 113), though this is almost certainly a mistake. Cooper cites an older transcription of the conversation books by Walther Nohl (which Nohl died before completing), and on the page he cites in Nohl's edition the work mentioned is *Von der Priesterweihung*, not *Neue Beyträge*, as Cooper claimed. (See W. Nohl, *Beethoven*, 1:100.) I have not been able to find a reference to *Neue Beyträge* anywhere else in the conversation books. Even so, it is striking to me that Cooper would have even heard of Sailer's *Neue Beyträge*, though without more information, I cannot tell how this was so. I shall discuss *Von der Priesterweihung* further below.
[126] Sailer, *Friedrich Christians Vermächtniß*, 1:50, 54.
[127] Sailer, 1:47.
[128] Sailer, 1:51–52: "Separirt ihr euch nicht selber von der heiligen Stätte.... [Aber] vergesset nicht, daß die äußern Tempel doch nur da stehen, um den innern in euch und in andern auszubauen."

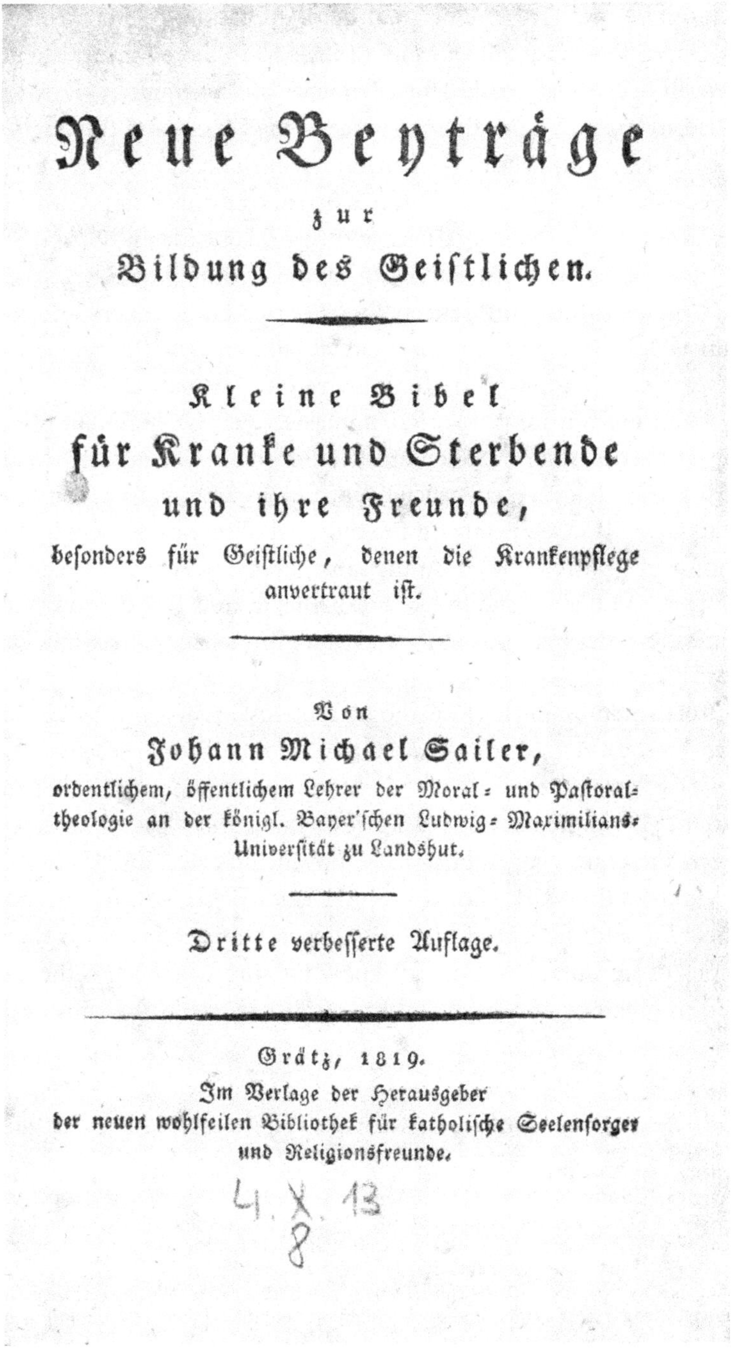

Neue Beyträge
zur
Bildung des Geistlichen.

Kleine Bibel
für Kranke und Sterbende
und ihre Freunde,
besonders für Geistliche, denen die Krankenpflege
anvertraut ist.

Von
Johann Michael Sailer,
ordentlichem, öffentlichem Lehrer der Moral= und Pastoral=
theologie an der königl. Bayer'schen Ludwig= Maximilians=
Universität zu Landshut.

Dritte verbesserte Auflage.

Grätz, 1819.
Im Verlage der Herausgeber
der neuen wohlfeilen Bibliothek für katholische Seelenforger
und Religionsfreunde.

Figure 5.2 Cover page showing the compilation of Johann Michael Sailer's *Kleine Bibel* and *Neue Beyträge zur Bildung des Geistlichen* in a single volume (Grätz, 1819). Image courtesy of the Austrian National Library.

your heart, be there."[129] The original Latin quotation, by Juan Luis Vives, reads: "Sacris intersis attente, ac pie" (Take part in sacred things attentively and piously). The *Kleine Bibel*, for all of its encouragement of private devotion, also stresses the central importance of the Mass—and the Eucharistic sacrifice that occurs within it—in encountering Christ, especially for those who are near death.[130] In general, the Christian who encounters Christ in the liturgy is then obliged to bring Christ to the world outside the liturgy: "Christ in the midst of his disciples, and his disciples a light in the midst of the dark world."[131] This exhortation reflects the need for both "inner" and "outer" religion as described above, for individual faith and the Church as a community. An equal emphasis on both active interior faith and exterior religious practice is apparent, too, in Thomas à Kempis's *Imitation of Christ*, whose connection to both Sailer and Beethoven has been described above. Thomas rejects an overly superficial approach to faith that cares only about ritual actions: "If we rely only on the outward observances of religion, our devotion will rapidly wane."[132] At the same time, however, he makes it clear that outward religious practice cannot be neglected: "We should carefully examine and order both our inner and outer life, since both are vital to our advance."[133]

It is worth mentioning here Beethoven's interest in a work by Sailer entitled *Von der Priesterweihung: Eine Rede* (On the ordination of priests: A speech), a homily exploring the nature of the Catholic priesthood, which Sailer gave in March 1817 on the occasion of a priest's inaugural Mass.[134] As described above, in the conversation books Beethoven indicated his desire to purchase a copy of this work, though—unlike *Goldkörner, Friedrich Christians Vermächtniß*, and the *Kleine Bibel*—it does not appear in the posthumous inventory of his library. We do not know for sure whether Beethoven did succeed in obtaining a copy of it, but we can say at least that his desire to

---

[129] Sailer, *Sprüche-Buch: Goldkörner*, 51: "Nicht dein Körper bloß sey in der Kirche; auch dein Verstand sey da... auch dein Herz, und vor allen dein Herz sey da."
[130] Sailer, *Kleine Bibel*, 134.
[131] Sailer, 88: "Christus in Mitte der Seinen, und die Seinen ein Licht in Mitte der finstern Welt."
[132] Thomas à Kempis, *Imitation of Christ*, 38 (I.11). See also Thomas von Kempen, *Das Buch*, 22: "Wenn wir unsere Religiosität, unser Fortschreiten im Guten nur in jene äußerlichen Übungen setzen, so wird unsere Frömmigkeit ein schnelles Ende nehmen."
[133] Thomas à Kempis, 48 (I.19). See also Thomas von Kempen, 35: "Wir müssen unser Inneres und Äußeres streng durchforschen und gewissenhaft ordnen; denn beides hilft uns auf dem Wege zum Guten weiter."
[134] Sailer, *Von der Priesterweihung*. A digitization of this text is available at https://www.digitale-sammlungen.de/en/view/bsb10591604, accessed August 1, 2024.

purchase it indicates a strong interest in Sailer's views on the Catholic liturgy. In this speech, Sailer translates the Latin rite of ordination into German and performs an exegesis of it. Though dedicated to seminarians, portions of the book are addressed explicitly to laypeople, and it is obvious that Sailer wishes lay readers, too, to understand the significance of the texts used in a Mass to ordain a priest.[135] This practice of translating and explaining liturgical texts in the vernacular is similar to what occurs in the *Kleine Bibel*—where, as has been discussed, Sailer performs this task in relation to the Sacrament of Extreme Unction—and reflects more broadly Sailer's goal of getting ordinary Catholics to know and understand the words of the Mass and other liturgical rites in their own language. At one point, for instance, he proposed the publication of the Latin Missal with German translations alongside the official liturgical text. He also supported the singing of Masses in German, and especially the development of appropriate German hymns (*Kirchenlieder*) for the Mass.[136]

Sailer's views on the liturgy, as with so much else in his "centrist" theological outlook, represented a nuanced and ambivalent relationship with the ideas of the German Catholic Enlightenment. His concern with the educative potential of the Mass reflects to a certain degree the emphasis on pastoral theology and ethical cultivation central to the Josephinist church reforms, but he rejected an *exclusively* didactic conception of the Mass that de-emphasized its mystical and emotional aspects, its status as a sacrament enabling the believer to encounter Christ.[137] In chapter 3, we saw how the extreme focus on the Mass text in Beethoven's Mass in C adhered conceptually to Josephinism's educative approach to church music—the notion that church music should teach the faithful what the liturgical text means—but, in its emotional exuberance, departed musically from the Josephinist emphasis on simplicity and restraint. I have previously mentioned that in this regard, Beethoven may have been influenced by the ideas of Ferdinand d'Antoine, who was active in Bonn during Beethoven's youth. But the parallels with Sailer's views on the liturgy are also noteworthy. Both the musical exegesis Beethoven performs on specific parts of the Mass text and the occasional dramatization of an individual's spontaneous emotional response

---

[135] Sailer, dedication page and 30–32.
[136] See Probst, *Gottesdienst in Geist und Wahrheit*, 87–88. As discussed in chapter 3, both for stylistic reasons and in the selection of poetry by Gellert in particular, Beethoven's Gellert Lieder alludes to the genre of the Catholic *Kirchenlied*.
[137] See Probst, 158; and Donakowski, "Age of Revolutions," 356, 358.

to the text—two important characteristics of the Mass in C that I highlighted in chapter 3—reflect a Sailerian desire for the believer to come to a deeper understanding of the liturgical text, while rejecting what might be described as the emotional aridity of Josephinism's approach to church music. In an emotionally vivid manner, Beethoven musically explains and dramatizes the Mass text in the same way that Sailer explains and elaborates on the meaning of liturgical texts in the *Kleine Bibel* (and in *Von der Priesterweihung*), not merely translating the Latin texts into the vernacular but responding to them with statements of his own in order to elucidate their broader spiritual implications. Also relevant in this regard are Beethoven's own efforts to ensure that the Mass in C was published with Christian Schreiber's German text. Though ostensibly meant for Protestant audiences, Schreiber's text could also function as a kind of exegesis of the Mass text for Catholics, suggesting other spiritual ideas that might be evoked through, or associated with, what is literally meant by the Latin words.

As with other aspects of his theological outlook, it is likely that Sailer's views on the Catholic liturgy resonated with ideas Beethoven already had prior to his engagement with Sailer's writings, in this case ideas about setting the text of the Mass that were reflected in his earlier Mass in C. Sailer's conception of the liturgy thus provides another possible reason for Beethoven's admiration for Sailer, an admiration which motivated his desire to send his beloved nephew Karl to study with the theologian. Beethoven's engagement with Sailer coincided with the beginning of his work on a new musical setting of the Catholic Mass—the *Missa solemnis*, which he would eventually describe as his greatest work. The *Missa* would perpetuate in some ways the composer's approach to the Mass in the Mass in C, but in other ways it would chart a new course. As we shall see in the next and final chapter of this book, in both of these respects, Sailer's ideas can help us understand what Beethoven's artistic and religious goals in the *Missa solemnis* might have been.

6
The *Missa solemnis*

Despite the usual marginalization of Beethoven's religious works and the related tradition of distancing the composer from the Catholic religion, the *Missa solemnis* has always been the one piece of religious music in Beethoven's output that has been impossible to ignore. Critics have had to reckon not only with the sheer scale and complexity of the work from a strictly musical perspective, but with copious evidence of its personal importance to the composer. In the first place, although the piece was originally intended for a specific liturgical occasion—the enthronement of Beethoven's friend, patron, and pupil Archduke Rudolph as Archbishop of Olmütz—it was not a commission, not something that Rudolph himself requested, but one that Beethoven himself decided to write. Indeed, it seems likely that Beethoven's desire to compose a mass long predated the news of Rudolph's episcopal appointment, which is first mentioned in Beethoven's correspondence in March 1819.[1] Documentary evidence of Beethoven's interest in learning more about older Catholic Church music exists from before this time. A conversation-book entry from February or March 1818 contains a brief sketch of a harmonization exercise in the Dorian mode.[2] This is probably connected to a written statement in the *Tagebuch* from the same year, in which Beethoven reminds himself, "In order to write true church music go through all the ecclesiastical chants of the monks."[3] A still earlier *Tagebuch* entry, from 1813, already shows Beethoven contemplating what the correct pronunciation of the word "eleison" should be in the Kyrie.[4] The Mass in C had been published by this time, so this entry cannot be a reference to that earlier mass. For most of the 1810s, then, Beethoven may well have harbored a wish to write a second mass: Rudolph's appointment, rather than being the

---

[1] Anderson no. 938 (*BGA* no. 1294), Beethoven to Ferdinand Ries, March 8, 1819. The earliest sketches for the *Missa* also appear around the same time. See Drabkin, *Beethoven: Missa solemnis*, 11.
[2] *BCB* 1:8 (*BKh* 1:34).
[3] *Tagebuch* no. 168, c. 1818: "Um wahre Kirchenmusik zu schreiben / alle Kirchenchoräle der Mönche ect."
[4] *Tagebuch* no. 10, c. 1813.

principal motivation for the *Missa*, merely provided an opportunity to compose a work that he had already wanted to write.

The amount of effort Beethoven expended on the *Missa* suggests that it meant more to him personally than simply a work for a special occasion, or even a gift for a beloved friend. Put simply, the composer worked harder on the *Missa solemnis* than on any other piece in his output. Six hundred pages of sketches for it survive, across four different sketchbooks, two hundred for the Credo alone.[5] Moreover, he regarded the *Missa* as so important that he was willing to put aside, for more than three years, completion of the Diabelli Variations, even though he had already drafted nineteen of the thirty-three movements that work would come to have.[6] As is well known, this lengthy and labored compositional process meant that Beethoven never even came close to finishing the *Missa* in time for Rudolph's enthronement—yet another fact that should encourage us to decouple the *Missa* from the occasion for which it was initially intended. Once he completed the *Missa*, Beethoven then went on to describe it more than once as his "greatest work."[7] While this description might cynically be regarded as merely an attempt to woo publishers, the fact that, as Adorno once stressed, Beethoven commented more often on the *Missa* than on any of his other works suggests that it may truly have been of special significance for him.[8] Joseph Karl Stieler's famous portrait of the composer, which Beethoven posed for in 1820, depicts him holding none other than a score of the *Missa*, opened to the beginning of the Credo movement (see figure 6.1; the portrait erroneously indicates the key of the work as D-sharp rather than D). As Silke Bettermann has noted, Stieler's painting is the only contemporary representation of the composer that includes an explicit reference to one of his musical works, a result of the

---

[5] Kinderman, "Beethoven's Symbol for the Deity," 103. See also Drabkin, *Beethoven: Missa solemnis*, 15.

[6] Winter, "Reconstructing Riddles," 233.

[7] See Anderson no. 1079 (BGA no. 1468), Beethoven to Carl Friedrich Peters, June 5, 1822: "The *greatest* work which I have composed so far is a grand Mass with choruses, four obbligato voices and a large orchestra" ("Das größte Werk, welches ich bisher geschrieben, ist eine große Meße mit Chören und 4 obligaten Singstimmen und großen Orchester") (Beethoven's emphasis). See also Anderson no. 1270 (BGA no. 1787), Beethoven to Bernhard Schotts Söhne, March 10, 1824: "In regard to my works which you would like me to send you, I offer you the following, but you must not delay too long in reaching a decision about this:—a new grand solemn Mass with solo voices and choruses and a full orchestra. Although I find it difficult to talk about myself, yet I must say that I consider this to be my greatest work" ("inansehung von neuen Werken, welche sie von mir zu haben wünschten, trage ich ihnen folgende an, nur müßte die Entschließung nicht lange ausbleiben—eine neue *solenne* Messe mit *Solo* u[nd] chorstimme[n samt] ganzen orchester an, so schwer e[s] mir wird über mich selbst zu reden, so halte ich sie doch für mein größtes werk").

[8] Adorno, *Beethoven*, 143–44.

Figure 6.1 Portrait of Beethoven by Joseph Karl Stieler (1820). Public domain, via Wikimedia Commons.

painter's desire to emulate the style of models with which he was familiar, not only paintings of other artistic figures but also traditional Christian religious portraiture.[9] In an April 1820 conversation-book entry, Beethoven's secretary Franz Oliva asks the composer whether he wanted the Credo or

---

[9] See Bettermann, "Mehr als nur ein Abbild."

the Gloria depicted in the painting, indicating that it was Beethoven himself who was responsible for the choice of the Credo as the specific part of the *Missa* to be included.[10] The available evidence does not clearly indicate whether it was Beethoven or Stieler who was behind the more fundamental decision to select the *Missa* rather than some other piece.[11] (Though the *Missa* was far from complete at the time, Stieler could have learned of the work from Beethoven's associates, without needing to have been told by Beethoven himself.) But even if the idea first came from Stieler, it would still have required Beethoven's explicit assent.

Notwithstanding its circumstantial connection to Rudolph's episcopal appointment, it is thus hard to deny that Beethoven regarded the *Missa* as some kind of deeply personal statement. Indeed, he declared explicitly that he wished the *Missa solemnis* to "awaken and permanently instill religious feelings not only into the singers but also into the listeners."[12] Not surprisingly, the question that has long preoccupied critics is precisely what these "religious feelings" were that Beethoven wished to encourage in both performers and his audience. This chapter seeks to grapple with this question by exploring a number of ways in which the *Missa solemnis* reflects important aspects of Johann Michael Sailer's theological outlook. As I mentioned briefly in the introduction and in chapter 5, Beethoven scholars have previously raised the possibility of a connection between Beethoven's engagement with Sailer and his work on the *Missa solemnis*, but a systematic and detailed consideration of this issue has yet to occur.

To be clear, in attempting to show links between the *Missa* and Sailer's theology, my aim is not to reduce the work to a mere vessel for Sailer's ideas, and certainly not to claim that Beethoven's engagement with Sailer's writings during the period he worked on the *Missa* prompted a sudden and decisive alteration in his religious views that is reflected in the piece itself. As I argued in the previous chapter, that key aspects of Sailer's outlook resonate with Beethoven's prior religious explorations suggests that his encounter

---

[10] See *BCB* 2:127–28 (*KH* 2:50).

[11] For the numerous references in the conversation books to Stieler and his portrait, see *BCB* 1:194, 217–18, 263, 271–73, 278, 314–15; 2:18–19, 48, 61, 64, 66, 75, 108, 114, 127–28, 131, 134, 160, 180, 181, 190–91, 204, 295 (*KH* 1:196, 216–17, 260–61, 268–69, 274, 308–9, 337–38, 372, 383, 385–86, 387, 397; 2:37, 40, 50, 52, 54, 78, 96, 97, 104–5, 118, 206). See also Bettermann, "'noch 10 Minuten,'" 30, 33.

[12] Anderson no. 1307 (*BGA* no. 1875), Beethoven to Johann Andreas Streicher, September 16, 1824: "Es bey Bearbeitung dieser großen Messe meine Hauptabsicht war, sowohl bey den Singenden als bey den Zuhörenden, Religiöse Gefühle zu erwecken und dauernd zu machen."

with Sailer's writings reinforced rather than fundamentally transformed elements of his worldview. In this regard, it is worth noting too that several of the features of the *Missa solemnis* that I shall discuss are not unprecedented in Beethoven's own output of religious works. Unsurprisingly, the only setting of the Mass that the composer previously completed, the Mass in C, is most relevant in this regard, even though indirect parallels can also be drawn with aspects of *Christus am Ölberge* and the Gellert Lieder. As will become apparent in my discussion of the *Missa*, Beethoven sometimes employs identical or near-identical compositional techniques as in his earlier mass, and at other times stresses the same religious ideas through different musical means. Notwithstanding these points of similarity between Beethoven's two masses, however, the *Missa* seems to employ particular compositional devices, or to emphasize certain religious concepts, in more extreme ways or with greater frequency. It is thus likely that Beethoven's engagement with Sailer did affect the composition of the *Missa* to some degree, even if it did not change his approach to setting the Mass Ordinary in some kind of revolutionary manner.

The one aspect of the *Missa solemnis* that does seem to represent a more decisive departure from Beethoven's practice in his earlier religious music is its very prominent evocation of what might be described as "archaic" church music styles: use of the church modes, plainchant, unaccompanied polyphony, and fugal counterpoint.[13] As I will argue, a potential parallel exists between this exploration of such older church music with Sailer's own support for ecclesiastical movements that sought a revival of the same, an aspect of Sailer's views on the liturgy not specifically discussed in the previous chapter but which I shall elucidate below. It is undeniable, as I have pointed out above, that Beethoven was already doing his own research into such archaic music in the years prior to 1819, the year from which we have the earliest documented proof of his connection with Sailer. But the precise way in which Beethoven employs this older music in the *Missa*—in synthesis with a highly personal, even radical, approach to setting the Mass text—seems to overlap with Sailer's nuanced views regarding liturgical tradition. In any event, to suggest that the *Missa solemnis* reflects religious themes of particular importance in Beethoven's cultural milieu calls into question the tendency to interpret this work in the kind of de-Catholicized manner I described in the introduction.

---

[13] Unlike Adorno, I do not employ this term in a pejorative way. Cf. Adorno, *Beethoven*, 146–49. I return to Adorno's evaluation of the *Missa* below.

Ecumenism and the *Missa solemnis*

Before delving into specific musical features of the *Missa solemnis*, it is worth mentioning an aspect of the compositional history of the *Missa* that might also be linked to Sailer's ideas—the fact that Beethoven expressed a desire to publish the *Missa solemnis* with a German text in addition to the liturgically prescribed Latin. This wish ultimately remained unfulfilled because of the premature death of Benedict Scholz, whom he had asked to produce the translation.[14] We know of this situation from a letter Beethoven wrote to Anton Schindler in June 1823.[15] But even as early as August 1820, before he was anywhere close to completing the *Missa*, Beethoven had already indicated his desire for a German translation in a letter to Nikolaus Simrock: "Should you wish to have a German translation of the Mass [the *Missa solemnis*], let me know by return of post; I will arrange for it to be done and will adapt it to my composition."[16]

We recall from chapter 3 that Beethoven's Mass in C had been published with a German text in addition to the usual Latin. It would not be surprising if the composer's interest in a German text for the *Missa* was motivated by similar factors as in the case of his earlier mass. Most obviously, the inclusion of such a text aligned with the German Catholic Enlightenment's encouragement of vernacular church music. Indeed, in specific relation to the *Missa*, this aspect of the Catholic Enlightenment can be tied directly to the work's dedicatee, Archduke Rudolph, who had Josephinist leanings when it came to ecclesiastical affairs. After becoming archbishop of Olmütz, he specifically advocated the singing of hymns in Czech within his diocese.[17] As with the

---

[14] As discussed in chapter 3, this same Benedict Scholz had previously sent Beethoven a new German text for the Mass in C, which had originally been published with a text by Christian Schreiber.

[15] Anderson no. 1188 (*BGA* no. 1662), June 1, 1823.

[16] Anderson no. 1029 (*BGA* no. 1407), August 30, 1820: "Wollten Sie eine deutsche Übersetzung der Messe haben, so schreiben Sie es mir umgehend, ich will es besorgen, und meiner *Composition* anpaßen."

[17] Körner, "Rossini, Erzherzog Rudolph und Beethoven." As Körner demonstrates, another aspect of Rudolph's Josephinist outlook was his emphasis on the pastoral and educative aspects of his role as archbishop, despite his own lofty hierarchical status in both the ecclesiastical sense (as a cardinal) and the political sense (as a member of the imperial family). Separate from his views on church affairs, he also encouraged the development of an independent Czech culture. Generally speaking, Rudolph seems to have inherited the broadly progressive outlook espoused by his father, the Holy Roman Emperor Leopold II (brother of Joseph II), discussed in chapters 1 and 2. Rudolph's brother was the emperor Francis II/I. Many historians have described Francis as more authoritarian than Leopold, but as previously mentioned it is possible that this characterization is overstated. See also Novotny, "Kardinal Erzherzog Rudolph," 345; Kagan, *Archduke Rudolph*, 164–67, 233–43; and Sehnal, "Kirchenmusik im Erzbistum Olmütz," 182–90.

Mass in C, however, Beethoven's plan for a German text might also reflect another facet of the Catholic Enlightenment: the movement's emphasis on ecumenical dialogue with Protestants. In a letter to Simrock concerning the *Missa* (different from the one cited in the previous paragraph), Beethoven remarked:

> As the translator [most likely Scholz] was overwhelmed with other literary tasks, I had to be patient, the more so as I have good reasons to be better pleased with the work he produces than if the Mass were to find its way into some translators' factory. Our Protestants have tired long ago of such factories, since their products have too little in common with the true original text.[18]

It is, of course, possible that Beethoven's outreach to Protestants had commercial motives: he might well have wanted the *Missa* to sell in Protestant markets as well as Catholic ones. As had been the case with the Mass in C, however, what is striking is the composer's level of concern about the quality of the translation. Beethoven cared deeply that the message of the work should be adequately communicated to Protestant listeners, a sentiment that resonates with the ecumenical attitudes espoused by Sailer.

Also noteworthy is one other sign of Beethoven's ecumenical outlook in the documentary evidence related to the composition of the *Missa solemnis*. In a previously cited *Tagebuch* entry from 1818, Beethoven expressed his desire to research traditional Catholic church music, especially plainchant. In Solomon's English translation the entry reads: "In order to write true church music go through all the ecclesiastical chants of the monks etc. Also look there for the stanzas in the most correct translations along with the most perfect prosody of all *Christian-Catholic* psalms and hymns in general."[19] What Solomon translates, somewhat awkwardly, as "Christian-Catholic" is the German word *christkatholisch*. The oddity of this term has escaped the notice of Beethoven scholars. It was a rare term and certainly not one often used in

---

[18] Anderson no. 1051 (*BGA* no. 1429), March 14, 1821: "Da der übersezer überhaüft mit andern schriftstellerschen Arbeiten, so mußte ich mich gedulden, um so mehr, da ich Ursache habe mit ihm zufriedener zu seyn, als wenn die Meße in eine übersezungsFabrik gerathen wäre, deren die Protestanten längs[t] müde sind, indem solche zu wenig mit dem wahrer Urtext übereinstimmen." It is not certain whether the translator referred to in this letter was Scholz, or somebody else.

[19] *Tagebuch* no. 168, c. 1818 (my emphasis): "Um wahre Kirchenmusik zu schreiben / alle Kirchenchoräle der Mönche ect. / durchgehen[,] wo auch zu suchen[,] wie die / Absätze in richtigsten Uibersetzungen / nebst vollkommener Prosodie aller / *christkatholischen* Psalmen und Gesänge / überhaupt."

everyday speech.[20] Much more common terms were the equivalents of those we use in English: *katholisch* and *römisch-katholisch*. A clue as to the possible significance of *christkatholisch* can be found in its only ordinary usage in present-day German. The "Christkatholische Kirche der Schweiz" is the name of a small denomination of "Old Catholics" in Switzerland.[21] "Old Catholic" Churches, which are mostly found in Germany, Austria, and Switzerland, are communities of Catholics that broke away from the Roman Catholic Church because of their opposition to the First Vatican Council's declaration of the doctrine of papal infallibility in 1870. This schism, in turn, had roots in various nineteenth-century movements within German Catholicism opposed to excessive centralization of Church authority in Rome, a topic discussed in chapter 1. As Michael Bangert has shown, *christkatholisch* was used polemically by figures within such movements, which were also frequently linked to political liberalism.[22] During Beethoven's time, the term did not yet have the more precise partisan or confessional meaning it would acquire later in the nineteenth century. Nevertheless, it was popular among theologians influenced by the German Catholic Enlightenment as a way of emphasizing that the "catholic" in the Catholic Church should first and foremost refer to a universal Church united in Christ and only secondarily to an institution governed by the Bishop of Rome—an emphasis that lent itself readily to an ecumenical outlook.

Christkatholisch actually appears in one other place in the documentary sources related to Beethoven's life: his brother Kaspar Karl, father of his beloved nephew Karl, used it in his will to describe the religious tradition in which he would like to be buried. In Theodore Albrecht's translation, the relevant passage reads: "I commend my soul to the mercy of God, but my body to the earth from which it came and desire that it be committed to the earth in the simplest manner in accordance with the rites of *Christian Catholicism* [*daß derselbe dem christkatholischen Gebrauche gemäß auf die einfachste Art zur Erde bestattet werde*]."[23] Beethoven's use of *christkatholisch* in the *Tagebuch*, as well as his brother's use of the same term, may well indicate a sympathy for an understanding of Catholicism that stressed the unifying

---

[20] I am grateful to Euan Cameron for alerting me to the rarity of the term "christkatholisch" in German Catholic writing, especially before the nineteenth century.

[21] See also Smit, *Old Catholic*, 59–69.

[22] Bangert, "Christkatholisch? Eine kleine Begriffsgeschichte—Teil I" and "Christkatholisch? Eine kleine Begriffsgeschichte—Teil II." Bangert traces the ultimate origins of *christkatholisch* to Augustine, who used the Latin description "homo christianus catholicus." The actual German word *christkatholisch* was first used during the Baroque period by a Premonstratensian canon named Leonhard Goffiné (1648–1719), then adopted by other Catholic theologians interested in more sentimentalist, mystical religious approaches that they believed could overcome theological conflict.

[23] Albrecht no. 213 (my emphasis). For the original German, see Thayer, *Ludwig van Beethovens Leben*, 3:517–19.

figure of Christ ahead of Roman primacy—a strand of Catholic thinking ultimately rooted in Beethoven's upbringing in Bonn, where the German Catholic Enlightenment was especially strong (see chapter 2).

Beethoven's use of *christkatholisch*, with its ecumenical and anti-ultramontane connotations, might thus be linked to the appeal that Sailer had for him, given the theologian's outreach to Protestants and discomfort with ultramontane visions of the Church, as described in the previous chapter. Though the word does not appear explicitly in Sailer's writings, it played a significant role in the theological outlook of one of his most prominent students, Ignaz Heinrich von Wessenberg, whom I mentioned in chapter 4 as a noted advocate for the establishment of a German national church with considerable autonomy from Rome.[24] An intriguing if tenuous connection can actually be established between Beethoven and Wessenberg: in 1815, Beethoven set one of Wessenberg's poems as the lied *Das Geheimnis* (The secret), WoO145:[25]

Wo blüht das Blümchen, das nie verblüht?	Where blooms the little flower that never withers?
Wo strahlt das Sternlein, das ewig glüht?	Where shines the little star, that glows eternally?
Dein Mund, o Muse! dein heil'ger Mund	Your mouth, O Muse! Your holy mouth,
Tu' mir das Blümchen und Sternlein kund.	Make the flower and the star known to me.
Verkünden kann es dir nicht mein Mund,	My mouth cannot announce it to you,
Macht es dein Innerstes dir nicht kund.	If your innermost self does not make it known to you.
Im Innersten glühet und blüht es zart	In the innermost self it glows and blooms tenderly
Wohl jedem, der es getreu bewahrt!	For him who faithfully keeps it.

---

[24] On Wessenberg's use of "christkatholisch," see Bangert, *Bild und Glaube*, 64–74, esp. 65–67; "Christkatholisch? Eine kleine Begriffsgeschichte—Teil I," 5; and "Christkatholisch? Eine kleine Begriffsgeschichte—Teil II," 6. On his connection to Sailer, see Baumgartner, "Bemühungen"; Bangert, *Bild und Glaube*, 22–24, 66, 112; and Printy, *Enlightenment*, 172–73, 184n69. I thank Michael Bangert for explaining to me the relevance of "christkatholisch" for Sailer's outlook, even if Sailer himself does not appear to have employed the term.

[25] A brief discussion of the song is provided in Reid, *Beethoven Song Companion*, 87–89. Reid also provides a short overview of Wessenberg's life (ibid., 288). Beethoven's setting was published in 1816 in the *Wiener Zeitschrift*, and was his first contribution to the recently founded journal: see B. Cooper, "Beethoven's 'Abendlied,'" 236.

Aside from his clerical career, Wessenberg also wrote and published secular poems such as this one. Indeed, the role of the arts in the dissemination of the Christian message was a major theme of his theological outlook and something he had in common with his teacher Sailer.[26] As far as I can tell, however, this particular poem, which appears to concern the mysterious nature of artistic inspiration ("The secret," "O Muse!"), does not have any explicit religious content, even if it is vaguely spiritual in its emphasis on interiority ("innermost self").[27] It is unclear the degree to which Beethoven was aware of Wessenberg's role in the ecclesiastical politics and theological debates of the time, but he was obviously at least familiar with Wessenberg's name.

Sailer's Liturgical Views and Beethoven's Treatment of the Mass Text

More compelling connections between the *Missa solemnis* and Sailer's ideas can be found by examining specific musical characteristics of Beethoven's work. Beethoven clearly aimed in the *Missa solemnis* to set the Mass text in as musically vivid and detailed a manner as possible. This attention to textual meaning occurs in two interrelated ways. First, Beethoven uses various musical devices to convey, explain, or highlight the significance of particular words in the Mass text, thereby performing a kind of musical exegesis. Second, he evokes the idea of a religious believer responding spontaneously to specific parts of the text, not least through making prominent alterations to the text in order to "personalize" its meaning.[28] As discussed in chapter 3, these features were also present in Beethoven's earlier Mass in C. But as I shall show, in the *Missa* they are more pervasive or manifest themselves in a manner that can be described as more extreme. Beethoven's approach to setting the Mass text reveals obvious affinities with Sailer's emphasis on educating ordinary Catholic believers about their faith, and on

---

[26] See Bangert, *Bild und Glaube*, 203, 223–26, 376–80.
[27] See also Bangert, *Bild und Glaube*, 111–12.
[28] Birgit Lodes has previously discussed these two features of the *Missa* but does not connect them to Sailer in the manner that I do below: see Lodes, *Das Gloria*, 152–64; and "'When I Try,'" 171, 176–77. While I refer below to some of the specific examples she cites, I also draw attention to other moments in the *Missa* where these features can be detected as well.

encouraging individual piety without neglecting communal participation in the church's public liturgical life.[29]

In a general sense, the *Missa*'s vivid, at times outright pictorial, treatment of individual words of the Mass text recalls Beethoven's efforts at musical exegesis in the Mass in C. Notwithstanding this similarity (and indeed the possible inspiration provided by Haydn's masses previously discussed), the attention to textual detail in the *Missa* exceeds what he attempted to do in his earlier mass. As Warren Kirkendale has commented, "Every textual concept, indeed almost every word is musically interpreted."[30] That Beethoven deliberately wanted the *Missa* to go further than the Mass in C in this regard is evident from some extra "homework" that he set himself during the earliest stages of the *Missa*'s composition. As discussed in chapter 4, Beethoven copied out a translation of the Latin words of the Credo, Sanctus, and Agnus Dei from Feßler's *Ansichten von Religion und Kirchenthum*. By itself, this action would be a sufficient sign of how devoted he was to understanding what the liturgical texts really meant. As Birgit Lodes has shown, however, he did not stop there.[31] For the Latin words, Beethoven marked not only the accented syllables but also the lengths of vowels. He might have been able to figure out the former from the Latin missal that he owned, but for the latter he would have had to consult his Latin–German dictionary (a book which happens to survive in Berlin).[32] Beethoven looked up vowel lengths for almost every single Latin word he wrote down; only for words not found in his dictionary are no vowel lengths given. From the same dictionary, Beethoven also copied out the meanings and exemplary usages of particular Latin words. For "vita" (life), for instance, he wrote down a quotation from Virgil's *Aeneid*: "tenues sine corpore vitae" (slender lives without bodies). And for "mundus" (world), he wrote "Himmel u[nd] Erde u[nd] alles, was Gott geschaffen hat" (heaven and earth and everything God created). For a number of words, Beethoven even wrote out declension and conjugation tables. The composer seems to have gone to quite extraordinary lengths to ensure that he really understood the texts he was going to set to music.

---

[29] Lodes has previously proposed such a link between the *Missa* and Sailer's views, but her discussion of the issue is very brief and does not directly cite any of Sailer's writings: see "Probing the Sacred Genres," 234–35. Lodes provides an accurate description of Sailer's view that "believers should not simply parrot the prayers from the liturgy, but rather try to penetrate intellectually their spiritual meaning" (235), though she does not cite a source for it.
[30] Kirkendale, "Ancient Rhetorical Traditions," 534.
[31] Lodes, "Composing with a Dictionary," 193–95.
[32] Berlin, Staatsbibliothek, Mus.ms.autogr. Beethoven, L.v. 40,8.

In the *Missa*, the end result of this attention to detail is reflected most explicitly in the Gloria and the Credo, where it also leads to a musical surface that is often extremely disjunct. In measure 42 of the Gloria, for instance, just before the words "et in terra pax" (and on earth peace), the music illustrates the shift from the heavenly heights—"Gloria in excelsis Deo" (Glory to God in the highest)—down to earth through a precipitous downward change of register in the string parts (see example 6.1). The first violins, cellos, and basses fall by more than two octaves, accompanied by a sudden dynamic change from fortissimo to piano. The texture also thins dramatically, from an orchestral tutti to just strings and first horn. A similar conjunction of extreme registral and dynamic contrasts occurs later in the Gloria, in the chorus parts in measure 80, on the words "adoramus te" (we adore you). Here, the effect is heightened by the entry of the sopranos one beat ahead of the other three voice parts and accompanying strings, such that for the briefest of moments the texture reduces abruptly from full chorus and orchestral tutti to sopranos alone. The sense of disjunction is increased further by the setting of the word "adoramus" to hollow open fifths in the chorus, creating a solemn, pretonal soundworld strikingly different from what comes both before and afterward. This quieter and lower-pitched music for "adoramus te" lasts barely four measures, before, in measure 83, a fortissimo dynamic and higher vocal register returns for "glorificamus te" (we glorify you). This shifting between "adoramus te" and "glorificamus te" is later repeated with similar music (mm. 100–3).

The opening section of the Gloria contains one other moment worth mentioning with regard to textual depiction. In measure 36, Beethoven inserts a surprising eighth rest between the words "excelsis" and "Deo," causing a striking and unexpected interruption in the vocal lines (again, see example 6.1). The effect of this hiccup is to isolate the word "Deo," a less than subtle way of highlighting the Latin word for God! The point that Beethoven seems to be making here about God's greatness is reiterated—more forcefully perhaps—in a later part of the movement, in his setting of "Deus Pater omnipotens" (God the Father Almighty), where he introduces the trombones for the first time in the *Missa* on the word "omnipotens" (mm. 185–90).[33] The other orchestral parts are marked *fff* at this point, an extremely rare marking in Beethoven's music and one that does not occur anywhere else in the *Missa*.

---

[33] This feature is also discussed in Kirkendale, "Ancient Rhetorical Traditions," 505.

THE *MISSA SOLEMNIS* 213

Example 6.1 *Missa solemnis*, op. 123, Gloria, mm. 35–48

Example 6.1 Continued

Similar attention to the meaning of individual words can be observed in the Credo. A sudden drop in texture, dynamics, and register occurs again for the word "mortuos," this time to depict the concept of death (mm. 232–38). And the same musical devices are used once more for "mortuorum" in measures 295–96, where just three beats of music at a soft dynamic, with a thinned-out texture, interrupt a section that is otherwise loud and thickly orchestrated. Musical symbolism in the Credo occurs at a larger temporal scale as well. The sheer length of the fugue on "et vitam venturi saeculi" (m. 306ff.), for instance, is an apt illustration of the eternity that the words describe.

Beethoven's vivid musical depiction of the liturgical text functions analogously to Sailer's exegeses of both liturgical and biblical texts in books like the *Kleine Bibel*. As described in the previous chapter, *Goldkörner* is also similar to the *Kleine Bibel* in this regard: though its Latin sayings are neither liturgical nor biblical, Sailer is concerned with interpreting their meaning for the reader. Sailer's aim is to render such texts accessible to the average believer, and the same could be said of Beethoven's musical exegesis of the Mass text, which encourages the listener to comprehend its meaning in a more profound way. It is worth repeating here a poignant passage from Sailer's *Goldkörner* already quoted in the previous chapter: "May not only your body be in church; but may your understanding also be there ... and may your heart, and above all things your heart, be there."[34]

Beyond using musical symbolism to depict the meaning of various parts of the liturgical text, the *Missa*, like the Mass in C, also dramatizes a kind of spontaneous, heartfelt response to the text. This type of intimate, personal engagement with the words of the Mass would have aligned with Sailer's theological outlook. Some of the methods Beethoven employs in this regard are strikingly similar to those found in his earlier mass. In the Kyrie, for instance, he twice has the choral sopranos enter ahead of the other parts (mm. 182 and 191; see examples 6.2a and b). That it is only *one* of the vocal parts that comes in at the "wrong" time makes these two moments stand out even in a movement where the use of metrical displacement is pervasive because of the syncopated nature of the motive for the word "Kyrie."[35] In these instances, the sopranos' "Kyrie" sounds as if it comes in too soon, as if it were a kind of uncontrollable outburst, an exclamation of something that cannot be held back.

Another feature from the Mass in C that reappears in the *Missa* is the surprising amount of emphasis placed on seemingly unimportant grammatical particles. As in his earlier mass, two such words are "et" (and) and "non" (not) in the Credo. (Earlier precedents for emphasizing these words in Haydn's masses were also discussed in chapter 3.) Unlike the Mass in C, the *Missa* extends the emphasis on "et" beyond a single instance ("et sepultus est").[36] The phenomenon occurs no fewer than nine times in the movement: in measures 30–31 (see example 6.3), 52, 107, 125 (see example 6.9 below), 141, 143–44, 179–80, 188, and 296–97. In these moments, Beethoven repeatedly

---

[34] Sailer, *Sprüche-Buch: Goldkörner*, 51: "Nicht dein Körper bloß sey in der Kirche; auch dein Verstand sey da ... auch dein Herz, und vor allen dein Herz sey da." This statement is a gloss on a Latin quotation by Juan Luis Vives: "Sacris intersis attente, ac pie" (Take part in sacred things attentively and piously).

[35] The dotted rhythm was a conventional topos for setting the word "Kyrie," but by beginning on a weak beat Beethoven makes a very deliberate alteration to this convention: see Kirkendale, "Ancient Rhetorical Traditions," 502–4.

[36] Daniel Chua interprets the repetition of "et" in Beethoven's setting of "et sepultus est" as "the dying stammer of [Christ's] suffering body" (*Beethoven and Freedom*, 239). As will become apparent, I offer here a different religious reading, based on Sailer's views on the liturgy, of Beethoven's emphasis on "et," not just in this instance, but elsewhere in the movement.

Example 6.2a *Missa solemnis,* op. 123, Kyrie, mm. 182–83

stresses the word "et" using repetition, sforzando markings, and rests that precede and/or follow the word. With regard to the word "non" in "cuius regni non erit finis" (of whose kingdom there will not be an end), to have multiple repetitions of "non" and/or the longer phrase "non erit finis" was a common practice in the Viennese mass tradition.[37] (The specific example of Haydn's *Nelson* Mass was mentioned in chapter 3.) As in the Mass in C, however, Beethoven in the *Missa* has the word "non" return *after* the phrase "non erit finis" has already been sung in full, producing a more drastic alteration to the liturgical text. And compared with his earlier mass, the level of dynamic and rhythmic emphasis applied here is exceptional, almost exaggerated: "non" is sung three times in succession, with sforzando markings the first and second time and rests between the three statements (see example 6.4).

---

[37] See MacIntyre, *Viennese Concerted Mass,* 396–99.

Example 6.2b *Missa solemnis*, op. 123, Kyrie, mm. 190–93

In the *Missa*, Beethoven extended his preoccupation with such grammatical particles as "et" and "non" to two other moments in the Mass text. In the Gloria, he inserted extra iterations of the word "quoniam" (since) after the initial phrase "Quoniam tu solus sanctus" (Since you alone are holy), such that "quoniam" is also added to the phrases "tu solus dominus" (you alone are Lord) and "tu solus altissimus" (you alone are the Highest): see measures 310–44. The repetition of this particular word is an unconventional choice for a Mass setting, as Günther Massenkeil has pointed out.[38] Like "et," "quoniam" is a conjunction, and might therefore seem a less obvious candidate for emphasis through repetition than other, more evocative words such as "sanctus," "dominus," or "altissimus." In the Sanctus movement, the word "qui" (who) in the Benedictus section is at one point sung three times on weak beats, separated by rests, and with a sforzando on each (mm. 170–71): "Benedictus qui, qui, qui venit in nomine Domini" (Blessed is he who, who, who comes in the name of the Lord). Repetition of the *two* words "qui

---

[38] Massenkeil, "Über Beethovens kirchenmusikalischen Stil," 187.

Example 6.3 *Missa solemnis*, op. 123, Credo, mm. 29–33 (vocal parts only)

venit"—rather than just the single word "qui"—was relatively common in earlier masses, often occurring in tandem with a musical emphasis on the word "venit" and/or the subsequent word "nomine."[39] Beethoven's repetition of only "qui," further highlighted using the musical techniques described above, is thus quite unusual.

Such repetition of words seemingly undeserving of repetition transforms the liturgical text from something formal and ritualistic into speech that sounds more conversational, evoking the artless sincerity of the occasional stutter, of stumbling over one's words. A similar conversational effect is

[39] See MacIntyre, *Viennese Concerted Mass*, 396, 473–75.

Example 6.4 *Missa solemnis*, op. 123, Credo, mm. 257–64 (vocal parts only)

created in a more extreme fashion by what is perhaps the most significant manipulation of the Mass text Beethoven makes in the *Missa*: the interpolation of the vocative particles "ah" and "o!" before the words "miserere nobis" in measures 296–305 of the Gloria. As Lodes has argued, this passage—which has no parallel in the Mass in C—comes across as a series of spontaneous exclamations, spur-of-the-moment repetitions of words already sung.[40] But the improvised quality of these interjections is also reinforced by the textual

---

[40] Lodes, *Das Gloria*, 158–62.

irregularity of the solo tenor's switching to "o!," having sung "ah" only four measures previously (compare measures 296 and 300). The words of the liturgy have been made to sound more like everyday speech. The text is no longer recited verbatim from the liturgical script, as it were, but comes across as one expressing the most sincere feelings of the believer. The words sound personalized, as if one has made the words of the liturgy one's own and truly internalized the meaning of an external ritual—an impression that accords with Sailer's ideal of liturgical participation.

The later sections of the Gloria present still other examples of Beethoven depicting a believer's spontaneous response to the text, in ways that were not foreshadowed by the Mass in C. In measures 514–17, with the chorus and orchestra at full volume, the soloists interject "Amen" four times (see example 6.5). Though they sing the same word as the chorus sings and though they might be heard to imitate or echo the "Amens" in the chorus, these interjected "Amens" otherwise seem disconnected from all the other parts of the musical texture. Not only are they rhythmically disjunct from the choral lines, but the soloists' lines are not doubled by any of the instruments at all. One has to strain to hear them. Overwhelmed by the rest of the texture, they sound almost a little out of place, a little superfluous. It is as if the soloists feel compelled to add their own frenzied, delirious exclamations of "Amen," to join in at a moment when it may not really be their turn to sing, regardless of how difficult it might be to get themselves heard.

Another example involves the famous return of "Gloria in excelsis Deo" at the end of the movement. As Lodes has demonstrated, this entire section has the character of an opening rather than an ending, a feeling reinforced by the metrical displacement of the chorus in the very last measures.[41] It is difficult to overstate just how out of place the return of the "Gloria" text feels. With a decisive-sounding A-to-D motion occurring in every single choral and instrumental part, the "Amen" in measures 524–25 could easily have brought the entire movement to a satisfying, rousing conclusion. In measure 525, none of the instrumental parts contains a rhythmically active line to keep propelling the music forward. A series of running eighth notes in the strings would, for instance, have done the trick, but absolutely no attempt is made to create a smoother transition from the previous section into the Presto in such a manner. Only the sounding of the "Gloria" motive in the trumpets signals that the movement has not actually ended. This motive begins on the tonic

---

[41] Lodes, "'When I Try,'" 155–61.

Example 6.5 *Missa solemnis*, op. 123, Gloria, mm. 514–17

note D—the same note sounded by everybody else—and this initial D is held for two quarter-note beats. On the downbeat of measure 525 it is thus not immediately apparent that this measure is, in fact, a new beginning rather than the end of the movement. That the music continues here, let alone continues with text that is totally unexpected, makes the concluding "Gloria" section sound like it has been brought in at the spur of a moment. The music does not need this return, but it simply could not help itself.

Example 6.5 Continued

The same effect has, moreover, already been experienced, though perhaps to a lesser degree, at three other moments before this one. The first occurs nearly two hundred measures earlier, in measure 359. Here, the initial syllable of "Amen" is held on a fermata, above which Beethoven marks first a diminuendo then a crescendo, a kind of reversed *messa di voce* that one is more accustomed to finding in a symphony by Mahler. This generates a kind of false-ending feeling, as if the composer teases us into thinking that the movement is about to end, before winding up the energy again to keep going. The fugue on "in gloria Dei patris" (in the glory of God the father) follows, but in measures 426–27, the music comes once more to a halt—a halt that we will soon realize is premature—with a diminuendo on the word "Amen" (see example 6.6). The soloists, who have not been heard from in the previous 123 measures, then re-enter unexpectedly, bringing back the "in gloria" fugue theme in stretto. Meanwhile, the chorus returns to the text "cum Sancto Spiritu" (with the Holy Spirit), which we thought had long been left behind when the fugue began. The abrupt nature of this transition is reinforced by the tonal disjunction between the C-sharp major chord in measure 427—functioning as the dominant of F-sharp minor (see the preceding measure)—and the D major clearly implied by the melody in measure 428. Beethoven has also been careful to confine the diminuendo on "Amen" to only the last two quarter-note beats of measure 426, making this dynamic change sound rather sudden: the music goes from fortissimo to piano in an extremely short amount of time. In measures 458 and 459, the music finally reaches a perfect authentic cadence on another "Amen." Indeed, there are few perfect authentic cadences in the entire *Missa* as conclusive as this one. And yet the music goes on, with the tempo quickened. What is more, the chorus brings back text that was originally introduced even before "cum Sancto Spiritu": "Quoniam tu solus sanctus...".

At the three striking moments I have just described (mm. 359–60, 426–28, 458–59), as well as with the concluding return of "Gloria in excelsis Deo," it is as if the movement could end—even *ought* to end—but feels compelled to keep going, repeating text that has already been sung aplenty. There is enough of a sense of disjunction each time, a noticeable stop-start feeling, to make each continuation sound somehow improvised, spontaneously conceived, as though the decision to keep going were made on the spot. This is a chorus of praise that simply does not wish to cease: the emotional impact calls to mind the title of a nineteenth-century American folk hymn: "How Can I Keep from Singing?"[42]

---

[42] My interpretation of the ending of the Gloria recalls the "'one more time' effect" described by James Webster in a study of the musical sublime in Haydn's late vocal music (*"The Creation"*). For Webster, this effect is produced through the "varied repetition of an earlier, simpler [passage]" (ibid., 83), and is one of several possible devices for generating a musical climax through evocation of the sublime. The examples I have cited from the Gloria in Beethoven's *Missa* utilize repetition of whole sections, not just shorter passages. In addition, unlike the Haydn examples Webster provides, in Beethoven's Gloria a musical unit is not elided into its repetition. It is not merely a case of music that keeps on going when we expect it to end; rather, the music does seem to come to a stop and then start up again. It is this feeling that makes each point of unexpected continuation sound improvised rather than preplanned.

Example 6.6 *Missa solemnis*, op. 123, Gloria, mm. 426–42

Christocentrism in the *Missa solemnis*

In certain specific cases, Beethoven's extreme attention to the meaning of the liturgical text is applied to moments in the Mass particularly associated with the person of Christ. We saw hints of this phenomenon in the Mass in C, as discussed toward the end of chapter 3. But in the *Missa solemnis*, Beethoven's

Example 6.6 Continued

setting of Christ-related parts of the Mass text comes across as significantly more vivid and emotionally exuberant. In this regard, the work can be seen to reflect the Christocentrism of Sailer's theological outlook.

In the Christe section of the Kyrie, Beethoven's text-setting places a relentless focus on the all-important name of Christ. The composer sharply distinguishes, both rhythmically and melodically, the word "Christe"

Example 6.6 Continued

(Christ) from the word "eleison" (have mercy). "Christe" is sung on two consecutive half notes, always with a downward melodic contour, most often a major or minor third. "Eleison" is sung on a series of quarter notes, usually beginning with a leap of a fourth. These two motives constitute the points of imitation that generate almost every measure of the entire section. Having musically created this distinction between the two words, Beethoven then

Example 6.6 Continued

chooses to place consistent emphasis on "Christe," rather than "eleison." The listener is encouraged to focus on "Christe" already by the curious way in which the section begins. The first iteration of the phrase "Christe eleison" is given to the soprano soloist. But just one quarter note after she starts singing, the tenor intrudes with the word "eleison" beneath her "Christe" line (see example 6.7). In this context, the quarter-note "eleison" motive sounds not

Example 6.6 Continued

like a continuation of the melodic idea that begins "Christe"—as the soprano line taken alone would imply—but like a counter-melody, independent of but subordinate to the half-note "Christe" motive.[43] This impression is subsequently reinforced by the greater prominence of the "Christe" motive in

---

[43] I know of no other setting of "Christe eleison" among Beethoven's forebears and contemporaries that treats the text in this manner. Haydn's *Theresienmesse* comes the closest (see m. 52ff. of the Kyrie

THE *MISSA SOLEMNIS* 229

Example 6.7 *Missa solemnis*, op. 123, Kyrie, mm. 88–93 (vocal parts only)

the overall texture. For most of the Christe section, and especially in the first ten or so measures after the soprano soloist begins singing (mm. 88–99), it is the half-note "Christe" motive that appears more often in the instruments, whether doubling or imitating the same motive in the voices. The two purely

movement). In that work, the alto soloist begins with "Christe," and the soprano soloist overlaps with the alto, entering on the first syllable of "eleison" on the same beat as the alto's "-ste." The alto herself continues singing "eleison," but unlike in Beethoven's *Missa*, this word is sung to *different* melodic material than the "eleison" sung by the soprano in her "interruption" of the alto. Even if one were to insist on Haydn's work as a potential model for Beethoven in this regard, or if some other example more akin to Beethoven's Christe were found that I have failed to consider, it would make no difference to my overall argument about the affective consequences of Beethoven's compositional choices in his setting of the "Christe" text.

instrumental measures preceding the first entry of the voices also reflect this situation (mm. 86–87; not shown in the example). The "eleison" motive occurs only in the bassoons and first and second horns, with the "Christe" motive, played by the other woodwinds and by all of the strings, dominating the texture. The textural hierarchy created between the two motives thus leads the listener to focus on the "Christe" motive throughout the section as the main melody. "Eleison," which always comes across as a counter-melody, seems an afterthought compared to the word "Christe," on which Beethoven places special stress.

Heard in this way, the name of Christ is repeated over and over and over again, like an insistent, pleading mantra, the half-note motive sounding especially ponderous when juxtaposed against the quarter-note "eleison." This is, after all, the desperate plea of a sinner begging for Christ's mercy. Even in the very few measures where "Christe" is not being sung by at least one vocal part, the mantra does not cease, for the half-note motive persists in the instruments (e.g., in measures 115–16). Beethoven brings the whole section to a close by saturating the chorus with the word "Christe," the individual parts sounding like they are interrupting each other as they sing Christ's name in close imitation (mm. 122–27). In the final two measures of this passage (mm. 126–27), the words "Christe eleison" are sung one last time, in chordal homophony by the entire chorus. The triple-piano dynamic marking (m. 126) might be a further way of emphasizing the name of Christ. Such a marking is very rare in Beethoven's output, and this moment is the only time in the *Missa* it occurs in the vocal parts.[44] Because of the brevity of the text, it is obvious that any setting of "Christe eleison" can be expected to utilize a fair bit of textual repetition. But Beethoven takes such repetition to an extreme here, with the word "Christe" appearing in almost every measure. This non-stop calling of Christ's name is reminiscent of Sailer's *Kleine Bibel*, where, as I discussed in the previous chapter, Christ is constantly the object of direct address.

In the Credo, Beethoven seems to pay particular attention to those parts of the text that relate to Christ's nature and earthly mission. As in the Mass in C, he appears fixated on the words "genitum, non factum" (begotten, not made), a reference to Christ's divine and eternal—that is, uncreated—nature (see example 6.8). Measure 68 sets "genitum" to homophonic chords in both

---

[44] The marking does appear one other time in the *Missa*, just before "Et resurrexit" in the Credo (m. 187), but in the instrumental parts only: see example 6.10 below.

Example 6.8 *Missa solemnis*, op. 123, Credo, mm. 67–71

chorus and orchestra, with the sopranos singing a high B-flat. Beethoven then emphasizes the importance of this word by having a full quarter note of complete silence, before the chorus continues with "non factum" in an imitative texture. As William Drabkin has pointed out, the subsequent measures also show Beethoven to be placing greater emphasis on the words "consubstantialem Patri" (consubstantial with the Father) than had been conventional in earlier mass settings.[45] Like "genitum, non factum," these words stress the divinity of Christ. Later in the same movement, as William Kinderman demonstrated in a classic study, Beethoven shifts his attention to Christ's *human* nature, vividly portraying it in his musical treatment of the lines of the Credo associated with Christ's time on earth—from "Et incarnatus" (And he was incarnate) to "Et resurrexit" (And he rose again).[46] This portion of the Credo is strongly distinguished from the rest of the movement by means of various musical features, including a slower tempo, modal harmony, and a lower overall register. The marked nature of the "earthly" section is reinforced through being bookended by a common F-major chord that Kinderman interprets as symbolic of heaven. This chord is sung on "coelis" (heaven; m. 117) just before the "Et incarnatus" begins. It then returns on the semantically identical word "coelum" (m. 200), shortly after the words "Et ascendit" (And he ascended) bring the section to a close by returning the music to a fast tempo (see examples 6.9 and 6.10). The chord spacing in the choral parts is almost exactly the same.

A closer examination of this "earthly" section of the Credo reveals further evidence of Beethoven's keen interest in Christ's incarnation and earthly mission. Beethoven dramatizes the various stages of Christ's life on earth in a strikingly detailed manner, as reflected both in the larger-scale tonal plan of this section and in certain more localized musical features. He sets the three subsections concerning Christ's conception in Mary's womb ("Et incarnatus"), his birth ("Et homo factus est"), and his death and burial ("Crucifixus"), in a different mode of the same tonic note: D Dorian, then D major, then D minor. Having the same tonic for all three events makes sense given that they each pertain to the life of the same person. At the same time, the modal alterations function as musical metaphors befitting the various events of Christ's earthly life. Kirkendale has argued that Beethoven's choice of the Dorian mode in setting the Et incarnatus was not accidental. According

---

[45] Drabkin, *Beethoven: Missa solemnis*, 55.
[46] See Kinderman, "Beethoven's Symbol for the Deity," 105–8.

Example 6.9 *Missa solemnis*, op. 123, Credo, mm. 117–36

234 THE CATHOLIC BEETHOVEN

Example 6.9 Continued

Example 6.9 Continued

Example 6.9 Continued

to Gioseffo Zarlino's famous 1558 treatise *Le istitutioni harmoniche*, a copy of which Beethoven probably owned, the Dorian was associated with chastity, making it appropriate for words describing the virgin birth.[47] But the very unfamiliarity of a non-tonal mode also lends the words describing the Incarnation an obvious sense of mystery, one that is reinforced by the way in which the mode is introduced. The previous section had ended in a fortissimo blaze of F major, the dominant of the movement's tonic B-flat (m. 123; again see example 6.9). We expect a perfect cadence in B-flat, but in the first measure of the new section, that cadence is thwarted, and the music lands abruptly on a first-inversion A-major chord (m. 124), with the bass having fallen by a tritone, from F to C-sharp. When the chorus tenors enter in the following measure, the harmony suddenly reduces to the single note A, followed by D. Only when the voices sing a B-natural passing tone in measure 126 does D get confirmed as the new tonic, albeit of the Dorian mode.

---

[47] Kirkendale, "Ancient Rhetorical Traditions," 511. The conversation books also make reference to Heinrich Glarean's *Dodecachordon*: see BCB 1:194–95 (BKh 1:196–97).

Example 6.10 *Missa solemnis*, op. 123, Credo, mm. 184–202

Example 6.10 Continued

Example 6.10 Continued

When the text moves on to describing the actual nativity of Christ—"homo factus est" (and was made man)—we return to the familiarity of the major mode with a decisive perfect cadence in D major: Christ is born, and now walks upon the earth. Beethoven was clearly attuned to the significance of this moment: in the sketches for this passage, he wrote "hier menschlich" (here human).[48] The subsequent move to D *minor* for the "Crucifixus" (He was crucified; m. 156) is unsurprising given the negative turn in the meaning of the text. Then, at the end of the Crucifixus section, on the words "et sepultus est" (and he was buried) the music arrives on the dominant of F, but to highlight the special, miraculous significance of Christ's resurrection, Beethoven does not have the music resolve in F major in any expected way (see example 6.10). In measure 186, the third (E) is suddenly removed from the C-major triad. A stepwise descent from C to G then occurs against a C held as a pedal point. The result, on the fermata in measure 187, is an open-fourth sonority (G–C). This harmonically unstable, tonally aimless dyad vividly depicts the sense of

---

[48] Kirkendale, "Ancient Rhetorical Traditions," 514.

uncertainty that surrounded Christ's disciples after his death and burial. The announcement of resurrection then takes place suddenly, with the chorus tenors declaiming "Et resurrexit" (And he rose from the dead) on a high G (m. 188). This declaration seems to come from another world. It is indeed a miracle: Christ is risen! A few measures later, the music pauses again, this time on a G-major chord (m. 193). This chord acts as the dominant of C (m. 194), which in turn acts as the dominant of F, and F major is finally regained at measure 200, on the word "coelum" (heaven).

In addition to this detailed musical treatment of Christ-related text in the Credo, the Christocentrism of Sailer's theology is also apparent in the next movement of the *Missa*, the Sanctus. Here Beethoven provides an unusually vivid depiction of the Eucharistic ritual that the movement is meant to accompany, in particular a dramatization of Christ's Real Presence in the Eucharist—a fundamental Catholic belief.[49] If the "earthly" section of the Credo concerned Christ's life on earth at a particular moment in history, the Sanctus is about his continued presence in the here and now. The heightened focus on Christ in the Eucharist in the Sanctus movement is reflected in two main ways. First, the overall structure of the movement is strongly directed toward its end, evoking the idea of a journey toward a goal that is significantly different in nature from its beginning. Second, both the instrumental "Präludium" connecting the Sanctus and Benedictus sections and the introduction of a solo violin at the conclusion of the Präludium display in almost pictorial fashion the closeness of Christ to the believer in the Eucharistic ritual. Such efforts to communicate the theological significance of the Eucharist find parallels in the books by Sailer in Beethoven's library, especially the *Kleine Bibel*, which, as I shall show below, connects the Eucharist to the theologian's broader Christocentric outlook by emphasizing the role it plays in drawing Christ and the human believer closer together.

The Sanctus movement is strongly goal-oriented, most obviously because of Beethoven's use of progressive tonality. It begins in D major but ends in G major, making it possible to hear the D major of the beginning as a dominant

---

[49] For clarity, I shall refer to the whole movement—which is divided into the Sanctus and Benedictus sections—as the "Sanctus movement," while using "Sanctus section" to refer specifically to the first part of the movement. Each section (Sanctus and Benedictus) concludes with an Osanna, and I shall follow the common practice of designating these as "Osanna I" and "Osanna II" respectively. Not all Mass settings treat the Sanctus and Benedictus together as a single Sanctus movement, at least in terms of the layout of the score: in Beethoven's own earlier Mass in C, for instance, the Sanctus and Benedictus are designated as two separate movements.

seeking eventual resolution in G major. Drabkin has observed that this teleological design may reflect the influence of Haydn's late masses.[50] But this claim overlooks the fact that in all of Haydn's masses—as well as in the masses of Mozart and in Beethoven's own earlier Mass in C—the Benedictus is indicated as a separate movement from the Sanctus in the score. In the *Missa solemnis*, Beethoven not only departs from this practice, but reinforces the idea of a single continuous Sanctus–Benedictus movement by connecting the Sanctus and Benedictus sections using an instrumental interlude labeled "Präludium." Such a substantial transition section at this point was unprecedented in the history of orchestrated masses.[51] In other respects, however, the Sanctus and Benedictus sections of the *Missa solemnis* still come across as separate and independent. Both sections are tonally closed: the Sanctus begins and ends in D; the Benedictus begins and ends in G. The self-contained nature of these two sections is reinforced by their striking differences in terms of tempo, melodic material, and general mood. The Benedictus maintains a gentle, leisurely 12/8 Andante lilt from beginning to end, while the Sanctus is more varied, starting with a slow Adagio in 2/4, quickening to an Allegro pesante in 4/4 for "Pleni sunt coeli" (m. 34), and culminating in a swifter 3/4 Presto for "Osanna in excelsis" (m. 53). Moreover, Beethoven sets the second Osanna to different music from the first, departing from his approach in the Mass in C, in which Osanna II is simply a verbatim repeat of Osanna I (a practice far from uncommon in Mass-settings).[52]

---

[50] Drabkin, *Beethoven: Missa solemnis*, 76–77, 80–81.

[51] See Kirkendale, "Ancient Rhetorical Traditions," 521. Earlier mass settings do provide precedents for beginning the Benedictus section with an extended instrumental ritornello that was meant to accompany the Consecration and Elevation of the Host: see MacIntyre, *Viennese Concerted Mass*, 419, 445. (As I discuss further below, Beethoven's "Präludium" also appears to be connected to this liturgical action.) In all the cases cited by MacIntyre, however, the Benedictus is labeled as a separate movement, so that the instrumental passage functions as an instrumental prelude, rather than as a transitional passage between the Sanctus and Benedictus sections. Moreover, in these examples the Benedictus music is related to the music heard in the instrumental section that precedes it, which is not true of Beethoven's *Missa*.

[52] In Bruce MacIntyre's study of early Viennese Classical masses, just under half (42%) of his representative sample of seventy-two masses by twenty-eight composers have an Osanna II that is an exact repeat of Osanna I. Overwhelmingly, even where repetition is not exact, Osanna II still tends to be a varied repeat of Osanna I. Only in a small number of cases does Osanna II use completely new musical material. See MacIntyre, *Viennese Concerted Mass*, 438, 445. Mozart wrote only one mass (the *Missa longa* in C, K. 292) in which Osanna II is substantially different from Osanna I. Haydn's masses made more frequent use of new material for Osanna II: four of his twelve authenticated mass settings do so (the *Paukenmesse*, *Heiligmesse*, *Theresienmesse*, and *Schöpfungsmesse*). It should be noted that in Beethoven's *Missa*, the Osanna II, while different from Osanna I, is based on the same musical material as the Benedictus. The only precedent I have found for this practice is in Haydn's *Heiligmesse*. In all other cases, when Osanna II is not an exact or varied repeat of Osanna I, it simply uses new material unrelated to the earlier portions of the Sanctus movement. Beethoven's decision

The whole movement is thus heard as one continuous journey, but also a journey that ends somewhere quite other than where it began. Perhaps this is why the return of the text "Osanna in excelsis" at the end of the Benedictus section (mm. 213ff.) evokes such a feeling of arrival and completion. The music here sounds nothing like the music heard at the first appearance of this text at the end of the Sanctus section (mm. 53ff.). Instead, it assumes the key, tempo, mood, and more conjunct melodic profile of the music associated from the beginning of the Benedictus section with the words "Benedictus qui venit in nomine Domini." It is as if the "world" of the Benedictus has replaced and superseded that of the Sanctus. The structure of the Sanctus movement thus depicts a particularly striking process of transformation. In doing so, it brings to life the Catholic doctrine of transubstantiation—the Eucharistic transformation of bread and wine into the Body and Blood of Christ.

Beethoven goes further in depicting this transcendent change by evoking, in the Präludium and at the beginning of the Benedictus section, the presence of Christ Himself in the Eucharist. The Präludium spans the period in the Eucharistic rite during which the Consecration of the sacred species would have occurred; in particular, it mimics the organ improvisation that occasionally accompanied this liturgical action, a practice Beethoven would probably have remembered from his youthful training as a church organist.[53] The small number of instruments and dense texture (divided cellos and violas, bassoons, flutes, and later clarinets) create an atmosphere of hushed intimacy, testifying to the awesome mystery of the moment at which the human transforms into the divine, and the divine is made present in the human world. The Präludium concludes with the sudden yet dynamically soft entry of a solo violin on a high G (m. 110; see example 6.11), which leads into the Benedictus proper. The use of a solo obbligato instrument for setting the Benedictus text occurs relatively often in earlier Mass-settings.[54] But the precise manner in which Beethoven makes use of the solo violin here goes far beyond simply emulating this established practice. To begin with,

---

to base the Osanna II on the Benedictus music is thus relatively unusual (the Haydn precedent notwithstanding).

[53] See Kirkendale, "Ancient Rhetorical Traditions," 521. Strictly speaking, to have the Consecration at this point—in effect, in the middle of the Sanctus—was not standard canonical practice but became customary for elaborate musical settings of the Mass text in order to avoid excessive delay to the moment of Consecration. Ordinarily, the Consecration would occur only after the Benedictus. See ibid., 521–23; and MacIntyre, *Viennese Concerted Mass*, 419.

[54] See MacIntyre, *Viennese Concerted Mass*, 462, 468.

this violin line exhibits a strikingly high degree of musical pictorialism. As Kirkendale has argued, the instrument's slowly descending entrance signifies the appearance of Christ himself in the consecrated species.[55] In Kirkendale's reading, the bright, luminous sound of the solo violin and flutes playing together in measure 110 evokes liturgical actions associated with the Elevation of the Host at the conclusion of the ritual of Consecration, namely the ringing of a bell and the lighting of a candle at the altar. In any event, as I showed in chapter 3, Beethoven had a history of using solo instruments in connection with texts associated with Christ: he at least considered the use of a solo cello for the Benedictus in the Mass in C, and also employed a cello in the duet between Christ and the Seraph in *Christus am Ölberge*. Kirkendale points out that an additional reference to Christ might be heard in the pastoral quality of the Benedictus itself, especially in its lilting 12/8 meter. The traditional association of the pastoral with Christ stems biblically from descriptions of Christ as the Good Shepherd, or alternatively from the shepherds who appear in Luke's account of Christ's Nativity. Musically, it might also be traced to the Austrian and south German tradition of pastoral masses—masses that made abundant use of pastoral idioms, often written specifically for Advent and Christmas. Words that Beethoven himself scribbled beneath a sketch for this passage provide additional support for Kirkendale's suggestion that the violin solo represents Jesus himself: "im Benedictus solo noch einmal das Herrliche kommt" (in the Benedictus solo that which is glorious comes again).[56]

Over the first six measures of the Benedictus, the solo violin line comes down from the heights, falling to earth. As Laura Dolp has pointed out, the otherworldly quality of its melody is reinforced by its taking a few measures to stabilize metrically.[57] The descending line soon "meets" the mortal voices of the softly intoned "Benedictus qui venit in nomine Domini" in the choral basses (mm. 114–17; again see example 6.11). Strangely, however, the singing does not continue, as if the awestruck believer feels first compelled to acclaim, "Blessed is he who comes in the name of the Lord," and then to return immediately to a state of pious speechlessness.[58] Eventually, words are heard again: after an instrumental interlude of fifteen measures dominated by the

---

[55] Kirkendale, "Ancient Rhetorical Traditions," 523–24.
[56] Drabkin, *Ludwig van Beethoven*, 2:27, 75.
[57] Dolp, "Between Pastoral and Nature," 220.
[58] Warren Kirkendale has remarked of this moment that "verbal expression [is] temporarily exhausted by the presence of Christ": see "Ancient Rhetorical Traditions," 524.

Example 6.11 *Missa solemnis*, op. 123, Sanctus, mm. 104–20 (organ part omitted)

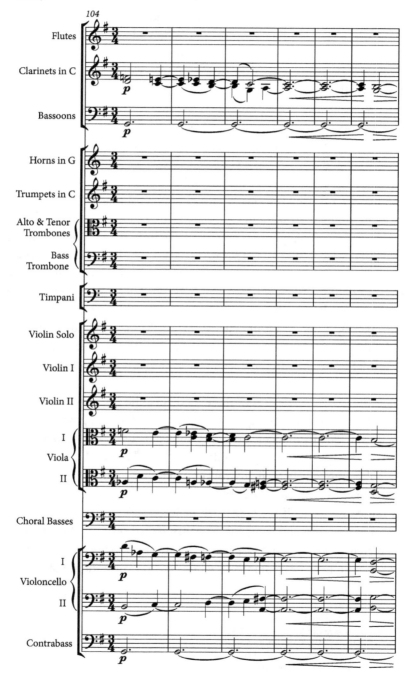

THE *MISSA SOLEMNIS* 245

Example 6.11 Continued

Example 6.11 Continued

Example 6.11 Continued

248 THE CATHOLIC BEETHOVEN

Example 6.11 Continued

Example 6.11 Continued

solo violin, the solo voices reenter (m. 133). Perhaps the believer finally feels able to continue with the remainder of the liturgical text. And some twenty measures later (m. 156), the chorus at last joins in, monotonically "chanting" in thirds, possibly depicting the uniting of the individual believer's faith with that of a larger community, the institutional church.

Accompanying all this is the solo violin, which remains for much of the rest of the movement, pointing to the continued presence of Christ (see example 6.12). Kirkendale's Christological reading of the violin's role can thus be extended beyond its initial entry at the end of the Präludium. While, as acknowledged above, there is ample precedent for the use of a solo obbligato instrument in the Benedictus, in earlier Mass-settings this instrument is almost always employed as part of an instrumental ritornello alternating with sung passages.[59] In Beethoven's Benedictus, although the solo violin part sounds like an introductory ritornello when it first appears, it continues to play when the singers re-enter, remaining present all the way to the final measure of the movement.

Moreover, the solo violin line does not function simply as accompaniment. Indeed, its melodic content is either the same as or an elaboration of the melodies of the singers. The extremely wide range of the violin melody means that it at times reaches down into the "human" range of the singers' voices, especially that of the soprano and alto and sometimes even that of the tenor. This mingling of the solo violin with the singers reinforces the idea of Christ as the Good Shepherd: the Shepherd stays close to his flock. At other times, however, the violin soars above the voices, and even sounds as if it is reaching beyond the soprano's melody, singing what is too high for her to sing. It sings as the singers do, and it sings with the singers, yet in terms of register and prominence it seems also to exist in a separate realm. It is hard to imagine a more vivid musical depiction of Christ as human *and* divine. Christ both goes down into the human world, and transcends it.[60]

---

[59] See MacIntyre, *Viennese Concerted Mass*, 419, 445.

[60] My interpretation here, which extends Kirkendale's reading, bears a resemblance to an 1828 review of the *Missa* by Georg Christoph Grossheim, published in the journal *Caecilia*. See Wallace, *Critical Reception of Beethoven's Compositions*, 31: "In the 'Benedictus' . . . a solo violin, along with these two flutes, descends from the greatest possible height, and they hover around us like a spring breeze. They proclaim the lovely path of the heavenly messenger. . . . The residents of earth greet the emissary of the Godhead. He ascends again, and flutes and whispering harp, with the thankful prayer of lips speaking benediction, accompany him to the clouds." For the original German, see Numaguchi, *Beethovens "Missa Solemnis,"* 128. Grossheim seems to take the solo violin as representing an angel rather than Christ himself. The fact that Beethoven subscribed to *Caecilia*, and the significance thereof, will be discussed in the conclusion.

Example 6.12 *Missa solemnis*, op. 123, Sanctus, mm. 140–50 (vocal parts and solo violin only)

Example 6.12 Continued

In both its overall structure and particular features such as the use of the solo violin, the Sanctus movement thus depicts, in an extraordinarily vivid and intense manner, theological ideas fundamental to the Catholic doctrine of transubstantiation—the mysterious process of physical and spiritual transformation associated with the Eucharist, as well as the closeness of Christ to the believer that results from this transformation. The movement's emphasis on the presence of Christ in the Eucharist resonates strongly with the Christocentric focus of Sailer's theological outlook, especially as reflected in his *Kleine Bibel*. In this text, Sailer stresses the connection between Christ's comfort for sick bodies and his salvific redemption of sick souls: "As the teaching of Christ, in its content and spirit, is medicine for humanity, through which it should recover from the sickness of sin: so is the same teaching, which strengthens the sick of soul, also a teaching of comfort for the sick of body."[61] The suffering induced by illness, Sailer suggests, should prompt reflection on one's sins:

The number, the magnitude of my sins, the depth of my corruption stands before my eyes. But the God of mercy and of comfort has granted me an awareness of a feeling of the shame and pain of my sins, a sense of remorse, and the powerful longing for a holy mind and life, and the resolve to forgo, suffer, shun, and accomplish everything that I must forgo, suffer, shun, and accomplish in order to become a new person.[62]

This sinfulness requires God's redemption, and Sailer points specifically to the Eucharist as a vehicle for that redemption: "This witness I bear in the sight of the church: through it I receive the Body and the Blood of our Lord with full devotion [*Andacht*], which instills in me faith in him, confidence in him, love for him, which the Lord himself will give me.... May the Body of our Lord Jesus Christ be for me a nourishing meal on my way to eternal life."[63] In the Eucharist, Christ heals the sinful soul. In the midst of suffering,

---

[61] Sailer, *Kleine Bibel*, 14: "So wie die Lehre Christi ihrem Inhalte und Geiste nach, eine Arzney für die Menschheit ist, dadurch sie von der Krankheit der Sünde genesen soll: so ist dieselbe Lehre, die die Geistlichkranken stärket, wohl auch eine Trostlehre für die Leiblichkranken."

[62] Sailer, 111: "Die Zahl, die Größe meiner Sünden, die Tiefe meines ganzen Verderbens steht vor meinen Augen. Aber der Gott der Erbarmung und des Trostes [hat] mir Erkenntniss der Sünde Scham- und Schmerzgefühl, Reusinn und das kräftige Sehnen nach einem heiligen Sinn und Leben, und den Entschluß, Alles zu entbehren, zu leiden, zu meiden, zu vollbringen, was ich entbehren, leiden, meiden, vollbringen muß, um ein neuer Mensch zu werden, geschenkt."

[63] Sailer, 134: "Dieses Zeugniß lege ich im Angesichte der Kirche dadurch ab, daß ich den Leib und das Blut unsers Herrn empfange mit aller Andacht, die mir der Glaube an Ihn, die Zuversicht auf Ihn,

both physical and spiritual, the believer is exhorted to seek succor at the Lord's table. The passage from the *Kleine Bibel* just quoted also makes an explicit connection between the Eucharist and what Sailer calls "Andacht"—religious devotion. In this regard, Beethoven's own use of the word "Andacht" in the performance direction "Mit Andacht" (with devotion) at the beginning of the Sanctus movement might well encode a specific reference to the personal feeling of piety associated with the Eucharistic ritual.[64] ("Mit Andacht" also appears as a performance direction at the beginning of the Kyrie—another part of the Mass text that emphasizes God's mercy for the sinner.) It is worth mentioning too that a strong emphasis on the Eucharist is apparent in Thomas à Kempis's *Imitation of Christ*, another book owned by Beethoven, probably in a translation by Sailer (see chapter 5). The last of the *Imitation*'s four books is devoted specifically to the topic of the Eucharist as a vehicle through which the Christian may enter into an intimate relationship with Jesus.[65]

Further evidence suggestive of Beethoven's keen interest in the Eucharist can be found in his sketches for the *Missa solemnis*, albeit for the Agnus Dei—the other part of the Mass Ordinary associated with the Eucharist. In the sketchbook Artaria 197, Beethoven wrote out a harmonization of the plainchant melody *Pange lingua gloriosi*, the text of which is known for its explicit articulation of the doctrine of transubstantiation and is liturgically associated with the Feast of Corpus Christi, which traditionally celebrates this doctrine.[66] To a greater degree than in the Sanctus, the text of the Agnus Dei associates the Eucharist with the forgiveness of sins. Beethoven's attention to this idea is detectable elsewhere in Artaria 197: above a sketch for the Agnus Dei just two pages after the harmonization of *Pange lingua*, he wrote the words "Scham der Sünden" (shame of sin).[67]

---

und die Liebe zu Ihn einflößen, die mir der Herr selbst schenken wird.... Der Leib unsers Herrn Jesu Christi, sey mir ein stärkendes Mahl auf den Weg in die Ewigkeit."

[64] As discussed in chapter 2, the word "Andacht" was also employed by Ferdinand d'Antoine, who was active in Bonn during Beethoven's youth, to describe what he believed church music should inspire.

[65] See Thomas à Kempis, *Imitation of Christ*, 183–217; and Thomas von Kempen, *Das Buch*, 191–230.

[66] See Kirkendale, "Ancient Rhetorical Traditions," 510. For the sketch, see Drabkin, *Ludwig van Beethoven*, 2:41.

[67] Drabkin, *Ludwig van Beethoven*, 2:43.

"Archaic" Features of the *Missa solemnis* and Sailer's Role in Catholic Liturgical Revival

So far, my discussion of the *Missa solemnis* and its resonances with Sailer's theological views has stressed features that have precedents in Beethoven's earlier religious music, especially the Mass in C: compositional techniques that draw special attention to the person of Christ, and that invoke an active engagement with the liturgical text, along with evidence of Beethoven's interest in ecumenical outreach to Protestants. But one prominent aspect of the *Missa* seems to have represented a genuinely new path for Beethoven: his employment of various "archaic" techniques associated with music of the relatively distant past, especially music associated with the traditional Catholic liturgy. As several commentators have argued, this aspect of the *Missa* constitutes by far the most significant point of contrast between the *Missa* and the Mass in C, other than the increased length and orchestration of the later work.[68] Famously, the work's archaic features were what most bothered Adorno, who scoffed at Beethoven's use of a "rudimentary church idiom retrieved from memory."[69] For Adorno, the archaism of the *Missa* represented a rejection of the "dynamic-dialectical" (*dynamisch-dialektische*) style and the "principle of development" (*Durchführungsprinzip*) that defined Viennese Classicism, and made the work pompous and anachronistic.[70] More recently, Lodes has echoed Adorno's view, albeit without the negative aesthetic judgment of Beethoven's approach. The composer, Lodes writes, "did not simply adopt these traditions: he chose them consciously, from a distance, as an alternative to the language of the Classical style."[71]

Documentary and biographical evidence clearly illustrates the deliberateness with which Beethoven sought to incorporate archaic church music styles in the *Missa*. The *Tagebuch* entry about studying Catholic psalms and hymns has been previously noted, as has Beethoven's harmonization of the plainchant melody *Pange lingua*, and his ownership of Zarlino's *Istitutioni harmoniche*. But, as Richard Kramer has pointed out, Beethoven also vigorously investigated Palestrina's music, in what Kramer describes

---

[68] McGrann, "Der Hintergrund zu Beethovens Messen," 133–37. See also Lodes, "Probing the Sacred Genres," 232.
[69] Adorno, *Beethoven*, 150.
[70] Adorno, 138, 144–46.
[71] Lodes, "Probing the Sacred Genres," 232.

as "an exercise bordering on the obsessive."[72] It should be pointed out, too, that Beethoven's use of church modes in the *Missa* was preceded by a number of preparatory exercises in modal harmony that have survived in the sketchbooks.[73] The composer's intense interest in the old modes seems, moreover, to have been animated by a belief that they were specially suited to evoking the divine. In an annotation he made while reading some theoretical writings concerning fugue, Beethoven wrote, "In the old church modes the devotion is divine, I called out, and may God let me express it someday."[74] Not surprisingly, perhaps, he thought of using the modes in more works than just the *Missa solemnis*. On the back of one of the sketches for the *Hammerklavier* Sonata, Beethoven wrote of his intention to compose a "pious song in a symphony in ancient modes—Lord God we praise Thee—alleluia ... *Cantique ecclesiastique*," though it is not clear whether this refers to the Ninth Symphony, or to a planned Tenth Symphony.[75] And Beethoven actually did employ the Lydian mode in the middle movement of the op. 132 quartet, whose full title is "Heiliger Dankgesang eines Genesenen an die Gottheit, in der lydischen Tonart" (Holy song of thanks of a convalescent to God, in the Lydian mode).[76] Just as with the case of the Dorian mode in the Credo, previously discussed, Beethoven chose the mode appropriate to the subject at hand, for Zarlino's *Istitutioni harmoniche* associates the Lydian mode with recovery from fatigue.[77] Given this symbolic meaning, the Lydian mode thus foreshadows Beethoven's own description of the movement's faster, tonal sections: "Neue Kraft fühlend" (Feeling new strength).

Finally, Beethoven's unusually detailed concern with the organ part in the *Missa solemnis* might be a further sign of his attention to traditional church music practice. As Norbert Gertsch has demonstrated, the composer tried

---

[72] Kramer, "In Search of Palestrina," 283. Beethoven's interest in Palestrina may have been inspired by E. T. A. Hoffmann's famous 1814 essay "Old and New Church Music" (*Alte und neue Kirchenmusik*), which exalted Palestrina's music as emblematic of proper church music style: see Hoffmann, "Old and New Church Music," 357–59. Carl Dahlhaus has acknowledged that we cannot be certain Beethoven read Hoffmann's essay, but he believes the likelihood is high given the composer's documented respect for Hoffmann's views: see *Ludwig van Beethoven*, 194. It should also be noted that Beethoven regularly read the *Allgemeine musikalische Zeitung* (see *Schätzungsprotokoll* no. 40), in which Hoffmann's essay was published.

[73] London, British Library, Add. MS 29997, fols. 13ʳ and 26ᵛ. See also Hans Schmidt, "Verzeichnis der Skizzen Beethovens," 73–74 (entry no. 187); and Biamonti no. 607.

[74] Quoted in Kramer, "In Search of Palestrina," 294: "In den alten Kirchentonarten ist die Andacht göttlich rief ich dabey aus, u[nd] Gott laße mich es einmal darstellen."

[75] Cook, *Beethoven: Symphony No. 9*, 13.

[76] The compatibility of the word "Gottheit" with Christian belief has been discussed in chapters 4 and 5.

[77] Kirkendale, "Ancient Rhetorical Traditions," 512.

to exercise an unconventional amount of control over the realization of the organ part by writing it out in full in many places, in addition to providing figured bass.[78] In contrast, for the Mass in C, the organ part had been notated using bass figures only. The specific mention of the organ in the full title of the *Missa* suggests further that in his later mass, Beethoven might have regarded the organ more as an obbligato instrument than a mere supplier of basso continuo.[79] The issue of the organ part in the *Missa* was so important to him that, even at a very late stage in the composition of the work, he was studying C. P. E. Bach's treatise on keyboard playing and setting himself figured-bass exercises to complete based on his reading of the treatise.[80]

At the broadest level, the archaic feel of the *Missa* as a whole owes much to the frequency of plagal cadences and avoidance of leading tones throughout the work.[81] But more localized allusions to older sacred styles can be found in all parts of the *Missa*. Some of these are relatively subtle, for instance the use of the archaic 3/2 meter in the Christe. A more explicit example is the use of ecclesiastical modes in the Credo. I have discussed above the setting of the Et incarnatus in the Dorian mode, but an argument can also be made for the use of a different mode, the Mixolydian, for the Et resurrexit (see example 6.10, mm. 188–93). It is true that in context this passage could be heard simply as a prolongation of a dominant chord in C major. But if that were the more appropriate interpretation, we might expect the presence of F-sharps to produce a local tonicization of G. Instead, not only are all Fs in this passage F-naturals, but F-natural is prominent in the highest voice (mm. 191–92). The ascending minor third in the soprano on the word "scripturas" (scriptures; mm. 192–93) adds further to the antiquated feel of this passage, for it resembles, at least melodically, a Landini cadence commonly employed in fourteenth- and early fifteenth-century music. Strictly speaking, for a true Landini cadence Beethoven would have had to have an F-sharp leading tone in the soprano in measure 192, and an A-natural held in the bass on both the third and fourth quarter-note beats. Nevertheless, the sound of a melody coming to a point of rest with an upward motion of a minor third is too distinctly pre-tonal not to be heard as anachronistic. One might be tempted to argue that the B-flat in the bass in measure 191 complicates a Mixolydian

---

[78] Gertsch, "Wer verfasste die Orgelstimmen," 297–98.
[79] Gertsch, 281–84. Beethoven did express dissatisfaction with the published organ part for the Mass in C and wanted to write a new one, but never got around to doing so.
[80] Gertsch, 295–96.
[81] Lodes, "Probing the Sacred Genres," 232.

reading here, but this note can easily be understood as an instance of *musica ficta*, a way of avoiding both a harmonic tritone with F in the soprano and a melodic tritone with the F that follows in the bass line.

This section of the Credo contains other examples of archaic music. The Et incarnatus sounds antiquated not just because of the use of the Dorian mode, but because a group of men's voices singing a single melody with uncomplicated rhythms evokes the sound of plainchant (mm. 125–31; see example 6.9). When this melody is then sung by multiple parts in close imitation (starting in m. 132), it is hard not to hear Beethoven mimicking Renaissance polyphony, the clarity of the choral texture reminding one especially of the music of Palestrina (again, see example 6.9). This polyphonic passage, sung by the four soloists, is followed by one of the most explicit evocations of plainchant in the entire *Missa*. In measure 141, the chorus enters at a hushed pianissimo dynamic to repeat the soloists' words "Et incarnatus est de spiritu sancto ex Maria virgine" (And he was incarnate by the Holy Spirit of the Virgin Mary; see example 6.13). Except for the bass part, these words are all sung on the same note (E), with the music's rhythm closely matching the spoken rhythm of the Latin, making this passage resemble a line of a psalm being chanted on a recitation tone. The fall of the bass from E to A in measure 142 might in this regard be historically inauthentic. But notwithstanding the C-sharp in the instrumental accompaniment (not shown in the example), the open fifth (A–E) created between the bass and the other three choral parts still evokes an antiquated, pre-tonal

Example 6.13 *Missa solemnis*, op. 123, Credo, mm. 141–42 (vocal parts only)

sound world. To these references to chant in the Credo can be added two further examples from the Sanctus: the brief entry of the choral basses at the beginning of the Benedictus already discussed above (see example 6.11), as well as the passage marked *mezza voce* immediately preceding the Pleni sunt coeli (mm. 29–33). Takashi Numaguchi has argued, moreover, that references to plainchant need not be as explicit as the examples I have cited so far.[82] Any unison singing might be heard to allude to chant, especially if it is at a slow or moderate tempo. In this regard one can point to several other unison passages elsewhere in the *Missa*: measures 51–54 in the Kyrie; 281–82 in the Gloria; 211–12 and 223–27 in the Sanctus; and 364–66 in the Agnus Dei. In a similar way, the two moments in the Agnus Dei when voices sing without any instrumental accompaniment (mm. 123–26 and 212–14) can also be heard as referring vaguely to a cappella polyphony, even if these passages are clearly tonal.

The fugue on "in gloria Dei patris" in the Gloria presents yet another instance of archaism in the *Missa*. As has been mentioned, at measure 429, in the middle of the fugue, Beethoven brings back the words "cum Sancto Spiritu." This textual return occurs in a slow-moving melody in the choral basses, mostly in whole notes (see example 6.6). Juxtaposed against the fugal stretto happening at the same time in the soloists, which is much more rhythmically active, this melody sounds like a cantus firmus. One might believe at first that we have here a new subject which turns the fugue into a double fugue, but this bass melody is not subsequently given imitative treatment. The "cantus firmus" melody never returns again. (The tenors do answer the basses in a rhythmically similar phrase in measure 436, but the tenor melody is different enough from what the basses sang that it is difficult to hear the tenors as imitating the bass melody.) Because the idea of a cantus firmus is referred to in such an isolated, one-off manner, it sounds self-conscious, unintegrated into the larger whole, as if Beethoven really wanted the listener to notice its intrusion, its stylistic foreignness. The same could be said of the other examples I have cited: the use of the church modes, and the hints of plainchant and unaccompanied polyphony. The relative brevity of the musical passages where these compositional devices pop up draws added emphasis to them. Beethoven does not just borrow musical ideas from the past; he seems intent on accentuating the "past-ness" of these ideas.

[82] Numaguchi, "Das instrumentale Fugato," 104.

This principle could also be applied to the "in gloria Dei patris" fugue taken as a whole, as well as to the concluding fugue in the Credo. Notwithstanding Beethoven's well-known obsession with fugues in his late works, the use of fugue to end the Gloria and Credo might be explained relatively straightforwardly as an attempt to abide by a long-established custom in musical settings of the Mass. But these fugues in the *Missa* are striking because of their sheer length and complexity. They are much more than an act of obedience to convention. Their extraordinary expansiveness seems intended to draw special attention to their generic identity. Beethoven stresses the fugue as fugue, such that it comes across as a particularly self-conscious evocation of the past. My interpretation here is strengthened by Michael Heinemann's observation that the Credo fugue builds up to its climax partly through a gradual accretion of younger and younger historical styles: sixteenth-century counterpoint gives way gradually to eighteenth-century counterpoint, and the fugue becomes more and more contrapuntally complex by providing a kind of chronological showcase of fugal technique.[83]

It might be possible to connect Beethoven's interest in traditional Catholic church music to the liturgical policies of Maximilian Friedrich, the earlier of the two elector-archbishops who ruled Bonn during the composer's youth. As discussed in chapter 2, Maximilian Friedrich, unusually for the time, promoted Gregorian chant, despite otherwise favoring Catholic Enlightenment policies concerning the simplification of the liturgy. But what is noteworthy about the archaic aspects of the *Missa* I have described is that they coexist with other features of the work that come across as personal and idiosyncratic, especially those features discussed earlier as reflective of Beethoven's intense engagement with the meaning of the Mass text. Faced with this apparent synthesis of the revolutionary and the reactionary, Carl Dahlhaus argued that the archaic musical devices are not archaic at all. Rather, they are appropriated and worked into what is essentially a modern, progressive musical style.[84] But an alternative framework for understanding this seeming tension in the *Missa solemnis* might be found, once again, in the theology of Johann Michael Sailer. In the previous chapter, I described how Sailer's attitude to the Catholic liturgy sought a balance between encouraging the private piety of individual believers ("inner religion") and maintaining the importance of the Church's age-old liturgical traditions,

---

[83] See Heinemann, "Suspended Time," 229–31.
[84] Dahlhaus, *Ludwig van Beethoven*, 194–201, esp. 194.

especially the Mass ("outer religion"). As it turns out, Sailer's approach in this regard also extended specifically to liturgical music. The same theologian who supported vernacular *Kirchenlieder* also loved plainchant and a cappella polyphony, and actively encouraged scholarly research into the history of Catholic church music, foreshadowing later developments in the nineteenth-century Church.[85] As Conrad Donakowski has written, Sailer was "a prophet both of progressive Catholicism and of liturgical revival based on historical research. He was the patron both of a program to restore old music and of popular participation in the liturgy."[86] Ironically, despite his own discomfort with ultramontane conceptions of the Church, Sailer's stress on the Church's traditions ended up exerting an impact on more conservative ultramontane theologians later in the nineteenth century.[87] In the realm of church music, this can be seen in Sailer's inadvertent role as an inspiration for the Cecilian movement (*Cäcilianismus*). This movement was established in 1868 to promote traditional Catholic liturgical music such as plainchant and unaccompanied polyphony, especially works composed by Palestrina, and actively sought to prohibit other forms of church music, including all church music in the vernacular.[88] (We shall return to this topic in the conclusion.)

For reasons discussed in the previous chapter, it is not entirely certain—though far from implausible—that Beethoven was aware of Sailer's views on the liturgy, as opposed to other aspects of his outlook. The same could be said of the theologian's attitudes to liturgical music in particular. Nevertheless, this blend of progressive and conservative elements in the *Missa solemnis* demonstrates striking parallels with Sailer's ideas. Josef Schuh has written the following pithy summary of Sailer's perspective: "The liturgy must be simultaneously traditional and current, history and event. It must be existential in the sense that one is engaged fully and completely in the present,

---

[85] Schuh, *Johann Michael Sailer*, 23.

[86] Donakowski, "Age of Revolutions," 384. Sailer's interest in traditional liturgical music may have been influenced to some degree by certain non-Josephinist strands of the German Catholic Enlightenment that fostered the study of liturgical history, in part because they wished to demonstrate the long-standing existence of specifically German liturgical traditions, separate from those mandated by Rome. However, such historical research, led by reformist figures such as Martin Gerbert (1720–1793), also led inadvertently to a better understanding even of traditional "Rome-centered" musical styles such as chant and polyphony. See Printy, *Enlightenment*, 157; and Kirkendale, "Ancient Rhetorical Traditions," 536.

[87] Hänsel, *Geistliche Restauration*, 61.

[88] For overviews of the Cecilian movement, and Sailer's role in its development, see Wiora, "Restauration und Historismus"; and Schwemmer, "Der Cäcilianismus."

but not in the sense that one loses sight of the past."[89] In a similar manner, the *Missa solemnis* combines a highly personal approach to setting the Mass text with references to church music from the past. Originality and tradition, new and old, are not in tension, but enliven each other.

The *Missa solemnis* at the Boundary of Sacred and Secular

Throughout this book I have referred often to the tendency of scholars to advance secularized readings of Beethoven's religious music, especially the *Missa solemnis*. The work's undeniable references to secular musical genres appears to support the idea that, fundamentally, Beethoven is reinterpreting a religious text in a secular way. Laura Dolp, for example, has described the violin solo in the Benedictus as evoking the "secular flourishes of the concerto cadenza."[90] Drabkin has further posited that the overall structure of the Benedictus approximates that of the opening movement of a classical concerto.[91] A more obvious intrusion from the world of secular music occurs in the Dona nobis pacem, where Beethoven employs accompanied recitative (mm. 174–89), a highly unconventional device to employ in a Mass-setting, even if it is not entirely unprecedented in the history of the mass as a musical genre.[92] It is particularly striking that these examples of secular music occur in the two movements associated with the Eucharist, the holiest part of the Mass. Indeed, if the interpretation of the violin solo that I put forward above is correct, concerto-like music is used in the Benedictus to represent Christ himself.

Even when commentators have not shied away from acknowledging the religious aspects of the *Missa*, it is usually assumed that it is at least not a piece of *liturgical* music. The sheer scale of the work, both in length and

---

[89] Schuh, *Johann Michael Sailer*, 78: "Liturgie muß traditionell und aktuell zugleich, Geschichte und Ereignis sein. Sie muß existentiell sein in dem Sinn, daß man sich voll und ganz in die Gegenwart engagiert, nicht aber in dem Sinn, daß man die Vergangenheit aus dem Blick verliert."
[90] Dolp, "Between Pastoral and Nature," 223.
[91] Drabkin, *Beethoven: Missa solemnis*, 78.
[92] Kirkendale, "Ancient Rhetorical Traditions," 531. Kirkendale cites two rare examples of the use of recitative in earlier masses: Cavalli's *Missa concertata* (at "Domine Deus") and Haydn's *Missa Cellensis* (*Cäcilienmesse*) (at "Et incarnatus"). Other isolated examples are identified in MacIntyre, *Viennese Concerted Mass*, 78, 310–11, 500–4. It should be noted that in none of the examples cited in these sources does the label "Recitative" appear in the score, as it does in Beethoven's *Missa*. Beethoven's sketches for this movement suggest that he thought of using recitative at a very early stage of the compositional process, and even considered opening the entire movement with a *secco* recitative. See Drabkin, "The Agnus Dei," 141.

performance forces required, suggests that it is better suited to the concert hall than to the church, notwithstanding the fact that Beethoven originally intended it for Archduke Rudolph's installation Mass.[93] As Lodes puts it, the *Missa* ended up going "far beyond the liturgically justifiable range of expression."[94] In several letters, Beethoven himself declared that it could be performed as an oratorio, possibly lending the composer's own endorsement to the idea that it is not really a liturgical work.[95]

Seen from the perspective of Sailer's theology, however, neither the secular aspects of the *Missa* nor its purported violation of liturgical propriety mean that the work should be conceived as entirely separate from the institutional Church or its liturgy. As discussed in the previous chapter, the fundamental distinction between "inner" and "outer" religion in Sailer's outlook leads to an equal emphasis on individual piety and public liturgy, as well as to the notion that one's inner faith, cultivated and nourished by the liturgy, should compel one to share that faith outwardly with others, including through good works. "It is not enough to know what the Good is," Sailer instructs in *Goldkörner*, "one must also do the Good."[96] The Church is not limited to physical buildings but should exist in the actions of individual Christians wherever they go. As Sailer writes in the *Kleine Bibel*, "Every Christian should be a Church in microcosm, and become in his place what the entire Church is in macrocosm."[97] Elsewhere in the same book, he also describes how service to others in everyday life turns individual believers themselves into a kind of liturgy.[98] By breaking the boundaries of the physical liturgy, the *Missa* might be seen to follow this broad conception of liturgy and its purpose. The work's merging of the sacred and the secular is no sacrilege or profanation. From Sailer's perspective, it points to the idea that the liturgy must reach out to the world beyond itself, for the divine can and should hallow the mundane.

---

[93] Rudolph's installation Mass featured enormous instrumental and vocal forces for the music that was performed, so the *Missa solemnis* may not have been as inappropriate as many commentators have believed for the liturgical setting for which it was originally intended. See Sehnal, "Kirchenmusik im Erzbistum Olmütz," 177–79.

[94] Lodes, "Probing the Sacred Genres," 224.

[95] See Anderson nos. 1134, 1135, 1139, 1260, and 1292 (*BGA* nos. 1550, 1563, 1571, 1773, and 1841).

[96] Sailer, *Sprüche-Buch: Goldkörner*, 39: "Es ist nicht genug, wissen, was gut ist; man muß auch das Gute thun."

[97] Sailer, *Kleine Bibel*, 66: "Jeder Christ soll eine Kirche im Kleinen seyn, an seiner Stelle das werden, was die ganze Kirche im Großen ist."

[98] Sailer, 97.

Beethoven's use of recitative in the Agnus Dei provides an especially compelling example of how the *Missa* enacts a liturgy that reaches out to the wider world. As is well known, the recitatives in the Dona nobis pacem are angst-ridden responses to threatening music evoking war (see mm. 164–74). This meaning is clear not just because of the march-like melody in the trumpets with a prominent timpani accompaniment, but also because of Beethoven's subtitle for this section of the movement—"Bitte um innern und äußern Frieden" (Plea for inner and outer peace)—a phrase that, incidentally, also calls to mind the distinction between "inner" and "outer" religion in Sailer's theology. War represents a threat to the peace (*pacem*) described in the text, and Beethoven's specific evocation of the idea of "outer peace" refers to the end of human conflict. "Outer peace" serves as an analog to the "inner peace" the believer finds through the mercy of Christ, whose presence in the Dona nobis pacem is signaled, as in the Benedictus, by the music's compound-duple pastoral lilt.

The influence of Haydn's *Missa in tempore belli* seems undeniable here, as many commentators have pointed out, but there is also a possible link between this military reference and allusions to war occurring in Beethoven's earlier religious music. The text of *Der Wachtelschlag*, for instance, encourages the listener to trust in God even amid the turmoil brought on by war:

Machen Gefahren der Krieger dir bang,	If the threats of warriors make you afraid,
Traue Gott!	Trust God!
Traue Gott!	Trust God!
Sieh, er verziehet nicht lang.	See, he will not be away for long.

The music accompanying this text features a repeated dotted-rhythmic motive, harmonically static on B-flat over four measures (mm. 51–54), undoubtedly an attempt to mimic the music of a military march. Beethoven also employs recitative (mm. 56–58)—another point of correspondence with the *Missa* (see example 6.14). Military music is prominent in *Christus am Ölberge* as well. In the oratorio, Beethoven seems to assign disproportionate attention to depicting the arrival of the soldiers who come to arrest Jesus (see Nos. 4 and 5). It is true that Beethoven's musical reference to the military in *Christus* could simply have been forced on him by the role of soldiers in the given narrative of Christ's Passion. But the strikingly vivid way in which the

Example 6.14 *Der Wachtelschlag*, WoO 129, mm. 51–58

Example 6.15 Mass in C major, op. 86, Agnus Dei, horn part (1st and 2nd horns doubled): (a) mm. 114–18; (b) mm. 178–82

arrival of the soldiers is depicted, with a dotted-rhythm march motive that repeats but gradually gets louder and louder, as well as the sheer amount of time Beethoven gives to this part of the narrative, points to a deliberate attempt to emphasize this aspect of the Passion story. Another reference to war might be heard in the Agnus Dei of the Mass in C, where a martial-sounding theme in the horns and bassoons seems, as in the *Missa*, to threaten the peace evoked in the text of the Dona nobis pacem (see example 6.15a). After four open-ended arrivals on the third scale degree in C major (mm. 115, 121, 138, and 145), the horn call returns yet again in the last five measures of the piece, but this time finally resolves to the tonic note, signaling the achievement of the peace to which the Mass text refers (see example 6.15b).

Whether in the *Missa* or in these earlier religious works, the use of military music to represent a force opposed to peace would, for both Beethoven and his listeners, have been more than just an abstract metaphor. For most of the composer's adult life, Europe was, after all, at war. "Curse this war," the composer remarked pithily in the aftermath of Napoleon's second occupation of Vienna in 1809.[99] To refer to war as blatantly as Beethoven does in the *Missa* would thus have been a way of making the liturgy relevant to contemporary events, to show how religion does indeed have real meaning for everyday life. It is easy to see how this gesture aligns with Sailer's belief that the liturgy and its traditions should not be mere rituals, but be responsive to the needs of individual believers in their daily lives. In the Dona nobis pacem, Beethoven's pleas for inner peace and outer peace are not separate, just as for Sailer religion meant both inner and outer religion. To encounter Christ in the Mass means also to understand what faith in Christ might mean in one's life beyond the physical boundaries of the liturgy.

---

[99] Anderson no. 226 (*BGA* no. 400), Beethoven to Breitkopf & Härtel, September 19, 1809: "verfluchter Krieg."

Beethoven as Musical Priest

The blurring of the boundary between sacred and secular in Sailer's liturgical views was also central to a broader theory of the relationship between religion and art that he put forward in a lecture entitled *Von dem Bunde der Religion mit der Kunst* (On the union of religion with art).[100] The text of this lecture was published as an appendix to *Neue Beyträge zur Bildung des Geistlichen*, with which, as discussed in the previous chapter, Beethoven may have been familiar. *Von dem Bunde* was one of Sailer's most influential writings, exerting an impact on numerous early Romantic artistic figures, especially the Nazarene painters.[101]

As evident in the lecture's title, Sailer regards religion and art as intrinsically and inextricably bound together.[102] Religion without art, Sailer states bluntly, is dead—"a corpse" (*eine Leiche*).[103] In his view, all true art is "holy art"—*heilige Kunst*—a term that he uses to refer both to the Catholic liturgy and to art that performs a similar function to liturgy in cultivating religious faith. On the one hand, the Church functions as a "holy art that reveals externally the life of religion" (*Eine heilige Kunst, die das Leben der Religion im Aeußern offenbaret*).[104] Just as a work of art is a physical manifestation of some inner emotional state, so the visible Church, especially in its liturgy, externalizes the inner faith of the believer. On the other hand, even art that is not explicitly religious has a fundamental religious basis. *All* art is, at its core, religious, precisely because it emerges from an interior, unsatisfied longing for the divine that is common to all human beings, regardless of whether they profess formal religious belief.[105] The Church's liturgy can be understood as the highest form of art, but all other art also plays a role in disseminating the Church's message and thus has an important pastoral purpose.[106] In a

---

[100] Sailer, *Neue Beyträge*, 207–18.
[101] Gajek, "Dichtung und Religion," 77–80; Peter Hrncirik also suggests that in early nineteenth-century critical debates about church music, Sailer's *Vom dem Bunde* was as influential as E. T. A. Hoffmann's "Old and New Church Music" (*Alte und neue Kirchenmusik*): see "Tendenzen der Kirchenmusik im Biedermeier," 24.
[102] Sailer, *Neue Beyträge*, 208: "Die Religion steht mit der Kunst in einem Bunde, der nicht zufällig, nicht verabredet, sondern nothwendig, wesentlich, der nicht heut oder gestern entstanden, sondern ewig ist" (Religion stands with art in a union, which is not accidental, not based on an artificial agreement, but necessary, essential; which does not emerge today or yesterday, but is eternal).
[103] Sailer, 214.
[104] Sailer, 210.
[105] Sailer, 211.
[106] Sailer, 211. See also Schuh, *Johann Michael Sailer*, 78. In this regard, Sailer's views echo those of Gellert, who also argued that secular art could be used legitimately to convey sacred truths, a view that Haydn found particularly appealing: see Schroeder, "Haydn and Gellert," 13.

discussion of architecture, Sailer argues that church buildings ought to reflect the human longing for what lies above in heaven, making use of that favorite image of Beethoven's—the stars:

> I see [holy art], how it . . . beholding and sensing the starry sky as the great cathedral of the temple of nature, emulates what no starry sky can express. It emulates on earth the same cathedral of the temple of nature, and what lies beyond the stars. It designs and produces a St. Peter's in Rome, a St. Paul's in London, or to climb down much further, a St. Stephen's in Vienna, a Frauenkirche in Munich, a St. Martin's in Landshut.[107]

A church building, in other words, evokes the heights of the starry sky in order to point to the God who lies beyond the stars. Sailer also explicitly points to music as a form of *heilige Kunst* that makes religion manifest.[108] Just like the liturgy, music "preserves, strengthens and elevates wherever it is found."[109]

At the same time, however, Sailer warns that union between art and religion should not be mistaken for a complete identity between them. Sailer opposes the idea of art for art's sake, and any notion that art itself could be its own religion.[110] The union of art with religion should ultimately be intended for the service of religion alone. Sailer wished to harness the emotional power of the arts to encourage a revival of Christianity: against the unfulfilled longing of much Romantic art, he believed that true art, holy art, showed how that longing can indeed be fulfilled through belief in Jesus Christ.[111]

---

[107] Sailer, *Neue Beyträge*, 210: "ich sehe [die heilige Kunst], wie sie . . . den Sternenhimmel als die große Domkirche des Naturtempels ansehend und ahnend, was kein Sternenhimmel ausdrücken kann, dieselbe Domkirche des Naturtempels, und was über den Sternen liegt, auf Erde nachbildet, und eine Peterskirche in Rom, eine Paulskirche in London, oder um tief, tief herabzusteigen, eine Stephanskirche in Wien, eine Frauenkirche in München, eine Martinskirche in Landshut entwirft und darstellt." Sailer's use of "Naturtempel" (nature-temple) recalls the phrase "Tempel der Natur" (temple of nature) in the Heiligenstadt Testament: "So lange schon ist der wahren Freude inniger widerhall mir fremd—o wann—o Wann o Gottheit—kann ich im Tempel der Natur und der Menschen ihn wider fühlen" (For so long now the inner echo of real joy has been unknown to me— Oh when—oh when, Almighty God—shall I be able to hear and feel this echo again in the temple of Nature and in contact with humanity). See E. Anderson, *Letters of Beethoven*, 3:1354; and *BGA* no. 106, p. 123. Lockwood has suggested that "temple of nature" might be taken as Masonic: see *Beethoven*, 120–21. Sailer's use of the phrase in a Christian context suggests the possibility that it might be innocent of any Masonic meaning.
[108] Sailer, *Neue Beyträge*, 212.
[109] Sailer, 213: "erhält, stärket und erhöhet sie auch da, wo sie ist."
[110] See Sailer, 207–8, 217.
[111] Sailer, 208. See also Schuh, *Johann Michael Sailer*, 35.

Art should thus encourage people to live lives thoroughly permeated by religious faith:

> Holy art reveals the inner life of religion not simply in temples that it erects, in heavenly songs that it supplies, in brilliant discourses that it utters, in paintings, statues that it enlivens, in wondrous harmonies that it creates in minds that listen. But it reveals the life of religion in a yet higher style of art—the very first style—where?—in the countenances, in the faces, in the gestures, in all actions, in the entire life of the person who is saturated by religion.[112]

These remarks by Sailer recall a statement that Bettina Brentano (Bettina von Arnim)—whose own personal contact with Sailer was noted in chapter 5—attributed to Beethoven: "So always art represents the divine [*Gottheit*], and the human relationship to art is religion: what we gain through art is from God, divine inspiration that sets up an aim for human capabilities, an aim that we can accomplish."[113] This statement, like much else that has come down to us from Bettina, is widely considered to be of doubtful authenticity.[114] But its content does resonate strikingly with Sailer's belief in the inseparability of art and religion.

As discussed in the previous chapter, in addition to the three texts by Sailer that Beethoven had in his library (*Goldkörner, Friedrich Christians Vermächtniß*, and the *Kleine Bibel*), the conversation books tell us of Beethoven's desire to obtain another work by Sailer on the nature of the

---

[112] Sailer, *Neue Beyträge*, 217: "Die heilige Kunst offenbaret das innere Leben der Religion nicht bloß in Tempeln, die sie erbaut, in himmlischen Gesängen, die sie eingiebt, in geistvollen Reden, die sie ausspricht, in Gemählden, Statüen, die sie beseelet, in wundervollen Harmonien, die sie in horchenden Gemüthern erzeugt: sondern sie offenbart das Leben der Religion noch in einem höhern Kunststyle—und allererst—worin?—in dem Antlitze, in dem Mienen, in den Geberden, in allen Handlungen, in dem ganzen Leben des von Religion durchdrungenen Menschen."

[113] Bettina Brentano, *Goethe's Briefwechsel mit einem Kinde* (1835), vol. 2, in Schmitz and von Steinsdorff, *Bettine von Arnim: Werke und Briefe*, 2:9–571, at 2:349: "So vertritt die Kunst allemal die Gottheit, und das menschliche Verhältnis zu ihr ist Religion, was wir durch die Kunst erwerben, das ist von Gott, göttliche Eingebung, die den menschlichen Befähigungen ein Ziel steckt was er erreicht."

[114] Bettina included this statement by Beethoven within a letter she claimed to have written to Goethe in May 1810, but even this letter is very likely to have been fictional: see Härtl, *Drei Brief von Beethoven*, 45–55. Bettina is also the source for an oft-cited anecdote about Beethoven—an incident at Teplitz where Beethoven purportedly refused to bow to the Austrian imperial family even though his companion Goethe did. Many scholars have questioned this account, and it is possible that this incident may never have occurred: see, e.g., Knittel, "Construction of Beethoven," 118–19. For examples of less skeptical views regarding Bettina's trustworthiness, see Kinderman, *Beethoven*, 169; Lockwood, *Beethoven*, 492n7; and Walden, "Authenticity."

Catholic priesthood, *Von der Priesterweihung*. Is it possible, then, that in writing the *Missa solemnis*, the composer thought of himself as a kind of musical priest? Such a suggestion is entirely in keeping with Sailer's belief that music, too, can act as a form of religious preaching. Beethoven does in music what Sailer demanded of Catholic priests in the *Von der Priesterweihung*: that they engage in "interpretation of God's Word" (*Dolmetschung des Wortes*) for their fellow believers.[115] Hence his wish that the *Missa* "awaken and permanently instill religious feelings not only into the singers but also into the listeners."[116] And hence his inscription of the words "Von Herzen—möge es wieder—zu Herzen gehn!" (From the heart—may it go to the heart!) on the first page of the autograph score.[117] Beethoven's heartfelt musical response to the meaning of the Mass text is meant to provoke a similar heartfelt response in his audience. In the same way, Sailer, in *Von der Priesterweihung*, writes of his desire to tell his reader what the words of the liturgy say "to our hearts" (*an unsere Herzen*).[118] In setting the Mass text in a deeply personal manner, Beethoven cannot be said to have been setting aside or even going against the Catholic religion, at least not Sailer's vision of it. Rather, he may have wanted to do his part to spread the Christian message far, far beyond the physical church, to show that music really could be a *heilige Kunst* as Sailer would have conceived it.

---

[115] Sailer, *Von der Priesterweihung*, 30.

[116] Anderson no. 1307 (*BGA* no. 1875), Beethoven to Johann Andreas Streicher, September 16, 1824: "Es bey Bearbeitung dieser großen Messe meine Hauptabsicht war, sowohl bey den Singenden als bey den Zuhörenden, Religiöse Gefühle zu erwecken und dauernd zu machen."

[117] The same phrase also appears in the sketches for the Gloria. See Lodes, "'Von Herzen,'" 300–1. In the same article, Lodes suggests that, contrary to what most scholars have believed, this inscription may not have been meant by Beethoven as an authorial message to all listeners, but rather simply a private dedicatory message to Archduke Rudolph. Lodes bases her argument on the fact that the inscription is found in only one manuscript source, and not in any of the later sources in which Beethoven made corrections (ibid., 295–96). Richard Kramer disagrees with Lodes's claim, and points out that the autograph in which the inscription occurs was not meant only for Rudolph but for many others as well. Indeed, it is missing from the dedication copy that was intended for Rudolph himself. See Review of *Missa solemnis*, 745. A recent essay by Mark Evan Bonds, while agreeing with Lodes's view, also points out that the phrase, or close variants of it, appears frequently in both Catholic and Protestant devotional books of the time: see "Heart to Heart," 232–39.

[118] Sailer, *Von der Priesterweihung*, 8.

Conclusion

The particular focus devoted to Johann Michael Sailer in the last two chapters of this book was motivated by several factors. Sailer is the only important religious figure of Beethoven's time who can be connected to the composer in a personal sense, even if that connection was indirect, with Antonie Brentano serving as an intermediary. Unlike other religious writers in his library, Beethoven owned multiple books by Sailer. And finally, Beethoven engaged with Sailer's writings while working on his most significant piece of religious music, the *Missa solemnis*, whose importance was declared by the composer himself and not just a matter of subsequent critical opinion. As I have explained, however, it is most likely that Sailer's views did not cause some kind of sudden or drastic change in Beethoven's attitude toward Catholicism. The main aspects of the theologian's outlook resemble ideas that Beethoven had been interested in earlier in his career: ecumenism and religious tolerance, ethical conduct, and active engagement with the liturgy. These were also ideas central to the German Catholic Enlightenment, which was prominent in Bonn during Beethoven's youth. Sailer did not fully embrace the Catholic Enlightenment: the fundamental Christocentrism of his theology, his insistence on the importance of dogma as a precondition for ethical conduct, and his interest in recovering traditional Catholic liturgical music represented a critique of the Catholic Enlightenment and possibly even an affinity for some aspects of the Catholic Restoration. But Beethoven, too, had shown signs going back to *Christus am Ölberge* of an openness to more conservative religious approaches. And aspects of the *Missa solemnis* that appear in tension with the Catholic Enlightenment offer a suggestive though not entirely conclusive hint that this openness increased in his final years. At least in a general sense, if Beethoven's religious outlook was defined primarily by a sympathy for the Catholic Enlightenment that was tempered by an attraction to certain aspects of the Catholic Restoration, it makes sense that Sailer's "middle way" between the two Catholic camps would have exerted a special appeal for him.

This book has focused overwhelmingly on a small number of musical works by Beethoven that set a text which can be connected to Catholic belief, even if briefer discussions of pieces that do not fit this criterion—the *Pastoral Symphony*, for instance—have been introduced where relevant. The Catholic connection is not obvious in all instances from the content of the text alone—as with Beethoven's two completed masses—but might derive instead from historical context, as in the case of the Gellert Lieder, whose poems (as has been explained in chapter 3) can be linked to the Catholic Enlightenment even if they were written by a Protestant author. Obviously, the limited scope of this study has been driven to a great extent by reasons of space, and I have simply chosen to concentrate on those Beethoven works most relevant to my aim of exploring Beethoven's Catholic interests. But focusing on texted works, I would argue, also enables a more accurate assessment of the exact nature of the religious content the composer might have been seeking to evoke through music. I have thus not given as much attention to examples such as the third movement of Beethoven's op. 132 string quartet. This movement's famous title, "Heiliger Dankgesang eines Genesenen an die Gottheit" (Holy song of thanksgiving of a convalescent to God), clearly points to some deep spiritual sensibility. But these words are too brief and too general to suggest a more specific confessional allegiance or theological viewpoint. Though the movement employs *stile antico* elements originally associated with the Renaissance polyphonic style of Palestrina—for example, carefully controlled use of dissonance, close imitation in the musical texture, and even modality—such features had long signaled a more generic "church style" rather than serving as unambiguously Catholic confessional markers—a fact demonstrated by J. S. Bach's appropriation of this style for some of his Lutheran works.[1]

Be that as it may, if Beethoven's worldview was shaped by Catholic beliefs to a greater degree than has been thought, those beliefs may also have influenced the ostensibly nonreligious works that make up the overwhelming majority of the composer's output. It has long been commonplace in the reception of Beethoven's music to describe many such works using religious imagery, albeit of an amorphous, nonspecific kind. This situation reflects the influential legacy of the Romantic concept of *Kunstreligion* (art-religion), most often defined as the notion that art can act as a substitute or replacement for traditional religion, a position frequently associated with

---

[1] See Wolff, "Bach and the Tradition." Robert Hatten is right to claim that in the "Heiliger Dankgesang" the use of *stile antico* "carries a religious connotation from its liturgical association": see *Musical Meaning in Beethoven*, 198–99. But, especially in the absence of text, to speak of a "religious connotation" (my emphasis) is not the same as claiming that the movement should be heard as explicitly religious music, let alone religious music that embraces a specific confessional or theological identity. For an overview of the *stile antico*, see Ratner, *Classic Music*, 159–61, 172–80.

figures such as Schopenhauer and Wagner. As Ruth Solie has described, Beethoven's music came to be increasingly sacralized over the course of the nineteenth century, a development that was closely tied to the deification of Beethoven himself: "It is because the figure of Beethoven—his character and his life as well as his music—was invested with religious and moral content that his works were pored over so earnestly in search of oracles."[2] The Ninth Symphony, for instance, was turned into "a source of moral instruction as the lives of the saints had been."[3] Recourse to religious ideas in writing about Beethoven's music can be traced at least as far back as E. T. A. Hoffmann's famous 1810 review of the Fifth Symphony, which described that work as showing how "music reveals to man an unknown realm."[4] But in later eras, much more extreme language was often employed. A 1927 book by the English writer J. W. N. Sullivan provides a notable example. In the op. 131 string quartet, Sullivan writes, "Beethoven had reached that state of consciousness that only the great mystics have ever reached, where there is no more discord."[5] In reference to the "Heiliger Dankgesang," Sullivan compares Beethoven to Christ: "We can well believe that no man ever saw the face of the transfigured Beethoven."[6] One character in Aldous Huxley's novel *Point Counter Point*, written around the same time as Sullivan's book, cites this same music as proof of the existence of God.[7]

That Catholicism played a more prominent role in Beethoven's religious attitudes than has long been assumed should encourage us to consider the possibility that even in the composer's nonreligious works, especially works of instrumental music, the sense of transcendence so many have detected is informed, at least to some degree, by a Catholic outlook, even if any attempt to understand a given work in this manner necessarily remains more speculative in the absence of a text that points to such an outlook.[8] My suggestion

---

[2] Solie, "Beethoven as a Secular Humanist," 4.
[3] Solie, 21.
[4] Hoffmann, Review of Beethoven's Fifth Symphony, 236.
[5] Sullivan, *Beethoven*, 161.
[6] Sullivan, 162.
[7] Huxley, *Point Counter Point*, 427.
[8] Daniel Chua has interpreted passages from the Cavatina of op. 130 and the *Grosse Fuge* as depictions of Christ's suffering: see *Beethoven and Freedom*, 189–248, esp. 231–48. At least as I perceive it, Chua's scholarly approach is less concerned with establishing the historical or biographical plausibility of his interpretations than with using Beethoven's music as a vehicle for theological contemplation. My demonstration of Beethoven's engagement with the Catholic theology of his own time would lend support to Chua's readings from a historical perspective: it is not at all far-fetched to suggest that the composer actually intended to communicate some kind of Christian message in writing these instrumental works.

here makes sense in light of recent research that has sought to complicate our understanding of the interaction of art with religion during the nineteenth century.[9] While it was undeniably important, the idea discussed above of art as replacement for religion was not the only way in which *Kunstreligion* was defined, especially not during the earlier decades of the nineteenth century. There were thinkers who advocated a more cooperative and equal relationship between art and religion, including Friedrich Schleiermacher, who appears to have been the first writer to employ the term *Kunstreligion*.[10] Indeed, as described at the end of the last chapter, Sailer himself believed that art, instead of being a replacement for traditional Christian belief, should serve as a vehicle for its revival. This perspective was typical for the Catholic Restoration and served to distinguish it from mainstream Romanticism, at least as it is usually understood. As Josef Schuh argues, while Romanticism's embrace of historicism and the irrational did exert some influence on the Catholic Restoration, the latter's emphasis on inner religious feeling did not entail the endless longing or the *Weltschmerz* typically taken to characterize the Romantic conception of subjectivity. Indeed, the historicist impulses of the Catholic Restoration sought a way of *fulfilling* human longing for the divine.[11]

Rethinking the nature of Beethoven's religious outlook, as I have sought to do in this book, is thus ultimately not simply an issue of narrow biographical interest, nor is it concerned just with the interpretation of certain musical works by a specific composer. Rather, it should encourage us to move beyond an aggressively secularizing narrative that defines the cultural history of the West over the last two centuries as simply a process by which religious belief has been replaced by art.

Beethoven's Religious Explorations after the *Missa solemnis*

The complexity of Beethoven's engagement with Catholicism continued to manifest itself in the very last years of his life, after he finished the *Missa solemnis*. On the conservative side of the ledger is evidence of an intensification of his interest in traditional Catholic church music that had begun in the

---

[9] See Garratt, "A Kingdom," esp. 146–51. See also Taylor, "Beyond the Ethical and the Aesthetic," 289–91.
[10] Garratt, "A Kingdom," 148–49.
[11] Schuh, *Johann Michael Sailer*, 33–35.

years just before he composed the *Missa*, and which is reflected in that work's allusions to "archaic" musical styles, discussed in chapter 6. Beethoven wanted to compose a third and possibly even a fourth mass, one of which would have been dedicated to the Austrian Emperor Francis I.[12] The project never came to fruition, but fragmentary sketches of mass movements survive from the years 1823 and 1824, including one for an Agnus Dei in C-sharp minor.[13] The composition of another mass after the *Missa* seems to have been particularly encouraged by Count Moritz Dietrichstein, who suggested in March 1823 that a new mass contain additional movements for the Mass Proper—a Gradual and an Offertory.[14] Beethoven's letters also contain hints that he contemplated adding similar movements to the *Missa solemnis* itself.[15] He planned to compose other works of Catholic liturgical music as well.[16] A conversation-book entry from September 1823 refers to a setting of the *Tantum ergo*, the last two verses of the longer *Pange lingua* hymn, normally sung during the Benediction and Veneration of the Blessed Sacrament.[17] The composer's interest in this text suggests that the special attention he devoted to the Eucharist, reflected in the *Missa solemnis* and in his harmonization of the *Pange lingua* melody (see chapter 6), persisted even after he had completed the *Missa*. Indeed, the conversation books tell us that just over a year later, in October 1824, Beethoven contemplated yet another setting of the *Tantum ergo*, for Anton Diabelli, along with settings of other hymn and psalm texts: *Jubilate Deo*, *Salve Regina*, and *Lauda anima mea Dominum*.[18] A sketch from 1825 survives for a setting of the hymn *Veni creator Spiritus*.[19] In addition, Beethoven planned to write a Requiem and a *Te Deum*, both of which are mentioned in the conversation books and the composer's correspondence.[20]

---

[12] See Solomon, *Beethoven*, 357. As described in chapter 1, before the dissolution of the Holy Roman Empire, Francis had ruled as the last Holy Roman Emperor, Francis II.
[13] Berlin, Staatsbibliothek Preußischer Kulturbesitz, Autograph 11, Bundle 2, fols. 17^v and 29^r (see Johnson, Tyson, and Winter, *Beethoven Sketchbooks*, 299–305); and Biamonti no. 730. See also Biamonti nos. 683 and 711.
[14] See Albrecht nos. 314 and 1170 (*BGA* nos. 1609 and 1610).
[15] Anderson no. 1203 (*BGA* no. 1686), Beethoven to the Archduke Rudolph, July 1, 1823; and Anderson no. 1206 (*BGA* no. 1697), Beethoven to Anton Felix Schindler, after July 9, 1823.
[16] See Ronge, "Beethoven's Ambitions in Church Music," 55–58.
[17] *BCB* 4:240 (*BKh* 4:169–70).
[18] *BKh* 7:19.
[19] Berlin, Staatsbibliothek Preußischer Kulturbesitz, Autograph 9, Bundle 2, fols. 35^r–35^v (see Johnson, Tyson, and Winter, *Beethoven Sketchbooks*, 430–34); and Biamonti no. 754.
[20] For the Requiem, see *BCB* 2:73 (*BKh* 1:395), c. March 20 to c. April 1, 1820; *BKh* 6:77, April 23 to end of April 1824; *BKh* 9:82, February 24–March 5, 1826; and Anderson no. 1399 (*BGA* no. 2016), Beethoven to Karl van Beethoven, c. July 20, 1825. See also Biamonti, Appendix II, no. 43; and Solomon, *Beethoven*, 322, 347, 354. For the *Te Deum*, see *BCB* 2:73 (*BKh* 1:395) and *BKh* 6:77. See

Aside from these unfulfilled plans for more Catholic liturgical settings, Beethoven also continued to study examples of church music by composers of earlier eras. In a conversation-book entry from July 1823, Wenzel Schlemmer refers to an Offertory, Gradual, and *Pange lingua* that Beethoven had ordered from a music publisher, though Schlemmer does not specify the composer.[21] (We also have here yet another sign of Beethoven's preoccupation with this Eucharistic hymn.) The conversation books tell us, too, that in the same year, Beethoven discussed Gregorio Allegri's *Miserere* with one of his house guests, the philologist Emmerich Thomas Hohler.[22] As Warren Kirkendale has suggested, the "Heiliger Dankgesang" in Beethoven's op. 132 string quartet also resembles the openings of four actual plainchant melodies, though it is unclear how the composer would have become familiar with these melodies.[23] As previously discussed, such an exploration of church music tradition on Beethoven's part would suggest at least a partial affinity for the Catholic Restoration, in the sense that it represented a departure from the Josephinist Catholicism that Beethoven had grown up in, which had instead encouraged vernacular liturgy. It can also be connected to Sailer's views on liturgy, which inspired movements, especially in Bavaria, that were precursors to the more organized Cecilian movement later in the nineteenth century (see chapter 6). Beethoven seems to have shared the views of such movements, which aimed at recovering and revitalizing older styles of Catholic liturgical music. In a letter to Carl Friedrich Zelter regarding the *Missa solemnis*, he encouraged Zelter to adapt the work so that it could be performed entirely unaccompanied:

---

also Biamonti, Appendix II, no. 44. The *Te Deum* may be mentioned in one other Beethoven source. In chapter 6, I quoted a written remark by Beethoven regarding his desire to compose a "pious song in a symphony in ancient modes—Lord God we praise Thee—alleluia . . . *Cantique ecclesiastique*." As Barry Cooper has pointed out, the original German for "Lord God we praise Thee" is "Herr Gott dich loben wir"—the first line of Luther's German version of the *Te Deum*: see *Beethoven*, 264–65. Though it was an oratorio rather than a piece of liturgical music, mention should also be made of the unfinished project *Der Sieg des Kreuzes* (The triumph of the Cross), a planned setting of a libretto by Karl Joseph Bernard that depicts the triumph of early Christianity over the pagans: see *BCB* 1:119 (*BKh* 1:131), December 7–12, 1819. A sketch for a bass recitative intended for this work survives in Dresden (Biamonti no. 738).

[21] *BCB* 4:115 (*BKh* 3:393).
[22] *BCB* 3:126 (*BKh* 3:36), c. February 6–11, 1823.
[23] Kirkendale, "Gregorian Style." Kirkendale's argument would lend credence to my suggestion above concerning the possibility of Catholic elements even in Beethoven's instrumental music. In contrast to Kirkendale, Sieghard Brandenburg has argued for a more indirect process of influence with regard to the relationship of the "Heiliger Dankgesang" to traditional church music: see "Historical Background."

Certainly a large portion of [the *Missa solemnis*] could be performed almost entirely *a la cappella*. But the whole work would have to be revised; and perhaps you would have the patience to do this—Besides there is in any case one number in this work which is performed entirely *a la cappella*. And indeed I should like to describe this style as preferably the only true Church style.[24]

There is, furthermore, evidence that Beethoven not only felt an affinity for these proto-Cecilian movements but may have been in personal contact with some of the people involved. The posthumous inventory of Beethoven's library, as well as his correspondence, indicates that the composer received several copies of the journal *Caecilia*.[25] Edited by Gottfried Weber from 1824 to 1842, this journal played an important role in proto-Cecilian campaigns to renew traditional Catholic church music.[26] In February 1827, weeks before his death, he wrote to one Gottlieb von Tucher in Nuremberg. Tucher was an avid collector of early church music, especially that by Palestrina, and had dedicated a compendium of such music—*Kirchengesänge der berühmtesten älteren italienischen Meister* (Hymns of the most famous old Italian masters)—to Beethoven.[27]

Though Beethoven's engagement with traditional Catholic liturgical music aligns with the Catholic Restoration, it should be noted that some of his other actions in the years after the *Missa solemnis* still reflect Catholic Enlightenment attitudes, including a continued interest in non-Christian sources of spiritual wisdom. The conversation books reveal that in 1823 he sought out two historical novels by Ignaz Aurelius Feßler for his nephew Karl to read: *Aristides und Themistocles* and *Marc-Aurel* (Marcus Aurelius).[28] Feßler, in addition to being a clergyman, was well known as a writer of such

---

[24] Anderson no. 1161 (*BGA* no. 1621), March 25, 1823: "gewiß ist daß viele beynahe bloß *a la capella* aufgeführt werden könnte, das ganze müßte aber doch hiezu noch eine Bearbeitung finden, u[nd] vielleicht haben sie die Geduld hiezu.—übrigens kommt ohnehin ein Stück ganz *a la Capella* bey diesem Werke vor, u[nd] mögte gerade diesen Styl vorzugsweise den einzigen wahren KirchenStyl nennen."

[25] See *Schätzungsprotokoll* no. 36; Anderson no. 1290 (*BGA* no. 1835), Beethoven to Bernhard Schotts Söhne, May 20, 1824; and Albrecht no. 361 (BGA no. 1819), B. Schotts Söhne to Beethoven, April 27, 1824.

[26] Numaguchi, *Beethovens "Missa Solemnis,"* 23. As David Wyn Jones has recently shown, articles concerning the history of traditional Catholic church music also featured prominently in another journal, the *Allgemeine musikalische Zeitung mit besonderer Rücksicht auf dem österreichischen Kaiserstaat*, which ran during a slightly earlier period (between 1817 and 1824): see Wyn Jones, "Shared Identities and Thwarted Narratives," 180–82. (This journal should not be confused with the better-known *Allgemeine musikalische Zeitung* published in Leipzig, which was referred to in chapters 3 and 6.)

[27] Albrecht no. 461 (*BGA* no. 2264), February 28, 1827.

[28] *BCB* 3:147 (*BKh* 3:56), February 12–22, 1823; and *BCB* 3:288 (*BKh* 3:204), c. April 20–26, 1823.

works, whose main point was not accurate historical reportage, but the communication of moral lessons relevant to Enlightenment thinking.[29] As the titles suggest, these books recounted stories from Greek and Roman antiquity. *Aristides und Themistocles* holds up the latter character as a model of moral duty who stands firm against the demands of a mob, choosing death in spite of his own political ambition.[30] *Marc-Aurel* depicts Marcus Aurelius rather ahistorically as a benevolent constitutional monarch who was tolerant of early Christians. This novel was very popular in its time, and seems intended to encourage both virtuous conduct and religious tolerance—critics saw in its title character parallels with Joseph II.[31] As Derek Beales has explained, Feßler's historical novels exemplify the way in which classical stoicism, in Christianized form, played a major role in various religious Enlightenments in the German-speaking lands.[32] Aside from this interest in Feßler's classically inspired novels, Beethoven's interest in non-Christian spirituality might also be seen in the postscript of a letter he wrote to Vincenz Hauschka in September 1824: "Yours in Christ and Apollo, Beethoven."[33] The fact that in the same year, the composer completed the Ninth Symphony, whose finale sets a text that mingles references to God the Father and Creator with evocations of Elysium, also cannot be overlooked.

A continued affinity for the Catholic Enlightenment may also account for Beethoven's apparently negative attitude toward Klemens Maria Hofbauer, the most important figure of the Catholic Restoration in Vienna.[34] In May 1826, Beethoven responded thus to accusations from the publisher Schott that he had engaged in double-dealing with regard to the publication of the *Missa*: "Such an accusation was really far too despicable for me to desire to defend myself against it. Something like that cannot be washed out even by the best Rhine wine. For that you must make in addition some Liguorian expiations such as we go in for here."[35] And some time in the summer of 1826, the composer wrote to Karl Holz, "Come to dinner with us tomorrow after you have made sufficient Liguorian expiations."[36] The word "Liguorian" in

---

[29] Barton, *Ignatius Aurelius Feßler*, 186.
[30] Barton, 204–7.
[31] Barton, 183–93.
[32] Beales, *Enlightenment and Reform*, 78–79.
[33] Anderson no. 1309 (*BGA* no. 1882): "Der eurige im Christo u[nd] apollo, *Beethoven*."
[34] See M. Cooper, *Beethoven*, 110–13.
[35] Anderson no. 1485 (*BGA* no. 2154): "Denn so etwas wäre wirklich zu schlecht, als daß ich mich darüber vertheidigen möchte. So etwas kann auch nicht durch den besten Rheinwein abgewaschen werden. Hiezu müßen noch *Liguorian*ische Büßungen, wie wir sie hier haben, kommen."
[36] Anderson no. 1509 (*BGA* no. 2158): "Begebt Euch morgen nach hinlänglichen *Liguorian*schen Abbüßungen zum Mittagsessen zu uns."

both these letters refers to Hofbauer's Redemptorist order, which had been founded in 1732 by St. Alphonsus Liguori, and Beethoven seems to be making fun of Hofbauer's religious community. An earlier letter to Tobias Haslinger, from September 1821, also includes an apparently sarcastic reference to Zacharias Werner, one of Hofbauer's most prominent followers (see chapter 4): "Sing every day the Epistles of St. Paul, go every Sunday to Father Werner who will tell you about the little book which will enable you to go straight to Heaven. You see how concerned I am about your spiritual welfare."[37] The conversation books show further that people in Beethoven's social circle held a very low opinion of Hofbauer and his followers, especially Werner. Josef Blöchlinger, on reporting Hofbauer's death in 1820, described the cleric as a "miserable, fanatical Dogmatist" (*elender fanatischer Dogmatiker*), before adding that Werner was a "monstrous hypocrite" (*abscheulichen Heuchler*).[38] In a similar vein, Franz Oliva told Beethoven that their mutual friend Franz Janschikh associated Werner with "rapture" (*Schwärmerey*) and "fanaticism" (*Fanatismus*).[39]

Given the conflicts within German Catholicism at the time, any antipathy that Beethoven felt toward Hofbauer and his followers, however strong, should not be equated with antipathy to the Catholic religion as a whole. We recall that Hofbauer was Sailer's chief opponent in the intra-ecclesial battles of the era: Beethoven would simply have been taking the side of a church figure that he admired. But complicating matters in this regard is the fact that Beethoven actually sought out a book by Zacharias Werner. In a conversation book entry from 1819, shortly after indicating his desire to purchase books by Sailer, Beethoven noted down the title of Werner's *Geistliche Übungen für drei Tage* (Spiritual exercises for three days), along with its price and publication information—just as he had for books by Sailer.[40] The possibility that Beethoven was interested even in religious figures who were considered more conservative and more aligned with the Catholic Restoration than Sailer thus cannot be entirely ruled out. As with other letters cited earlier in this book, we may need to be more cautious in interpreting Beethoven's remarks about Werner and the Redemptorists. It is entirely possible that they were meant as innocent humor rather than biting critique. Regarding evidence from the

---

[37] Anderson no. 1056 (*BGA* no. 1439): "Singt alle Tage die *Episteln* des Heil. Paulus, geht alle Sonntage zum *pater* Werner, welcher euch das Büchlein anzeigt, wodurch ihr von Mund an in Himmel kommt, ihr seht meine Besorgniß für euer SeelenHeil."
[38] *BCB* 2:31 (*BKh* 1:352–53), March 11–19, 1820.
[39] *BCB* 1:190 (*BKh* 1:194), c. January 7–January 26, 1820.
[40] *BCB* 1:21 (*BKh* 1:43), March 17 to after May 15/16, 1819.

conversation books, it is also possible that Beethoven did *not* share the negative opinions of his interlocutors toward the Hofbauer circle.[41]

In the end, wherever we wish to locate Beethoven on the theological spectrum of his time, the composer's worldview, as well as his religious works, were shaped by the Catholicism of the era to a greater degree than most accounts of his life and works have recognized. His outlook seems to have been dominated by the ideas of the German Catholic Enlightenment, a historical framework that also helps us reconcile his ostensibly progressive political views with a continued allegiance to the Catholic religion. At the same time, he was not entirely closed off from more conservative versions of Catholicism—a situation that may have been influenced by the broader cultural changes that took place in his society, in reaction to the upheavals wrought by the French Revolution and the decades of warfare that followed.

The Lost Voice of the Catholic Beethoven

I began this book with a discussion of Ernst Julius Hähnel's Beethoven monument in Bonn. I noted the way the monument specifically highlights sacred music on its pedestal, and the prominent role Beethoven's religious works played in the festivities surrounding the monument's unveiling in 1845. At this point in the nineteenth century, less than two decades after Beethoven's death, the composer's religious music—his Catholic music—remained an important part of his public image. The early reception history of the sacred works adds to this impression. Both *Christus* and the Mass in C were more popular during Beethoven's lifetime and in the immediate decades following his death than their subsequent critical marginalization would suggest. *Christus*, as Anja Mühlenweg has demonstrated, was very often performed during the first two-thirds of the nineteenth century, including during Beethoven's lifetime.[42] Between 1800 and 1840, for instance, the only

---

[41] There are additional references to both Hofbauer and Werner in the conversation books that seem entirely neutral. Josef Köferle reported to Beethoven simply that "the Redemptorists rule" ("die *Ligorianer* regieren"), probably a description of the popularity of the order, or of their political influence: see *BCB* 2:278 (*BKh* 2:189), c. July 7/8–August 19, 1820. (*BCB* translates "Ligorianer" as "Ligorians," but the order is most commonly known in English as the Redemptorists.) In 1823, when both Schindler and Karl Joseph Bernard told the composer about Werner's death, neither man expressed any opinion about Werner himself: see *BCB* 3:55 (January 19–26, 1823), *BCB* 3:65 (January 21–26, 1823). Theodore Albrecht has argued that the former entry was falsified by Schindler, though it was not identified as such in the supplement to vol. 7 of *BKh*: see *BCB* 3:54n87.

[42] Mühlenweg, "Ludwig van Beethoven, *Christus am Oelberge*," 1:5, 112–13.

oratorios more frequently performed in the German-speaking lands were Haydn's *Seasons* and *Creation*, and the publication of foreign editions and translations of *Christus* demonstrates the work's popularity elsewhere.[43] The Mass in C does not appear to have been as popular as *Christus* in the initial years after its premiere, but it became much more widely known after 1817.[44] There was significant demand for it from individual parish churches, even those in rural areas.[45] Prior to the twentieth century, as Jens Peter Larsen has shown, Beethoven's first mass was better regarded than any of Haydn's late masses.[46] Perhaps owing to its scale and difficulty, the *Missa solemnis*, in contrast, took a relatively long time to cement its place in the repertoire of Beethoven's most often performed works.[47] This is quite ironic given that this work would subsequently end up proving the exception to the rule that Beethoven's sacred music was not authentically Beethovenian. Even so, as Gerhard Poppe demonstrates, if one takes into account partial performances of the *Missa*—that is, those where not all of the movements were performed—the work actually established itself in the repertoire much faster than is often believed. Indeed, in the earliest period following its composition, such partial performances took place more frequently in actual liturgical settings than in the concert hall.[48]

When it came to critical opinion regarding Beethoven's religious music, the story was much the same. Among professional music critics in the first half of the nineteenth century, there were undoubtedly those who expressed negative views of individual sacred works by Beethoven, or of specific aspects of those works. (*Christus am Ölberge* was especially controversial, as discussed in chapter 3.) The important issue, however, is not whether the works were liked or disliked, but the terms on which they were judged. As Helmut Loos has shown, even when criticizing Beethoven's sacred music, most commentators treated it as sacred music: they had absolutely no problem with the idea of Beethoven as a composer for the church.[49]

The marginalization of Beethoven's religious works and the related de-Catholicization of the image of Beethoven that has become conventional

---

[43] Mühlenweg, 1:112–13.
[44] Wyn Jones, "Shared Identities," 184.
[45] Riedel, "Kirchenmusik," 57.
[46] Larsen, "Beethovens C-Dur-Messe," 12–13.
[47] Poppe, *Festhochamt, sinfonische Messe*, 192–93. See also Numaguchi, *Beethovens "Missa Solemnis,"* 15–20.
[48] Poppe, *Festhochamt, sinfonische Messe*, 61–80.
[49] Loos, "Religiöse Aspekte der Beethoven-Rezeption," 302–4.

thus did not always exist. There was a time when the idea that sacred music played an important role in Beethoven's compositional identity was not as strange as it sounds to us now, when the fact that the composer of the *Eroica* Symphony described the *Missa solemnis* as his greatest work would not have been considered puzzling. Despite its age, what eventually became the standard view of Beethoven's religious outlook and his sacred music was not always standard. So how did it come about?

To answer this question requires us to return to a topic discussed at the end of chapter 1: the history of German Catholicism in the second half of the nineteenth century. Put simply, this history was the triumph of the Catholic Restoration whose seeds had been planted as early as the 1790s. Mirroring similar developments elsewhere in Europe, German Catholicism became more and more hostile to ideas construed as modern and progressive, especially political liberalism. It also became more ultramontane, and thus supportive of increasing centralization of church governance in the hands of the pope in Rome instead of preserving some amount of local or regional autonomy. Within this context, what was acceptable as Catholicism came to be defined much more narrowly than had been the case at the turn of the nineteenth century. The fear of modernity that prompted this broad conservative turn in the German Catholic Church was not unfounded, for the growth of liberalism in the German lands often went hand-in-hand with anti-Catholic sentiment. A decisive moment in this process occurred in 1866, when Catholic Austria was defeated in the Austro–Prussian War, cementing the hegemony of Prussia—a Protestant state in which liberal political forces were especially strong—over the German lands.[50] Five years later, in 1871, German unification would occur under Prussian leadership, with Austria excluded. Almost immediately after this event, the Prussian chancellor Bismarck launched his so-called *Kulturkampf*—a systematic, though ultimately unsuccessful, persecution of the Catholic minority within the newly formed German nation.[51] In Bismarck's view, German unification required curbing papal power, and hence also the power of the Catholic Church in the new German nation.[52]

The triumph of Prussia in the late nineteenth century meant that German identity came to be defined through a Protestant lens. Many historians now

---

[50] Sperber, *Popular Catholicism in Nineteenth-Century Germany*, 155.
[51] See Gross, *War against Catholicism*.
[52] Chadwick, *Secularization of the European Mind*, 129, 134.

point to a long-standing Protestant bias in historical approaches to modern German history.[53] In effect, these approaches have bought into the same myths that Bismarck and his liberal allies propagated in their anti-Catholic *Kulturkampf* in the 1870s: Protestantism represented progress and lent itself to political liberalism, while Catholicism was authoritarian, regressive, antimodern.[54] Ironically, this same historical narrative also came to dominate the Catholic Church. For if liberalism and modernity were such evils as leading Catholic figures in the late nineteenth century proclaimed them to be, then to be considered antimodern and even authoritarian was no insult. This state of affairs is clearly illustrated by the historiography of the German Catholic Enlightenment, which did not fit the liberal or the Protestant view of Catholicism as antimodern and thus anti-Enlightenment, nor did it fit the view of conservative Catholics that the principles of the Enlightenment broadly defined were irreconcilable with Catholic belief. "Josephinism" was actually coined as a pejorative term by Catholic conservatives in the 1830s, and by the late nineteenth century the accepted view within the Church of the Catholic Enlightenment as a whole was that it was an attack on the Church that had been successfully countered.[55] Indeed, when Sebastian Merkle introduced the term "Catholic Enlightenment" in 1908 (as described in the introduction), it was intended as a deliberate challenge to this narrative and to the ultramontane orthodoxy still reigning at that time.[56]

The reception history of Beethoven's religious music maps neatly onto the two parallel victors' histories I have just outlined. On the one hand, it did not fit the growing conception, well documented in studies of Beethoven reception history, of Beethoven and his music as symbols of German national unity.[57] As the nineteenth century progressed, not only did German cultural identity come to be defined in Prussian terms as secular, liberal, Protestant, and bourgeois, but traditional Christianity in German culture was also gradually eclipsed by a kind of sacralized conception of the arts that conceived of the Catholic Church as culturally backward.[58] In this context, as Loos has pointed out, German nationalists were faced with the inconvenient truth

---

[53] See Lehner, "Introduction," 8; and Anderson, "Limits of Secularization," 649. See also Printy, "History and Church History," 257.

[54] See Gross, *War against Catholicism*, 5; and Forster, *Catholic Germany*, 2.

[55] Beales, *Joseph II*, 2:684; Forster, *Catholic Germany*, 197.

[56] See Printy, "History and Church History," 248, 257; Burson, "Introduction," 2–5; and Lehner, "Introduction," 3–4.

[57] See Dennis, *Beethoven in German Politics*, esp. 1–85.

[58] Poppe, *Festhochamt, sinfonische Messe*, 253–55. See also Nipperdey, *Germany from Napoleon to Bismarck*, 389–98.

that Beethoven's sacred works came from a "Catholic milieu."[59] The religious music posed a problem for attempts to turn Beethoven into a good bourgeois composer, so critics started to find ways of emphasizing Beethoven's separation from Catholicism.[60] Sacred works other than the *Missa solemnis* began to be downplayed.[61] And the *Missa* itself, which seemed too important a work to ignore, was soon reinterpreted as something other than a work of Catholic church music.

This was, it should be stressed, quite a feat of critical reimagining, for in the early years of the work's reception, Protestants had often stressed, and had even been irked by, its Catholic identity. Felix Mendelssohn found the *Missa* too Catholic for his tastes.[62] Other Protestant critics frequently tried to explain aspects of the *Missa* they found puzzling by pointing their readers to the supposed theatricality intrinsic to the Catholic liturgy, an interpretation that echoes the criticism of *Christus am Ölberge* discussed in chapter 3.[63] In the second half of the nineteenth century, however, critics from the same Protestant cultural orbit managed to embrace the *Missa* by reconceiving it as a work that belonged in the concert hall rather than the church, even (however counterintuitively) as a work of absolute instrumental music.[64] Some of the reviews of the performances that took place at the dedication of Hähnel's monument in 1845 already began to reflect an increasingly secularized view of the *Missa*, but a decisive moment came with the criticism of A. B. Marx. Writing in 1859, Marx insisted that Beethoven was no Catholic, and thus the *Missa* departed from traditional church-music practice by being completely based on models from instrumental music.[65] The de-Catholicization of the *Missa* was no doubt helped by the aforementioned fact that the *Missa* took longer than other works to settle into the canon of Beethoven masterpieces. Therefore, by the time the *Missa* became firmly established in the repertoire, the secular-liberal Beethoven myth had already become highly influential. Despite the contradictions involved, the *Missa* was simply made to fit the myth.[66] In addition, the scale and difficulty of the *Missa* meant that the

---

[59] Loos, "Zur Rezeption," 59: "katholischen Milieu."
[60] See Loos, "Religiöse Aspekte der Beethoven-Rezeption," 301; and Poppe, *Festhochamt, sinfonische Messe*, 255.
[61] Loos, "Religiöse Aspekte der Beethoven-Rezeption," 301.
[62] Poppe, *Festhochamt, sinfonische Messe*, 255.
[63] Poppe, 98.
[64] See Loos, "Religiöse Aspekte der Beethoven-Rezeption," 58–59.
[65] See Marx, *Ludwig van Beethoven*, 2:224–59, esp. 2:237–56; and Loos, "Religiöse Aspekte der Beethoven-Rezeption," 304–5. A similar claim was made by Ludwig Nohl: see L. Nohl, *Der Geist der Tonkunst*, 204–5; and Poppe, *Festhochamt, sinfonische Messe*, 233.
[66] Poppe, *Festhochamt, sinfonische Messe*, 18.

increased frequency of complete, rather than partial, performances of the work relied on its performance in secular venues such as the concert hall and on the growth of secular choral organizations in the German lands during the nineteenth century.[67] The *Missa* eventually became more popular, then, for reasons that had nothing to do with its Catholic content. By the end of the nineteenth century, the decoupling of the *Missa solemnis* from its Catholic roots, emblematic of the separation of Beethoven from Catholicism, was largely complete.[68] Writers such as Paul Bekker, who described the work as a "monument of a subjectively critical religiosity,"[69] then carried this view into the twentieth century, and it has since been perpetuated by numerous commentators on Beethoven's music.

While liberals sought to distance Beethoven and the *Missa* from Catholicism, many German Catholic commentators during the second half of the nineteenth century sought to do the same.[70] The main factor in this regard was the growth of the Cecilian movement, a reflection of the broader conservative turn in the Church's stance toward modernity, discussed above. The official movement, which was formally organized in 1868, advocated the banishment from the Catholic liturgy of all music other than plainchant and unaccompanied polyphony. But predecessor movements, which were inspired by Sailer and of which Beethoven seems to have been aware, were not nearly as rigid. *Caecilia*, the proto-Cecilian journal mentioned above, was active in promoting the *Missa* in the years immediately following Beethoven's death. In its pages, a 1828 review by Franz Joseph Fröhlich expressed praise for the work. Some other critics who wrote in *Caecilia* were less positive but focused their criticism on specific compositional choices, not on the work's religious propriety.[71] As proto-Cecilian attitudes toward "nontraditional" Catholic music hardened, however, the *Missa* began to receive fewer and fewer performances, partial or complete, in church.[72] Once-regular liturgical performances in places such as Koblenz and Cologne ceased.[73] The founding of the official Cecilian movement confirmed the exclusion of the *Missa* from the realm of permissible Catholic church music.

[67] Numaguchi, *Beethovens "Missa Solemnis,"* 29–30.
[68] Poppe, *Festhochamt, sinfonische Messe*, 252.
[69] Bekker, *Beethoven*, 373: "Denkmal einer subjective kritischen Religiosität." In contrast, Bekker dismissed the Mass in C for reflecting a "naive and unscrupulous churchly faith" (*naiv skrupelloser kirchlicher Gläubigkeit*).
[70] Loos, "Religiöse Aspekte der Beethoven-Rezeption," 305.
[71] Numaguchi, *Beethovens "Missa Solemnis,"* 23–25.
[72] Poppe, *Festhochamt, sinfonische Messe*, 126.
[73] Poppe, 61, 75.

Writing in 1894, the Cecilian critic Paul Krutschek attacked the *Missa* in specific detail: features such as the concluding repeat in the Gloria, the military music in the Dona nobis pacem, and the strange treatment of "et" in the Credo rendered the work unliturgical. Krutschek did not deny Beethoven's artistic accomplishments in the *Missa*, but believed that its status as art was precisely what made it inappropriate for church use.[74] Ludwig Nohl, though not a card-carrying member of the movement, expressed similar opinions, calling the *Missa* a "pseudo-mass" (*Scheinmesse*).[75]

As has been mentioned, the Cecilian movement was closely tied to the increasing dominance of more conservative, ultramontane strands in the German Catholic Church, a phenomenon that was at least partially a defensive reaction to the persecution of German Catholics by Protestant Prussia. The same development contributed to the historiographical marginalization of the Catholic Enlightenment, as well as Sailer's posthumous fall from favor. This link between the fortunes of the Catholic Enlightenment and those of Beethoven's religious music can be observed in the fact that the regions where Catholic Enlightenment ideas had been the most popular, such as Bonn and the Rhineland, were those where favorable Catholic attitudes toward the *Missa* were most common and prevailed the longest.[76] The Cecilian movement ultimately sought the exclusion not just of Beethoven's *Missa solemnis*, but all church music of the Viennese Classical era, motivated by a belief that that era had been one of religious indifferentism and decline.[77] The Catholic Enlightenment had become a tainted concept, and so had the music that was perceived to have emerged from it. With mainstream German identity becoming more secular, liberal, and Protestant on the one hand, and German Catholicism becoming more conservative and rigid in its liturgical views on the other, the idea of Beethoven as a composer of sacred music was caught in between, and loved by neither. Unless a way could be found to secularize that music, as occurred with the *Missa*, Beethoven's religious music was too Catholic for Prussian liberals, and not Catholic enough for many German Catholics. As with the historiography of the Catholic Enlightenment, both these parties managed to come to a similar view, but for entirely different, even opposing, reasons.

---

[74] Poppe, 347.
[75] See L. Nohl, *Beethoven's Leben*, 3:219; and Numaguchi, *Beethovens "Missa Solemnis,"* 44.
[76] Poppe, *Festhochamt, sinfonische Messe*, 200.
[77] Poppe, 340.

The conventional view of Beethoven's religious attitudes that this book has sought to challenge is thus not a product of the composer's own historical context but of what subsequent periods wanted to believe about that context. It reflects particular cultural biases that emerged later in the nineteenth century, biases that arguably persist today, not just in Beethoven studies but in humanistic scholarship more generally. This persistence is unsurprising given that the issues at stake concern such things as the relationship between modernity and religion, liberalism and secularism—topics that remain ideologically, even personally, sensitive. But whatever our own views on such topics, we must recognize that the assumptions of past cultures may not exactly match our own, that concepts such as religion or Catholicism, or Enlightenment, may not have meant in those cultures what we take them to mean today. In doing so, we enrich our understanding of what Beethoven was trying to communicate through his religious music, and allow that music to serve as a window into the complex history of a time whose conflicts and debates are still very much alive in our own.

Works Cited

Aaslestad, Katherine. "Napoleonic Rule in German Central Europe: Compliance and Resistance." In Broers, Hicks, and Guimerá, *Napoleonic Empire*, 160–72.
Addison, Bland, Jr. "The *Bibliographie liégeoise*: From Jansenism to Sans-culottism in the Book Industry of Eighteenth-Century Liège." *Primary Sources & Original Works* 1 (1992): 117–36.
Adorno, Theodor W. *Beethoven: The Philosophy of Music*. Edited by Rolf Tiedemann. Translated by Edmund Jephcott. Stanford, CA: Stanford University Press, 1998.
Agten, Els. *The Catholic Church and the Dutch Bible: From the Council of Trent to the Jansenist Controversy (1564–1733)*. Leiden: Brill, 2020.
Albrecht, Theodore. "Anton Schindler as Destroyer and Forger of Beethoven's Conversation Books: A Case for Decriminalization." In *Music's Intellectual History*, RILM Perspectives I, edited by Zdravko Blažkovic and Barbara Dobbs Mackenzie, 169–81. New York: Répertoire International de Littérature Musicale, 2009.
Albrecht, Theodore, ed. and trans. *Beethoven's Conversation Books*. Rochester, NY: Boydell and Brewer, 2018– (4 of 12 projected volumes published so far).
Albrecht, Theodore. "The Fortnight Fallacy: A Revised Chronology for Beethoven's *Christ on the Mount of Olives*, Op. 85, and Wielhorsky Sketchbook." *Journal of Musicological Research* 11, no. 4 (1991): 263–84.
Albrecht, Theodore, ed. and trans. *Letters to Beethoven and Other Correspondence*. 3 vols. Lincoln: University of Nebraska Press, 1996.
Anderson, Emily, ed. and trans. *The Letters of Beethoven*. 3 vols. New York: St. Martin's Press, 1961.
Anderson, Margaret Lavinia. "The Limits of Secularization: On the Problem of the Catholic Revival in Nineteenth-Century Germany." *Historical Journal* 38, no. 3 (1995): 647–70.
Appel, Bernhard R., and Julia Ronge, eds. *Beethoven liest*. Bonn: Beethoven-Haus, 2016.
Assmann, Jan. *Kult und Kunst: Beethovens Missa Solemnis als Gottesdienst*. Munich: C. H. Beck, 2020.
Balisch, Alex. "The *Wiener Zeitung* Reports on the French Revolution." In Brauer and Wright, *Austria in the Age*, 185–92.
Bangert, Michael. *Bild und Glaube: Ästhetik und Spiritualität bei Ignaz Heinrich von Wessenberg*. Stuttgart: Kohlhammer, 2009.
Bangert, Michael. "Christkatholisch? Eine kleine Begriffsgeschichte—Teil I: Eine ganzheitliche Frömmigkeit." *Zeitschrift der Christkatholischen Kirche der Schweiz*, October 31–November 13, 2009, No. 22: 4–6.
Bangert, Michael. "Christkatholisch? Eine kleine Begriffsgeschichte—Teil II: Liberalität und Spiritualität." *Zeitschrift der Christkatholischen Kirche der Schweiz*, November 14–27, 2009, No. 23: 6–7.
Barnett, S. J. *The Enlightenment and Religion: The Myths of Modernity*. Manchester: Manchester University Press, 2003.
Barton, Peter F. *Ignatius Aurelius Feßler: Vom Barockkatholizismus zur Erweckungsbewegung*. Graz: Hermann Böhlaus Nachf., 1969.
Barton, Peter F. "Ignatius Aurelius Feßler: Vom ungarischen Kapuziner zum Bischof der Wolgadeutschen." In *Kirche im Osten: Studien zur osteuropäischen Kirchengeschichte und Kirchenkunde*, edited by Robert Stupperich, 7:107–43. Göttingen: Vandenhoeck & Ruprecht, 1964.

Barton, Peter F. "Ignatius Aurelius Feßlers Wertung der Konfessionen in seinen *Ansichten von Religion und Kirchenthum* (1805)." In *Kirche im Osten: Studien zur osteuropäischen Kirchengeschichte und Kirchenkunde*, edited by Robert Stupperich, 13:133–76. Göttingen: Vandenhoeck & Ruprecht, 1970.

Baumgartner, Konrad. "Bemühungen um Seelsorge und Seelsorger im Kreis um Sailer und Wessenberg." *Beiträge zur Geschichte des Bistums Regensburg* 35 (2001): 22–27.

Baumgartner, Konrad, ed. *Johann Michael Sailer: Leben und Werk*. Kevelaer: Topos Plus, 2011.

Beales, Derek. *Enlightenment and Reform in Eighteenth-Century Europe*. London: I. B. Tauris, 2005.

Beales, Derek. *Joseph II*. 2 vols. Cambridge: Cambridge University Press, 1987–2009.

Beales, Derek. *Prosperity and Plunder: European Catholic Monasteries in the Age of Revolution, 1650–1815*. Cambridge: Cambridge University Press, 2003.

Beck, Dagmar, and Grita Herre. "Anton Schindlers fingierte Eintragungen in den Konversationsheften." In *Zu Beethoven: Aufsätze und Annotationen*, vol. 1, edited by Harry Goldschmidt, 11–89. Berlin: Verlag Neue Musik, 1979.

Beghin, Tom. "*Credo ut intelligam*: Haydn's Reading of the Credo Text." In *Engaging Haydn: Culture, Context, and Criticism*, edited by Mary Hunter and Richard Will, 240–78. New York: Cambridge University Press, 2012.

Bekker, Paul. *Beethoven*. 2nd ed. Berlin: Schuster & Loeffler, 1912.

Bell, David A. *The First Total War: Napoleon's Europe and the Birth of Warfare as We Know It*. Boston: Houghton Mifflin, 2007.

Beller, Steven. *The Habsburg Monarchy, 1815–1918*. Cambridge: Cambridge University Press, 2018.

Bettermann, Silke. "Mehr als nur ein Abbild: Ikonografische Besonderheiten und gedanklicher Hintergrund des Beethoven-Porträts von Joseph Stieler." In *In bester Gesellschaft: Joseph Stielers Beethoven-Porträt und seine Geschichte*, edited by Silke Bettermann, 48–57. Bonn: Beethoven-Haus, 2019.

Bettermann, Silke. "'noch 10 Minuten, dann sind wir fertig': Die Entstehung des Beethoven-Porträts von Joseph Stieler." In *In bester Gesellschaft: Joseph Stielers Beethoven-Porträt und seine Geschichte*, edited by Silke Bettermann, 24–39. Bonn: Beethoven-Haus, 2019.

Beutel, Albrecht. *Aufklärung in Deutschland*. Göttingen: Vandenhoeck & Ruprecht, 2006.

Biamonti, Giovanni. *Schema di un catalogo generale cronologico delle musiche di Beethoven, 1781–1827*. Rome: Mezzetti, 1954.

Biba, Otto. "Gottfried van Swieten." In *Europas Musikgeschichte: Grenzen und Öffnungen; Vorträge des Europäischen Musikfestes Stuttgart 1993*, edited by Ulrich Prinz, 120–37. Kassel: Bärenreiter, 1997.

Biermann, Joanna. "Bonn *Aufklärer* Nikolaus Simrock and Beethoven." In Chua and Chong, *Rethinking Beethoven and the Enlightenment*, forthcoming.

Biermann, Joanna. "*Christus am Ölberge*: North–South Confrontation, Conflict, Synthesis." In Tomaszewski and Chrenkoff, *Beethoven 3*, 275–98.

Biermann, Joanna. "Cyclical Ordering in Beethoven's Gellert Lieder, Op. 48: A New Source." *Beethoven Forum* 11 (2004): 162–80.

Black, David. "Mozart and the Practice of Sacred Music." PhD diss., Harvard University, 2007.

Blanchard, Shaun. *The Synod of Pistoia and Vatican II: Jansenism and the Struggle for Catholic Reform*. New York: Oxford University Press, 2020.

Blanning, T. C. W. *The French Revolution in Germany: Occupation and Resistance in the Rhineland, 1792–1802*. Oxford: Clarendon Press, 1983.

Blanning, T. C. W. *Reform and Revolution in Mainz, 1743–1803*. Cambridge: Cambridge University Press, 1974.

Blanning, T. C. W. "The Role of Religion in European Counter-Revolution, 1789–1815." In *History, Society and the Churches: Essays in Honour of Owen Chadwick*, edited by Derek Beales and Geoffrey Best, 195–214. Cambridge: Cambridge University Press, 1985.

Blaschke, Olaf. "Das 19. Jahrhundert: Ein Zweites Konfessionelles Zeitalter?" *Geschichte und Gesellschaft* 26, no. 1 (2000): 38–75.
Bonds, Mark Evan. "The Court of Public Opinion: Haydn, Mozart, Beethoven." In Lodes, Reisinger, and Wilson, *Beethoven und andere Hofmusiker*, 7–24.
Bonds, Mark Evan. "Heart to Heart: Beethoven, Archduke Rudolph, and the *Missa solemnis*." In *The New Beethoven: Evolution, Analysis, Interpretation*, edited by Jeremy Yudkin, 228–43. Rochester, NY: University of Rochester Press, 2020.
Bory, Robert, ed. *Ludwig van Beethoven: Sein Leben und sein Werk in Bildern*. Zurich: Atlantis, 1960.
Bowman, William David. "Popular Catholicism in *Vormärz* Austria, 1800–48." In Robertson and Beniston, *Catholicism and Austrian Culture*, 51–64.
Bradley, James E., and Dale K. Van Kley. Introduction to *Religion and Politics in Enlightenment Europe*, 1–45.
Bradley, James E., and Dale K. Van Kley, eds. *Religion and Politics in Enlightenment Europe*. Notre Dame, IN: University of Notre Dame Press, 2001.
Brandenburg, Sieghard. "Beethovens Oratorium *Christus am Ölberg*: Ein unbequemes Werk." In *Beiträge zur Geschichte des Oratoriums seit Händel: Festschrift Günther Massenkeil zum 60. Geburtstag*, edited by Rainer Cadenbach and Helmut Loos, 203–20. Bonn: Voggenreiter, 1986.
Brandenburg, Sieghard. "The Historical Background to the 'Heiliger Dankgesang' in Beethoven's A-Minor Quartet Op. 132." In *Beethoven Studies 3*, edited by Alan Tyson, 161–91. Cambridge: Cambridge University Press, 1982.
Brandenburg, Sieghard, ed. *Ludwig van Beethoven: Briefwechsel Gesamtausgabe*. 7 vols. Munich: Henle, 1996.
Braubach, Max. "Beethovens Abschied von Bonn: Das rheinische Erbe." In *Beethoven-Symposion Wien 1970: Bericht*, edited by Erich Schenk, 25–41. Vienna: Hermann Böhlaus Nachf., 1971.
Braubach, Max. "Neue Funde und Beiträge zur Kulturgeschichte Kurkölns im ausgehenden 18. Jahrhundert." *Annalen des historischen Vereins für den Niederrhein* 172 (1990): 155–77.
Braubach, Max, ed. *Die Stammbücher Beethovens und der Babette Koch*. 2nd printing ["Auflage"], with a transcription by Michael Ladenburger. Bonn: Beethoven-Haus, 1995.
Brauer, Kinley, and William E. Wright, eds. *Austria in the Age of the French Revolution, 1789–1815*. Minneapolis: Center for Austrian Studies, 1990.
Broers, Michael. *Europe under Napoleon, 1799–1815*. London: Arnold, 1996.
Broers, Michael, Peter Hicks, and Agustín Guimerá, eds. *The Napoleonic Empire and the New European Political Culture*. New York: Palgrave Macmillan, 2012.
Brophy, James M. *Popular Culture and the Public Sphere in the Rhineland, 1800–1850*. New York: Cambridge University Press, 2007.
Bunnell, Adam. *Before Infallibility: Liberal Catholicism in Biedermeier Vienna*. Cranbury, NJ: Associated University Presses, 1990.
Burnham, Scott. *Beethoven Hero*. Princeton, NJ: Princeton University Press, 1995.
Burnham, Scott. "The Four Ages of Beethoven: Critical Reception and the Canonic Composer." In *The Cambridge Companion to Beethoven*, edited by Glenn Stanley, 272–91. Cambridge: Cambridge University Press, 2000.
Burson, Jeffrey D. "Introduction: Catholicism and Enlightenment, Past, Present, and Future." In Burson and Lehner, *Enlightenment and Catholicism in Europe*, 1–37.
Burson, Jeffrey D., and Ulrich L. Lehner, eds. *Enlightenment and Catholicism in Europe: A Transnational History*. Notre Dame, IN: University of Notre Dame Press, 2014.
Caeyers, Jan. *Beethoven: A Life*. Translated by Brent Annable. Berkeley: University of California Press, 2020.
Chadwick, Owen. *The Popes and European Revolution*. Oxford: Clarendon Press, 1981.
Chadwick, Owen. *The Secularization of the European Mind in the Nineteenth Century*. 1975. Reprint, Cambridge: Cambridge University Press, 1990.

Chapin, Keith, and David Wyn Jones, eds. *Beethoven Studies 4*. Cambridge: Cambridge University Press, 2020.
Chédozeau, Bernard. *La Bible et la liturgie en français*. Paris: Éditions du Cerf, 1990.
Chédozeau, Bernard. "Bibles in French from 1520 to 1750." In *The New Cambridge History of the Bible*, vol. 3, edited by Euan Cameron, 285–304. New York: Cambridge University Press, 2016.
Chédozeau, Bernard. *Port-Royal et la Bible*. Paris: Nolin, 2007.
Chen, Jen-Yen. "Catholic Sacred Music in Austria." In *The Cambridge History of Eighteenth-Century Music*, edited by Simon P. Keefe, 59–112. Cambridge: Cambridge University Press, 2009.
Chong, Nicholas. "Beethoven and Kant's *Allgemeine Naturgeschichte*." In *Beethoven Perspectives: Proceedings of the International Conference, Bonn, 10–14 February 2020*, edited by Christin Heitmann, Jürgen May, and Christine Siegert. Bonn: Beethoven-Haus, forthcoming.
Chong, Nicholas. "Beethoven's Theologian: Johann Michael Sailer and the *Missa solemnis*." *Journal of the American Musicological Society* 74, no. 2 (2021): 365–426.
Chua, Daniel K. L. *Beethoven and Freedom*. New York: Oxford University Press, 2017.
Chua, Daniel K. L., and Nicholas Chong, eds. *Rethinking Beethoven and the Enlightenment*. New York: Cambridge University Press, forthcoming.
Clark, Christopher. "The New Catholicism and the European Culture Wars." In *Culture Wars: Secular-Catholic Conflict in Nineteenth-Century Europe*, edited by Christopher Clark and Wolfram Kaiser, 11–46. Cambridge: Cambridge University Press, 2003.
Clubbe, John. *Beethoven: The Relentless Revolutionary*. New York: Norton, 2019.
Comini, Alessandra. *The Changing Image of Beethoven: A Study in Mythmaking*. New York: Rizzoli, 1987.
Cook, Nicholas. *Beethoven: Symphony No. 9*. Cambridge Music Handbook. Cambridge: Cambridge University Press, 1993.
Cook, Nicholas. "The Other Beethoven: Heroism, the Canon, and the Works of 1813–14." *19th-Century Music* 27, no. 1 (2003): 3–24.
Cooper, Barry. *Beethoven*. The Master Musicians. New York: Oxford University Press, 2000.
Cooper, Barry. "Beethoven's 'Abendlied' and the 'Wiener Zeitschrift.'" *Music and Letters* 82, no. 2 (2001): 234–50.
Cooper, Barry. "Beethoven's Oratorio and the Heiligenstadt Testament." *Beethoven Journal* 10, no. 1 (1995): 19–24.
Cooper, Martin. *Beethoven: The Last Decade, 1817–1827*. London: Oxford University Press, 1970.
Coreth, Anna. *Pietas Austriaca*. Translated by William D. Bowman and Anna Maria Leitgeb. West Lafayette, IN: Purdue University Press, 2004.
Cowan, Robert Bruce. "Fear of Infinity: Friedrich Schlegel's Indictment of Indian Philosophy in *Über die Sprache und die Weisheit der Indier*." *German Quarterly* 81, no. 3 (2008): 322–38.
Crahay, Roland. "Les tensions religieuses dans une Wallonie catholique." In *La Wallonie, le pays et les Hommes: Histoire, Économie, Sociétés*, 2nd ed., edited by Hervé Hasquin, 1:371–87. Brussels: La Rénaissance du Livre, 1975.
Dahlhaus, Carl. *Ludwig van Beethoven: Approaches to His Music*. Translated by Mary Whittall. Oxford: Clarendon Press, 1991.
De Dijn, Annelien. "The Politics of Enlightenment: From Peter Gay to Jonathan Israel." *Historical Journal* 55, no. 3 (2012): 785–805.
Delforge, Frédéric. *La Bible en France et dans la Francophonie: Histoire, traduction, diffusion*. Paris: Publisud/Société Biblique de France, 1991.
Dennis, David B. *Beethoven in German Politics, 1870–1989*. New Haven, CT: Yale University Press, 1996.
Dietrich, Donald J. *The Goethezeit and the Metamorphosis of Catholic Theology in the Age of Idealism*. Bern: Peter Lang, 1979.

Dolp, Laura. "Between Pastoral and Nature: Beethoven's *Missa solemnis* and the Landscapes of Caspar David Friedrich." *Journal of Musicological Research* 27, no. 3 (2008): 205–25.
Donakowski, Conrad L. "The Age of Revolutions." In *The Oxford History of Christian Worship*, edited by Geoffrey Wainwright and Karen B. Westerfield Tucker, 351–94. New York: Oxford University Press, 2006.
Dotzauer, Winfried. "Die Illuminaten im Rheingebiet." In *Der Illuminatenorden (1776–1785/ 87): Ein politischer Geheimbund der Aufklärungszeit*, edited by Helmut Reinalter, 125–67. Frankfurt am Main: Peter Lang, 1997.
Drabkin, William. "The Agnus Dei of Beethoven's *Missa Solemnis*: The Growth of Its Form." In *Beethoven's Compositional Process*, edited by William Kinderman, 131–59. Lincoln: University of Nebraska Press, 1991.
Drabkin, William. *Beethoven: Missa solemnis*. Cambridge Music Handbook. Cambridge: Cambridge University Press, 1991.
Drabkin, William, ed. *Ludwig van Beethoven: A Sketchbook from the Year 1821 (Artaria 197)*. 2 vols. Bonn: Beethoven-Haus, 2010.
Eakin, Travis. "Between the Old and the New: Friedrich Gentz, 1764–1832." PhD diss., University of Missouri–Columbia, 2019.
Edelstein, Dan. *The Enlightenment: A Genealogy*. Chicago: University of Chicago Press, 2010.
Eigenauer, John D. "A Meta-Analysis of Critiques of Jonathan Israel's Radical Enlightenment." *The Historian* 81, no. 3 (2019): 448–71.
Eyerly, Sarah. *Moravian Soundscapes: A Sonic History of the Moravian Missions in Early Pennsylvania*. Bloomington: Indiana University Press, 2020.
Eyerly, Sarah. "Mozart and the Moravians." *Early Music* 47, no. 2 (2019): 161–82.
Fellerer, Karl Gustav. "Beethoven und die liturgische Musik seiner Zeit." In *Beethoven-Symposion, Wien, 1970: Bericht*, edited by Erich Schenk, 61–76. Vienna: Hermann Böhlhaus Nachf., 1971.
Ferraguto, Mark. "Beethoven *à la moujik*: Russianness and Learned Style in the 'Razumovsky' String Quartets." *Journal of the American Musicological Society* 67, no. 1 (2014): 77–123.
Feßler [Fessler], Ignaz Aurelius. *Ansichten von Religion und Kirchenthum*. 3 vols. Berlin: Johann Daniel Sander, 1805.
Fillion, Michelle. "Beethoven's Mass in C and the Search for Inner Peace." *Beethoven Forum* 7 (1999): 1–15.
Forster, Marc R. *Catholic Germany from the Reformation to the Enlightenment*. Basingstoke: Palgrave Macmillan, 2007.
Frank, Mitchell Benjamin. *German Romantic Painting Redefined: Nazarene Tradition and the Narratives of Romanticism*. Aldershot: Ashgate, 2001.
Gajek, Bernhard. "Dichtung und Religion: J. M. Sailer und die Geistesgeschichte des 18. und 19. Jahrhunderts." In *Johann Michael Sailer: Theologe, Pädagoge und Bischof zwischen Aufklärung und Romantik*, edited by Hans Bungert, 59–85. Regensburg: Mittelbayerische Druckerei- und Verlagsgesellschaft, 1983.
Garratt, James. "A Kingdom Not of This World: Music, Religion, Art-Religion." In *The Cambridge Companion to Music and Romanticism*, edited by Benedict Taylor, 146–62. Cambridge: Cambridge University Press, 2021.
Gay, Peter. *The Enlightenment: An Interpretation*. 2 vols. New York: Knopf, 1966–1969.
Gellert, Christian Fürchtegott. *Geistliche Oden und Lieder*. 1757. Hamburg: Tredition, [2012].
Gertsch, Norbert. "Wer verfasste die Orgelstimmen in Beethovens Messen?" In *Beethoven und die Rezeption der Alten Musik: Die hohe Schule der Überlieferung*, edited by Hans-Werner Küthen, 281–302. Bonn: Beethoven-Haus, 2002.
Graf, Friedrich Wilhelm. *Die Politisierung des religiösen Bewußtseins: Die bürgerlichen Religionsparteien im deutschen Vormärz; Das Beispiel des Deutschkatholizismus*. Stuttgart-Bad Cannstatt: Frommann-Holzboog, 1978.
Gregory, Brad S. *The Unintended Reformation: How a Religious Revolution Secularized Society*. Cambridge, MA: Belknap Press of Harvard University Press, 2012.

Grewe, Cordula. *The Nazarenes: Romantic Avant-Garde and the Art of the Concept.* University Park: Pennsylvania State University Press, 2015.

Grewe, Cordula. *Painting the Sacred in the Age of Romanticism.* Farnham: Ashgate, 2009.

Grigat, Friederike. *Beethovens Glaubensbekenntnis: Drei Denksprüche aus Friedrich Schillers Aufsatz* Die Sendung Moses. Bonn: Beethoven-Haus, 2008.

Gross, Michael B. *The War against Catholicism: Liberalism and the Anti-Catholic Imagination in Nineteenth-Century Germany.* Ann Arbor: University of Michigan Press, 2004.

Gülke, Peter. "'mein Größtes Werk': Glaubensprüfung in Musik; Die Missa Solemnis." In *". . . immer das Ganze vor Augen": Studien zur Beethoven*, 269–78. Stuttgart: J. B. Metzler, 2000.

Haag, John J. "Beethoven, the Revolution in Music and the French Revolution: Music and Politics in Austria, 1790–1815." In Brauer and Wright, *Austria in the Age*, 107–23.

Hänsel, Markus. *Geistliche Restauration: Die nazarenische Bewegung in Deutschland zwischen 1800 und 1838.* Frankfurt am Main: Peter Lang, 1987.

Härtl, Heinz. *"Drei Briefe von Beethoven": Genese und Frührezeption einer Briefkomposition Bettina von Arnims.* Bielefeld: Aisthesis, 2016.

Hatten, Robert. *Musical Meaning in Beethoven: Markedness, Correlation, and Interpretation.* Bloomington: Indiana University Press, 1994.

Heer, Joseph. "Zur Kirchenmusik und ihrer Praxis während der Beethovenzeit in Bonn." *Kirchenmusikalisches Jahrbuch* 28 (1933): 130–42.

Heim, Manfred. "Nachwort." In *Anleitung zum Leben und Sterben: Aus dem Buch von der Nachfolge Christi*, by Thomas von Kempen [Thomas à Kempis], translated by Johann Michael Sailer, edited by Manfred Heim, 113–24. Munich: C. H. Beck, 2008.

Heine, Heinrich. "The Romantic School." Translated by Helen Mustard. In *The Romantic School and Other Essays*, edited by Jost Hermand and Robert C. Holub, 1–127. New York: Continuum, 1985.

Heinemann, Michael. "Suspended Time: The Fugue on 'et vitam venturi saeculi' in the Credo of the *Missa solemnis*." *Journal of Musicological Research* 32 (2013): 225–32.

Herttrich, Ernst. "Beethoven und die Religion." In *Spiritualität der Musik: Religion im Werk von Beethoven und Schumann*, edited by Gotthard Fermor, 25–44. Rheinbach: CMZ-Verlag, 2006.

Hettrick, Jane Schatkin. "Antonio Salieri's Requiem Mass: The Moravian Connection." In *Mozart in Prague: Essays on Performance, Patronage, Sources, and Reception*, edited by Kathryn L. Libin, 31–43. Prague: Mozart Society of America, 2016.

Hinrichsen, Hans-Joachim. *Beethoven: Musik für eine neue Zeit.* Kassel: Bärenreiter, 2019.

Hinske, Norbert. "Katholische Aufklärung—Aufklärung im katholischen Deutschland?" In *Katholische Aufklärung—Aufklärung im katholischen Deutschland*, edited by Harm Klueting, 36–39. Hamburg: Felix Meiner, 1993.

Hochstrasser, T. J. "Cardinal Migazzi and Reform Catholicism in the Eighteenth-Century Habsburg Monarchy." In Robertson and Beniston, *Catholicism and Austrian Culture*, 16–31.

Hoffmann, E. T. A. *E. T. A. Hoffmann's Musical Writings:* Kreisleriana, The Poet and the Composer, *Music Criticism.* Edited by David Charlton. Translated by Martyn Clarke. Cambridge: Cambridge University Press, 1989.

Hoffmann, E. T. A. "Old and New Church Music." In *E. T. A. Hoffmann's Musical Writings*, 351–76.

Hoffmann, E. T. A. Review of Beethoven's Fifth Symphony. In *E. T. A. Hoffmann's Musical Writings*, 234–51.

Hoffmann, E. T. A. Review of Beethoven's Mass in C. In *E. T. A. Hoffmann's Musical Writings*, 325–41.

Hofmeier, Johann. "Gott in Christus, das Heil der Welt—die Zentralidee des Christentums im theologischen Denken Johann Michael Sailers." In *Johann Michael Sailer: Theologe, Pädagoge und Bischof zwischen Aufklärung und Romantik*, edited by Hans Bungert, 27–43. Regensburg: Mittelbayerische Druckerei- und Verlagsgesellschaft, 1983.

Holzem, Andreas. *Christianity in Germany, 1550–1850: Confessionalization, Enlightenment, Pluralization.* 2 vols. Translated by Charlotte P. Kieslich and Ansgar Hastenpflug. Paderborn: Brill Schöningh, 2023.

Höyng, Peter. "The Codependent Polarity Between Light and Darkness: Beethoven's *Bildung* in the Midst of Censorship." In Chua and Chong, *Rethinking Beethoven and the Enlightenment*, forthcoming.

Höyng, Peter. "'Denn Gehorsam ist die erste Pflicht freier Männer': Eulogius Schneider as a Paradigm for the Dialectic of Enlightenment." In *The Radical Enlightenment in Germany: A Cultural Perspective*, edited by Carl Niekirk, 310–27. Leiden: Brill, 2018.

Hrncirik, Peter. "Tendenzen der Kirchenmusik im Biedermeier." In *Kirchenmusik im Biedermeier: Institutionen, Formen, Komponisten*, edited by Andrea Harrandt and Erich Wolfgang Partsch, 9–60. Tutzing: Hans Schneider, 2010.

Huxley, Aldous. *Point Counter Point.* New York: Literary Guild of America, 1928.

Ingrao, Charles W. *The Habsburg Monarchy, 1619–1815.* 3rd ed. New York: Cambridge University Press, 2019.

Israel, Jonathan I. *Democratic Enlightenment: Philosophy, Revolution, and Human Rights, 1750–1790.* Oxford: Oxford University Press, 2011.

Israel, Jonathan I. *Enlightenment Contested: Philosophy, Modernity, and the Emancipation of Man, 1670–1752.* Oxford: Oxford University Press, 2006.

Israel, Jonathan I. *Radical Enlightenment: Philosophy and the Making of Modernity, 1650–1750.* Oxford: Oxford University Press, 2001.

Israel, Jonathan I. *A Revolution of the Mind: Radical Enlightenment and the Intellectual Origins of Modern Democracy.* Princeton, NJ: Princeton University Press, 2010.

Ito, John Paul. "Johann Michael Sailer and Beethoven." *Bonner Beethoven-Studien* 11 (2014): 83–91.

Jäger-Sunstenau, Hanns. "Beethoven-Akten im Wiener Landesarchiv." In *Beethoven-Studien: Festgabe der österreichischen Akademie der Wissenschaften zum 200. Geburtstag von Ludwig van Beethoven*, edited by Erich Schenk, 11–36. Vienna: Hermann Böhlaus Nachf., 1970.

Jander, Owen. "The Prophetic Conversation in Beethoven's 'Scene by the Brook.'" *Musical Quarterly* 77, no. 3 (1993): 508–59.

Janz, Tobias. "Das romantische und das gegenrevolutionäre Beethovenbild." *Archiv für Musikwissenschaft* 79 (2022): 98–121.

Johnson, Douglas, Alan Tyson, and Robert Winter. *The Beethoven Sketchbooks: History, Reconstruction, Inventory.* Berkeley: University of California Press, 1985.

Johnson, Paul. *The Birth of the Modern: World Society, 1815–1830.* New York: HarperCollins, 1991.

Jones, Rhys. "Beethoven and the Sound of Revolution in Vienna, 1792–1814." *Historical Journal* 57, no. 4 (2014): 947–71.

Judson, Pieter M. *The Habsburg Empire: A New History.* Cambridge, MA: Harvard University Press, 2016.

Jung, Hermann. "'Wahr' Mensch und wahrer Gott': Zum Christusbild in Beethovens Oratorium *Christus am Ölberge*." In *Beethoven 5: Studien und Interpretationen*, edited by Mieczysław Tomaszewski and Magdalena Chrenkoff, 47–59. Kraków: Akademia Muzyczna w Krakowie, 2012.

Kagan, Susan. *Archduke Rudolph, Beethoven's Patron, Pupil, and Friend: His Life and Music.* Stuyvesant, NY: Pendragon Press, 1988.

Kant, Immanuel. *Kants gesammelte Schriften.* Vol. 1. Edited by the Royal Prussian Academy of Sciences. Berlin: Georg Reimer, 1910.

Kant, Immanuel. *Natural Science.* Edited by Eric Watkins. Cambridge: Cambridge University Press, 2012.

Kinderman, William. *Beethoven.* 2nd ed. New York: Oxford University Press, 2009.

Kinderman, William. *Beethoven: A Political Artist in Revolutionary Times.* Chicago: University of Chicago Press, 2020.

Kinderman, William. "Beethoven's Symbol for the Deity in the *Missa solemnis* and the Ninth Symphony." *19th-Century Music* 9, no. 2 (1985): 102-18.

Kirkendale, Warren. "Ancient Rhetorical Traditions in Beethoven's *Missa solemnis*." In *Music and Meaning: Studies in Music History and the Neighbouring Disciplines*, by Warren and Ursula Kirkendale, 501-37. Florence: Leo S. Olschki, 2007. (Updated and expanded version of "New Roads to Old Ideas in Beethoven's *Missa solemnis*," *Musical Quarterly* 56, no. 4 [1970]: 665-701.)

Kirkendale, Warren. "Gregorian Style in Beethoven's String Quartet Op. 132" (1980). In *Music and Meaning: Studies in Music History and the Neighbouring Disciplines*, by Warren and Ursula Kirkendale, 539-43. Florence: Leo S. Olschki, 2007.

Klueting, Harm. "The Catholic Enlightenment in Austria or the Habsburg Lands." In *A Companion to the Catholic Enlightenment in Europe*, edited by Ulrich L. Lehner and Michael Printy, 127-64. Leiden: Brill, 2010.

Klueting, Harm. "'Der Genius der Zeit hat sie unbrauchbar gemacht': Zum Thema *Katholische Aufklärung*—Oder: Aufklärung und Katholizismus im Deutschland des 18. Jahrhunderts: Eine Einleitung." In *Katholische Aufklärung—Aufklärung im katholischen Deutschland*, edited by Harm Klueting, 1-35. Hamburg: Felix Meiner, 1993.

Knapp, J. Merrill. "Beethoven's Mass in C Major, Op. 86." In *Beethoven Essays: Studies in Honor of Elliot Forbes*, edited by Lewis Lockwood and Phyllis Benjamin, 199-216. Cambridge, MA: Harvard University Press, 1984.

Knittel, K. M. "The Construction of Beethoven." In *The Cambridge History of Nineteenth-Century Music*, edited by Jim Samson, 118-50. Cambridge: Cambridge University Press, 2001.

Knittel, K. M. "Wagner, Deafness, and the Reception of Beethoven's Late Style." *Journal of the American Musicological Society* 51, no. 1 (1998): 49-82.

Koch, Jakob Johannes. *Heiliger Haydn? Der Begründer der Wiener Klassik und seine Religiosität*. Kevelaer: Topos Plus, 2009.

Koch, Jakob Johannes. "'Von Herzen – möge es wieder – zu Herzen gehn!': Der biografische und biblisch-theologische Hintergrund der Missa solemnis." In *Ludwig van Beethoven: Missa Solemnis*, edited by Meinrad Walter, 35-92. Stuttgart: Carus-Verlag and Deutsche Bibelgesellschaft, 2019.

Köhler, Karl-Heinz, Grita Herre, and Dagmar Beck, eds. *Ludwig van Beethovens Konversationshefte*. 11 vols. Leipzig: VEB Deutscher Verlag für Musik, 1968-2001.

Komlós, Katalin. "Miscellaneous Vocal Genres." In *The Cambridge Companion to Haydn*, edited by Caryl Clark, 164-75. Cambridge: Cambridge University Press, 2005.

Konrad, Ulrich. "Der 'Bonner' Beethoven." *Bonner Beethoven-Studien* 12 (2016): 65-80.

Kopitz, Klaus Martin, and Rainer Cadenbach, eds. *Beethoven aus der Sicht seiner Zeitgenossen*. Munich: Henle, 2009.

Körner, Axel. "Rossini, Erzherzog Rudolph und Beethoven: Musik und österreichische Staatsidee im Zeitalter Metternichs." In *Beethoven und Rossini in ihrer Epoche*, edited by Arnold Jacobshagen and Christine Siegert. Bonn: Beethoven-Haus, forthcoming.

Korsyn, Kevin. "J. W. N. Sullivan and the Heiliger Dankgesang: Questions of Meaning in Late Beethoven." *Beethoven Forum* 2 (1993): 133-74.

Kramer, Richard A. "Beethoven and Carl Heinrich Graun." In *Beethoven Studies*, edited by Alan Tyson, 18-44. New York: Norton, 1973.

Kramer, Richard A. "In Search of Palestrina: Beethoven in the Archives." In *Haydn, Mozart, and Beethoven: Studies in the Music of the Classical Period: Essays in Honour of Alan Tyson*, edited by Sieghard Brandenburg, 283-300. Oxford: Clarendon Press, 1998.

Kramer, Richard A. Review of *Missa solemnis*, by Ludwig van Beethoven, edited by Norbert Gertsch, *Neue Beethoven-Gesamtausgabe*, Abteilung VIII, vol. 3. *Notes* 59, no. 3 (2003): 743-46.

Kraus, Beate Angelika. "Beethoven liest international: Wege aus der Sprach(en)losigkeit." In Appel and Ronge, *Beethoven liest*, 73-104.

Lamm, Julia A. "Romanticism and Pantheism." In *The Blackwell Companion to Nineteenth-Century Theology*, edited by David Fergusson, 165–86. Chichester: Blackwell, 2010.
Landon, H. C. Robbins. *Haydn: The Years of "The Creation," 1796–1800*. Bloomington: Indiana University Press, 1977.
Landon, H. C. Robbins. *Mozart and Vienna*. London: Thames & Hudson, 1991.
Larsen, Jens Peter. "Beethovens C-Dur-Messe und die Spätmessen Joseph Haydns." In *Beiträge '76–78: Beethoven-Kolloquium 1977; Dokumentation und Aufführungspraxis*, edited by Rudolf Klein, 12–19. Kassel: Bärenreiter, 1978.
Lehner, Ulrich L. "Benedict Stattler (1728–1797): The Reinvention of Catholic Theology with the Help of Wolffian Metaphysics." In Burson and Lehner, *Enlightenment and Catholicism in Europe*, 167–89.
Lehner, Ulrich L. *The Catholic Enlightenment: The Forgotten History of a Global Movement*. New York: Oxford University Press, 2016.
Lehner, Ulrich L. "Introduction: The Many Faces of the Catholic Enlightenment." In *A Companion to the Catholic Enlightenment in Europe*, edited by Ulrich L. Lehner and Michael Printy, 1–61. Leiden: Brill, 2010.
Lehner, Ulrich L. *On the Road to Vatican II: German Catholic Enlightenment and Reform of the Church*. Minneapolis: Fortress Press, 2016.
Leisinger, Ulrich. "C. P. E. Bach and C. C. Sturm: Sacred Song, Public Church Service, and Private Devotion." In *C. P. E. Bach Studies*, edited by Annette Richards, 116–48. New York: Cambridge University Press, 2006.
Leitzmann, Albert. "Beethovens Bibliothek." In *Ludwig van Beethoven: Berichte der Zeitgenossen, Briefe und persönliche Aufzeichnungen*, edited by Albert Leitzmann, 2:379–83. Leipzig: Insel-Verlag, 1921.
Link, Dorothea. *The National Court Theatre in Mozart's Vienna: Sources and Documents, 1783–1792*. Oxford: Clarendon Press, 1998.
Link, Dorothea. "Zinzendorf, Count Karl Zinzendorf und Pottendorf." In *The Cambridge Mozart Encyclopedia*, edited by Cliff Eisen and Simon P. Keefe, 553–54. Cambridge: Cambridge University Press, 2006.
Lockwood, Lewis. *Beethoven: The Music and the Life*. New York: Norton, 2003.
Lockwood, Lewis. *Beethoven's Symphonies: An Artistic Vision*. New York: Norton, 2015.
Lodes, Birgit. "Composing with a Dictionary: Sounding the Word in Beethoven's *Missa solemnis*." In Chapin and Wyn Jones, *Beethoven Studies 4*, 189–208.
Lodes, Birgit. *Das Gloria in Beethovens Missa solemnis*. Tutzing: Hans Schneider, 1997.
Lodes, Birgit. "Probing the Sacred Genres: Beethoven's Religious Songs, Oratorio, and Masses." In *The Cambridge Companion to Beethoven*, edited by Glenn Stanley, 218–36. Cambridge: Cambridge University Press, 2000.
Lodes, Birgit. "'So träumte mir, ich reiste . . . nach Indien': Temporality and Mythology in Op. 127/I." In *The String Quartets of Beethoven*, edited by William Kinderman, 168–213. Urbana: University of Illinois Press, 2006.
Lodes, Birgit. "'Von Herzen – möge es wieder – zu Herzen gehn!': Zur Widmung von Beethovens *Missa solemnis*." In *Altes im Neuen: Festschrift Theodor Göllner zum 65. Geburtstag*, edited by Bernd Edelmann and Manfred Hermann Schmid, 295–306. Tutzing: Hans Schneider, 1995.
Lodes, Birgit. "'When I Try, Now and Then, to Give Musical Form to My Turbulent Feelings': The Human and the Divine in the Gloria of Beethoven's *Missa solemnis*." Translated by Glenn Stanley. *Beethoven Forum* 6 (1998): 143–79.
Lodes, Birgit, Elisabeth Reisinger, and John D. Wilson, eds. *Beethoven und andere Hofmusiker seiner Generation: Bericht über den internationalen musikwissenschaftlichen Kongress Bonn, 3. bis 6. Dezember 2015*. Bonn: Beethoven-Haus, 2018.
Lodes, Birgit, Elisabeth Reisinger, and John D. Wilson. Introduction to *Beethoven und andere Hofmusiker*, 1–5.
Loidl, Franz. *Geschichte des Erzbistums Wien*. Vienna: Herold, 1983.

Loos, Helmut. "Arnold Schmitz as Beethoven Scholar: A Reassessment." *Journal of Musicological Research* 32, nos. 2–3 (2013): 150–62.

Loos, Helmut. "Christian Gottlob Neefe (1748–1798) und seine Bedeutung für Ludwig van Beethoven." In *Beethoven: Die Bonner Jahre*, edited by Norbert Schloßmacher, 389–416. Vienna: Böhlau, 2020.

Loos, Helmut. "Religiöse Aspekte der Beethoven-Rezeption zwischen Nord und Süd." In Tomaszewski and Chrenkoff, *Beethoven 3*, 299–308.

Loos, Helmut. "Zur Rezeption von Beethovens *Missa solemnis*." In *Beethoven: Studien und Interpretationen*, edited by Mieczysław Tomaszewski and Magdalena Chrenkoff, 55–64. Kraków: Akademia Muzyczna, 2000.

MacIntyre, Bruce C. *The Viennese Concerted Mass of the Early Classic Period*. Ann Arbor, MI: UMI Research Press, 1986.

Maier, Franz Michael. "Beethoven liest Littrow." In Appel and Ronge, *Beethoven liest*, 251–88.

Marx, Adolf Bernhard. *Ludwig van Beethoven: Leben und Schaffen*. 2 vols. Berlin: O. Janke, 1859.

Massenkeil, Günther. "Katholischer deutscher Passionsgesang im 18. und 19. Jahrhundert" (1997). In *Wort und Ton*, 165–83.

Massenkeil, Günther. "Religiöse Aspekte in den Gellert-Liedern von Ludwig van Beethoven" (1978). In *Wort und Ton*, 193–204.

Massenkeil, Günther. "Über Beethovens kirchenmusikalischen Stil: Ein Vortrag" (1970). In *Wort und Ton*, 185–91.

Massenkeil, Günther. *Wort und Ton in christlicher Musik: Ausgewählte Schriften*. Paderborn: Ferdinand Schöningh, 2008.

Mathew, Nicholas. "Beethoven's Political Music, the Handelian Sublime, and the Aesthetics of Prostration." *19th-Century Music* 33, no. 2 (2009): 110–50.

Mathew, Nicholas. "History under Erasure: *Wellingtons Sieg*, the Congress of Vienna, and the Ruination of Beethoven's Heroic Style." *Musical Quarterly* 89, no. 1 (2007): 17–61.

Mathew, Nicholas. *Political Beethoven*. New York: Cambridge University Press, 2013.

McCool, Gerald A. *Catholic Theology in the Nineteenth Century: The Quest for a Unitary Method*. New York: Seabury Press, 1977.

McGrann, Jeremiah W. "Beethoven's Mass in C, Opus 86: Genesis and Compositional Background." 2 vols. PhD diss., Harvard University, 1991.

McGrann, Jeremiah W. "Der Hintergrund zu Beethovens Messen." *Bonner Beethoven-Studien* 3 (2003): 119–38.

McGrann, Jeremiah W. "Kritischer Bericht." In *Messe C-Dur: Opus 86, Neue Beethoven-Gesamtausgabe*, Abteilung VIII, vol. 2, by Ludwig van Beethoven, 163–294. Munich: G. Henle, 2003.

McGrann, Jeremiah W. "Zum vorliegenden Band." In *Messe C-Dur: Opus 86, Neue Beethoven-Gesamtausgabe*, Abteilung VIII, vol. 2, by Ludwig van Beethoven, ix–xiii. Munich: G. Henle, 2003.

McManners, John. *Church and Society in Eighteenth-Century France*. 2 vols. Oxford: Clarendon Press, 1998.

Mellers, Wilfrid. *Beethoven and the Voice of God*. London: Faber & Faber, 1993.

Melton, James van Horn. "Pietism, Politics, and the Public Sphere in Germany." In Bradley and Van Kley, *Religion and Politics in Enlightenment Europe*, 294–333.

Meyer, Michael A. "Judaism and Christianity." In *German-Jewish History in Modern Times*, edited by Michael A. Meyer, 2:168–98. New York: Columbia University Press, 1997.

Mühlenweg, Anja. "Ludwig van Beethoven, *Christus am Oelberge*, op. 85: Studien zur Entstehungs- und Überlieferungsgeschichte." 2 vols. PhD diss., Julius-Maximilians-Universität, Würzburg, 2004.

Nettl, Paul. "Erinnerungen an Erzherzog Rudolph, den Freund und Schüler Beethovens." *Zeitschrift für Musikwissenschaft* 4 (1921): 95–99.

Nichols, Aidan. *Catholic Thought since the Enlightenment: A Survey*. Pretoria: University of South Africa, 1998.
Nichols, Aidan. *The Thought of Pope Benedict XVI: An Introduction to the Theology of Joseph Ratzinger*. London: Burns & Oates, 2007.
Nipperdey, Thomas. *Germany from Napoleon to Bismarck, 1800–1866*. Translated by Daniel Nolan. Princeton, NJ: Princeton University Press, 1996.
Nohl, Ludwig. *Beethoven's Leben*. Vol. 3. Leipzig: Ernst Julius Günther, 1877.
Nohl, Ludwig. *Der Geist der Tonkunst*. Frankfurt am Main: J. D. Sauerländer, 1861.
Nohl, Walther, ed. *Beethoven: Konversationshefte*. Vol. 1. Munich: Allgemeine Verlagsanstalt, 1924.
November, Nancy. *Beethoven's Theatrical Quartets: Opp. 59, 74 and 95*. New York: Cambridge University Press, 2013.
Novotny, Alexander. "Kardinal Erzherzog Rudolph (1788–1831) und seine Bedeutung für Wien." *Wiener Geschichtsblätter* 4 (1961): 341–47.
Numaguchi, Takashi. *Beethovens "Missa Solemnis" im 19. Jahrhundert: Aufführungs- und Diskursgeschichte*. Cologne: Verlag Dohr, 2006.
Numaguchi, Takashi. "Das instrumentale Fugato im 'Dona nobis pacem' der *Missa solemnis*: Beethovens Dialog mit der Tradition." In Tomaszewski and Chrenkoff, *Beethoven* 3, 103–7.
Okey, Robin. *The Habsburg Monarchy c. 1765–1918: From Enlightenment to Eclipse*. Basingstoke: Macmillan, 2001.
O'Meara, Thomas Franklin. *Romantic Idealism and Roman Catholicism: Schelling and the Theologians*. Notre Dame, IN: University of Notre Dame Press, 1982.
Pauly, Reinhard G. "The Reforms of Church Music under Joseph II." *Musical Quarterly* 43, no. 3 (1957): 372–82.
Petersen, Nils Holger. "*Sepolcro*: Musical Devotion of the Passion in 17th–18th Century Austria." In *Instruments of Devotion: The Practices and Objects of Religious Piety from the Late Middle Ages to the 20th Century*, edited by Henning Laugerud and Laura Katrine Skinnebach, 145–56. Aarhus: Aarhus University Press, 2007.
Plantinga, Leon. "Beethoven, Napoleon, and Political Romanticism." In *The Oxford Handbook of the New Cultural History of Music*, edited by Jane F. Fulcher, 484–500. New York: Oxford University Press, 2011.
Poppe, Gerhard. *Festhochamt, sinfonische Messe oder überkonfessionelles Bekenntnis? Studien zur Rezeptionsgeschichte von Beethovens Missa solemnis*. Beeskow: Ortus Musikverlag, 2007.
Printy, Michael. *Enlightenment and the Creation of German Catholicism*. New York: Cambridge University Press, 2009.
Printy, Michael. "History and Church History in the Catholic Enlightenment." *Modern Intellectual History* 18 (2021): 248–60.
Probst, Manfred. *Gottesdienst in Geist und Wahrheit: Die liturgischen Ansichten und Bestrebungen Johann Michael Sailers (1751–1832)*. Regensburg: Friedrich Pustet, 1976.
Rady, Martyn. *The Habsburgs: To Rule the World*. New York: Basic Books, 2020.
Ratner, Leonard G. *Classic Music: Expression, Form, and Style*. New York: Schirmer Books, 1980.
Ratzinger, Joseph [Pope Benedict XVI]. "What Will the Future Church Look Like?" In *Faith and the Future*, 101–18. San Francisco: Ignatius Press, 2006.
Reid, Paul. *The Beethoven Song Companion*. Manchester: Manchester University Press, 2007.
Reinalter, Helmut. "Die Freimaurerei zwischen Josephinismus und frühfranziszeischer Reaktion: zur gesellschaftlichen Rolle und indirekt politischen Macht der Geheimbünde im 18. Jahrhundert." In *Freimaurer und Geheimbünde im 18. Jahrhundert in Mitteleuropa*, edited by Helmut Reinalter, 35–84. Frankfurt am Main: Suhrkamp, 1983.
Reisinger, Elisabeth. *Musik machen, fördern, sammeln: Erzherzog Maximilian Franz im Wiener und Bonner Musikleben*. Bonn: Beethoven-Haus, 2020.
Reisinger, Elisabeth. "The Prince and the Prodigies: On the Relations of Archduke and Elector Maximilian Franz with Mozart, Beethoven, and Haydn." *Acta Musicologica* 91, no. 1 (2019): 48–70.

Reisinger, Elisabeth. "Sozialisation, Interaktion, Netzwerk: Zum Umgang mit Musikern im Adel anhand des Beispiels von Erzherzog Maximilian Franz." In Lodes, Reisinger, and Wilson, *Beethoven und andere Hofmusiker*, 179–98.
Reisinger, Elisabeth, Juliane Riepe, and John D. Wilson, eds. *The Operatic Library of Elector Maximilian Franz: Reconstruction, Catalogue, Contexts*. Bonn: Beethoven-Haus, 2018.
Riedel, Friedrich Wilhelm. "Kirchenmusik in der ständisch gegliederten Gesellschaft am Ende des Heiligen Römischen Reiches." In *Kirchenmusik zwischen Säkularisation und Restauration*, edited by Friedrich Wilhelm Riedel, 47–57. Sinzig: Studio Verlag, 2006.
Roberts, Andrew. *Napoleon: A Life*. New York: Viking, 2014.
Robertson, Angus. *The Crossroads of Civilization: A History of Vienna*. New York: Pegasus, 2022.
Robertson, Ritchie. "Johann Pezzl (1756–1823): Enlightenment in the Satirical Mode." In Burson and Lehner, *Enlightenment and Catholicism in Europe*, 227–45.
Robertson, Ritchie, and Judith Beniston, eds. *Catholicism and Austrian Culture*. Edinburgh: Edinburgh University Press, 1999.
Ronge, Julia. "Beethoven's Ambitions in Church Music: Plans, Ideas and Fragments." *Beethoven Journal* 30, no. 2 (2015): 52–61.
Ronge, Julia. "'When Will the Time Finally Come When There Will Only Be Humans': An Unknown Letter from Beethoven to Heinrich von Struve." *Beethoven Journal* 35 (2022), Article 2. https://doi.org/10.55917/2771-3938.1002.
Rowe, Michael. *From Reich to State: The Rhineland in the Revolutionary Age, 1780–1830*. Cambridge: Cambridge University Press, 2003.
Rowe, Michael. "A Tale of Two Cities: Aachen and Cologne in Napoleonic Europe." In Broers, Hicks, and Guimerá, *Napoleonic Empire*, 123–31.
Rumph, Stephen. *Beethoven after Napoleon: Political Romanticism in the Late Works*. Berkeley: University of California Press, 2004.
Sailer, Johann Michael. *Friedrich Christians Vermächtniß an seine lieben Söhne: Deutschen Jünglingen in die Hand gegeben von J. M. Sailer*. 2 vols. 2nd improved printing ["Zweyte verbesserte Auflage"]. Grätz: Verlag der Herausgeber der neuen wohlfeilen Bibliothek für katholische Seelsorger und Religions-Freunde [Ferstl], 1819.
Sailer, Johann Michael. *Kleine Bibel für Kranke und Sterbende und ihre Freunde, besonders für Geistliche, denen die Krankenpflege anvertraut ist*. 3rd improved and expanded printing ["Dritte verbesserte und vermehrte Auflage"]. Grätz: Verlag der Herausgeber der neuen wohlfeilen Bibliothek für katholische Seelsorger und Religionsfreunde, 1819.
Sailer, Johann Michael. *Neue Beyträge zur Bildung des Geistlichen*. 3rd improved printing ["Dritte verbesserte Auflage"]. Grätz: Verlag der Herausgeber der neuen wohlfeilen Bibliothek für katholische Seelsorger und Religionsfreunde, 1819. Bound as part of *Gesammelte Werke*, vol. 8.
Sailer, Johann Michael. *Sprüche-Buch: Goldkörner der Weisheit und Tugend: Zur Unterhaltung für edle Seelen*. 3rd improved printing ["Dritte verbesserte Auflage"]. Vol. 2 of *Deutsches Sprichwörter- und Sprüchebuch: Ein Lehr- Lese- und Unterhaltungsbuch für Deutsche*. Grätz: Verlag der Herausgeber der neuen wohlfeilen Bibliothek für katholische Seelsorger und Religionsfreunde, 1819.
Sailer, Johann Michael. *Von der Priesterweihung: Eine Rede*. Landshut: Weber'schen Buchhandlung, 1817.
Sanda, Anna. "The Enlightened Practice of Sacred Music in Bonn and the Role of Andrea Luchesi." In Chua and Chong, *Rethinking Beethoven and the Enlightenment*, forthcoming.
Sayce, R. A. "Continental Versions from c. 1600 to the Present Day: French." In *The Cambridge History of the Bible: The West from the Reformation to the Present Day*, edited by S. L. Greenslade, 347–52. Cambridge: Cambridge University Press, 1963.
Schaefer, Richard. "A Critique of Everyday Reason: Johann Michael Sailer and the Catholic Enlightenment in Germany." *Intellectual History Review* 30, no. 4 (2020): 653–71.

Schaefer, Richard. "Program for a New Catholic *Wissenschaft*: Devotional Activism and Catholic Modernity in the Nineteenth Century." *Modern Intellectual History* 4, no. 3 (2007): 433–62.
Schiel, Hubert, ed. *Johann Michael Sailer: Leben und Briefe*. 2 vols. Regensburg: Friedrich Pustet, 1948.
Schindler, Anton Felix. *Beethoven as I Knew Him: A Biography*. Edited by Donald W. MacArdle. Translated by Constance S. Jolly. New York: Norton, 1972.
Schindler, Anton [Felix]. *Biographie von Ludwig van Beethoven*. 1st ed. Münster, Westphalia: Aschendorff'schen Buchhandlung, 1840.
Schindler, Anton [Felix]. *Biographie von Ludwig van Beethoven*. 2nd ed. Münster, Westphalia: Aschendorff'schen Buchhandlung, 1845.
Schindler, Anton [Felix]. *Biographie von Ludwig van Beethoven*. 3rd ed. 2 vols. Münster, Westphalia: Aschendorff'schen Buchhandlung, 1860.
Schindler, Anton F[elix]. *The Life of Beethoven*. Translated by Ignace Moscheles. 2 vols. 1841. Reprinted with both volumes combined into a single edition. Mattapan, MA: Gamut Music Company, 1966.
Schlosser, Johann Aloys. *Beethoven: The First Biography*. Edited by Barry Cooper. Translated by Reinhard G. Pauly. Portland, OR: Amadeus Press, 1996.
Schmidt, Hans. "Verzeichnis der Skizzen Beethovens." *Beethoven-Jahrbuch* 6 (1965/1968): 7–128.
Schmidt, Hugo. "The Origin of the Austrian National Anthem and Austria's Literary War Effort." In Brauer and Wright, *Austria in the Age*, 163–83.
Schmidt-Biggemann, Wilhelm. "Johann Michael Sailer als Aufklärer." In *Aufklärung: Interdisziplinäres Jahrbuch zur Erforschung des 18. Jahrhunderts und seiner Wirkungsgeschichte*, edited by Martin Mulsow, Gideon Stiening, and Friedrich Vollhardt, 33:81–116. Hamburg: Felix Meiner, 2021.
Schmitz, Arnold. *Das romantische Beethovenbild: Darstellung und Kritik*. Berlin: Ferdinand Dümmlers, 1927.
Schmitz, Walter, and Sibylle von Steinsdorff, eds. *Bettine von Arnim: Werke und Briefe*. 4 vols. Frankfurt am Main: Deutscher Klassiker Verlag, 1992.
Schneiderwirth, Matthaeus. *Das katholische deutsche Kirchenlied unter dem Einflusse Gellerts und Klopstocks*. Münster, Westphalia: Verlag der Aschendorffschen Buchhandlung, 1908.
Scholz, Gottfried. "Die geistigen Wurzeln von Gerard und Gottfried van Swieten." *Studien zur Musikwissenschaft* 55 (2009): 169–94.
Schroeder, David P. "Haydn and Gellert: Parallels in Eighteenth-Century Music and Literature." *Current Musicology* 35 (1983): 7–18.
Schuh, Josef. *Johann Michael Sailer und die Erneuerung der Kirchenmusik: Zur Vorgeschichte der cäcilianischen Reformbewegung in der ersten Hälfte des 19. Jahrhunderts*. PhD diss., University of Cologne, 1972.
Schwaiger, Georg. *Johann Michael Sailer: Der bayerische Kirchenvater*. Munich: Schnell & Steiner, 1982.
Schwemmer, Johannes. "Der Cäcilianismus." In *Geschichte der katholischen Kirchenmusik*, edited by Karl Gustav Fellerer, 2:226–36. Kassel: Bärenreiter, 1976.
Sehnal, Jiří. "Kirchenmusik im Erzbistum Olmütz unter Kardinal Erzherzog Rudolph." In *Kirchenmusik zwischen Säkularisation und Restauration*, edited by Friedrich Wilhelm Riedel, 177–93. Sinzig: Studio Verlag, 2006.
Shantz, Douglas H. *An Introduction to German Pietism: Protestant Renewal at the Dawn of Modern Europe*. Baltimore: Johns Hopkins University Press, 2013.
Sheehan, Jonathan. "Enlightenment, Religion, and the Enigma of Secularization: A Review Essay." *American Historical Review* 108, no. 4 (2003): 1061–80.
Skwara, Dagmar. "Cum versus ex: Ein Lapsus im Credo-Text beider Beethoven-Messen." *Musik und Kirche* 78 (2008): 46–47.

Smit, Peter-Ben. *Old Catholic and Philippine Independent Ecclesiologies in History: The Catholic Church in Every Place*. Leiden: Brill, 2011.
Smither, Howard E. *A History of the Oratorio*. 4 vols. Chapel Hill: University of North Carolina Press, 1977–2000.
Solie, Ruth A. "Beethoven as a Secular Humanist: Ideology and the Ninth Symphony in Nineteenth-Century Criticism." In *Explorations in Music, the Arts, and Ideas: Essays in Honor of Leonard B. Meyer*, edited by Eugene Narmour and Ruth A. Solie, 1–42. Stuyvesant, NY: Pendragon Press, 1988.
Solomon, Maynard. *Beethoven*. 2nd ed. New York: Schirmer Books, 1998.
Solomon, Maynard. *Beethoven Essays*. Cambridge, MA: Harvard University Press, 1988.
Solomon, Maynard, ed. and trans. "Beethoven's Tagebuch." In *Beethoven Essays*, 233–95.
Solomon, Maynard, ed. *Beethovens Tagebuch*. Bonn: Beethoven-Haus, 1990.
Solomon, Maynard. "The Healing Power of Music." In *Late Beethoven*, 229–41.
Solomon, Maynard. "Intimations of the Sacred." In *Late Beethoven*, 198–212.
Solomon, Maynard. *Late Beethoven: Music, Thought, Imagination*. Berkeley: University of California Press, 2003.
Solomon, Maynard. "The Masonic Imagination." In *Late Beethoven*, 159–78.
Solomon, Maynard. "The Masonic Thread." In *Late Beethoven*, 135–58.
Solomon, Maynard. "The Quest for Faith." In *Beethoven Essays*, 216–29.
Solomon, Maynard. "Some Romantic Images." In *Late Beethoven*, 42–70.
Sorkin, David. *The Religious Enlightenment: Protestants, Jews, and Catholics from London to Vienna*. Princeton, NJ: Princeton University Press, 2008.
Sperber, Jonathan. *Popular Catholicism in Nineteenth-Century Germany*. Princeton, NJ: Princeton University Press, 1984.
Sturm, Christoph Christian. *Betrachtungen über die Werke Gottes im Reiche der Natur und der Vorsehung auf alle Tage des Jahres*. 2 vols. Reuttlingen [Reutlingen], 1811.
Sturm, Christoph Christian. *Betrachtungen über die Werke Gottes im Reiche der Natur und der Vorsehung auf alle Tage des Jahres*. Edited by Bernard Galura. 2 vols. Augsburg: Moy'schen Buchhandlung, 1813.
Sturm, Christoph Christian. *Reflections on the Works of God and of His Providence throughout All Nature*. Translated by the Rev. Dr. Balfour. 2 vols. London: G. and W. B. Whittaker, 1823.
Sullivan, J. W. N. *Beethoven: His Spiritual Development*. 1927. Reprint, New York: Vintage, 1960.
Swafford, Jan. *Beethoven: Anguish and Triumph; A Biography*. Boston: Houghton Mifflin Harcourt, 2014.
Swidler, Leonard. *Aufklärung Catholicism, 1780–1850: Liturgical and Other Reforms in the Catholic Aufklärung*. Missoula, MT: Scholars Press, 1978.
Taylor, Benedict. "Beyond the Ethical and Aesthetic: Reconciling Religious Art with Secular Art-Religion in Mendelssohn's *Lobgesang*." In *Mendelssohn, the Organ, and the Music of the Past*, edited by Jürgen Thym, 287–309. Rochester, NY: University of Rochester Press, 2014.
Thayer, Alexander Wheelock. *Ludwig van Beethovens Leben*. Edited by Hermann Deiters and Hugo Riemann. 5 vols. Leipzig: Breitkopf & Härtel, 1901–1917.
Thayer, Alexander Wheelock. *Thayer's Life of Beethoven*. Edited by Elliot Forbes. 2 vols. Princeton, NJ: Princeton University Press, 1967.
Thomas à Kempis. *The Imitation of Christ*. Translated by Leo Sherley-Price. London: Penguin, 1952.
Thomas von Kempen [Thomas à Kempis]. *Das Buch von der Nachfolge Christi*. Translated by Johann Michael Sailer. Edited by Walter Kröber. Ditzingen: Reclam, 2019.
Tomaszewski, Mieczysław and Magdalena Chrenkoff, eds. *Beethoven 3: Studien und Interpretationen*. Kraków: Akademia Muzyczna, 2006.
Tyson, Alan. "Beethoven's Heroic Phase." *Musical Times* 110, no. 1512 (1969): 139–41.
Van Kley, Dale K. "Piety and Politics in the Century of Lights." In *The Cambridge History of Eighteenth-Century Political Thought*, edited by Mark Goldie and Robert Wokler, 110–43. Cambridge: Cambridge University Press, 2006.

Vilanova, Evangelista. *Histoire des théologies chrétiennes*. 3 vols. Translated by Jacques Mignon. Paris: Éditions du Cerf, 1997.

Walden, C. Edward. "The Authenticity of the 1812 Beethoven Letter to Bettina von Arnim." *Beethoven Journal* 14 (1999): 9–15.

Walden, C. Edward. *Beethoven's Immortal Beloved: Solving the Mystery*. Lanham, MD: Scarecrow Press, 2011.

Walker, Colin. "Zacharias Werner and the Hofbauer Circle: The Question of Toleration." In Robertson and Beniston, *Catholicism and Austrian Culture*, 32–50.

Wallace, Robin, ed. and trans. *The Critical Reception of Beethoven's Compositions by His German Contemporaries, Op. 123 to Op. 124*. Center for Beethoven Research, Boston University, 2020. Available for download at https://www.bu.edu/beethovencenter/publications-by-the-center/.

Wallnig, Thomas. "Franz Stephan Rautenstrauch (1734–1785): Church Reform for the Sake of the State." In Burson and Lehner, *Enlightenment and Catholicism in Europe*, 209–25.

Wangermann, Ernst. *The Austrian Achievement, 1700–1800*. London: Thames & Hudson, 1973.

Wangermann, Ernst. "The Austrian Enlightenment and the French Revolution." In Brauer and Wright, *Austria in the Age*, 1–10.

Ward, W. R. "Late Jansenism and the Habsburgs." In Bradley and Van Kley, *Religion and Politics in Enlightenment Europe*, 154–86.

Webster, James. "*The Creation*, Haydn's Late Vocal Music, and the Musical Sublime." In *Haydn and His World*, edited by Elaine Sisman, 57–102. Princeton, NJ: Princeton University Press, 1997.

Webster, James. "Haydn's Sacred Vocal Music and the Aesthetics of Salvation." In *Haydn Studies*, edited by W. Dean Sutcliffe, 35–69. Cambridge: Cambridge University Press, 1998.

Wegeler, Franz Gerhard, and Ferdinand Ries. *Beethoven Remembered: The Biographical Notes of Franz Wegeler and Ferdinand Ries*. Translated by Frederick Noonan. Arlington, VA: Great Ocean Publishers, 1987.

Weise, Dagmar, ed. *Beethoven: Ein Skizzenbuch zur Chorfantasie Op. 80 und zu anderen Werken*. Bonn: Beethoven-Haus, 1957.

Weise, Dagmar, ed. *Beethoven: Ein Skizzenbuch zur Pastoralsymphonie Op. 68 und zu den Trios Op. 70*. 2 vols. Bonn: Beethoven-Haus, 1961.

Weise, Dagmar, ed. *Beethoven: Entwurf einer Denkschrift an das Appellationsgericht in Wien vom 18. Februar 1820*. 2 vols. Bonn: Beethovenhaus, 1953.

Weiss, Otto. *Begegnungen mit Klemens Maria Hofbauer, 1751–1820*. Regensburg: Friedrich Pustet, 2009.

Werner, Zacharias. "Geistliche Uebungen für drei Tage." In *Sämtliche Werke*, 3:88–132. Grimma: Verlags-Comptoir, n.d.

White, James F. *Roman Catholic Worship: Trent to Today*. 2nd ed. Collegeville, MN: Liturgical Press, 2003.

Will, Richard. *The Characteristic Symphony in the Age of Haydn and Beethoven*. New York: Cambridge University Press, 2002.

Wilson, John D. "From the Chapel to the Theatre to the *Akademiensaal*: Beethoven's Musical Apprenticeship at the Bonn Electoral Court, 1784–1792." In Chapin and Wyn Jones, *Beethoven Studies 4*, 1–23.

Winter, Robert. "Reconstructing Riddles: The Sources for Beethoven's *Missa solemnis*." In *Beethoven Essays: Studies in Honor of Elliot Forbes*, edited by Lewis Lockwood and Phyllis Benjamin, 217–50. Cambridge, MA: Harvard University Press, 1984.

Wiora, Walter. "Restauration und Historismus." In *Geschichte der katholischen Kirchenmusik*, edited by Karl Gustav Fellerer, 2:219–25. Kassel: Bärenreiter, 1976.

Witcombe, Charles. "Beethoven's Markings in Christoph Christian Sturm's *Reflections on the Works of God in the Realm of Nature and Providence for Every Day of the Year*." *Beethoven Journal* 18, no. 1 (2003): 10–17.

Witcombe, Charles. "Beethoven's Private God: An Analysis of the Composer's Markings in Sturm's *Betrachtungen*." MA thesis, San Jose State University, 1998.

Wolf, Hubert. *Johann Michael Sailer: Das postume Inquisitionsverfahren*. Paderborn: Ferdinand Schöningh, 2002.

Wolff, Christoph. "Bach and the Tradition of the Palestrina Style." In *Bach: Essays on His Life and Music*, 84–104. Cambridge, MA: Harvard University Press, 1991.

Wolfshohl, Alexander. "Beethoven liest Autoren und Texte mit Bezug zu Religion und Theologie." In Appel and Ronge, *Beethoven liest*, 105–41.

Wolfshohl, Alexander. "Nichts weniger als Atheisten und Gottesschänder? Oder: Hundert thätige Männer, der Kern des Volkes? Intellektuelle Gruppierungen in Bonn unter den letzten Kurfürsten." In *Beethoven: Die Bonner Jahre*, edited by Norbert Schloßmacher, 213–40. Vienna: Böhlau, 2020.

Wyn Jones, David. *Beethoven: Pastoral Symphony*. Cambridge Music Handbook. Cambridge: Cambridge University Press, 1995.

Wyn Jones, David. *The Life of Beethoven*. Cambridge: Cambridge University Press, 1998.

Wyn Jones, David. *Music in Vienna, 1700, 1800, 1900*. Woodbridge, Suffolk: Boydell Press, 2016.

Wyn Jones, David. "Shared Identities and Thwarted Narratives: Beethoven and the Austrian *Allgemeine musikalische Zeitung*, 1817–1824." In Chapin and Wyn Jones, *Beethoven Studies 4*, 166–88.

Zalar, Jeffrey T. *Reading and Rebellion in Catholic Germany, 1770–1914*. New York: Cambridge, 2019.

Index

For the benefit of digital users, indexed terms that span two pages (e.g., 52–53) may, on occasion, appear on only one of those pages.

Abendlied unterm gestirntem Himmel, WoO 150 (Beethoven), 81–82
Abschiedsgesang an Wiens Bürger, WoO 121 (Beethoven), 68–69
absolutism, 40–41, 42–43
Adorno, Theodor, 202–4, 255
    on Beethoven's religious beliefs, 8
Albrecht, Theodore, 60, 73–74
Allegri, Gregorio, *Miserere*, 276
Allgemeine musikalische Zeitung (*AmZ*) (Leipzig), 115–16, 256n72
Allgemeine musikalische Zeitung mit besonderer Rücksicht auf dem österreichischen Kaiserstaat (*AmZÖ*) (Austria), 277n26
Anysius, Janus, 164–65, 167, 177–80
Arnim, Bettina von. *See* Brentano, Bettina (Bettina von Arnim)
Artaria (publisher), 9, 71n1, 122
Assmann, Jan, 10–11
Austro-Prussian War, 282
Averdonk, Severin, 50, 56–57

Bach, C. P. E. (Carl Philipp Emanuel), 72, 130, 256–57
Bach, J. S. (Johann Sebastian), 271–72
Baroque Catholicism, 25–27
Barton, Peter, 149–51
Bavaria, 48, 162, 171–73, 276
Beales, Derek, 14–15, 277–78
Beethoven, Johann van (Beethoven's brother), 9
Beethoven, Johanna van (wife of Kaspar Karl van Beethoven), 128–29
Beethoven, Karl van (Beethoven's nephew), 128–29, 277–78
    proposed study with Johann Michael Sailer, 160–62, 164–65
Beethoven, Kaspar Karl van (Beethoven's brother), 128–29, 208–9
Beethoven, Ludwig van (Beethoven's grandfather), 60–63

BEETHOVEN, LUDWIG VAN
    Akademie concert, December 1808, 96–97
    Artaria 197 (sketchbook), 254
    "Beethoven Myth," 21–23, 284–85
    Bible in French, ownership of, 60–63 (*see also* Bible de Port-Royal ("Sacy Bible"))
    Catholic background, 5–6
    and church modes, 201–2, 232–36, 255–56, 257–58
    church music training, 5–6, 51–52, 57–59
    deafness, 12n44, 71–72, 73–74, 87, 121–22
    Grasnick 3 (sketchbook), 87n53, 94, 97–98n78
    Heiligenstadt Testament, 12n44, 71–72, 73–74, 85–86, 86n52, 87, 121–22, 137, 138–39, 145–46, 186, 193, 268n107
    "Immortal Beloved," 128–29
    Landsberg 10 (sketchbook), 87n53
    library, 9–10 (*see also* Feßler, Ignaz Aurelius; Kant, Immanuel; Sailer, Johann Michael; Sturm, Christoph Christian; Thomas à Kempis)
    lieder, 72
    and Palestrina, 255–56, 258–59
    political views, 21–22, 63–70
    portrait by Joseph Karl Stieler, 202–4
    religious references in correspondence, 5–6, 8–9, 64–66, 67–68, 71–72
    religious views, conventional accounts of, 6–8
    Schwarzspanierhaus (final residence), 35–36
    sketches for incomplete works, 73, 74–75, 255–56, 274–75
    statue by Ernst Julius Hähnel (Bonn Münsterplatz), 1–4, 280–81
    Tagebuch, 6–7, 130–31, 139–46, 186, 190–91, 201–2, 207–9
    Teplitz incident, 269n114

BEETHOVEN, LUDWIG VAN (*cont.*)
works (*see Abendlied unterm gestirntem Himmel*, WoO 150 (Beethoven); *Abschiedsgesang an Wiens Bürger*, WoO 121 (Beethoven); *Christus am Ölberge*, op. 85 (Beethoven); *Der freie Mann*, WoO 117 (Beethoven); *Das Geheimnis*, WoO 145 (Beethoven); *Der glorreiche Augenblick*, op. 136 (Beethoven); *Kantate auf den Tod Kaiser Josephs II.*, WoO 87 (Beethoven); *Kantate auf die Erhebung Leopolds II zur Kaiserwürde*, WoO 88 (Beethoven); *Kriegslied der Österreicher*, WoO 122 (Beethoven); Mass in C major, op. 86 (Beethoven); *Missa solemnis*, op. 123 (Beethoven); *Sechs Lieder von Gellert*, op. 48 (Beethoven); String Quartet in A minor, op. 132 (Beethoven); String Quartet in B-flat major, op. 130 (Beethoven); String Quartet in C-sharp minor, op. 131 (Beethoven); String Quartet in E-flat major, op. 127 (Beethoven); Symphony No. 3 in E-flat major, op. 55 "Eroica" (Beethoven); Symphony No. 5 in C minor, op. 67 (Beethoven); Symphony No. 6 in F major, op. 68 "Pastoral" (Beethoven); Symphony No. 9 in D major, op. 125 (Beethoven); *Der Wachtelschlag*, WoO 129 (Beethoven); *Wellington's Victory*, op. 91 (Beethoven))
Zehrgarten Circle, 48–50, 53–54, 66
Zehrgarten Stammbuch, 48–50, 55–56
Bekker, Paul, 284–85
Bell, David A., 40–41
Bernadotte, Jean-Baptiste, 66
Bernard, Karl Joseph, 161–62, 164, 275–76n20, 280n41
Bettermann, Silke, 202–4
Bible de Port-Royal ("Sacy Bible"), 60–63
Bible reading, 33–34, 60–61, 63, 77–78, 174, 184
Biermann, Joanna, 114–15
Bismarck, Otto von, 282–83
Blöchlinger, Josef, 278–79
Boldrini, Carlo, 9
Bonaparte, Napoleon. *See* Napoleon Bonaparte
Bonn
  Catholic Enlightenment in, 51–57
  church music, 57–59
  political environment, 47–51
  university, 50, 51–52, 53–54, 55–56, 159
Brandenburg, Sieghard, 117
Breitkopf & Härtel, 5–6, 12, 74n21, 75, 82–84, 93–94, 95, 100–1, 116–18, 150n85

Brentano, Antonie, 5–6, 160, 168–69
Brentano, Bettina (Bettina von Arnim), 171n34, 269
Brentano, Clemens, 157–58, 168
Brentano, Franz, 168
Buddhism, 142–43
Burke, Edmund, *Reflections on the Revolution in France*, 43

Cäcilianismus. See Cecilian movement
Caecilia (journal), 250n60, 277, 285–86
Caeyers, Jan, 8
Calvinism, 33–34, 154–55, 192
Catholic Enlightenment. *See* Catholic Enlightenment in German lands; Enlightenment historiography
Catholic Enlightenment in German lands, 28–32
  Bonn, 51–57
  Josephinism, 32–37
  opposition to, 37–45 (*see also* "Catholic Restoration")
  Vienna, 33–34, 37, 38, 58–59, 77–78
"Catholic Restoration," 37–45, 156–59, 278–80
  in Vienna, 39–40, 63–70, 156–59, 278–79
Cecilia, St., 1
Cecilian movement, 260–61, 276–77, 285–86
Chadwick, Owen, 27
Cherubini, Luigi, 65–66
christkatholisch, 207–10
Christkatholische Kirche der Schweiz, 207–8
Christocentrism
  and Beethoven's *Missa solemnis*, 224–54
  and Johann Michael Sailer, 177, 180, 186–89, 193
Christus am Ölberge, op. 85 (Beethoven), 71–72
  Christ, depiction of, 114–20, 121–22, 192, 193
  as dramatic oratorio, 114–16
  and ethical conduct, 88–92, 192
  and Heiligenstadt Testament, 73–74
  libretto, 73–74, 114–15, 117–20
  as lyric oratorio, 92–93
  military music in, 264–66
  reception history, 11–12, 115–16, 280–81
Clemens August of Bavaria (Elector-Archbishop of Cologne), 60n80
Clement XIV, Pope, 35
Clubbe, John, 14
Cologne, 5–6, 47–48, 53–54, 172–73, 285–86
congregational singing, 26–27, 36–37, 58–59, 69–70, 206–7
Congress of Ems, 53–54
Congress of Vienna, 21–22, 40–41, 42–43, 68–69

Cooper, Barry, 69, 73–74
Cooper, Martin, 22–23
Cowan, Robert Bruce, 142–43

d'Antoine, Ferdinand, 58–59, 101–2, 199–200, 254n64
Dahlhaus, Carl, 260–61
deism
    and Beethoven, 4, 7, 8, 23–24
    and Enlightenment, 13–14, 16, 30–31, 175, 185–86
Deutschkatholizismus, 44–45
Dietrichstein, Count Moritz, 274–75
divine providence. *See under* nature
Dolp, Laura, 243–50, 262
Donakowski, Conrad, 30–31, 260–61
Drabkin, William, 230–32, 240–41, 262

ecumenism
    and Beethoven's religious music, 76–79, 93–99, 190–91, 206–10
    and Catholic Enlightenment, 31–32, 139
    Ignaz Aurelius Feßler on, 149–55
    Johann Michael Sailer on, 173–74, 177, 183–84, 191–92
    and Thomas à Kempis, 187–88
Eichhoff, Johann Joseph, 55–56
Emmerich, Anna Katharina, 157–58
Enlightenment historiography, 13–18
    Catholic Enlightenment, history of concept, 17–18 (*see also* Catholic Enlightenment in German lands)
    "religious Enlightenment," 15–16
Eroica Symphony (Beethoven). *See* Symphony No. 3 in E-flat major, op. 55 "Eroica" (Beethoven)
Esterházy, Prince Nikolaus, 74–75
ethical conduct
    and Beethoven's *Christus am Ölberge*, 88–92, 192
    and Beethoven's *Sechs Lieder von Gellert*, 87–88, 192–93
    and Catholic Enlightenment, 29–30
    Christian Fürchtegott Gellert on, 77–78
    Christoph Christian Sturm on, 134–35, 136–37
    Ignaz Aurelius Feßler on, 154–55
    Johann Michael Sailer on, 175–78, 180, 185–86, 199–200
    Thomas à Kempis on, 190
Eucharist
    and Baroque Catholicism, 25–26, 27
    and Beethoven's Mass in C, 96–97, 100, 126–27

    and Beethoven's *Missa solemnis*, 240–54
    Ignaz Aurelius Feßler on, 153–54
    Johann Michael Sailer on, 174–75, 183–84, 196–98, 253–54

fanaticism, 48–50, 56, 182, 278–79
Febronianism, 34–35, 53–54, 146–47
Febronius. *See* Hontheim, Johann Nikolaus von ("Febronius")
Feßler, Ignaz Aurelius, 146–47
    Ansichten von Religion und Kirchenthum, 146–56, 191–92
    Aristides und Themistocles, 277–78
    on ecumenism, 149–55
    on ethical conduct, 154–55
    on Eucharist, 153–54
    and Freemasonry, 146–47, 148–50
    and Johann Michael Sailer, 191–92
    and Kant, 146–47, 149–50
    Marc-Aurel, 277–78
Feuerbach, Ludwig, 173
Fillion, Michelle, 100–2
Forster, Marc, 45–46
Francis I (Francis Stephen, Holy Roman Emperor), 32n41
Francis II (Holy Roman Emperor) / Francis I (Emperor of Austria), 39–41, 65–66, 67–68, 69–70, 206n17, 274–75
Franz, Ignaz, 78n39
Freemasonry
    and Beethoven, 6–7, 51
    in Bonn, 48–50, 54–55
    and Catholic Enlightenment, 31–32, 37, 54–55
    and Ignaz Aurelius Feßler, 146–47, 148–50
Der freie Mann, WoO 117 (Beethoven), 51, 56
French Revolution
    and Beethoven, 64–66, 68–69
    and "Catholic Restoration," 38–39, 40–43, 156–57
    and Enlightenment, 13–14
    and Johann Joseph Eichhoff, 55–56
    and Eulogius Schneider, 50–51
French Revolutionary Wars, 38–39, 40–41
    and Rhineland, 47–48
Fröhlich, Franz Joseph, review of Beethoven's *Missa solemnis*, 285–86
fugue, 214, 222–23, 259–60

Gallicanism, 34
Gay, Peter, 13–14
Das Geheimnis, WoO 145 (Beethoven), 209–10

Gellert, Christian Fürchtegott, 71–72, 77–78, 190–91, 267n106
Gellert Lieder (Beethoven). *See Sechs Lieder von Gellert*, op. 48 (Beethoven)
Gentz, Friedrich von, 43
German Catholic Enlightenment. *See* Catholic Enlightenment in German lands
German unification, 282
Gertsch, Norbert, 256–57
Der glorreiche Augenblick, op. 136 (Beethoven), 21–22, 68–69
Goethe, Johann Wolfgang von, 39, 142–43, 170–71, 269n114
Gottesdienstordnung of 1783. *See under* Josephinism
"Gottheit," 86–87, 144, 145–46, 186
Graun, Carl Heinrich, *Der Tod Jesu*, 92–93
Gregorian chant
  Beethoven and, 207–8, 254, 258–59, 276
  in Bonn, 57–59
  and the Cecilian movement, 285–86
  Johann Michael Sailer and, 260–61
Grillparzer, Franz, oration at Beethoven's funeral, 1–4
Grossheim, Georg Christoph, review of Beethoven's *Missa solemnis*, 250n60

Hähnel, Ernst Julius, statue of Beethoven (Bonn Münsterplatz), 1–4, 284–85
Hamann, Johann Georg, 173
Haslinger, Tobias, 278–79
Hauschka, Vincenz, 277–78
Haydn, Joseph
  and Christian Fürchtegott Gellert, 72–73n10, 267n106
  Kaiserhymne ("Gott erhalte Franz den Kaiser"), 69–70
  masses, 100–1, 102–5, 228–29n43, 240–41, 262n92, 264, 280–81
  oratorios, 28–29, 73–74, 124n110, 280–81
Heiligenstadt Testament. *See under* BEETHOVEN, LUDWIG VAN
"Heiliger Dankgesang." *See* String Quartet in A minor, op. 132 (Beethoven)
Heine, Heinrich, "The Romantic School," 43–44, 142–43
Heller, Ferdinand, 58–59
Hermes, Georg, 159
Herttrich, Ernest, 144–45
Hinduism, 142–45
Hinrichsen, Hans-Joachim, 14
Hofbauer, Klemens Maria, 157–59, 174–75, 278–80

Hoffmann, E. T. A., 95n70, 115–16, 256n72, 267n101, 272–73
Hoffmeister & Kühnel (publisher), 71n1, 122n109
Hoffmeister, Franz Anton, 8, 64, 67–68
Hohler, Emmerich Thomas, 276
Holz, Karl, 278–79
Hontheim, Johann Nikolaus von ("Febronius"), 34
Höyng, Peter, 55–56
Huber, Franz Xaver, 73–74, 114–15, 116–18
Huxley, Aldous, *Point Counter Point*, 272–73

Ignatius, Father, prior of the Michaelskirche, Vienna, 161–62
Illuminati, 48, 174
Ingrao, Charles, 67–68
Israel, Jonathan, 16–17
Ito, John Paul, 164–65, 168–70

Jacobi, Friedrich Heinrich, 173
Janschikh, Franz, 278–79
Jansen, Cornelius, 33–34, 63n89. *See also* Jansenism
Jansenism
  and Beethoven's French Bible, 60–63
  and Catholic Enlightenment, 30n31, 33–36, 53–54
  and Ignaz Aurelius Feßler, 146–47, 149–50, 152–53, 155–56
Jena Romantic circle, 43–44, 157–58
Jesuit Order, 27, 34–36, 146–47, 171–72, 174
  Suppression of, 35, 53–54
Joseph II, Holy Roman Emperor, 27, 32–34, 35–37, 39–40, 48, 52–54, 58–59, 277–78. *See also* Josephinism; *Kantate auf den Tod Kaiser Josephs II.*, WoO 87 (Beethoven)
Joseph Cantata (Beethoven). *See Kantate auf den Tod Kaiser Josephs II.*, WoO 87 (Beethoven)
Josephinism, 32–37
  and Archduke Rudolph, 206–7
  Bonn, influence in, 58–59
  Gottesdienstordnung of 1783, 36–37
  and Ignaz Aurelius Feßler, 146–47, 148–50, 153–54, 158–59
  and Johann Michael Sailer, 177, 181–82, 199–200
  opposition to, 38, 43–44 (*see also* "Catholic Restoration")
  origin of term, 282–83
  suppression of monastic orders, 35–36
Judson, Pieter, 40–41

Kant, Immanuel
  critical philosophy, 14–15
  and Ignaz Aurelius Feßler, 146–47, 149–50
  influence on university in Bonn, 50, 53–54, 159
  Johann Michael Sailer on, 167, 175–76
  Benedikt Stattler on, 171
  Universal Natural History and Theory of the Heavens, 133n29
Kantate auf den Tod Kaiser Josephs II., WoO 87 (Beethoven), 50, 56, 67
Kantate auf die Erhebung Leopolds II zur Kaiserwürde, WoO 88 (Beethoven), 56–57, 67
Kempen, Thomas von. *See* Thomas à Kempis, *The Imitation of Christ*
Kempis, Thomas à. *See* Thomas à Kempis, *The Imitation of Christ*
Kinderman, William, 10–11, 14, 51, 230–32
Kirchenlied, 36–37, 58–59, 77–79, 87, 198–99, 260–61
Kirkendale, Warren, 211, 232–36, 242–50, 276
Klopstock, Friedrich Gottlieb, 48–50, 55–56, 77–78
Koch, Jakob Johannes, 22–23, 28–29
Koch, Matthias, 48–50
Koch, Willibald, 57–58
Kohlbrenner, Johann, *Deutsche Singmesse*, 58–59
Konrad, Ulrich, 51–52
Kramer, Richard, 255–56
Kraus, Beate, 60
Kreutzer, Rodolphe, 66
Kriegslied der Österreicher, WoO 122 (Beethoven), 68–69
Krutschek, Paul, 285–86
Kulturkampf, 282–83
Kunstreligion, 272–74

Larsen, Jens Peter, 280–81
Lavater, Johann Kaspar, 173
Leopold II, Holy Roman Emperor, 38, 39–40. *See also Kantate auf die Erhebung Leopolds II zur Kaiserwürde*, WoO 88 (Beethoven)
Leopold Cantata (Beethoven). *See Kantate auf die Erhebung Leopolds II zur Kaiserwürde*, WoO 88 (Beethoven)
Lesegellschaft, Bonn, 48–50, 52–53, 54–55, 56–57, 58–59
Lockwood, Lewis, 8, 23–24, 130–31, 136, 167–68
Lodes, Birgit, 47, 144–45, 147–48, 211, 218–21, 255, 262–63

Loos, Helmut, 23–24, 54–55, 281, 283–84
Ludwig, Crown Prince (later King Ludwig I) of Bavaria, 172–73
Lutheranism, 30–31, 77–78, 92–93, 130, 146–47, 154–55, 271–72

Mainz, 47–48, 50, 55–56, 69
Maria Theresa, Holy Roman Empress, 32–33, 35, 37, 58–59, 77–78
Martin of Braga, St. 164–65, 178–79
Marx, A. B. (Adolf Bernhard), 284–85
Masonry. *See* Freemasonry
Mass in C major, op. 86 (Beethoven)
  Agnus Dei, 96–97, 100, 105–9, 262, 264–66
  Christ, texts related to, 122–27
  compositional history, 74–76
  Credo, 96n75, 96–97, 102–9, 125–27
  and ecumenism, 93–99, 190–91
  exegesis of Mass text, 99–102, 199–200
  German text, 93–99
  Gloria, 94, 95–97, 98–101, 105–9
  Kyrie, 75–76, 95–97, 98–100, 105–9, 122–25, 126
  military music in, 264–66
  "personalization" of Mass text, 102–14, 199–200
  reception history, 11–12, 280–81, 283–84
  Sanctus, 96–97, 126–27
  sketches, 94, 124–25
Massenkeil, Günther, 78–79, 217–18
Mathew, Nicholas, 14, 21–22, 69–70
Maximilian Franz, Elector-Archbishop of Cologne, 48, 52–54, 57–59, 67
Maximilian Friedrich, Elector-Archbishop of Cologne, 53–54, 57–58, 260–61
McGrann, Jeremiah, 75–76, 96–97, 125–26
Melancthon, Philipp, 154–55
Mellers, Wilfred, 8
Mendelssohn, Felix, 284–85
Mendelssohn, Moses, 55n52
Merkle, Sebastian, 17–18, 282–83
Metternich, Clemens von, 40–41, 42–43, 158–59
Migazzi, Cardinal Christoph Anton Graf von, 33–34
military music, 264–66, 285–86
Minervalkirche, Bonn, 48–50, 52–53, 54–55, 58–59
Missa solemnis, op. 123 (Beethoven)
  Agnus Dei, 258–59, 262, 264, 285–86
  "archaic" features, 255–61
  and Archduke Rudolph, 201–4
  and Christocentrism, 224–54
  church modes, use of, 232–36, 255–56, 257–58
  Credo, 214, 215–16, 230–40, 257–59, 260, 285–86

Missa solemnis, op. 123 (Beethoven) (*cont.*)
   and ecumenism, 206–10
   exegesis of Mass text, 211–15, 224–54
   German text, 206–7
   Gloria, 212, 217–23, 258–60, 285–86
   Kyrie, 215, 225–30, 253–54, 258–59
   military music in, 264, 285–86
   organ part, 256–57
   "personalization" of Mass text, 215–23
   reception history, 10–11, 280–81, 283–86
   recitative, use of, 262, 264
   Sanctus, 217–18, 240–54, 258–59, 262
   secular references in, 262–66
   sketches, 147–48, 201–4, 239–40, 242–43, 254
Moravian Church (Moravian Brethren), 150–51, 155
Mühlenweg, Anja, 114–15, 116, 280–81
Müllner, Amandus, 144–45
Muratori, Ludovico Antonio, 33–34

Napoleon Bonaparte, 39, 40–41, 65, 66, 156–57, 266
Napoleonic Wars, 38–39, 40–41, 171–72
   War of the First Coalition, 40–41, 68–69
nature
   and Beethoven's music, 79–87, 135
   and Catholic Enlightenment, 28–29
   and Christoph Christian Sturm, 131–36
   divine providence, 84–86, 133–34
   quail call, 82–84, 86–87, 135
   stars, 81–82, 96n75, 131–33, 267–68
Nazarene movement, 157–58, 267
Neefe, Christian Gottlob, 48–50, 51–52, 53–55, 77, 92–93
Nohl, Ludwig, 284n65, 285–86
Novalis, 142–43, 173
Numaguchi, Takashi, 258–59

Old Catholics, 207–8
Oliva, Franz, 162, 202–4, 278–79
oratorio
   dramatic oratorio, 92, 114–16
   lyric oratorio, 92–93
   sepolcro, 115–16
   in Vienna, 73–74, 115–16

Palestrina, Giovanni Pierluigi da, 255–56, 258–59, 260–61, 271–72, 277
Pange lingua (Gregorian chant), 254, 274–75, 276
pantheism, 4, 23–24, 44n115, 136, 174–75
papal infallibility, 33–34, 44–45, 152–53, 207–8

pastoral mass, 242–43
Pastoral Symphony (Beethoven). *See* Symphony No. 6 in F major, op. 68 "Pastoral" (Beethoven)
Pfeffel, Gottlieb Conrad, 51
Pietism, 30–31, 92–93, 146–47. *See also* Lutheranism
Piuk, Franz Xaver, 164–65
Pius VI, Pope, 37
Pius VII, Pope, 65
Pius IX, Pope, 44–45
Plainchant. *See* Gregorian chant
Plantinga, Leon, 136
Poppe, Gerhard, 280–81
Probst, Manfred, 174–75
Protestantism
   and Baroque Catholicism, 25–27, 34–35
   and Catholic Enlightenment, 31–32, 37, 47–48, 54–55
   and German historiography, 282–84
   Ignaz Aurelius Feßler on, 151–55
   Johann Michael Sailer and, 173, 174–75, 177
   and oratorio, 92–93
   and Prussia, 282
   and "religious Enlightenment," 15–16
   See also Calvinism; ecumenism; Lutheranism; Moravian Church
Prussia, 42–43, 282–84, 286

Razumovsky, Count (Beethoven's patron), 43
recitative
   in Beethoven's *Christus am Ölberge*, 90–91, 117
   in Beethoven's *Missa solemnis*, 262, 264
   in Beethoven's *Der Wachtelschlag*, 264–66
Redemptorist order, 157–58, 278–80
Reid, Paul, 51, 72, 82–84
Reisinger, Elisabeth, 52–53
"religious Enlightenment." *See under* Enlightenment historiography
Revolutions of 1848, 44–45, 63–64
Rhineland, 27, 47–48, 54–55, 60, 286
   French occupation of, 69–70
Ries, Ferdinand, 7
Ries, Franz Anton, 48–50
Ries, Johann, 58–59
Rochlitz, Friedrich, 54n50, 116
Romanticism, 43–44, 142–43, 157–58, 272–74
   Johann Michael Sailer and, 170n32, 174–75, 267, 268–69
Ronge, Julia, 66
Rowe, Michael, 52–54
Rudolph, Archduke (of Austria), 161, 162, 262–63

and Beethoven's *Missa solemnis,* 12, 201–4, 270n117
and Josephinism, 206–7
Rumph, Stephen, 21–22, 73, 122

Sacy, Louis-Isaac Lemaistre de, 60–61. *See also* Bible de Port-Royal ("Sacy Bible")
Sailer, Johann Michael, 170–73
  and Antonie Brentano, 160
  and Beethoven, 160–69
  Christocentrism, 177
  ecumenism, 173–74, 177, 183–84, 191–92
  on ethical conduct, 175–78, 180, 185–86, 199–200
  on Eucharist, 174–75, 183–84, 196–98, 253–54
  Friedrich Christians Vermächtniß an seine lieben Söhne, 162–64, 181–82, 194, 196–98
  Goldkörner der Weisheit und Tugend, 162–67, 177–80, 190–91, 196–98, 214–15, 263
  on Kant, 167, 175–76
  Kleine Bibel für Kranke und Sterbende und ihre Freunde, 162–64, 183–87, 193, 196–200, 214–15, 230, 253–54, 263
  and liturgy, 195–200, 260–62
  Neue Beyträge zur Bildung des Geistlichen, 195–96, 267–69
  posthumous reputation, 172–73
  theological views, 173–77
  and Thomas à Kempis, 164
  Von dem Bunde der Religion mit der Kunst, 267–69
  Von der Priesterweihung: Eine Rede, 162–64, 198–99, 269–70
Sauter, Samuel, 82–84
Schelling, Friedrich, 44n117, 142–43, 149–50, 174–75
Schiller, Friedrich, 7n17, 14, 39, 48–50
  "An die Freude," 66
Schindler, Anton, 5–6, 23–24, 131n19, 147n77, 206, 280n41
  biography of Beethoven, 7
Schlegel, Dorothea, 157–58
Schlegel, Friedrich
  and Klemens Maria Hofbauer, 157–59
  Über die Sprache und Weisheit der Indier, 142–43
Schleiermacher, Friedrich, 149–50, 273–74
Schlemmer, Wenzel, 276
Schlosser, Johann Aloys, biography of Beethoven, 7
Schmitz, Arnold, 23–24
Schneider, Eulogius, 50–51, 55–56, 69

Schneiderwirth, Matthaeus, 77–78
Scholz, Benedict, 96, 206–7
Schreiber, Christian
  and Beethoven's *Christus am Ölberge,* 116–18
  German text for Beethoven's Mass in C, 93–100, 136, 138–39, 179–80, 199–200
Schuh, Josef, 18–19, 261–62, 273–74
Sechs Lieder von Gellert, op. 48 (Beethoven), 71–72
  "Bitten" (no. 1), 77–79
  "Bußlied" (no. 6), 122
  and Christ, 121, 122, 192–93
  and ecumenism, 76–79, 190–91
  "Die Ehre Gottes aus der Natur" (no. 4), 78–79, 81–82, 85–86
  and ethical conduct, 87–88, 192–93
  "Gottes Macht und Vorsehung" (no. 5), 77–79, 84–86, 122, 138–39
  and Heiligenstadt Testament, 73–74
  "Die Liebe des Nächsten" (no. 2), 77–79, 87–88, 192–93
  and nature, 79–82, 84–86
  reception history, 11–12
  sketches, 73, 78–79
  "Vom Tode" (no. 3), 73, 77–79, 121, 138–39
sepolcro. See under oratorio
Simrock, Nikolaus, 48–50, 55–56, 66–67, 69, 162, 206–7
Singmesse, 36–37, 58–59
Smither, Howard, 92
Society of Jesus. *See* Jesuit Order
Solie, Ruth, 272–73
Solomon, Maynard
  on Beethoven's *Missa solemnis,* 10–11
  on Beethoven's religious beliefs, 8, 23–24, 52–53, 71–72
  on Beethoven's *Tagebuch,* 142, 144–45, 207–8
  on Heiligenstadt Testament, 87
  on Johann Michael Sailer, 167
Sorkin, David, 15–16
stars. *See under* nature
Stattler, Benedikt, 171–72, 175–76
Stieler, Joseph Karl, portrait of Beethoven, 202–4
stile antico, 100–1, 271–72
Streicher, Nanette, 8–9
String Quartet in A minor, op. 132 (Beethoven), 145–46, 255–56, 271–73, 276
String Quartet in B-flat major, op. 130 (Beethoven), 273n8
String Quartet in C-sharp minor, op. 131 (Beethoven), 272–73
String Quartet in E-flat major, op. 127 (Beethoven), 144–45

Struve, Heinrich, 53–54, 55n52, 66
Sturm, Christoph Christian, 130
   Betrachtungen über die Werke Gottes im Reiche der Natur und der Vorsehung, 130–39, 192, 193
   on ethical conduct, 134–35, 136–37
   on nature, 131–36
Sullivan, J. W. N. 272–73
Sulzer, Johann Georg, 54–55, 92–93, 116
Swafford, Jan, 8
Swieten, Gerard (Gerhard) van, 33–34
Swieten, Gottfried van, 28–29, 33–34
Symphony No. 3 in E-flat major, op. 55 "Eroica" (Beethoven), 12n44, 65
Symphony No. 5 in C minor, op. 67 (Beethoven), 120, 272–73
Symphony No. 6 in F major, op. 68 "Pastoral" (Beethoven), 86–87, 131n19
Symphony No. 9 in D major, op. 125 (Beethoven), 81–82, 96n75, 255–56, 272–73, 277–78

Thomas à Kempis, *The Imitation of Christ*, 164, 187–91, 196–98, 253–54
Tucher, Gottlieb von, 277

ultramontanism, 42–43, 44–45, 174–75, 209, 260–61, 282–83, 286
Ursulines (religious order), 9, 35–36

Varena, Joseph, 9
Vatican Council, First, 44–45, 207–8
Vatican Council, Second, 44–45, 172–73
Veit, Philipp. *See* Nazarene movement
vernacular church music. *See* congregational singing; *Kirchenlied*; *Singmesse*
Victoria, Queen, 1
Vienna
   and Catholic Enlightenment, 33–34, 37, 38, 58–59, 77–78
   and "Catholic Restoration," 39–40, 63–70, 156–59, 278–79
   French occupation of, 156–57, 266
   oratorio in, 73–74, 115–16
   See also Congress of Vienna
Virgil, *Aeneid*, quoted by Beethoven, 211
Vives, Juan Luis (Ludovicus Vivis), 164–65, 167, 177–78, 179–80, 198–99, 215n34

Der Wachtelschlag, WoO 129 (Beethoven), 71–72
   and nature, 82–84, 85, 135
   recitative, use of, 264–66
   and war, 264–66
Waldstein, Count, 48–50, 52–53
War of the First Coalition. *See under* Napoleonic Wars
Wegeler, Franz, 7, 51
Weishaupt, Adam, 48
Wellington's Victory, op. 91 (Beethoven), 21–22, 68–69
Werner, Zacharias, 157–58, 278–80
Wessenberg, Ignaz Heinrich von, 159, 209–10
Wiener Zeitung, 40n97, 97–98n78, 161–62
Wilson, John, 47, 57–59
Witcombe, Charles, 130–31
Wolff, Christian, 171
Wolfshohl, Alexander, 60
Wyn Jones, David, 67–70

Zalar, Jeffery, 187
Zarlino, Gioseffo, *Le istitutioni harmoniche*, 232–36, 255–56
Zehrgarten Circle. *See under* BEETHOVEN, LUDWIG VAN
Zehrgarten Stammbuch. *See under* BEETHOVEN, LUDWIG VAN
Zelter, Carl Friedrich, 276–77
Zinzendorf, Karl von, 150n85
Zmeskall, Nikolaus, 5–6